Praise for 2020's breakout YA fantasy
WOVEN IN MOONLIGHT

"*Woven in Moonlight*—appropriately—weaves a beautiful spell that takes culturally specific details and spins them into an engaging fantasy world."

—NPR

★ "A nuanced and empathetic fantasy. . . . Touching on ideas of restorative justice in a unique and vivid setting, Isabel Ibañez delivers a confident, subtle, and inspiring debut about what it takes to move a divided society forward."

—BookPage, starred review

★ "Builds a world that feels true to life with a distinctive magic system at its core. *Woven in Moonlight* spins a satisfying tale of adventure, romance, and magic."

—Shelf Awareness, starred review

"With its slow burn romance and simmering intrigue, *Woven in Moonlight* kept me reading long into the night. Pure magic."

—Shelby Mahurin, *New York Times* bestselling author of *Serpent & Dove*

"A lush, vibrant feast of a book."

—Margaret Rogerson, *New York Times* bestselling author of *Sorcery of Thorns*

"Immersive prose, original magic, and characters as rich as the Bolivian culture that constructs the story. A wholly unique book for the YA shelf."

– Adrienne Young, *New York Times* bestselling author of *The Girl the Sea Gave Back*

THIS ONE IS FOR YOU, PAPA.
I never tire of hearing your stories of growing up in the jungle.

PAGE STREET
PUBLISHING CO.

Copyright © 2021 Isabel Ibañez

First published in 2021 by
Page Street Publishing Co.
27 Congress Street, Suite 105
Salem, MA 01970
www.pagestreetpublishing.com

Distributed by Macmillan, sales in Canada by The Canadian Manda Group.

25   24   23   22   21   1   2   3   4   5

ISBN-13: 978-1-64567-132-9
ISBN-10: 1-64567-132-1

Library of Congress Control Number: 2020936367

Cover and interior illustration © Isabel Ibañez

Printed and bound in the United States

Written in Starlight

ISABEL IBAÑEZ

PAGE STREET
PUBLISHING CO.

CAPÍTULO

uno

Legend says if the jungle wants you, it will have you.

The tree line looms ahead, smothering and terrifying in the dying light. Long tentacles of fog snake around thick trunks, as if readying to choke the life from anyone foolish enough to enter. The sharp trill of birds and buzzing locusts are the only sounds coming from the jungle fringes, but even I know there are monsters lurking beneath the vivid green canopy.

Anacondas. Jaguars. Black caimánes with teeth the length of my palms. And that's only the bigger creatures. I've read books about toads capable of bringing a grown man to the brink of insanity. Piranhas that ravage flesh straight to the bone in seconds. Then there are the rumors of terrible dark magic—magic that comes from the earth, hungry and wanting to devour. Only the Illari know how to survive it, becoming monsters themselves in order to reign over the forest.

I've been sentenced to die here.

My final resting place, cut off from the life I've always known back in La Ciudad Blanca. There's nothing I could have done to prepare for my journey. No books to read. No conversations to be had. No amount of training to defend myself. A sharp screech echoes beyond the trees. My stomach swoops as if I've launched myself off the Illustrian tower, screaming the whole way down.

Don't be a coward, Catalina. You're the condesa, born to rule Inkasisa. You will survive this.

Or you'll die with dignity, damn it.

I force out a long exhale and shove all thoughts of the jungle's creatures far from my mind. But the pressure in my chest curls, tight like a clenched fist. *What do you know about being brave?* The voice is close and intimate, utterly resistant to silencing. It's been one week since my fate was decided, and I'm still coming to terms with my exile and how badly I messed up my life and my people's future.

I study the six guards crowding me. They are my enemies, armed with swords and pikes and knives, traveling close at my elbows and high up on their horses, while I clutch the reins of my poor sweaty mule. Not one of them has offered me anything to drink or eat in hours. As for taking a minute to rest, forget it. We've been riding nonstop since dawn. At least my ride is cute. The sweetest animal I've ever seen, with big brown eyes and soft tufts of hair. I lean forward and curl my fingers in her thick mane, wishing I could take her far away from this place.

Maybe the guards will leave her behind with me. At least I'd have a friend.

"Adelante," one of the guards says. I dig my heels and attempt to move us forward. Diosa, I *hate* being told what to do. The creature whines but obeys the sharp whistle that comes from the captor on my right. I shoot the Llacsan a disgruntled look while attempting to hold on as the mule propels us forward.

My heart thuds painfully in my chest as we approach the tree line. The tall grass slowly transitions to the dappled jungle floor under the mule's hooves. Thick fog descends, casting the ropy vines as villainous snakes. Panic curls deep in my belly, like the mist clutching the tree trunks. My dark hair sticks to the back of my neck, a knotty mess. I want to take the time to properly braid it, to coil it high on the crown of my head, but no one spares a minute for grooming or bathing. All I need is twenty minutes to look presentable.

Maybe then I'd feel more like myself.

I shift my attention from the chokes of leafy bushes and the serpentine vines clogging the path to stare at Rumi—the boy responsible for the mess I'm in, and a last-minute addition to my entourage. He's dressed in typical Llacsan gear: darker-hued pants and a long-sleeved tunic with a striped vest bursting in vibrant colors and a broad hat hiding an abundance of brown hair. Tied around his waist are a wooden slingshot with leather straps and a long sword.

Dirt and sweat stain my once startling white tunic and trousers. No one thought to pack me a change of clothes. My palms are filthy, and there's grime caked under my nails. Dirty half-moons. I shove at my tangled mess of hair, again, sighing heavily. Rumi feels my gaze and his coffee-colored eyes flicker to mine, assessing the curves of my face. His intent study of my features startles me until I realize what he's doing. He's searching for Ximena.

The friend who betrayed me.

We were like sisters, in appearance and friendship, if not in blood. I avert my gaze. He can look all he wants. He won't

3

find *her* in me. I'd never dishonor the memory of my parents, conspiring with our enemy to put a Llacsan princesa on the throne—instead of me, the rightful heir. I'd never turn against my people for a *boy*. I'd soon as take a knife to my heart. And I'd never hurt the one person I was closest to.

Best friends aren't supposed to do that.

My voice scratches the air, hoarse from disuse. "Why'd you volunteer to escort me? Shouldn't you be off on a harebrained adventure, dressed as El Lobo?"

This *Llacsan* was a popular vigilante who once drove Atoc, my enemy, mad with his antics. The discovery of his identity still sours my mood. I assumed, like all Illustrians, the vigilante was one of us. I thought he could be a friend to my cause. A brave hero to fight alongside my people. I was very wrong. I've been wrong about too many things.

He cuts me a look. "The days of El Lobo are over. No one needs a vigilante, not when we can all work toward peace." His expression is pointed and loaded. "All you had to do was accept Princesa Tamaya as your queen. You and I both know she's the better ruler."

His judgment stings like the angry bite of a fire ant, and his words are flavored with my worst fears. I'm not enough. I'm not a leader worth following and not a queen people will love and respect. I swat away a fat mosquito, but another three replace it, buzzing loudly.

I grip the reins tighter. "I *can't*."

He's already shaking his head, discarding my words as if they're fruit rotted through. "You don't know her like we do. She'll—"

"You don't know me either."

A hint of a smile plays at his mouth. "Oh, I don't know, Catalina. I think I know enough."

He doesn't use my official title: condesa, countess. "I hardly think whatever *she*"—there's no reason to speak her name out loud—"told you is an accurate picture of my person."

Rumi hesitates. "Maybe. It certainly was gracious."

A guard behind us snorts loudly. Blood rushes to my cheeks. I turn away from the Llacsan and focus on remaining upright on the mule. We cross the tree line in single file. I'm somewhere in the middle, with three guards ahead and three at the tail. Rumi is directly behind me. The canopy overhead tangles together until not even a ray of moonlight escapes its snares. Twilight disappears and only the living dark remains.

"Luna," I whisper to my diosa. "Where are you?"

But the jungle is skilled at blocking out the heavens.

The horses are skittish, neighing every so often, stomping against the hard earth. Ahead, the guards have lit torches and the firelight draws angry shadows against the prickly leaves surrounding us. It only illuminates a few yards into the dark depths of the forest. Past its glow, the jungle hides its sinister face.

The guard at the front of the line holds up a hand and we all come to a stop.

I frown and turn to peer over my shoulder. The tree line is still visible. Do they mean to leave me within sight of it? The pressure in my chest eases, and I almost laugh. This was the plan all along. It's a scare tactic. That princesa never wanted me to actually *die*. Once they're gone, I'll head back, reach the nearest village, and—

"We walk from here," one of the guards up front calls over his shoulder. "Too thick for the horses."

My jaw clenches. Rumi softly laughs as he throws a leg over, sliding off his mare in one fluid motion. "You didn't really think it'd be that easy, did you?"

"No," I mutter, my cheeks flushing.

"Do you need help climbing down?"

Because he's being polite, I'm compelled to answer in kind, even if it grates me. "I can manage. Gracias." I hop off the mule. I gently pat her neck and she swerves, offering me her rump instead. Despite the danger, I smile and scratch her soft fur. "Are we stopping to rest?" I shake my head and use my most commanding voice. "I *insist* we stop to rest."

No one within hearing range replies.

Rumi motions to my small leather pack, attached to the mule's saddle. "Don't forget that." He throws it at me and then turns his attention to the last guard in line. He gives him the reins of my mule and says, "We'll join you after we leave behind . . ." He trails off. "Be alert. Nothing in this jungle wants you here. Take care on the journey back out. And touch nothing."

It's almost time. They're leaving me tonight.

I have to come up with a plan before then. Maybe I can follow them back out? Maybe I can read the constellations, even without my telescope. The idea crashes before it can fully take flight. I've never been good at reading the stars, despite my calling.

My shoulders slump as the guard nods and takes hold of all the reins and leads the horses and my sweet mule back the way we came, back to the little light that remains. Rumi nudges my shoulder, and I reluctantly turn away from the sight of freedom and march alongside him as the rest of the guards use thick swords to cut at the dense foliage. Rotted logs peppered with white mushrooms and yellow mold block our trek. My boots tread on a decaying mulch of damp leaves and cloying vines. Buttress roots supporting massive trees curl under the greeneries. If I somehow don't twist my ankle, it'll be a miracle.

A guard ahead slaps at his neck. "Damn mosquitos."

They're bothering me too. Annoying pricks I feel up and down my arms and legs. My thin trousers and tunic are a paltry shield.

"Be thankful it wasn't a black scorpion," another guard says. "The rainy season brings them out."

I shudder and pull the sleeves of my tunic down as far as they can go. Then I shove away a thick batch of tangled branches, slick with slime. Luna knows what I'm touching, what I'm seeing. Nothing looks familiar.

"Want me to explain what you're staring at?" Rumi asks conversationally.

"¿Qué?"

He gestures to the surrounding plant life. "That's a foxtail fern. Over there are orchids. I've always thought they looked graceful. These rope-like vines are called *lianas*. Ever seen them before?"

I haven't seen much of *anything* before. For most of my life I've been hidden behind the Illustrian fortress walls. I shake my head. He's a walking guidebook. Prudence tells me to set aside my aversion to this Llacsan and listen closely. Because after tonight, I'll be alone, and the idea of dying in this jungle makes fear seep into the very marrow of my bones. Whatever knowledge of the forest this Llacsan knows, I should learn also.

My life may depend on it.

Rumi spends the next few minutes pointing out the various wildlife. Jungle yams, avocado, orange and fig trees, and my personal favorite, maracuyá. I listen and study each one, knowing my small pack of food won't last forever. I'm amazed by the amount of sustenance readily available at my fingertips.

"How far in are we going?"

"We walk until we're too tired to continue," he says over his shoulder. "Keep up."

"I'm moving as fast as I can." I stumble after him, noting how Rumi moves like *her*. Sure-footed, weapon raised, ready to face the world. I'm cowering in his shadow, flinching as the branches scratch at my face, tangling in my hair. He ducks under the liana vines and skirts around thorny bushes that are sharp enough to tear flesh. I try to mimic his steps but end up slipping on a particularly slimy stretch of forest floor.

"Oh, cielos." I lurch forward, reaching for a vine to stop my fall—

"Don't!" Rumi yells, jerking me away. The tips of my fingers brush the vine and the effect is instant. Hot, searing pain flares, burning the skin where I touched the plant. I try to wipe my hand on something, but Rumi grabs my wrist like a manacle.

"¡Para!" he yells to the other guards. "Necesito fuego."

The guards encircle us, torches raised, as Rumi examines my fingertips. "Don't touch anything—it'll spread and only make it worse. I'll be right back."

I'm hardly listening. The pain is excruciating. Blisters form as each finger swells, and my palm feels as if it's on fire. Carajo, it hurts. My breath comes out in sharp pants as I try to stop myself from crying. They already think I'm weak—spoiled, even. Maybe it's true. A hoarse laugh escapes me in between huffs. Look at me. I'm a joke. I'm not strong or brave like my friend. I'm not a warrior.

I'm a condesa without a country.

CAPÍTULO

dos

The guards start mumbling in the old tongue, and I catch a few disgruntled looks. I'm slowing them down. They want to leave the jungle as much as I do. The farther in we go, the longer the journey back. There isn't a stretch of safe ground in this forest. I could literally hide under a rock, but then a frog might croak and douse me in, I don't know, poisonous spit.

I glance down at my fingers, the skin a blotchy red that slowly spreads down to my wrist. I let out a small whimper and raise my head to search for relief amid the heavy greenery. I want to find a pond to sink my whole hand into.

Rumi returns carrying thick leaves. He tears them apart and crushes the bundle into an oily pulp. He smears the slick moisture over my hand and down the length of my forearm.

The burning feeling fades. My relief nearly sends me to my knees. "Gracias."

He spreads the rest of the oily mess onto his own hands and I wonder if, by touching me, his hands were infected too. "De nada."

"How did you know what to do?"

"I know plants," Rumi says. "The one you touched exudes an irritant that keeps insects at bay." He holds up the crushed oily leaves. "And this one comes from the violet family. It dulls pain by numbing the area."

I stare at my hand in wonder. It's still swollen and marred with blisters, but at least it doesn't sting anymore.

"He's the best healer we have," one of the guards says proudly. "My son's cough has disappeared—"

"I hardly did anything, Usuy," Rumi says. "Your son is strong."

At his words, the guard's chest puffs up. I turn my attention to the crushed leaves, trying to commit the color and shape to memory. This is a plant I don't want to forget. One of the guards nudges my back, and we form a single-file line and continue our trek. We walk seemingly for hours. My pants are a shredded mess, my tunic soaked with sweat. The mosquitos are endless. Buzzing in my ear, sticking to my skin, riding my breath. My clothing isn't the fortress I think it is either. I slide the fabric up my arm and discover several welts marring my skin.

I'm not used to the exercise, long as it is from the miles we're traveling. I'm not told where we're heading, how much farther there is to go, or if I'll be given a weapon to defend myself against the jungle once they leave. But then, that's the point.

The princesa wants me dead.

At last, *at last*, one of the guards signals and we stop. The Llacsan turns to look at the healer, who gives a slight nod. I look around, but the forest is as dense as ever. I thought we'd find a clearing, or someplace close to a water source. But no. They're dumping me in a nondescript area. A single column of stone is the only landmark, made nearly invisible by the amount of foliage suffocating it.

"You're leaving me *here*?"

Rumi ignores me as he rummages in his pack. I tilt my head back to study the overhang of tangled branches and leaves. I can't find a single star through the tree limbs. The constellations are useless to me under the canopy. Any messages from Luna are hidden, not that I have much success in interpreting the stars. My first and foremost failure as the only remaining Illustrian seer.

Fear grasps at my heart. I'm so close to unraveling, and the urge to give in to my frustration and hurt nearly overwhelms me. I want to drop to my knees and howl and sob and scream out everything that's in me, but I can't—I'm terrified they won't care. That their last sight of me will be a crying mess on the ground.

Pride keeps my back straight. Lifts my chin and fortifies me for the night ahead.

Rumi finds two items in his pack, both wrapped crudely in fraying fabric. Wordlessly, he hands them to me. I open the smaller one—rolls of bread, smashed together from being tossed around in his bag. The second bundle is longer, and when the wrapping falls softly to my feet, my breath hitches at the back of my throat.

It's my dented bronze telescope. The one tool I need to properly read the constellations.

"From Ximena," he whispers.

I bite down hard on my bottom lip. I want to hurl both gifts into the dark jungle. Let the beasts devour her pity. But my fingers clutch the telescope as if on their own accord, refusing to let go. I lift my eyes as they fill with tears. I dash at them angrily. Rumi stares for a moment, deliberating, until something in his gaze changes—softens and bends like a slash of starlight.

"Help her settle in for the night." He slings his pack off his shoulder. "I'll start a fire."

The guards stiffen, their mouths opening at the mandate. Apparently, helping me set up camp wasn't part of the plan. They divvy up the tasks—clearing the area and setting up a perimeter. Someone thrusts a hammock into my arms, and motions toward two trees a few yards apart. There's rope on either end and I set about tying each to a trunk, careful not to touch any of the vines.

"Damn it," I say as each end slides down the trunk. "Wouldn't bedrolls be easier? I'd rather sleep in one of those."

One of the guards barks out a laugh and says something to another, who promptly rolls his eyes in my direction. Rumi looks over at me, his hands at work making a fire. When it roars to life, he comes over to help with the hammock.

"If you sleep on the ground, you'll wake up with several nasty bed companions. Scorpions, snakes, and spiders." He finishes tying each end, and somehow the rope doesn't slide. "Still think it'd be easier?"

I shake my head, shuddering.

"This is the jungle, Condesa," he says softly. "Don't you forget it. Have you had any water?"

I shake my head again, and now that he's mentioned it, my throat suddenly feels dry, my tongue hot and swollen.

Rumi half turns and one of the guards tosses him a sac, the

liquid sloshing loudly. He hands it over, and I drink my fill, not caring how the water is slightly warm. When I'm done, he passes the bag back to the owner.

"Why are you being so nice to me?" I ask. "Because of her?"

I still can't say her name. I've finally reached my breaking point. I went from having nearly everything to having nothing in a matter of days. For a few moments I was invincible. In my hands I had the power to reclaim our throne, and my people believed in me.

It still wasn't enough.

"Because of her," he echoes. "I want to be able to look her in the eye when she asks me how I left you."

His words hit me oddly. I don't want her empty pity, I didn't need her to send Rumi—

"She sent me because she cares," he says softly.

I flinch in surprise and it makes Rumi smile.

"You wear everything on your face." He picks up the fine netting. "Drape this over your hammock, but not too close. The bugs will bite you right through it." I stare at the bundle, despairing. His jaw clenches, but then he lets out a slow exhale, as if attempting to control his impatience. "Here, let me show you how to do it."

Rumi places the netting up and over the hammock, using rocks and twigs to spread the fabric out into a canopy. Then he removes everything and hands over the netting so I can do it on my own. I imitate what he does, collecting various flotsam to hold my netting away from the hammock. Rumi nods in approval. I duck under my netting for a few minutes of respite from the mosquitos, and after a couple of wobbly attempts, manage to encase myself inside the hammock. The material is rough and scratchy.

My gaze returns to the fire, oddly reassuring as it pushes the dark heart of the forest away. Hunger flares deep in my belly, but I leave the rolls alone. What am I going to do after they leave? I peer into the steaming jungle, away from where the guards have convened around the cozy fire. All I see is a flat darkness that sends a chill down my spine.

My fingers curl around the edges of the hammock. How am I going to survive on my own? I'm optimistic, always have been, but making it out of the forest in one piece—*alone*—sounds foolish at best. If a menacing vine almost did me in earlier, imagine something with *claws*.

Unless . . . I turn to Rumi. Could I persuade him to stay with me? I nearly scoff at the idea until I remember that he really does seem to care for *her*. He might stay if it meant pleasing my former friend—the traitorous rat. As if he can sense my thoughts, the healer meets my gaze over the flickering fire. He slowly shakes his head, as if I'd asked the question out loud. His kindness has its limits, it seems.

I avert my gaze. *What did I expect?*

"Catalina," he calls softly. I climb out of the hammock and make my way toward the group. My steps are heavy on the tangled brush under my boots. The guards are fidgeting, eager to be on their way. They have to survive the trek back out—follow the trail before the jungle swallows the way home.

"So this is it," I say numbly. "Lovely meeting you all."

"Don't stay here for longer than a night," Rumi says, ignoring my jab. "Keep moving and head downhill; eventually you'll find water. Don't touch any vines." He thrusts his pack at me. "There's a blanket inside, and a weapon. Do you know how to defend yourself with a dagger?"

"Not against anything with teeth."

He shoots me a pointed look. "Do you?"

I grudgingly nod. "*She* taught me."

"Good." He gestures to my sleeves. "Keep those down to avoid bugs and scratches. If you're bitten, and the wounds become infected, maggots will appear." He hesitates. "If maggots appear . . . Just try to avoid infection, all right? Once that happens, find somewhere to hide and then—"

"Die peacefully," I cut in. "That's what you mean?"

"Actually, yes. The maggots are an indicator of a serious problem."

I gag as a shudder rips through me.

He steps closer and, in an undertone, whispers, "This is your last chance, Catalina. Say you'll accept Princesa Tamaya as your queen, and you'll be welcomed back to La Ciudad. Don't let your pride—"

"Rumi," one of the guards says. "It's time."

He's wrong, this vigilante. It isn't my pride. I have to think of what's best for my people, and another Llacsan on the throne is not the answer—I am. The last Llacsan ruler murdered my family and destroyed our city.

It will be a moonless black night before I give up my birthright. I shake my head.

The Llacsan healer nods and drops a hesitant hand onto my shoulder. I pull away—gently. He may have stayed longer than planned, showed me where to find food, and built me a fire, but he's still *leaving* me here.

And I'll never forget the role he played in my downfall.

They leave in a single file, Rumi at the back. He shoots me one last look over his shoulder before the jungle's long arms encircle him. The sounds of their departure settle into the night, my ears straining to hear every grunt, every footstep, until there's nothing more. Only the song of the jungle: toads and insects screeching, owls hooting, leaves rustling in the heavy wind. There's moisture in the air and a moment later a deep rumble bears down from above.

A storm comes.

I need to find shelter from the approaching storm, but I can't make myself move away from the fire's warm glow. It's my final link to humanity. This fire pit, this half-hidden stone pillar, is my last known location. The moment I step away, I'll become untethered and truly alone. Lost forever. I sink to my knees, holding out my hands to the flames. What if the Llacsans change their mind? What if they grow a conscience and decide it's *inhumane* to leave me here?

Maybe they'll come back if I wait long enough.

Thunder roars in the treetops as I think through my options. Rumi and his companions will meet a torrential downpour on the way out. The trail will disappear from under their feet. *They may not even survive the night.* And if they can't, how will I? I let myself have a few minutes, my thoughts skittering from one thing to another. If I don't pack now, if I don't move, I'll lose whatever meager possessions I have left in the dark once the storm douses the fire. I inhale deeply, the scent of dirt, decaying plants, vegetation, and wood filling my nostrils.

Move, Catalina.

Another roar crashes from above. I jump to my feet, throwing the telescope and bread into the pack. I run to the hammock, untying the knots, and then fold the delicate netting. I jam everything into my bag and sling it over my shoulder. I take one last look around to make sure I'm not leaving anything useful behind. The fire's heat beckons, but I ignore the call. I leave the safety of the small clearing and march into the jungle, where darkness engulfs me. I need a cave, a hollow in a tree, anything to shield me from the downpour. From the sound of the booming thunder, the storm will be immense.

I've taken ten steps before it becomes nearly impossible to see anything in the cloying night. Only my little fire is visible in the distance.

A sudden rumble roars overhead. The treetops dump water, soaking everything. I jerk wildly and race for a tree, but there's no escaping the pouring rain. It drowns my fire, creating a muddy sludge in the center of the clearing. My camp site disappears, becoming part of the jungle as if it'd never existed.

Water slides from the top of my head and travels down my body. Every article of clothing is sopping wet in seconds, including my boots. My tunic and pants stick to my skin as I continue walking away from the clearing. My long wet hair is a weight on my shoulders. The strap of my pack digs into my skin, but I ignore the discomfort and push on. Leaves bigger than half my body block the way, but I use my covered shoulder and arm to push through. With every step, my feet squish inside my leather boots.

Squish, squish, squish.

The heavy downpour slows my progress, but I refuse to let

it defeat me. Everyone else may have, but not this damn rain. I keep walking, forcing myself to take slow, steady steps, every now and again tipping my head back to catch water in my mouth. I climb over fallen logs, traverse long stretches of sodden grass. At least the mosquitos have disappeared. Small mercies. Thunder rumbles again above the treetops, promising more rain, and the heavens deliver. I imagine a bucket, the level of water rising and rising. Soon my bucket will overflow. But at least I'm getting plenty of water.

I keep moving. Anytime the terrain veers upward, I readjust and go in the opposite direction so that I'm consistently walking downhill. Even in the gloom, the hazy outline of a mountain ridge looms in the distance. I decide to head away from it, but only Luna knows if I'm heading toward a river or a stream. My meandering walk takes me deeper and deeper into the jungle. The rain slows, the water no longer pounding the top of my head.

When the downpour stops altogether, a miracle happens.

The forest slowly lights up, a buttery, soft yellow. I let out a gasp, my bag dropping to my feet. Surrounding me, a shimmery gleam dusts the tree trunks, the grassy knotted floor, the curling vines. I venture closer to one of the plants—it's covered in glowing fungus.

Fungus.

"Imagine that," I whisper. I pick up my pack, dismiss the stabbing pain coming from the bottoms of my feet—the miles walked are catching up to me—and set off, seeking a way that won't take me up the mountain. At last I find an overhang of rock and duck under, nestling close to the stone. I use the sodden pack as a makeshift pillow, and, ignoring the hunger pains, force myself to shut my eyes.

My first night in the jungle.

I wake with a start. Somewhere in the distance a rustling draws near. Branches parting, twigs snapping. I sit up and rub my eyes. The rain has started again, thick and incessant. Is it morning? I peep out into the dark. The rain casts a heavy gloom on the forest. Impossible to tell what time it is. The sound of the water slapping the overhang almost drowns out the rustling, but it continues drawing closer and louder.

The ground shakes.

What beast makes that kind of racket? I slowly exhale as I reach into my pack for the dagger. The blade is dirty with dried blood. I grip the leather-wrapped handle and wait for whatever predator is stalking me. The seconds stretch as my heart slams against my ribs, painful and fast like the onslaught of a battering ram.

The rustling grows louder. The jungle carpet quakes.

I climb out from under the overhang, clutching my weapon at the level of my heart. Water blurs my vision, but I don't soften my stance. "Come out if you're going to eat me!" My voice is a wail against the rain, against the forest.

The rustling is deafening now.

My legs are shaking, the grip on the weapon trembling. I swallow back a painful lump. Maybe I can outrun the creature?

From the bushes come dozens of rabbits, howling monkeys, wild guinea pigs, and—are those *anteaters*? They rush past, veering around me and escaping from whatever approaches.

I'm not waiting around to find out. I bend to pick up my pack, my fingers clutch the strap—

The floor shifts and slides. A scream tears out of me as I'm knocked off my feet and swept into a thick mudslide. The sludge thrusts me toward a sleek hill covered in a mess of greenery and twigs. Trees whip past, a distorted painting on either side. The current propels me to a steep decline.

"Luna!" I shriek as I'm flung into the air, and I plummet down, down, down into a canopy of trees. I land on a branch with a hard thud. My pack and dagger slip from my grasp. Mud continues to pour from above, splattering onto my back in thick disgusting plops. I let out a shuddering breath. I'm curled around the tree, doubled over, facing the ground below. Most of the impact was on my stomach. I grip the tree and slowly climb down, my booted feet sliding on the slick wood.

Grime seeps into the corner of my mouth, cakes under my eyes, settles into my hair. My stomach hurts from when I landed on that branch. Which probably saved my life.

When I reach the ground, I drop to all fours and force my breath to even out. It hurts to inhale. Hurts to exhale. I catch sight of my pack and I crawl toward it, groaning as if I were a hundred years old and not eighteen. The rain rids my skin and hair of some of the mud, but my clothes will forever be stained in the color of filth.

Exhaustion blankets my vision, and fatigue overcomes my bones. From this tiny corner of the jungle, the sky is visible. I gingerly get on my knees and tilt my head backward. It's dark and ominous, pouring rain, but comforting all the same. It's a lifeline, an answer to my prayer. I'm not moving from this spot, rain be damned. Clutching the pack, I search for my dagger and find it perched on a rock. Then I attempt to set up camp.

But the hammock won't stay up no matter how many knots I make.

I can't start a fire in the rain.

And I'm not sure how one sets up a perimeter.

In the end, I prop against a tree trunk and wrap myself in the hammock, my pack tucked between my legs. I open my mouth to catch streams of water pouring down from overflowing bowl-shaped leaves. Then I reach into my bag and pull out the soggy bread rolls. I force myself to eat them all even though the texture reminds me of mushy rice. I finish my meal, reposition the bag, and clutch the dagger. The itchy, damp material of the hammock scratches the bottom of my jaw as I curl deeper into my cocoon.

This is how I fall asleep: alone, wet, hungry, and vulnerable to attack.

I try not to think about it as my eyes drift closed.

The next time I wake, it's silent. I lean forward and peer up to the sky. Only a half circle is visible through the tangled tree canopy, but the night is as clear as if I were gazing into the unmarred surface of Lago Yaku. The hammock cocoon has dried stiff and smells like clothes that have been trapped in a trunk for a century. I shove at the fabric until I'm free, and then rummage through the bag for my telescope. If there was ever a time to seek Luna, it's now.

I peer into the bronze scope and aim for the stars.

Luna is characteristically aloof, ever changing the shimmery lines that connect one star to another, forming constellations. The stars have their own language, and our diosa communicates through the heavens by creating symbols in the night sky. A celestial alphabet taught only to Illustrian seers. My great-aunt was a seer, and if I ever have a daughter, I'll sit down and give her the test. Maybe she'll inherit Luna's blessed gift.

But for now I am the last seer of my people. The only one who survived the Llacsan revolt.

And though I'm fluent in Luna's heavenly language, the constellations shift on me—in a moment, in a blink—leaving me unsure if I read the symbols right. This never happened to my aunt. The stars were always constant and true for her.

What am I doing wrong?

"Luna," I whisper as the mosquitos return in full force. "Help me. Show me a way out of this place."

I stand still and continue reading the shifting stars. They move slowly, lines connecting and disconnecting, rearranging themselves and changing shape, changing size and direction. It's a mess up there. With a disgusted sound, I stop looking through the telescope. Why can't I make any sense of what she's trying to tell me?

I inhale and slowly shut my eyes. The jungle harmony surrounds me, clamoring for attention, but I ignore the constant chatter of the toads and owls and focus on feeling the heavens. Dwelling on the pressure building in my chest. Feeling the air trapped in my lungs. Thinking of the endless night, and the way the moon conquers all shadows. My hands tingle, tiny pricks that shoot awareness deep into my belly. I exhale, and once again peer through the scope. The stars have moved again. This time, they stay put. A single word is made clear, as if Luna herself whispers it in my ear.

Danger.

It comes to me breathless and urgent, impossible to ignore. I'm plunged back to earth, back to the heart of the jungle. I lower the scope and turn toward my discarded dagger, lying next to the hammock.

Something moves in the dark. Disturbs the tall leaves.

A noise climbs up my throat, shrill and panicked. The shadow I'm watching materializes, and he's massive. Almost the size of a *horse*. He looks ancient—from another time. A hint of red glows from the depths of his eyes. The jaguar crouches next to my tree, lambent gaze steady on mine. A feral growl rents the air. Luna save me. It's going to be a slaughter.

I have no defense against this beast.

We are both impossibly still. *Run*, someone whispers in the night, the voice soft but powerful. *Go.* As if by their own accord, my feet slowly angle away from the jungle cat. In response, he crouches lower, readying to strike.

I bolt, taking only my telescope.

The jaguar roars from somewhere behind me. My legs pump harder, and I run as fast as I can. The trees spread out enough for me to see where I'm going—there's a cliff ahead. For the first time, Luna shines down on me. Moonlight reveals a path parallel to the edge. I pivot, my hands shooting out to catch my fall. My fingers find purchase and I propel myself forward, feet pushing against the ground to give me a head start.

The jaguar leaps.

I drop to the ground as the big cat sails above me. I get to my feet and dart away, stumbling back through the jungle bush. The moonlight disappears. Darkness blankets my vision. Sharp leaves scratch my cheeks, but I push on, the jaguar snarling at my heels. Above our heads, monkeys screech, startled by the jungle cat. My eyes adjust to the darkness as I'm about to touch a prickly vine. I use my covered shoulder to push the bulk aside.

A log blocks my path. I climb over, but as soon as my feet touch the other side, the beast slashes my shoulder blades. A bloodcurdling scream escapes me. Hot liquid slides down my back. I take a few steps forward, my vision blurring from the pain. The ground under my feet gives way, sending me down, down, down into a pit. I land hard, my temple hitting something jagged and rough.

The world blinks to black.

CAPÍTULO

Cuatro

When I wake, it's to the frantic sounds of growling and scratching. I open my eyes slowly, disoriented. The gloom prevents me from seeing anything clearly. I'm lying on hard dirt, the scent of rocks and worms assaulting my nose. I'm in a narrow pit, slumped over on my back, my legs above me.

Dimly, I notice a creature at the top of the hole, digging to widen the opening. With a gasp I bring in my legs, pressing my knees against my chest. Clumps of dirt land on my face from the jaguar's incessant movements.

The hole is barely big enough to fit me, and the jaguar's size prevents him from jumping in. But not for long. I have minutes, maybe, before he tunnels inside.

There's nothing left in me to block my fear, the rising panic, the tears streaming down my face. I'm going to die in this pit, mauled by a jungle cat. I'm going to die a failure. Betrayed by my people. A blight to my family name.

The jaguar widens the hole big enough to slip in its massive paw. His claws spread, scrambling for my leg, inches away.

27

My hands are shaking, imagining his teeth ripping at my skin, sipping the gushing blood as it pours out of me. If Ximena could see me now, would she care? Would my death even matter to her now that she has her new friends, and she supports another queen? Tears carve tracks down my cheeks.

I tip my head back and scream as loud and as long as I can.

The jaguar startles but resumes his digging. My gaze snags on the rock I hit on the way down. Using both hands, I launch it upward toward the jungle cat. The rock smacks his face, sending him back from the opening. Then the rock plummets and hits my leg and I wince. The beast returns in seconds and continues digging, furious now that I'm defending myself.

I throw everything within reach. Rocks, twigs, handfuls of dirt. Much of it rains back down onto me, but I don't care. I keep throwing whatever I find, but my assault barely slows down the big cat. My arm tires and I stop, breathing heavily. There's nothing left to throw.

All I can do is curl up and wait to die.

Without warning the jaguar slumps forward. Blood splatters my legs. Someone shoves the creature away from the opening and a face appears in its place. Narrowing my gaze, I try to discern if it's one of my guards—or Rumi.

The face belongs to a man half hidden by a wide-brimmed hat. Patches of scattered moonlight illuminate the bottom half of the stranger's countenance: scruffy beard and a strong jaw. Someone young—the skin on his arms is smooth.

"Rumi?" My voice is shaky. Did the healer have a beard? I can't remember. I clutch at the dirt walls, trying to stand. "Is it you?"

"I'm going to get you out," he says, but then moves away.

"No!" My limbs are tangled in the small space. "Por favor. No me dejes."

"Listen to me," he says calmly as his face reappears. "I'm not going to leave you down there."

His voice is low and rough, as if he's not used to talking. It also doesn't sound the least bit like Rumi's. The stranger disappears again, and I stifle a sob. What if another jaguar attacks him— what if he can't come back?

"Espera! Come back!"

A heavy vine drops, landing in a coil on my stomach.

"I told you I wasn't going to leave you. Hold on to the vine," he calls. Amusement threads his tone like the night sky stitched with stars. It soothes me because it radiates confidence. He's really going to pull me out of this hole.

"Sí," I say, and yank on the vine to let him know I'm ready. It snaps, taut, against the dirt wall. I concentrate on his heavy breathing as the man slowly drags me out of this infernal pit.

When I'm close to the top, he hooks his hands under my armpits and pulls me out the rest of the way. He underestimates my size, because we topple forward, him onto his back and me crashing against his chest. His wide-brimmed hat flounces off, revealing his face, his softly glowing eyes. Twin fires against rich olive skin. A chill skips down my spine as my mouth goes dry.

I *know* him.

The man squints up at me and then gasps. *"Catalina?"*

I blink at him, feeling his chest rise and fall underneath me. My hands are on either side of his head. He has black wavy hair that reaches his shoulders. Dark eyebrows shaped in surprise are set over a pair of brown eyes, fringed by even darker lashes.

His nose is broken—that's new—and a rough beard hides the bottom half of his face, but I'd recognize him anywhere. It's been years, though.

My heart does an odd flip. Even after all this time.

"Manuel," I whisper.

My former general's only son. A ranger and scout for the Illustrian throne. I frown. He's wearing black clothing, not our traditional white. A leather vest is set over a long-sleeved shirt, and there's a machete poking out from behind his back, attached by a leather strap that crisscrosses his chest. His leather boots ride up to mid-calf, and the only thing that remotely looks Illustrian is a pendant hanging from his neck.

A silver crescent moon his mother gave him on his seventeenth birthday three years ago.

"What are you doing *here*?" He clutches my arms and hauls us both to our feet. Then he starts shaking me. "What's happened? You look like you've fought in a battle."

Which is entirely correct. I open my mouth to say so, but a laugh escapes instead. Suddenly I'm giddy with relief. My skin flushes, growing warmer. I'm not alone in this jungle. I'm not going to die. More laughter erupts and Manuel frowns at me.

"Catalina." He shakes me again, but I can't stop the giggling. Tears stream down my face. My giggles turn to gut-wrenching sobs. "What's wrong with—"

He breaks off with a low curse, staring at something over my shoulder. I turn and stiffen.

A tall girl is staring at us. She's outfitted in various shades of green, from her wide-leg pants to the black-and-white checked tunic covering her powerfully built frame. A circlet of gold sits on her dark hair. She's carrying a slingshot in one hand. There's a small pouch attached to her leather belt, I'm guessing filled with polished stones.

"We have to move," Manuel whispers. "Ahora. Right now."

But the girl vanishes into the jungle, tucking herself behind the tree and out of sight. It happens so fast, for a moment I think I must have imagined her.

"Who was that?" I try to take a step forward, but Manuel places a heavy hand on my shoulder.

"An Illari tracker," he says grimly, still staring at the spot where she disappeared.

I gasp. "She's *Illari*? You mean they actually exist in here?"

"Yes, and where there's one, several more will follow. She's been hunting me for days." He removes his hand from my shoulder. His voice drops to a whisper. "Follow me. You can tell me what in diablos is going on when we get to safety."

"Is there such a thing in this place?"

His lips quirk.

Again, my heart does that odd flip.

Manuel uses his machete to hack through the jungle. He doesn't hesitate where to strike, or where to step and what to touch, seeing clearly in the dark. He has Moonsight, a gift from Luna, the ability to never get lost at night. As a little girl, I watched him from the Illustrian tower. Out at night, doing various tasks. He comes alive when the sun goes down. We have that in common.

Manuel half turns, one eyebrow raised, his eyes illuminated in their soft, warm glow.

"I'm all right," I say. I don't mention my wounds. There's

nothing he can do about them right now anyway, what with the Illari tracking us.

He nods and faces forward again, hacking at jungle foliage. I let myself smile. He was always protective, even when we were children. I have so many questions—and I know he must feel the same, but neither of us talks again. I personally can't, trying to keep up with his brisk pace. It's the dead of night, and I'm having a hard time remaining upright, let alone searching for menacing vines. My skin feels feverish and clammy, and black dots dance across my vision.

We're descending around the cliff I almost ran into earlier. My back feels raw, stinging sharply with each of my steps. Damn that jungle cat. Every now and again, Manuel helps me navigate the shifting, jagged rocks. Callouses cover his palms. Overhead, the night sky turns cloudy and gray, dripping rain and mist onto my head. Manuel tips his head back and catches raindrops in his mouth. The line of his neck looks strong, connecting to a softly rounded jawline all but hidden by his dark stubble.

I turn away to hide my blush.

I can still remember the day he left, a few days after his birthday. My general—Ana—had given him the little money she had, a machete that belonged to his father, and a small bag of provisions. Whatever we could spare. We'd celebrated that whole day, not that we had much in the way of food. But we'd played music and danced around a roaring fire. And then he'd pulled me behind a tree, away from prying eyes, and kissed me. It was the best night of my life.

Three days later he was gone.

And the only thing I had left was a forbidden kiss between a condesa and her guard, behind a tree while everyone else danced through the night. How many times did I think about that evening? Replayed a conversation I'd overheard between Ana and Manuel, just a day before he left? Perhaps thousands. Even now, the words come unbidden.

We're all counting on you, she had said. *Never forget who you are, and why you're fighting.*

She sounded stern, though her expression was anything but. Manuel reached for her, hugging her tightly. She'd bitten her lip so hard I thought she might draw blood. I didn't realize she'd been saying goodbye to her son.

The memory is a cruel one, because I know what happens next. Manuel left early the next morning and Ana never saw her son again. She was captured and killed by the Llacsan king Atoc in a public execution in the middle of the main plaza. Ximena didn't do a thing to stop it.

Suddenly I'm terrified by the questions Manuel's bound to ask. I don't want to tell him about his family and how every one of them died; I don't want to hurt him that way. I don't want him to know how everyone deserted me. I've failed him and it's my fault.

I trusted the wrong people.

Manuel lifts a branch after carefully examining it. I wonder if he's ever felt the same horrible sting from the plant I'd touched. I want to ask, but the jungle is a thief and it steals all of my breaths. I've never been so thirsty in my entire life, and no matter how much rainwater I catch in my mouth, it never seems to be enough. Manuel hands me a big palm leaf filled with water and I drink from it greedily.

We continue the climb down, heading for a narrow riverbed that winds outward into the jungle. At last Luna becomes visible amid swollen dark clouds hanging low in the sky. A constant hum of croaking frogs reverberates around us, accompanied by buzzing locusts. Graceful branches arch over the river while fireflies dance overhead, looking like fairies in the mist. We reach the bottom and Manuel leads us along the bank, eyes scanning the area.

The mist creates a moonbow that hovers above the surface of the flowing stream. I wipe raindrops from my eyes and smile. Parts of the jungle are truly breathtaking.

Manuel stops abruptly.

"We cross here," he says. "Watch where you step. Stingrays like to hide in the shallows, and a single prick will kill you if you're unlucky enough to disturb one."

My smile fades. Damn this jungle.

He takes my hand. We cross slowly and carefully, and the water is cool and clear, reaching almost to my knees. It feels delicious against my heated skin. I step on something smooth and slippery and let out a shriek. "I think I touched a stingray!"

Manuel doesn't turn around. "Nope. Just a rock."

"How do you know?"

"You wouldn't be alive if you'd stepped on one."

Oh.

He gently tugs me across. We reach the other side and he helps me find firmer ground as we move up and away from the river. My boots are sodden, and my poor feet are in a worse state. Pinched and cramped, the balls of them are sore and bruised. But the pain coming from my back is overwhelming, stinging and raw.

Manuel points upward. "Our destination."

I follow the length of his finger. Nestled above the tree line is a small cave situated near the top of a vertical wall made of sheer granite. An expanse that stretches higher than the tallest tower of the Illustrian fortress. We're mere specks against its great height. Ants considering an elephant. One miscalculation with the rope, and we'll plummet to our deaths.

"Hilarious," I say. "Where are we really going?"

Manuel continues to point to the cave, his expression infinitely patient, as if I were a child and not a rational being pointing out the dangers of climbing impossible heights. "Who *are* you right now?"

He quirks a dark brow and then drops his hand.

"Even with a rope, it's too risky."

"Don't be silly, Catalina," Manuel says calmly. "We'll be climbing without one."

My jaw drops, but he merely marches toward the wall. With quivering steps, I follow in his wake, my gaze latching onto the immense slab of rock, illuminated in cold moonlight. The stone is smooth and polished, but even so, I can't help feeling as if the face of it salutes me with a sinister smile.

Cinco

I scramble after Manuel, my heart thumping hard against my ribs. My feet ache and sting—I must have blisters. He hacks off branches and makes a clear path for me to follow after his brisk pace. He doesn't look back, as if he knows the current expression I'm wearing on my face.

Utter dismay. Shock. Terror.

When I finally catch up to him, I get a better glimpse of the rock wall. It's an odyssey of cracks and grooves, some gaping, but most barely a fist wide. I look higher and there's a smattering of ledges that appear to be the width of shoes meant for children. My eyes strain in the dim light to catch sight of every possible way up, but there aren't that many footholds.

"Can we talk about this?" I ask. "I mean, logically, I physically *cannot* climb this wall. Even without my injured back, this is impossible. I'd rather face another jaguar."

Manuel frowns, turning me around. His quiet gasp makes my stomach lurch. He uses gentle fingers to part my tunic where it's sticking to dried blood. I wince as some of the cloth refuses to budge.

"How bad is it?" I ask. I can tell he's trying to hide his concern, because he's not quite successful. That deep line appears between his brows.

"Bad," he says, his voice grim. "Come on."

He leads us back the way we came and down to the river, motioning for me to kneel beside it. Manuel looks to the left and then to the right. Satisfied the coast is clear, he squats next to me and proceeds to cup water into his hands, then gently washes the areas around my wound. It doesn't matter how soft his touch is—tears drip down my cheeks.

I can't seem to stop crying. My head is pounding.

"Three deep gashes," he says quietly. "You'll have scars, but I'm more worried about you contracting a fever. ¿Cómo te sientes?"

"Feverish."

He falls silent and continues to wash my back. "Can you stand?"

I nod, and with his help I'm back on my feet. His forearm rests against my forehead, and his lips thin to a narrow slash. He mutters a low curse.

I can't believe he's touching me. Manuel.

"I'm so glad you're here," I whisper. "She banished me."

Manuel's face darkens. He removes his arm slowly, his eyes never leaving mine. A muscle in his jaw jumps. "What do you mean, *banished?*"

We're standing close, inches apart. He's grown up since he left the Illustrian keep. Filled out in the shoulders, his features no longer soft from boyhood. There're new lines that cross his forehead. Manuel's gaze is intent on mine. His anger is palpable, radiating heat like steam coming from a boiling pot.

I don't know what to say. Part of me wants to have it all out right now. But it's the middle of the night, and who knows what monsters are hunting us. He seems to realize the same because he tugs me away from the water and back up the riverbank. We reach the wall and he stands with feet braced apart, fists on his hips, head tilted back to better study it.

"I can't climb it."

"I know," he says. "But we can't stay on the ground. The cave is our best hope for survival. There's only one entry point, and I can defend us from any dangers. Down here . . ." He trails off. Manuel comes to a decision and turns to face me. "Get on my back."

"Impossible," I say. "It's raining."

"Barely misting."

"It's a long way up—"

"You either get on my back or we stay down here. If we do, it's over." There's a hint of a challenge in his tone. "Don't tell me you're ready to quit. The condesa I knew wasn't afraid of heights."

"This is very different from climbing the Illustrian tower and you know it." As children we'd race to the craggy walls and finagle our feet into the grooves, reaching high for the next bit of stone and continuing upward until we'd reached the top. Manuel always teased me that I'd never do it, but of course I did. He quickly learned never to say I couldn't do something.

"Are you through?" Manuel waits for my reply, patient and quiet.

I summon whatever stubborn energy I have left. I shake my head. He nods, satisfied, and then turns. I place my arms on his shoulders, then wind my legs around his waist. Manuel bounces me up higher. "Do you have a strong enough hold?"

I study the spidery cracks in the wall. "Will *you?*"

He reaches for the first ledge. My cheek softly glides against the back of his head under the brim of his hat, rustling his dark hair. "Don't let us fall," I whisper. My lips almost brush his neck. I'm half out of my mind with fever, my back is raw, but all I can think about is how soft his olive skin looks. It was soft then too, the night he kissed me all those years ago. I'd been surprised, delighted.

Overwhelmed.

I've thought about him every day for three years. And now he's here with me. Inches away. I'm such an idiot. I think it even as I slowly dip forward. I place a feathery kiss right under his left ear.

He immediately stiffens, his arm still outstretched. "Do *not* do that again."

Heat floods my cheeks.

"Lo siento," I say. What was I thinking? It's been a long time since we played as kids, protected by fortress walls, a long time since we stayed awake all night making up stories about the constellations. He knew my secret and called me by my real name behind closed doors. All the other boys thought I was just a maid, a helpmate to who they *thought* was the condesa. My proximity to Ximena made me attractive to them, but I knew their attentions were as fickle as thunderstorms. Manuel was the steady ray of light that cut through the fog.

But the Manuel in front of me lost his sense of humor a long time ago. I can see it in the tight lines around his eyes, in the straight edge of his shoulders, straight enough to measure with. There's only one thing I recognize: his protectiveness.

Always my guardian.

And here he is now, saving me again.

It must be my fever, the lack of sleep. The terror I'm trying to keep deep within me, buried with the rest of my secrets. The realization of how much I missed him. I'm such a fool.

"It's fine," he says gruffly. "I'm starting. Don't . . ." He clears his throat. "Don't make any sudden movements."

Don't kiss me again. That's what he means.

I squeeze my eyes shut. "All right."

He climbs with me clutching at him like a baby monkey. It's slow going, but he's sure-footed, as if he's made this climb many times before. I open my eyes and peer over my shoulder when we're about halfway up. I'm not afraid of heights, but the view is terrifying. The canopy of trees looks like tiny shrubs meant for a doll's house. Broccoli tops on cinnamon sticks.

The wind is our constant companion, and with every gust, I cringe. If Manuel were to slip . . . I try not to think about it. His skin is clammy with sweat. Under the leather vest, the muscles in his back move as he continues the climb. I try not to breathe too heavily. I try to remain still. Manuel groans softly under his breath as he heaves us upward, inch by inch, groove by groove.

We reach the ledge of the cave.

"Catalina," he says, in between huffs. "You need to climb in first. Do you see the coiled vine near the edge?"

"Yes."

He doesn't say anything else in order to conserve his strength.

"I can't do this," I whisper. "What if I make us fall?"

"Do it. Ahora, por favor."

My body is trembling, but so is his, from exertion and wariness. I can't burden him further. I reach for the vine, drawing it closer. It scratches against the hard rock.

Manuel reaches for the vine, wrapping it around his wrist. His arm is faintly vibrating.

"Go. Anda," he says, his voice rough, as if it's been scraped against rocks. "Rápido, rápido."

I haul myself up and over him. My knees scrape against the rock, and once I'm crawling on the ledge, he lets out a sigh of relief. He heaves himself over the ledge, and collapses next to me, legs dangling out of the cave entrance.

I poke his shoulder. Manuel grunts, and the noise startles a laugh out of me. He turns his head, his eyes crinkling with amusement, a soft almost-smile on his lips.

My breath catches. Like his mother, he rarely smiles.

"You did it," I say. "I don't know how you did it, but you did it."

He climbed a vertical slab of granite, without a rope, and with me on his back. He's kind of amazing. And unrecognizable. The soft boy I remember no longer exists.

Manuel nods as he half drags, half crawls away from the edge. I stare out into the night, the shreds of my pant legs whipping in the breeze. My vision darkens, making everything seem as if it's touched by shadows. He grabs me by the crook of my elbow and pulls me farther into the cave.

It's narrow, with no room overhead to stand upright. There's a single bedroll, along with a small pack—I recognize it as the one he'd left the Illustrian keep with. A pair of stone bowls are stacked against the curved wall, next to a pile of avocados, oranges, and figs. As hungry as I am, I can't make myself reach for the food.

"Why were you limping?"

I blink at him. "Was I?"

"I've never seen you this way," he says softly. "What's happened to you?"

The cave doesn't shield us from the jungle's steady roar. Monkeys howling, louder and worse than a thunderstorm. Frogs and owls and insects that croak, hoot, and buzz every second. None of this feels real.

I lift the hem of my tattered tunic. "You've never seen me in what way?"

I know what I must look like. But his words sink into my flesh like claws. Because he doesn't mention what's wrong with my appearance on the outside. He finds the part of me that's broken, hidden deep.

"I've never seen you look so defeated." He leans forward and taps the top of my leather boot. "Take off your shoes and socks."

I stare down at my feet. Pain shoots up from the tips of my toes. "I'm not used to all the walking. That's why I was limping."

"Take them off," he says in a harder voice.

The blisters on my fingers make it hard to untie the leather laces. My vision blurs, and no amount of blinking makes my eyesight clearer. Exhaustion drags my eyelids down. Manuel scoots closer and gently pushes my fingers away from my shoes.

"Let me do this." He gently tugs the boots and drenched socks off, and then, with the same gentle touch, lifts my right foot onto his knee. I survey the damage through my watery gaze. Blisters mar the tops of every single toe and the bottom heel. Same on the left foot. He reaches for a bowl filled with a poultice, then brushes a thin amount onto each foot.

"You need rest," he says grimly. "Lots of it."

Manuel unrolls the slim bedding and gently helps me lie down on my stomach. He rubs the same mixture onto my back, peeling the fabric away with hesitant fingers. "You're burning up."

"I feel like I'm on fire."

He continues running his palms across my wounded back. The medicine feels cool. I want to roll around in it naked.

"Better?"

"Sí. Gracias," I whisper. "I still can't believe—"

"Silencio. Descansa."

"Don't leave me." My voice drops to a soft hush. "No me dejes."

Don't leave me like you once did, without word. Without a goodbye.

I never hear his response. My eyes shut, and I fall asleep.

CAPÍTULO
Seis

I wake to the sight of Manuel studying me. He's propped against the curved wall, a bowl of mashed avocados in his lap. His hat is off, and I realize my head is using it as a pillow. I'm lying on my stomach, cool air brushing against my exposed back. I try to push myself up, but my arms are weak and not working properly.

"Easy," he says softly. "You've been out for two days."

My eyes widen. "¿Dos días?"

He nods once, his lips tight.

Everything comes back in an instant. Arriving to the jungle, my escorts—Rumi the vigilante—the infernal jaguar, the rock wall.

Manuel.

"Where have you been?" I ask. "Three years without word."

He raises an eyebrow. "I sent word."

I shut my eyes, realizing my mistake. Of course he wrote—*to his mother*. Never anything personal to me. Again, I tell myself, why would he? He's probably forgotten all about the kiss. I don't say anything; I've already been behaving like a besotted fool and I don't want to pile it on.

Manuel wasn't easy like the other boys back at the Illustrian camp. Earning smiles from them took nothing. Kisses were even easier. This scout, this ranger of the Illustrian throne, doesn't hand out his grins to just anyone.

Or his kisses, for that matter. I'd never once heard of him kissing anyone else except me. Why can't I stop thinking about that night? He's certainly never going to bring it up.

"Here's what's going to happen next," he says. "I'm going to feed you, and you're going to eat what you can. And then we're going to talk. I've been sitting here, imagining the worst, and I can't take not knowing anymore."

He scoots closer, bringing the stone bowl with him.

Manuel coaxes me into a sitting position. He gently lifts a bowl filled with water to my dry, cracked lips. I gulp it loudly, wanting every last drop, but Manuel firmly keeps me from drinking all of it. I reach for the container, but he shakes his head. "Despacio."

"But I'm so thirsty."

"I know," he says. "You'll get more. *Slowly*."

I cross my arms and eye the bowl.

"Let's try some food." Using a wooden spoon—which he probably whittled himself—he feeds me a few bites of the mashed avocado.

My stomach roars to life.

"Not that I'm not thankful," I say in between chewing. "But do you have anything heartier than avocado?"

He smiles. My heart flutters once, twice, and I tell it to behave. It's just a smile. Manuel turns to a small fire pit, where a rabbit is propped, ready to be eaten. He cuts small chunks and drops them into the bowl. Silently, he hands everything over to me. He probably realizes that if I'm asking for a heavier meal, then I can feed myself.

He waits patiently, watching me eat, and I'm so hungry, I don't care if I've gotten any of the food on my face or in my hair, which has long since escaped its braid and hangs in a frizzy mess down my shoulders. I must look a sight.

When I'm finished, he takes the bowl and spoon from my hands, and lets me have more water. "Do you want to lie down again?"

I shake my head. Outside, it's raining still, the clouds heavy and dark. Thunder sounds off in the distance. "Any monsters come calling?"

"No visitors, unless you count the vultures."

"Vultures?"

He nods. "An enormous flock of them flew past, heading to where I found you. Turkey, yellow-heads, and even a few king vultures. They were excited, fighting among themselves, nearly tearing one another apart to get to whatever was dead on the ground. From the size of the flock, I'd say there was quite a bit of food for them to find."

"A dead beast, do you think?"

He shakes his head. "Too many vultures for just one animal. I'd say it was a small group of people traveling through."

I swallow bile. My entourage. They didn't make it out alive. I shut my eyes. Rumi the healer. My friend and I are done, but my heart splinters for her.

"Catalina," he says softly. "What is it?"

Goose bumps crawl over my skin. He calls me by name only

when he's thinking of me as a friend and not as his queen. The moments are rare: meals shared with his mother and sister in a closed room, the few times he'd taken me riding around the perimeter of our land, somehow sensing when I needed to be free of the stone walls trapping us inside. Again, times alone were rare. But he's been calling me by my name since he found me.

"I came in with a group of guards—Llacsans. They were my escorts. One of them was nice to me. I think he's dead. He must be. What could have attacked them? Another jaguar?"

"There are many monsters in this jungle."

"I don't know how anyone can survive this place," I say, shuddering, remembering the size of the jaguar, its gleaming claws.

"You're still alive."

"With your help," I say. "Luna's ray of moonlight, too. She led me to that hole, I think."

"One of my traps," he says. "It's how I found you."

"How long have you been in the forest?"

He waves his hand impatiently. "Later. I need to know—"

"I know you do," I say. "And I promise I'll tell you, but I . . ." I swallow. "Can we just talk about what you've been doing first?"

He leans back against the wall, his eyes moving upward to the ceiling. "My mission was to recruit allies by assimilating into the various tribes of the Tierra Baja. I thought that if I could earn their trust, they'd rise against Atoc. But no one dared join us. Every village I lived at, they spoke, one way or another, about the Illari. The tribe driven to the jungle by the Llacsans. They said maybe they'd support us. Out of all the tribes in the Lowlands, the Illari have good reason to hate the Llacsans. I only had to survive the jungle and find the legendary city, Paititi."

"Did you?" I ask. "Did you find it? Is it really made entirely of gold?"

His gaze drifts downward and lands on mine, oddly flat. "I've never seen it. I've only ever made it to the outside border of their perimeter. Their *heavily* guarded perimeter. They don't take to outsiders, especially Illustrians. My attempts at communication only made them angry and hostile. Eight months in this place and all I have to show for it is a broken nose."

My mind whirs. There has to be a way to convince the Illari to side with us, to take back the throne. Maybe if they met me, an Illustrian royal, the message would have more weight.

"Your turn, Catalina," he says. "Why aren't you at the keep? Is my family safe?"

His words are like shooting arrows, one right after the other, hitting their target.

I take a deep breath. "I don't quite know where to start. How do I . . ." I trail off. Should I begin with his family? I shake my head. I don't have the courage. "We learned that the Estrella—Atoc's powerful weapon—might be hidden somewhere in the castle. Ximena . . . Ximena was sent as my decoy. She went to find information, and—" My throat thickens. Thinking about her is too painful; speaking her name makes my heart *hurt*.

Manuel frowns. "Why would Atoc willingly allow Ximena access to the castle?"

"She went under the guise of posing as Atoc's fiancée."

His mouth drops in surprise. "What?"

"Please let me finish," I say. "It's a lot and I'm trying to . . ." I take a deep breath. "Here's what you need to know. Ximena betrayed me . . . all of us, and helped place Atoc's sister, Tamaya, on the throne. Who is now queen of Inkasisa. I refused to accept her as my sovereign, so she banished me. To the jungle. To my *death*."

He reacts like I expect him to. Growing silent and wooden as the seconds pass. His light brown eyes shut away behind half-mast lids, and his fingers curl into tight fists. Manuel looks out to the entrance of the cave, his expression carefully blank. He doesn't want to ask me about his family again. He's afraid to ask me. I don't blame him, so I keep the knowledge of their deaths to myself for however much longer he wants to hold on to the hope that they're alive.

I'm not going to destroy his hope like that, not when I'm the one responsible.

"And what happened to Atoc?"

"Ximena killed him," I whisper.

His face clears, as if a long-shouldered weight has been lifted off his back. "There's some good news, at least."

"Some," I agree. Until Ximena placed Atoc's sister on the throne. But Manuel knows that already. When he returns his attention to me, I nearly flinch. His expression is decided and resolved, and I brace myself for what will come next.

"We're leaving this place and heading back to the keep."

I blink. Not what I want to hear. At all. He starts throwing things into his pack, the bowls and spoon, leftover food. He puts on his hat and tightens the laces of his worn boots.

Through it all I can only stare.

"Be ready to leave in fifteen minutes," he says. "Your back has healed enough to travel, I think. But we'll move slow." He hesitates. "As slow as we can, anyway. I've been searching for a way out of this damned jungle and it's possible your tracks leading from the outside are still visible."

I shake my head. "I have to stay here."

He brushes off my comment. "How long were you traveling before you arrived at the jungle?"

"A week," I say. "But it doesn't matter because I'm not leaving."

"Can you scoot over? I want that bedroll."

"Manuel."

"Is the keep still standing?"

"Manuel," I say. "I'm not going with you."

His gaze narrows. He props a hand on one bent knee, the other leg tucked under him. "Haven't you been listening? It's pointless. The Illari can't stand having me in their jungle, let alone having a conversation. Every day is a test to stay alive. Their perimeter isn't just guarded with warriors capable of doom and death. They use the very jungle to fortify their borders—*with Pacha magic.* We can't get to them."

"We have to," I say angrily. "There're no other moves left. You want to head to the keep? Be my guest. You'll find no one there. It's *empty.* And I can't go back with nothing, without an army. I can't."

"Where is everyone?" he asks. "Damn it, Catalina. What aren't you telling me?"

"I've told you—"

His hand slashes the air. "No, *no.* Not everything. You haven't said a word about my family," he snaps. "You haven't mentioned what happened to our people."

I let out a sigh that could have been a sob. "They've accepted Princesa Tamaya as their queen."

"Why?" he asks. "There has to be a reason. Not one Illustrian would give up everything we've worked for this past decade for nothing."

"Their *reina* said she wanted peace," I snap. "That we'd be treated equal, that we'd have rights and a new life in La Ciudad Blanca. They believed her. The fools. As if we could ever agree with the Llacsans after what they've done to us. That girl is dreaming if she thinks she'll achieve peace."

He's quiet for a long moment. "When I lived among the various tribes in the Tierra Baja, I learned quite a bit about Llacsans. No, stop," he says, holding up his hand. "Maybe some of them are different than Atoc? Aren't you curious to know why our people would accept her as queen? Observe with your own eyes what others have seen?"

Something in me dies. Whatever I felt, whatever I yearned for in this moment—his smiles, to be seen by him as a girl and not just his queen—all of that vanishes like yesterday's sunrise.

It's another betrayal. I can't look at him. Can't speak to him anymore. Why am I the only one who still cares about what happened to us during the revolt? We lost family. We lost our homes. Our way of life. The throne. My parents were murdered.

"I'm going to find the Illari. With or without you."

"Don't do this to me," Manuel whispers. "It's been three years. I need to go home."

"I know you do." I look away. "So go."

"You're still not listening to me." His hands reach toward me as if he wants to shake me. "It will mean your death."

I'm supposed to die here anyway. But I don't say the words out loud. "I have nothing and no one left, Manuel."

"Let me take you—"

"Don't you dare finish that sentence," I say, my voice cold and frozen over as if I were made of solid ice. "Do not."

"My mother isn't one to suffer fools," he says gently. "She may have seen this as the best way forward—"

I slap my palms on the ground. "Your mother is dead!"

My words ricochet off the walls, clamoring in my head, ringing in my ears.

His face goes deadly white. "No."

"Ana and Sofía both died at the hands of Atoc," I say. "Do you still want to accept Atoc's sister as your queen? If you do, then I guess I never knew you at all. Your mother would be ashamed, Manuel. Ashamed. Do you want to know how she died? She was executed while Ximena *stood by and watched.*" I pause. "Don't tell me *you're* ready to quit."

He flinches at my words, at my tone.

There are tears running down my face. I've hurt him. I've hurt us both. He stands, head ducked to keep from bumping into the cave ceiling, and marches farther into the dark until he's out of sight.

I don't know how long I sit without him. The rain hasn't stopped; neither has the roaring thunder. In the distance I catch sight of the flock of vultures, feasting on death. My back is sore and tired from not having anything to lean on, but the idea of pressing my wounds against the cool rock is not appealing.

I turn my head and gaze into the darkness where Manuel went. I never should have told him about his family that way. Impatient and frustrated beyond belief. Back at the Illustrian keep, when I was just the personal maid to Ximena's condesa act, I helped soothe tempers, and tried my best to care for each family under my supervision. I was everyone's friend, the person they came to when approaching Ximena was unthinkable.

I should have spoken to him gently, but he was starting to sound like *her*.

I'm tired of being the only one holding on to the Illustrian dream of reclaiming La Ciudad Blanca for ourselves. I want him to feel the same hurt I felt. I want him to remember what we've been fighting for. But more than anything I want to remember who I am: the condesa. Ruler of Inkasisa. I am the best answer to who will protect the Illustrians who survived the revolt.

Footsteps sound in the dark and draw closer. I stiffen, bracing myself. If he insists on leaving the jungle, I won't fight him. But I'm going to stay and try to reach the Illari. I will not go home empty and without a plan.

I will not.

There's iron in my blood, after all.

Manuel reappears, eyes bloodshot and red-rimmed. My heart pinches, sharp and painful. He's been crying and he didn't want me to see. He drops to his knees in front of me and lifts his chin, daring me to say something. But I don't. Instinct tells me to keep my hands close, no matter how much I want to offer some comfort.

I need him angry.

"I'll take you as far as I've gone, Condesa," he says quietly. I stiffen at his use of my title. "I'll help you and protect you with my body. Whatever I can do to give you access to the Illari, I'll do it. I'll do it for them—my family." His voice nearly breaks, and he takes a deep breath. "But I'm in control. Whatever I say, you do. That's the only way we'll survive. If I say to stop, hide, or run, you obey me. Do you agree with my terms?"

"Yes."

Manuel nods, and gone is his harrowed look. Now he lets me see his fury. The expression on his face steals my breath. The scant lines around his eyes are tight and his mouth is a white slash against olive skin. Gone is my friend. He won't call me by my name anymore. I'm looking at a soldier, born and raised by a warrior mother.

I'm almost sorry to have pushed him.

Almost.

Once again, I hold on to Manuel's back as we climb down the impossible granite wall, this time using the coiled vine from within the cave. His shoulders are tight beneath my arms, probably from the exertion, but maybe also because of my decision to find the Illari. I try to forget about the disappointment in his eyes, the apparent despair in their depths. He's homesick, missing his family, and terrified we won't survive the jungle.

I ought to cut him loose. Force him to go home and mourn his family. But I need him with me. I can't survive this place without him. He's been living in this nightmare for eight months—living and somehow surviving.

Manuel's faster on the way down, even while carrying me and the canvas bag, filled with his meager possessions and my dented telescope. The second his booted feet touch the jungle carpet, I drop my legs to the floor and back away from him as if he were a feral jaguar. He glances up to the cave, an unreadable expression on his face.

"What is it?"

Grudgingly, he turns away from the rock wall and pulls out his machete. "For three years I've kept moving, never staying longer than a few weeks in each village. That cave was my home for two months."

I squeeze my eyes shut. Three years is a long time to be away from home. I want to hug him, offer some encouragement. The words bubble to the surface, but his walls are up. He's suffering. I know he is, and now I'm the burden he has to carry. "Tell me how to find the Illari, and after you do, go back to La Ciudad, Manuel. You don't need to be here."

He hacks at thick liana vines, and then glances at me from over his shoulder. "Did you come here with supplies?"

I nod, my heart sinking. This is it: He's changed his mind. "I lost them though."

"¿Dónde?"

"Over the cliff. Near that pit you found me in," I say. "The way out is about a day's walk from there. Maybe less."

He looks away and hacks at several broad palms. "Anything worth saving?"

I'm not sure if I'm supposed to be following him, so I stay put. "Hammock and mosquito net. Dagger. Some food."

He pauses, his hand held high over his head. "Supplies are hard to come by in the jungle, especially a weapon." Then his arm swoops down and slices away at the dense foliage. "We'll search the area for your things before crossing the river."

I barely hear his words, except for the one that matters most: *we*. He's made his choice; I gave him a way out. I even told him how far of a journey it was to the border.

Manuel turns around and I have to blink at the sight of him.

Sweat drips from his brow, and his arms are corded with muscle. He towers over me, grim and silent, appraising me not as his sovereign, but as a weakness he'll have to compensate for.

"I can defend myself," I say.

His gaze drops to my slim hands, the blisters gone, the skin soft once more. I drag them behind my back. Embarrassment sweeps across my cheeks.

He swears under his breath.

"I'll keep up." I lift my chin, pride demanding it of me, even as the blood rushes to my face. "Try not to worry."

"This is the height of stupidity," he says. "You know that, right?"

"It's not *that* bad of an idea."

"You're right. It's the worst."

"Then how else will I help my people, Manuel? Hmm? How else will I take back the throne? I don't have an army. Do you want to help me, or don't you? Don't you want to avenge your mother and sister?"

He flinches. "Try to understand something for me, por favor: Above all else, my mother would have wanted you to *survive*. Aside from securing allies, I had one other job. And that was to watch over you. Make sure no harm came to you inside the Illustrian keep."

"Who would have hurt me?"

"Hundreds of Illustrian refugees, hungry and near starving? Desperate and bored? Without your title, you were just a girl among hundreds. Anything could have happened to you."

Memories of the few moments we were alone together resurface. I thought he just enjoyed my company. Thought of me as a friend. "All those years . . . I was just a job to you?"

His brow rises. "What else would you be?"

I shrug, my cheeks flaming. Again, the memory of our kiss sweeps all other thoughts from my mind. He's completely forgotten. "It doesn't matter. We should keep going."

A muscle in his jaw ticks. "Follow close behind me. We must *always* stay together. Don't touch or lean on anything. Don't wander away, even if you have to relieve yourself. Not every predator can be seen or anticipated. Do not talk until I say it's safe. I need to listen to the jungle. Understand?"

I nod and try to keep my face neutral, because his tone isn't one I'm used to, especially coming from him. He's always been respectful, but now he's erected a careful barrier between us, reminding me that I'm his sovereign and the only thing I should be thinking about is acquiring an army.

He whips around and plunges into the mat of trees and hanging vines as thick as his arm. I stumble forward and through the tiny path forged, my gaze trained on the strong lines of his back. He's uneasy; I can see it in every one of his movements, the hard press of his feet on the tangled mess of leaves, the downward motion of his hand as he cuts into the face of the jungle, thick with heat and the scent of mildew and rotting mushrooms. We are enveloped by the various shades of greens and browns under our feet and over our heads. There's no sunlight under the canopy, only the chronic gloom cast by the broad palms and tangled branches. More vines unspool at my feet. I carefully step around or over each one, minding for a snake—or worse.

This is the same way we'd gone two days earlier, but the path has already been swallowed by the ravenous jungle. By now, the trail leading out of this place is long gone as well. He must know that. But I guess it doesn't matter anymore. The trickling sound of water comes softly at first, but with every step closer, the noise transforms into a gentle roar.

Manuel stops at the tree line, looking from one end to the other and back again. His machete is an extension of his arm. Every few minutes he looks back to see if I'm still trudging along in his footsteps, or to check if I'm hurt. I scramble down the bank and for once we walk alongside each other, toward the cliff I thought I'd left behind.

My expression sours. More climbing.

"That won't be the worst of it," he says, and then he quickens his step until we are at the base of the cliff. It's nothing like the wall we climbed, with me on his back and the howling wind tousling my hair. But it's still steep. The boulders are jagged and large, emitting a sweet smell. "Step where I step."

I'm not used to following orders. Not used to being looked at as if I were a burden, an annoying nuisance. Back home, I'd been a favorite. Everyone's friend, the person they turned to for a listening ear or encouragement. While in public, I was free to be myself, but *even then* I knew that no one could order me around.

Manuel lifts his foot high, hooking it between the rocks, and hauls himself up. I follow, surveying his technique, where he places his hands and feet. We're halfway up when the distinct sound of thunder rumbles overhead. Seconds later raindrops plop onto the rocks, splattering and dripping down the craggy surface. The rain is relentless, a steady pattering that infiltrates every line and curve of my body. If I ever make it out of here, I'm going to stand in the sun for an eternity, I swear it.

Manuel reaches the top first and then bends to help me up the rest of the way. I consider ignoring his offered hand, but my legs and arms are shaking too much. I reach up, and he clasps my palm, his callouses rubbing against my skin. As soon as I'm upright, he lets me go, then he yanks out his machete and slices a way through. I follow close behind, his dutiful shadow, until we arrive at the pit he found me in.

The jaguar has been picked clean; all that remains are chewed-up bones half hidden by thick twigs and branches. Manuel studies the area and places a light hand on the log I'd climbed over. "You came from the direction of the cliff."

My breath comes out in pants. "But I was moving toward it at first. Trying to get away. I didn't run far."

He takes this in and then heads away from the pit. Once again I follow him. He stops every so often to examine crushed leaves still attached to their stems, overturned twigs, and any tracks on the ground. We're at it for what feels like hours, without a word spoken between us. It finally stops raining, but then the heat is stifling. I sip hot gulps of air while birds chatter close by, only stopping to listen for the sounds of an approaching predator.

I can't take the silence or my growing thirst. All I can picture is a frosty glass of water, something I'll never have in here.

"Manuel," I whisper. "I need water."

He glances at me from where he's crouching, examining a nondescript patch of jungle floor that looks exactly the same as all the rest. In fact, I think it *is* the same as all the rest. "Yo también."

"Don't you carry any?"

"There's plenty if you know where to look." He stands and

surveys the area for a long moment. He points with his machete. "This way."

I trail behind him, the familiar thwacking noise of his machete ever present, like my own heartbeat. Manuel leads us into a swampy grove where bamboo shoots up from the ground, towering above us, over double his height. The bamboo shoots are perfectly segmented and parallel to one another. He hacks off a piece exactly at the joint, two segments high, and then grabs a leaf, proceeding to wipe down the bamboo from top to bottom and all the way around.

He hands the heavy column to me. "Some bamboo can irritate skin. Safer to wipe it down with something."

The bamboo weighs more than I thought it would. Its shade is a bruised yellow, and when I tilt the bamboo, liquid sloshes from within. He lops off one more stalk at the joint, wipes it down, and then holds the plant at arm's length, chopping the top with one fluid motion. Silently, he hands it to me in exchange for the other. The bamboo is now a sort of wooden cup, and inside laps astonishingly clear water. I bring the stalk to my lips and drink the whole thing down, and while it's this side of warm, it tastes refreshing, like diluted herbal tea. Manuel finishes his drink and turns the stalk around to chop off the top of the other end. Again, he hands it over to me and I eagerly polish off every drop. As soon as I'm done, my stomach rumbles.

Manuel rummages in his pack and pulls out a handful of walnuts and a banana. I scarf both down in a matter of seconds. I'm still hungry, but now the feeling is bearable. What I wouldn't give for a bowl of hot quinoa piled high with fried eggs and diced red onion and locoto. I want to ask for more food, but he's already turned away, examining the landscape. He doesn't eat anything, and guilt settles onto my shoulders, weighing them down further. I must have eaten his meager supply.

His back is still facing me. "Lista?"

"Ready," I say, trudging after him. His disapproval picks at me like a vulture nibbling on raw flesh. It hurts, more than I'd like, and as I carefully step my way through the path he's blazing, I try to hold on to my reasons for staying. I've failed my people, failed to keep my promise that I'd return their lives to the way they were before the Llacsan revolt. My people lost everything and wanted revenge; they wanted the Illustrian royal family back in power.

I am the only survivor. Their last hope to reclaim our way of life, our culture.

If I'm not their condesa, then who am I? I've only known one future. Behind closed doors, Ana—Manuel's mother—trained me to be worthy of the title, and I soaked up her knowledge as if I were a starving plant in the desert. Memorizing history texts, studying geography and the many countries surrounding Inkasisa, categorizing them into compartments in my mind labeled "enemy" or "friend." I speak the foreign languages of our neighbors passably well, but I've mastered the most important one: diplomacy.

When I turned seventeen, Ana sat me down and we discussed suitable marriage candidates from neighboring countries. Manuel had been gone for two years then, and I didn't know if I was ever going to see him again. So I paid attention, remembering their names and ranks. And on top of all that, I've studied the stars, worshiping our goddess, Luna. I love her as if she were my own mother, even if she doesn't love me like the dutiful daughter I hope I am.

Everything I've done has been for the throne. For the future of my people, so that our traditions and beliefs will survive the ravages of time.

I'm nothing if I'm not the condesa.

Manuel stops abruptly, and I reach out to keep myself from slamming into him, my fingers barely skimming his shoulders. The line of his back stiffens at my touch. I pull away and peer around him, stuffing my hurt deep within me. It has no place in this jungle.

Manuel thinks like Ximena—wanting to see this Llacsan queen with his own eyes and come to his own conclusion. He might end up being completely fine with having yet another Llacsan on the throne, even though the last ten years have been demoralizing. Barely living behind the fortress, biding our time to take back the throne while we fought starvation and boredom.

Like my former friend, he doesn't believe in me either.

I shove the thought out of my mind. Manuel drops to his haunches, peering around, and eventually finds my pack, half hidden under a tangle of brush, the dagger lying discarded and nearly forgotten next to it. He hands both things to me and stands, frowning at a nearby tree. Something else has gotten his attention.

"What is it?"

Manuel takes a step closer to the massive trunk, its timber a reddish brown. "This is a mahogany tree. Take a look, and tell me what you see." I step closer, inspecting the ragged bark. There's nothing of note. When I tell him so, he raises a brow.

"Try again."

It's painfully hot, the mosquitos are lunching on my skin, and my stomach grumbles loudly, demanding a hearty meal. I'm in no mood for one of his lessons. "Just tell me."

He remains still and stubbornly silent, his expression grim.

I sigh and study the bark again. Deep grooves run up and down the length of the trunk, some curving and deep, others shallow and straighter. I place my fingers into the marks and Manuel snarls. I jump back, alarmed. He maneuvers me behind him in a flash.

"What did I say about touching anything?"

"It's only a tree," I mutter.

The sharp hiss is the only warning.

Manuel slams his machete against the trunk. Something falls to the ground, and he scoops it up using his weapon. On the steel blade rests the trapezoidal head of a snake, brilliant yellow with brownish flecks near its cleft mouth. Surrounding its diamond-shaped eyes are ridges that look like eyelashes. Even dead, the pellet gaze is focused on mine. Its vermillion forked tongue rests languidly against Manuel's steel.

"Oropel," he says. "One of the vipers. I would have had to cut off your hand if it'd bitten you. Never touch anything without looking *everywhere* first. Understand?"

I nod.

"Now tell me what you see."

I don't touch the bark this time. My knees shake, but somehow I remain upright. This time, I finally see what captivated his attention. Along the trunk are faint claw marks that run high over my head and down to my knees.

"There," I say, jerking my chin at the wood. "An animal made them."

He nods. "Jaguar marking her territory. Probably the one who hunted you."

I shudder. "Why is this important?"

He points to the large plants surrounding the tree trunk. "It's not, but those are."

After I take a step back, I finally see the entire picture. What wasn't visible to me when only studying the timber. All the stalks have been cut in half. Deliberately and in plain sight once you know where to look.

"I don't understand."

"It means we're being hunted," Manuel whispers. "By the Illari."

I press closer to Manuel, thankful for his presence, and for the blade curled tightly in his palm. He stands with his feet braced apart, his attention flicking to several gaps in the immense green. His chest rises and falls, and I mimic his quiet breathing, straining my ears to listen for any signs of the approaching threat.

But the jungle song rises around us, making it impossible to detect any irregular movements in the brush.

"They've tracked you before then left you alone, right?" I clutch his tunic sleeve, trying to keep an even tone but failing.

Manuel shoots me an exasperated glance. "What makes you think they left me alone? I've been in *hiding.*"

"But—"

"Quiet." He slowly turns, machete raised, and peers into the jungle gloom. "They're waiting."

My voice is a soft hush. "For what?"

"You said we were close to the border, right? A day's walk?"

I nod.

"That's it then," he says in an undertone. "They're waiting to see if we leave. If we do, they'll leave us alone."

"And if we don't?"

Manuel's gaze locks with mine. "Think carefully. The odds are stacked against us. One or both of us will die here. Decide, Condesa."

I drag in a deep gulp of steaming air, feel it press against my lungs, and slowly push my breath from my lips until I'm empty. "I have to try."

His lips flatten. "I was afraid you'd say that."

"Manuel, go home." My eyes prick with tears, but I force myself not to lower them. "I've lost everything, and this is my only chance to get it back. This isn't your fight anymore. Go."

He glances toward the immense trees surrounding us, perhaps imagining taking that first step away from me. My heart cracks. I can't ask him to risk his life for a cause he doesn't believe in. I can't ask him to stay because he *pities* me.

Maybe I'm supposed to do this alone.

"I can't leave you," he whispers.

"Why?" My voice holds one squeeze of lemon, enough to make his shoulders tighten. "Clearly you're curious about the Llacsans, and why our people have chosen to live alongside them in La Ciudad."

Manuel doesn't refute it. "I made a promise to my mother to keep you safe."

I blink. Right, this is his reason for staying. His code of honor won't allow him to ignore his word. Which means *everything* to him. But I can't deny how much it hurts that he would potentially accept an enemy as his queen, and not the friend and sovereign he'd grown up with.

"Take your pack, keep that dagger close. We have to move." He steps around me, heading back toward the cliff. I sling the strap over my shoulder, twisting it so the bulk rests on my back and not my hip.

I look around, staring into the flat green, sure there are a hundred pairs of eyes looking back. "Manuel."

"Move it." He sets off running.

A bellowing cry roars to life. The sound is lightning cracking against stone. I bolt after him, my pack bouncing against my lower back. He jumps over tree roots, hacking at dangling vines and enormous broad leaves. Gone is his caution—the Illari are at our heels.

A sharp whistle is my only warning.

I instinctively flinch as something rushes past my ear, the gust of air rustling my hair. I scream as arrows smack against trunks. *Thwack, thwack, thwack.*

Manuel spins, arm already outstretched, reaching for me. The warm clasp of his hand does nothing to settle the frantic beating of my heart. My breath comes out in shuddering gasps. He yanks us behind a tree.

Someone rushes past, spear raised high. A blur of dark hair, toned olive legs encased in leather sandals, and muscled arms gripping a long wooden spear. The man stops just beyond our tree and whirls around.

Manuel shoves me out of the way as the spear comes barreling at us. I land on the ground, full of terror, and suppress a scream. My fingers dig into the dirt, my knees sink into the thick padding of decaying leaves.

The Illari warrior charges with a ferocious war cry.

Manuel steps forward with his machete raised, drawing his attacker away from me. The clash of their weapons rents the air. Birds caw and swoop away from the fight. I scramble onto my feet, back away until I meet the solid strength of the oak tree. I hunch my shoulders, trying to conceal myself under the low-hanging branches.

Manuel fights with every inch of his body. Every jab of his weapon lands—until his opponent bleeds from wounds on his hip and stomach and forearm. Manuel's feet never stop moving until he disarms the Illari. I look away as he uses the butt of his machete to knock out the Illari fighter.

Someone grabs my arm, screams unintelligible words into my ear. They hold my wrist in a tight snare. A man's voice speaks Quechua, but I'm too rattled to understand a word of it. My captor drags me away from my hiding spot, and I stumble.

"Let go!" I shriek.

Manuel bends and yanks out a dagger hidden in his boots. He launches the blade and it somersaults through the air. The weapon sinks into the belly of my assailant, and the force catapults him off his feet. I dash to Manuel, my bag smacking against my hip.

He takes my hand. "Run!"

More arrows fly. I let out a small cry. Embedded in the muck is a long wooden arrow with black and white feathers stitched at the end. How many of the Illari are there? I pump my legs, my arms swinging wildly, expecting to feel the sudden smack of an arrow. But it never comes. The Illari's yelling grows louder, and the sound of rustling leaves rings in my ears. We reach the cliff's edge and Manuel runs alongside it. He slows to a jog, peering down the other side.

Thunder blasts overhead.

Damn this wet season.

Manuel continues searching for something. He stops at a sparse area as water pours from above, pounding everything in sight with a great watery fist. He wraps both arms around me, tucking my hands against his chest, and walks me backward to the cliff.

"What are you doing?" I cry over the bellowing storm.

"Trust me!"

We're at the edge, my heels in the air. The water softens the dirt and it gives. "Manuel!"

The jungle floor turns to sludge and we slide down, mud splattering our faces. He tightens his hold around me as we follow the muddy current. Trees zip by on either side, and I scream. This is madness. We're going to hit one.

We slow toward the bottom and Manuel uses his feet to push us away from a jagged rock at the foot of the hill. Then he yanks me upright, both of us covered in brown muck. The rain is relentless; I can barely see a foot in front of my face. Manuel urges me forward, toward the black river.

Manuel mutters a curse under his breath and half turns, surveying the strong current, the corners of his mouth deepening. "We can't go back up—they've surrounded us."

He pulls me behind him, facing the hill that envelops the craggy cliff on either side. Trees punctuate the soggy jungle floor, and while I know the Illari are close, I can't find a single one of them through the pouring rain. But I can't trust my eyes in the forest. I swallow hard, afraid to stare into that hill, afraid of what I'll find. Any moment I expect a group of Illari warriors to burst through the tree line. But the seconds stretch into minutes, even as my heart continues to batter my ribs. Only the growing murmur of birds in the distance disrupts the silence.

"What are they doing? Why don't they attack?" I ask. I don't know how long we stand there, at the base of the hill, the river at our backs. But no one comes. There's no more yelling. Only the splattering of heavy rain and the croaking red frogs jumping happily in puddles. Probably poisonous, every single one of them. The birds' murmuring grows louder and louder.

Manuel narrows his gaze. "Something's happened."

"What—"

Loud cawing drowns out my voice. I turn to face the water, and in the distance, I catch sight of a massive billowing cloud. It shifts erratically, the bulk moving up and down. It takes me a moment to understand: I'm not staring at a cloud.

Hundreds of birds soar above the canopy of trees, shrieking as one. The sight is extraordinary and terrifying all at once. I slap my palms against my ears to deafen their panicked call. Manuel lowers his weapon, and his jaw loosens. Without knowing how or why, I know that we're all gazing at the sight. The Illari have stopped attacking us because of the unusual noise coming from the birds, the bizarre flying.

A second later the sound stops. The birds cease their flapping, and fall to the earth.

Dead.

Every single one of them.

"What just happened?" I ask, clutching Manuel's arm.

"Shhh," he says, tilting his head. We listen for signs of the Illari's approach, but there's nothing. No more yelling, or the whistle of arrows. The gradual song of the jungle returns.

"I think . . . I think they've gone," he says. "Maybe to investigate the birds?"

"What could have killed them all?" I ask. "I've never seen anything like it."

"Whatever it was, it most likely saved our lives." Manuel studies the river. "Can you swim?"

The Illustrian fortress is surrounded by mountains at the rear, and an abysm several hundred feet deep at the front. No water anywhere. Even if I wanted to, there's never been enough to drink my fill, let alone swim in. I shake my head.

"Can you float?" he asks. "It's easy—just flip onto your back, keep your arms outstretched, and position your body parallel to the water. Your head is half in the water, chin lifted up—"

"I don't know how to do it."

"Fine," he says. "Can you cook?"

I glance away, a flush rising to my cheeks. I can boil water and eggs, but that's it. Every attempt leads to burnt bread and tasteless mush. Somehow I don't think he'd like any of that. "No."

"Well, we have your telescope," he says, brightening.

I nearly crumble. What will he say when he learns that I'm not much of a seer? Yet another thing I can't do. Shame climbs up my throat, spreads across my cheeks, and makes my eyes burn. My education didn't prepare me for the jungle—or basic survival.

"We're stuck here. Want to learn how to cook?"

"What? *Now?*"

"The sun will set in the next hour and we need to build a shelter to spend the night. We can't be anywhere near the river during dusk."

"Why not?"

"Caimán feeding hour. And the piranhas." He reaches for my pack, and I hand it to him. "I'll hunt for food." He flips the machete, handle in my direction. "Take it and cut down thin liana vines for me to use."

I take the weapon, my hand dropping automatically because of its weight. "What if there are more of them out there?"

But Manuel shakes his head. "We'd be dead if there were."

The rain is a soft patter now. I swallow hard and avoid looking at the water where stingrays live buried in the mud, and schools of bone-scouring fish hunt in the depths. "Are we going to cross the river?"

"We have to in order to find Paititi."

I squint into the gloom. "Do you think we'll make it to the lost city?"

His expression turns stony. "I told you, the odds are stacked against us, Condesa. Cut those vines, I'll be close. Scream if you need me." Manuel turns, but pauses for a moment. "Remember to look carefully where you touch. Only the liana. And stay around here, on the bank."

I nod.

Then he bounds up the bank, vanishing behind the trees. No arrows come. I shudder at the sight of all those birds falling from the sky as one. What kind of monster could have killed so many at once? What else is out there? Terror makes my skin crawl. I want to yell Manuel's name the moment he disappears from my line of sight. The churning water roars in my ears, and somewhere close by the monkeys begin their howling. Mosquitos swarm around me, happy now that the rain has let up. Steaming fog curls around the tree trunks, hissing softly.

I hate this place. Hate how the ground slithers, how the lethal water runs like veins throughout the jungle. But I won't let it defeat me—I can't fail again. I can't be as weak and useless as they all think. I take a step forward and another, until I'm close to the end of the bank. Vines hang from nearly every branch, or lie spooling on the ground. The machete is awkward in my smooth palms, nothing like the slim daggers I'm used to. I squint into the green darkness and catch sight of thinner vines. I'm close enough to inspect nearly every visible inch of the plant, and seeing nothing threatening or with sharp teeth, I swipe at several all at once. They plop onto the ground. Manuel didn't say how many he'd need, but this has to be enough.

I scoop up the vines, and half carry, half drag them back toward the bank. I'm several feet away when something shrieks, the noise slicing the air. A mewling cry follows.

Whatever it is, it isn't human.

I don't think.

Goose bumps flare up and down my arms. Another scream, and the sound is heartbreaking, full of suffering and terror and defeat. There's a menacing growl and then leaves stirring. My feet can't take me back to the sandbank fast enough, the vines dragging behind me like the tail of an anaconda.

When I emerge from the tree line, the sky blazes orange gold, a heavenly bonfire for the gods. I drop the vines and the machete onto the sand and clap my hands over my ears to block out the eternal song of the jungle: rustling leaves, hoots, high trills, coughing grunts, and croaks.

A soft tickle creeps along the back of my right hand. Slowly,

I lower my arm to inspect the sensation. A four-inch-long murky-green scorpion clings to my skin, spiral tail quivering. I fling my hand, screaming, and it snaps into the air. I squeeze my eyes shut as another rustling noise grows louder, someone crashing out from beneath the jungle canopy.

Strong arms grip my hands and shake me.

"Stop screaming," Manuel says. "Condesa! What's wrong?"

I reopen my eyes, and his mud-splattered face is inches from mine, dark eyes deep pools of calm water. "S-scorpion."

"Where were you bit?" he asks, releasing me. "Show me."

"I wasn't, I don't think." I thrust my hand toward him, and he takes it into his, and warmth spreads to every inch of my skin. He turns over my palm, carefully examining the flesh.

"You're fine." He releases my hand, and then scoops up an enormous speckled egg from the ground, which he gives to me, and then picks up six bamboo stalks, eight segments high each. "I'm going to build shelter before it gets dark, come on."

I trudge behind him, cradling the egg, my pack swaying behind me. He finds two trees close together and beckons me closer with the crook of his finger. "Hammock and net." I awkwardly wrest it from within my bag and toss the canvas bundle to him. He sets up the hammock and then secures one of the bamboo stalks above it.

"Stay here," he says. "You can put the egg in the hammock if you're tired of carrying it."

But I'm not. It seems bizarre to be holding something so fragile in such a dangerous place. Manuel returns carrying the bundle of vines and the machete and proceeds to attach the rest of the stalks to the one above the gently swaying hammock, forming a kind of roof with the bed underneath. He cuts large palm fronds and layers several over the bamboo, then he finally sets the mosquito net over all the greenery. Layers of protection from the jungle.

"Cozy," I say.

He holds out his hand for the egg. "Hungry?"

The poor little creature. "What's inside?"

"Ostrich."

I bite my lip, and he snorts. When my stomach grumbles, I pass the egg to him and he sets it down onto the floor. Then he lops off a segment of bamboo and hands it to me. I drink the water in one long gulp while he uses his machete to scrape the sides of another stalk until there's a small pile of tinder.

"Will you grab the pan from my bag?" He jerks his chin in the direction of the shelter, where the pack is nestled against a tree trunk. I march over, watching where I step. The pan is near the bottom. I yank it out and turn around in time to catch the soft wisps of smoke curling from the scraped-up bamboo. I hand over the pan and Manuel cracks the giant egg into it, and the food slowly cooks above the fire.

My stomach growls, demanding to be fed. The size of the egg can feed ten people, but I swear I might finish it off by myself. I haven't eaten anything since that one banana and the handful of nuts. Neither has he, for that matter. Manuel stomps out the fire once the food is done cooking, and we eat the egg using chopped bamboo stalks as makeshift spoons. It's plain but somehow delicious, and in moments there's nothing left but an empty pan, my stomach finally full. We put everything away into our bags and duck under the shelter.

He and I will be sharing a hammock.

I flush to the roots of my hair, but Manuel doesn't notice. He checks the bed for any creeping insects and then motions for me to get in. Once I'm in, he settles into the opposite end, booted feet dangling off the edge and away from my face. I position mine the same way, the hammock swinging wildly as we try to get comfortable.

But that's impossible. The long line of Manuel's body is pressed against mine and I'm suddenly thankful for the darkness hiding my red cheeks. His matter-of-fact demeanor helps. Everything is about survival with him, and sleeping above the ground is part of that. His heart's probably a steady drum in his chest while mine dances against my ribs.

"Sleep, Condesa," he says gruffly.

I stare up at the canopy of tight leaves. "I have a name."

"Yes, I know."

Neither of us says a word, but I know he's still awake. It's pitch black underneath the palm fronds and maybe that's why I say what I do. "Why didn't you say goodbye?"

Manuel remains quiet. The words he won't say too loud in this shelter. I lie thinking, remembering that night, remembering how he'd been the one to pull me behind that tree. I'd been laughing, and he'd kissed me before I'd stopped. I remember laughing still as his lips moved earnestly against mine, until it was no longer funny. Until I could no longer feel the ground beneath my feet. The way he'd looked at me after, as if I were the best thing he'd ever seen in his whole life.

How can anyone forget something like that?

All day he's kept me at arm's distance. No private jokes, or reminiscing about our childhood. Calling me by my title, and not my name. Treating me as a sovereign and not a friend. Manuel doesn't want me poking at that wall he's erected, trying to get through. Maybe he's afraid of what I'll find on the other side.

"Whatever it is you're thinking about, it's not helpful," he says at last, and in a voice that brooks no argument.

"You don't know a thing about my thoughts."

"Want to bet?" he says, his voice hard. "Sleep, Condesa. Tomorrow we face the river."

My stomach clenches. For a moment I'd forgotten about the rushing water, and the Illari watching us, waiting for our next move. I exhale, willing my body to relax, but I can't get that arrow out of my mind. Quick and deadly, coming from out of nowhere.

CAPÍTULO

nueve

When I wake, Manuel is gone. I stumble out of the hammock
and duck under the netting and broad leaves, frantic, my heart
thudding against my ribs. The dappled jungle floor steams under
my boots, alive and noisy with the sounds of buzzing locusts
and rustling bushes. Our measly campfire has disappeared,
swallowed whole during the night. From down the hill comes
a steady thwacking noise, and I walk toward the river, careful
not to touch anything. My clothes are a mess, the scent truly
frightening. I haven't bathed in maybe a week, not since I first
arrived in this place.

Birds trill as I continue, my stomach grumbling. I slept as
well as I could have expected, if a little cramped, squished against
Manuel's lean shape. Several times I woke, having to wipe the
sweat from my face with my dirty tunic.

The immense tree trunks become sparse as the black river
comes into view, long and wide from one end to the other.
Manuel kneels in front of a rectangular raft made of bamboo
and liana vines, and he cuts at smaller stalks. His hair is wet

underneath his hat, for some unaccountable reason. The rest of him is dry, and while I wouldn't say he's precisely clean, most of the mud and grime has disappeared from his face and arms.

"Buenos días," I say.

He doesn't look up. "If you're hungry, there's scrambled eggs in the pan. I found papaya, too."

No good morning. Not even a glance in my direction. "You've been busy."

He grunts and moves over to a smaller pile of liana vines. The shorter stacks are tied to the bottom of the longer one, and the shape of an oar emerges. He quickly creates another one while I eat the rest of the food, still warm in the pan. I watch him work, his movements brisk, neat, and efficient. Always the same, no matter what he's doing. Ana used to tell her children, "The way you do anything is the way you do everything." Her mandate governs Manuel to this day. No matter what he does, he does it with excellence. In this jungle, that's a gift. But for my heart? His duty and honor are devastating.

He stands and pushes the raft toward the river. I bend over to help and together we get our makeshift transportation close to the edge, only a foot away from the lapping water. "We need to pack up," he says.

As we walk back up the hill, I shoot him a glance. His shoulders are tense, jaw locked tight. He's still angry I didn't leave the jungle when I had the chance. "You're not happy with me."

"It doesn't matter if I'm happy or not. All that matters is your safety."

"And yours."

"No," he says ruefully. Then he stops, forcing me to stop,

but I'm grateful to catch my breath. "Have you been paying attention to where we are?"

"Aren't you doing that?"

His lips thin. "What if I'm dead?"

"Then chances are, I'll be dead too."

"I never want to hear that from you again. If I'm dead, it's because I was protecting you, and you need to live no matter what."

"You'd die for me, wouldn't you?" I hate the idea of how much trouble I'm putting him through, by remaining here with me in this jungle, risking his life.

"Without hesitation."

"I hope it doesn't come to that."

"Me too."

"I wish you'd been there," I say softly. "During the fight for the throne, when I'd lost and Ximena betrayed me. Things might have ended differently."

"Had I known, I would have fought with you." He straightens and lifts his chin toward the trees. "Do you know where the jungle border is? Just in case you need to walk back out."

I take a moment to think. "We've been going in a straight line, so it's this way." I point behind me.

If I weren't his sovereign, I swear he'd start laughing. The corners of his mouth twitch, but he manages to fight the lurking smile. He ticks my arm several notches to the right. "This way. The jungle will eat you alive, Condesa, if you're not constantly aware and careful and vigilant. Want to survive out here? You need to pay attention."

I reach out and grab his arm. He looks down at my fingers and then slowly upward to meet my gaze.

"It's Catalina."

His mouth hardens as he pulls away. "I can't call you by your name as if I were some lord."

"You can call me by my name because you're my friend." I don't care what he says. The times we spent together in the Illustrian fortress were more than just him following orders. If that had been true, we wouldn't have talked at all. But we did. I told him about the books I'd read, the stories I loved and the characters I admired. Once, I even caught him reading by candlelight. One of my favorite tales about a creature of the jungle who used his persuasive call to lure people off well-traveled paths.

He remains stubbornly silent. I want to shake him.

"You called me Catalina before. Right after you rescued me."

"That was before."

Ah. *Before* I told him my plan to stay here. When his sense of duty kicked in after he found out about his family's horrible fate. "We might die here, and you can't call me by my name?"

"What difference does it make? Both are true. I prefer addressing you with the respect your status requires. What about that upsets you?"

I gesture to all of him. "Your aloofness upsets me. Back at the keep, we were friends," I amend. "We talked *all* the time. Every day."

This seems to amuse him. "We did?"

"Yes, we—" I break off, flushing. He doesn't remember any of our conversations, while I carried them in my heart, dreamed about him for years. That hurt. "You really don't remember?"

Manuel stills, his expression remote and blank. If he were a house, it'd be empty and haunted. I take the tiniest step forward.

His nostrils flare at my approach. He's *lying*. And the hurt I feel transforms, taking over my body, overruling my better judgment. I'm tired of being protected, sheltered, of having my experiences dictated.

"You want to pretend we weren't friends? That we never danced together or stayed up talking most nights? That you didn't *kiss* me?" At this, his eyes narrow into slits, the gleam in them hard. "You're not fooling me. But if you insist on carrying on, have the decency to explain why."

"There's nothing to explain."

I tug at the ends of my hair. "It was your choice to stay here."

"I didn't really have a choice."

I step close to him and poke his chest. "You always have a choice. Why do people think they don't have choices? You're not standing in a river with the current dragging you one way or another. You're on solid ground and responsible for what you do. Ximena had a choice. You have a choice, and so did I. You can still leave."

"I won't do that."

I press my fingers to my throbbing temples. "If we have to travel together, the least you can do is say good morning. Honestly, you're as pleasant to be around as an angry swarm of bees."

He clenches his jaw. "Are you finished?"

I nod.

"Any moment in the jungle could be our last," he says with fire in his voice. "I have to listen, to pay attention. I don't have room to engage you in conversation, not when we have a tribe of people hunting us and predators with teeth, with poison in their systems. I can't *entertain* you."

Is that what he thinks? No better than a child, demanding amusement? The thought spikes my blood, and tears prick my eyes. Whenever I feel frustrated, I tend to angry cry until the emotion is swept away. "That's not fair. I'm not asking you to do that."

"Then what do you want from me?" he asks, genuinely confused. "I'm a ranger and your guard. I'm trying to protect you. That's *all* I'm trying to do." Manuel shoots me a look loaded with meaning.

He doesn't want to talk about the kiss. He'd rather I forget all about it, as if I hadn't dreamed about that moment for years. As if I hadn't cried when he left without a word.

"I understand."

His eyes narrow. "Then why do you look like you're about to cry?"

I bite my lip. Struggle to contain my emotions. Manuel is all I have left. Ana and Sofía are gone, Ximena betrayed me. My people are living in La Ciudad under the reign of an enemy queen, the sister of the man who took away everything from us.

"I don't mean to hurt you," he says softly. "But I need you to let me do my job. If I'm short or unwilling to talk, it's because I need to concentrate. We both need to be prepared for the worst. I'm not going to coddle you."

He's telling me the truth—but not all of it. There was a time when he used to tease me, sneak me stolen food from La Ciudad. That's the person I miss. I can sense that he's keeping himself tucked away from me, blocking my way with an impenetrable wall. Leaving me out in the cold. "You used to be kinder."

He rears back as if I've struck him.

I wince. "Manuel. I only meant—"

"We're losing light," he says, moving away, as if an emotional distance isn't enough. I trudge after him, lonely and hurt and unsure of how to make things less awkward between us. Confusion filters into my mind, and I try to parse through our conversation. He never answered my question. I still consider him a friend, but maybe he doesn't feel the same way.

We pack up our meager belongings and double back to the river as thunder rumbles from above. The clouds are heavy with rain, and I prepare myself for another wet day. What I wouldn't give to bathe with gardenia-scented soap and put on fresh, clean clothing. My fingers are caked with mud, and all over my body are red welts from the mosquitos ravaging my skin. Manuel pushes the raft into the water and easily hops on. He turns, his hand reaching for mine.

But I stay put on the sandbank.

"Condesa," he says. "Come on."

"Am I your friend?"

His brow darkens. "You can't be serious." The raft moves slowly away from the edge and he uses one of the oars to keep it still. "Condesa."

I fold my arms across my chest. "Catalina."

"We don't have time for this."

"Then say my name, and stop calling me by my title."

"¿Por qué?"

Because I've loved you all of my life, and if I can't have you that way, then at least be my friend. I want to scream. I'm so tired of keeping this secret. I never told anyone, not even Ximena. "It's important to me. Por favor. Say my name."

"Catalina," he growls.

My name on his mouth is like hissing coals, smoke curling and twisting high into the air. I jump onto the raft, arms windmilling. He glares at me, and I can't help the laugh that bubbles up to the surface.

I grab the other oar and help him maneuver away from the bank. The water runs swiftly and carries us out and away, until both sides of the thirty-foot-wide river transform into dense walls of vegetation: mosses and vines, bushes and enormous palms. There's no sight of the Illari, only intuition's insistence whispering in my ear that they'll be back.

My paddling needs work and Manuel calls out instructions. When I finally get the rhythm right, I'm ready for more conversation. "Tell me about your time here."

"What do you want to know?" His voice is wary, as if not trusting I'll keep to subjects that won't end in an argument.

"Well, you've been in this jungle for eight months." I pause. "Did you make any friends?"

He lets out a crack of laughter. "No one. The Illari were suspicious of me from the day I stepped foot in here. Not too long ago, I saw a man in a purple robe walking through, but I didn't like the look of him so I didn't attempt to make my presence known. I'm sure it was for the best. I never saw him again, so he must have died."

I shudder. "And before you arrived to the jungle?"

Manuel sinks the paddle deep into the water, navigating us away from the bank. "Yes, I made friends. But I was constantly moving from place to place. Hard to stay in touch with anyone."

There's a subtle note of bitterness that seasons his words.

"Sounds lonely."

"I had a job to do."

I swivel around on the bamboo and study him. He permits himself to lower his eyes for half a second before returning his attention to our surroundings. "You look older. Tougher."

This time, he lets his eyes linger on my face. Assesses every curve, every line. "So do you."

His scrutiny warms the blood in my cheeks. Part of me wants to sink into the moment, but I'm worried he'll pull back. So I draw away first. "Do you know where we're going?"

Manuel considers the area. "Somewhat. I wouldn't have gone by river; it's too easy to veer far away from where we need to stop the raft." He points to a large hill with a dip in the middle. "We need to walk toward the hill. On the other side there's a large grove of mahogany trees."

"And beyond?"

His expression darkens, as if a veritable shadow has crossed his face. "We'll cross that bridge when we get there. Literally."

"We're crossing a bridge?"

He shrugs, his attention on the muddy banks.

"Why won't you just tell me?"

"Trust me," he says grimly. "It's not something you need to think about right now."

"I thought you said I was your sovereign."

"And I thought you wanted to be *friends*."

"Do you enjoy being cryptic?" I burst out. "Honestly. I fully understand that you're mysterious and handsome and amazing at everything, but do you have to treat me like I'm three years old *all* the time—"

His eyes widen. But he's not looking at me.

"What?" I follow the line of his gaze and let out a smothered cry. The river curves, and along the right muddy bank lies an enormous black caimán. A predator from another world, another time, sunning in the gloomy morning, its black scales shining dully. Ragged yellow teeth line its maw, bigger than Manuel's palm. We drift past, and I drag in a mouthful of hot air; I'm rooted to the bamboo as we gently bob with the current.

"About twenty feet long," Manuel whispers. "A male, by the look of his nostrils. I've never seen one so big."

I shudder as our raft glides in front of the monster. He remains stone still, seemingly unaware of our presence. My attention stays fixed on the caimán, and when we pass him by, I let out a sigh of relief. But I still can't tear my eyes from the sight of him. Beautiful and deadly.

His armored head swings around as the tail end of our boat glides by.

"Cielos! He's woken up," I say.

"What made you think he was sleeping?" Manuel dips the oar into the black water and urges us forward.

"What do we do?"

"We do nothing. If we leave him alone, chances are he'll leave us—"

The caimán lunges quickly down the bank, splattering mud, and then slides into the water, vanishing completely below the surface. I yank my oar out of the water and turn to stare at Manuel, my jaw dropping.

"Stay calm," he says, yanking out his machete. "He's probably nervous and wants to get away from us."

My palms are slick with sweat and my hair hangs limply down my back, damp from the humid air smothering every living thing. I clutch the bamboo stalk as if it were a weapon. Manuel stands at the front of our raft, the machete tucked between his legs, and propels us faster down the river, dipping the oar on the left and then right side, and back again. I face the other way, staring into the rippling depths. Terror shoots to every inch of my body.

The head of the caimán rises, cresting the water.

"Manuel!"

He turns, lays the oar on the raft, cradled by the bamboo, and then pulls me away from the edge. We huddle together in the center, down on our knees, bodies pressed tightly, our packs against us. "Hold on," he whispers in my ear.

The black caimán sweeps past, nudging the raft, sending it gently spinning. Manuel clutches my waist, preventing any movement. His fingers dig into my sides. I peer over the edge as the monster doubles back, and even through the river's murky water, twin lines of ridges are visible.

"He's testing us."

"I don't understand," I say, my voice low. I'm afraid to speak louder. "What does he want?"

"He's curious if he's found food."

Manuel grips me tighter. A rippling wave disturbs the water, long and foreboding. My breath lodges at the back of my throat, my lungs burning. The air grows thick with heat, our bodies baking. Sweat drips into my eyes. Overhead, the clouds swell, any moment threatening to burst.

The beast's head reemerges as he circles us one, two, three

rotations. He bumps us again—harder this time—and we bob up and down roughly, the water sloshing around us.

"Hold on," Manuel whispers again. "He's not done yet."

I press closer to the bamboo and let out a soft whimper, praying the raft will hold us, praying we'll survive this moment. Time stretches. I slap a mosquito on my neck.

The raft bucks underneath us and I scream—we lift up high into the air, and then slam down. Manuel's hold loosens, jarred from the impact. I land hard on the bamboo, and pitch sideways, rolling away from him.

He reaches for me. "Condesa!"

I tumble into the murky river.

CAPÍTULO

diez

The water's strong current envelops my writhing body, dragging me under. I can't see anything beneath the surface. My limbs tangle together as I twist amid bubbles and flailing arms, trying to find the right way up. The water is murky and warm, and strangely alive. Something brushes against my leg and I scream, losing precious air.

I can't swim.

My heart slams against my chest, panic clawing at my skin like a hungry vulture. I kick once, twice, and break free. I reach up, my gaze focused on the smattering of light above my head, my pack helping me draw toward it. When I break the surface, terror coursing through my veins, rioting my blood and thundering in my ears, the raft is several feet up the river.

The current steals me farther away.

Manuel is on his hands and knees at the edge of the raft, furiously maneuvering it closer and shouting at me, but I can't make sense of the words. This doesn't feel real. I'm not in this river with an enormous predator close by. My vision blurs as water sweeps over my head. I fumble and swing my arms, trying to remain afloat. Once again, my head pops above the surface. I gasp, coughing up water.

"Condesa!" Manuel yells. "Stop moving! Tuck your arms and legs and float!"

My body can't stop shaking. I sense movement, a sudden surge against the river.

If the jungle wants me, it will have me.

I squeeze my eyes shut, fighting to remember how to float. What did Manuel say? *Lie on your back, parallel to the water.* I slowly move into position, but the river is too strong for me to remain still.

Manuel urges the raft toward me, his movements controlled and ever so slow. He's only a few feet away. But the black caimán swims in between us, grazing my body, taunting me. A scream rips out of me. A few yards away, his snout appears, midnight scales gleaming dully. His black eyes appear next, and slowly he inches forward, water rippling around his yawning jaw.

I turn away, moaning, my fear nearly swallowing me whole. The raft is so close. If I reach for it, I might be able to latch on. Manuel is just above me, his face set, his sole attention on the approaching beast. He yanks out a dagger tucked within his boot, looking so much like his mother, I can't breathe for a second.

There's no way I'll make it without the caimán reaching me first. I start kicking wildly, my fingers outstretched. They slide against the slick bamboo.

Manuel leaps over my head with a sudden roar. I grip the raft and haul myself up, my legs thrashing. I whip around as the caimán rears, Manuel glued to his head and upper back with one arm while the other slashes, sinking into one of the beast's black eyes. The caimán snarls, his tail whipping back and forth, trying to buck the ranger.

Quickly, Manuel yanks his weapon free and stabs the monster's other eye. A loud howl of fury and pain escapes from the caimán as Manuel jumps into the water. He swims for the raft, and I scoop up one of the oars, hold it out for him to hold on to.

Manuel ignores my offering and makes quick work of climbing on board. He sheathes the dagger and picks up the second oar. The caimán bellows again. The water surges, violently rocking us.

"We have to get off the river!" he yells, pointing to the opposite sandbank. "Rápido!"

I help him row the raft toward the shore. Something hits the bamboo and I glance down. There's a sudden swelling of water underneath—

"Get down!" I cry, dropping to my knees.

The raft kicks up and slams onto the water; somehow we remain on board. Another caimán circles the raft, its eyes unharmed. It's slightly smaller than the other.

"His mate!" Manuel says. "Hit her snout!"

The female approaches and I slap the paddle, making contact with her nose and she immediately ducks below the surface. We furiously row to the muddy bank and jump from the raft. My boots slip against the sludge as I race upward toward the tree line.

I turn around to find Manuel gaping at the water. A man rides on the back of the small caimán, blood snaking down both cheeks where his eyes used to be.

"No," I whisper, fear twisting my stomach.

Manuel backs away from the edge as the caimán emerges from the water, slowly following him up. The man is ancient—grizzly gray beard, wrinkled skin clinging to a lean, muscular frame. He's naked, carrying only a wooden staff. Around his neck hangs a black cord with an amber amulet dangling between his collarbone. He climbs off the back of the caimán—his mate?—and slams the end of his staff into the ground, murmuring something in the old language. The water behind him swells and rises, up to his ankles. He's using Pacha magic—magic that bursts from deep within Mother Earth, their goddess.

"He's calling up the river," I say quickly.

"Run, Condesa," Manuel says.

"You can't fight them both!"

He shoots me a look of such withering scorn, it almost knocks me sideways. The caimán charges, heading straight for me. I whip around, my pack swinging wide. The creature follows, snapping her jaws, snarling at my heels as I race into the jungle. I dart around fallen logs, shoving vines out of the way, not caring what I touch. I glance over my shoulder. The beast struggles to navigate the dense jungle floor, slowing down. There are rocks and decaying timber clogging the path.

I stop and turn, breathing hard, protected by the immense trunks surrounding me. The sound of her frustrated snarls echoes in my ears. I'm trapped here, vulnerable to attack by other predators lurking in the gloom. My dagger! I reach into my pack, rummaging, until my finger nicks the sharp blade.

"Damn it," I mutter as I pull my weapon from my bag. I clench the handle tightly, ignoring the blood dripping down my index finger. My ears strain to hear anything ominous, but it's nearly impossible. I've forgotten how loud the jungle is, the constant thrum of activity and life, bursting and straining like a bird clamoring against its cage, desperate for freedom.

"Condesa," someone says, from my left.

I drop the dagger with a sharp scream.

Manuel rolls his eyes and bends to scoop up the weapon. His tunic is stained red.

"You're hurt." I step toward him, but he waves me off.

"It's not my blood—"

Another loud snarl comes from the direction of the female caimán.

Manuel takes my hand and leads me away from the sound. With his other, he uses his machete to clear a path. I follow, one miserable step at a time. The ground transforms into a muddy sludge, hard to walk through. I don't know how Manuel knows where we're going. Nothing is visible from above; the tangled branches are too thick with knots and hanging vines.

We walk for hours, until my legs scream with fatigue. Until the wounds across my shoulders protest every step, every inch of movement. My boots are sodden, and the bottom of my feet scream in protest. My blisters are back, probably bursting, the whole lot of them. I want to ask Manuel to stop, but I recognize the set of his shoulders, the determined strides to push on. A reminder that we aren't safe. There's no stopping to eat, but we do drink our fill of rainwater.

Manuel stops at last. "We need to set up camp."

"Are we lost?"

His shoulders sag. "Maybe—none of this looks familiar.

It's best we stop for the night, and I can reassess in the morning."

"How can I help?"

"It's my problem, not yours."

"Pardon me, but I think your current problems are mine also." I nudge my shoulder against his. "Let me help. I can pay attention to our surroundings—"

"Wait. You *aren't* paying attention?"

"Better attention," I add quickly. "I'll be careful to remember any funny-looking trees we walk by." I let out a crack of grim laughter. "I mean, they *all* look funny, I guess."

Manuel looks like he's trying not laugh. "Just help me set up camp."

"That I can do," I say.

We find two trees the right distance apart to hang the hammock. Neither of us has eaten, and I think our stomachs are competing to see which is the loudest and most annoying.

Mine is currently winning.

Once our shelter is secure, Manuel looks over at me with an expression I've learned means: *Pay attention to what I'm about to teach you.* "Come on, Condesa," he says. "Time to learn how to fish."

My stomach drops. "We're heading back to the river?"

"There's a small stream nearby." He pauses. "Can't you hear it?"

I close my eyes and attempt to hear the sound of water. But the only noises clogging my senses are from the howling monkeys and hooting owls. Overhead, the canopy sweats; water plops onto the top of my head. I don't think I've been completely dry since arriving.

"I don't hear anything."

He turns away from me, grabbing another bamboo stalk, and calls over his shoulder for me to follow him. The jungle's heat clings to my skin, irritating the wounds across my shoulder blades. I can barely catch sight of Manuel as he darts through the forest, leading us down and away from camp. But then the trees spread farther apart, and at last Luna and all her glittering companions finally make an appearance through patches of wispy clouds. When I hold my hand up to my face, I can actually see it.

There might be a way for me to help, after all.

I call out to Manuel. He immediately stops and looks over his shoulder. I rummage in my bag and pull out my dented telescope. A smile breaks through Manuel's grim features, like the dawn rising free from the horizon. He thinks I can finally be of some use.

Unease flickers through me.

He's betting on me being a capable seer. But I'm not even that. I try not to let my dismay show—maybe by some miracle Luna will reveal her whole self to me, the stars perfectly aligning and staying in place long enough for me to interpret them. Manuel keeps away from me, giving me space to relax and empty my mind.

How many times has he watched me read the constellations? Watched me fail at nearly every attempt? The hope sparking in his gaze fills me with dread. He must think I've improved in the three years since he's been gone.

I don't want to disappoint him.

I drag in sips of warm air, and somehow it tastes sweet and clean. My breath fills my lungs, gently stretching and pulling, and then I exhale, releasing my worries. Slowly, I tilt my head back, my chin greeting the open sky, and I lift the telescope to my right eye. The magic pulses in my veins, wanting to connect and latch onto a current only I can see. It glides upward, riding the wind, searching for the faint lines between each glimmering star.

A scrambled word appears, then transforms into another and then another, shifting and changing, like curls of smoke coming from a burning candle. I want to lower the telescope in frustration, but I'm keenly aware of Manuel's hopeful presence. Waiting for me to come through. To contribute and do something right.

My gaze remains on the heavens. Until, finally, my shoulders slump. I stuff the scope back into my bag, fingers shaking. I sense him take a step toward me.

"Well?"

I force myself to meet his eyes. They're guarded once more, already shifting to our surroundings, as if remembering that he alone is responsible for our fate.

"Unclear," I say, miserable.

His gaze flickers to mine. His voice is unfailingly kind. "It's fine."

It's not the least bit fine. I know it, and he knows it. I'm the reason he's here, and I can't even lead us in the right direction.

"I can try again."

"Let's catch dinner." He turns away, but not before I see his face. Worry is carved into his features, in every line, down to the set of his jaw. I want to hurl the telescope into the flat darkness, but I can't make my fingers let go.

We're lost in the jungle.

There's nothing I can do about it.

I follow after him and the stream finally comes into view, Luna's watery portrait glimmering on the surface. Manuel stops at the water's edge and plucks his dagger from within his boot. He carves the end of the bamboo, shaping it into a sharp prong. I peer into the water, but because I have only Luna's light, I can't make out anything in the depths. Manuel's vision at night is a whole other story.

"I can't see the fish," I mutter.

"Just because you can't see them, doesn't mean they aren't watching you."

He takes the dagger's blade and slices his forearm—the cut is shallow, but I wince anyway. Then he wades into the water, staying close to the bank. He holds out his arm over the stream and blood drips into its depth. Next, he grips the bamboo with both hands and stares intently into the water.

Moments later the water churns, bubbling, and little fins splash the surface. The swarm of fish swims closer to Manuel and I hold my breath. With poised alertness, he lifts the bamboo high, prong side angled down, his feet spread apart, and then slams the stalk into the water. He leaps backward, coming out of the water and hurrying up the bank.

Something definitely writhes on the end of that bamboo stalk, the fish stabbed through the center, probably about a foot in length, maybe a bit more. I step closer as Manuel draws near. He's caught a piranha. Moonlight glints off its shiny scales, and even in the dim ray of light, I can make out its teeth, each one shaped like the tip of a dagger. It snaps weakly in my general direction before it's carried off by my companion.

We reach the campsite, my stomach growling. Manuel hands me the bamboo, the scary fish finally dead, and settles into starting the fire. I hold the stalk with one hand while I rummage in his pack for the pan, every now and again checking to make sure the piranha isn't moving.

Manuel keeps the fire small and manageable, and I hand over the fish and the pan. He points to a rock close to the pit. "Have a seat. It will only be a minute." He glances around, surveying our surroundings, his eyes a soft pearlescent glow. I've always envied his ability to see clearly in the dark, and even more so now that it's keeping us safe. "There should be a lemon in my bag."

I dig around and produce a naranja. He looks over and says, "That'll work."

He makes quick work of gutting the fish, ridding the bones and the skin. Then he drops it into the pan, where it promptly sizzles. "Remember how my mother made this amazing salsa to go with fish? Papaya and mango, thin slices of the locoto pepper. She likes everything spicy." His expression clouds. "Liked. My mother *liked* everything spicy."

My throat seems to close up. I remember that salsa, but instead of fish, she paired it with quinoa and fried eggs. That was when food wasn't as hard to come by, before we made the switch to plain rice and potatoes. I want to talk about her, I miss her so much. She was our guiding force back at the Illustrian keep, a constant presence who kept me safe and fed, fighting to keep the memory of my family alive in the minds of all survivors of the revolt. It was her idea for Ximena to be my decoy. Her idea to keep me hidden as a small child, reintroducing me as the companion to the condesa.

Manuel must see the anguish on my face. "She loved you like a daughter."

"I know." My voice is careful and hesitant. "I'll never forget her and everything she sacrificed. Risking the lives of her children for my chance at the throne. I want to honor her, too."

"Do you ever wonder how she inspired such loyalty?"

"I don't wonder at it," I say. "I know how."

He lifts a brow, silently asking me to elaborate.

"She never asked anyone to do something she wouldn't do herself. We all loved her because she fought in the revolt, and then routinely snuck into La Ciudad to steal bags of grain and beans for us, despite the danger. She participated in training, ran the same miles as the other soldiers. There was nothing she wouldn't do for any one of us." My voice turns wistful. "If she were here, she'd never take the easy way out. She'd face a hundred jungles if it meant a better future for Illustrians. She wouldn't have run from that jaguar or screamed at the sight of a scorpion."

Manuel's tone is gentle. But his words still hurt. "Condesa, you are not my mother."

As if I didn't know. I'm not Ana, Ximena, or Sofía. Warriors, all of them. "It was my fault Sofía died." I keep my gaze away from his, unable to look him in the eye. "It was my idea to have her escort Ximena to the castillo."

"My sister never did anything she didn't want to do," he says firmly.

I frown. "That's not true—she was following orders. *My* orders."

"Because she *wanted* to honor you. As her sovereign, as her future queen. Sofía would have done anything to keep you safe.

That was her choice." He clears his throat. I can tell the next words will cost him. "I only wish I'd been around to see her grow up."

I grimace at the undercurrent of longing and regret in his voice. And the sad thing is that I *know* he would have made the same decision to leave all over again if he could. He believed in our cause that much. He believed in *me* that much.

"As she grew up, she looked more and more like your mother," I whisper. "She fought the same way you do. If there was a cup of coffee around, she'd drink it, no matter the time. She liked to train at night when everyone else slept."

"Like me," he says.

"Like you."

I look at the trees enveloping us. He reaches for his pack, pulls out the bamboo utensils. "Why don't you ever talk about Ximena?"

I'm tempted to answer him. Ximena made a fool of me, told me I don't have what it takes to be a leader. Manuel thinks the same—probably. I don't want to know for sure.

"You haven't wanted to talk," I say instead. "Remember?"

Manuel falls silent, but I don't think it's because I've made my point.

He hands me the fork. "We'll share it. You first."

I take the plate and utensil and cut a large chunk of the fish. It tastes crispy and delicious, the hint of orange bursting on my tongue. Manuel sits next to me on the large rock, checking for snakes or ants, or whatever else might kill us with a bite or sting. "I don't mean *about* her. Not exactly. She was your best friend. How are you feeling?"

"Are you asking me a question as my friend?"

A sheepish expression settles onto his features. "Sort of. I need to know how you're doing, because if we do somehow reach Paititi, which would be a miracle, whatever requests you make of the king ought to be for the good of all Illustrians and not motivated by revenge."

I shove the plate of food at him. "You don't have a very good opinion of me, do you?"

His eyes widen. "Of course I do. Condesa, anyone would feel betrayed and hurt by Ximena's actions. I feel betrayed and angry. It'd be hard to separate wanting to cause pain from the need to do right by your people. But that doesn't mean our emotions need to rule our thoughts and our decisions."

"You were furious when you found out about your family."

"I didn't say don't *feel* the emotions; I'm saying don't be ruled by them."

"I haven't thought about revenge," I insist. "My only thought has been to displace the new Llacsan queen and install myself as the queen of Inkasisa. I want Illustrians to have their homes back, to walk freely in La Ciudad without risking arrest or persecution. I don't believe that Llacsan queen will treat our people fairly."

"Ximena's loyalty to the new queen may mean you'll have to fight her all over again. Are you prepared for that?"

"Today I'm not," I admit softly. "But when I need to be ready, I will be."

He nods, satisfied. "I will be with you when the time comes."

My lips part. I want to reach out and smooth the lines across his brow. This is why I care about him: his noble heart that beats to keep me safe. I know it's his job; I know it's a result of Ana's long training and his desire to make his mother proud. But he's here for me when no one else is, and that counts more than anything.

We take turns devouring the fish, enjoying having something warm fill our bellies. When we're done, I stuff the pan back into his bag while he smothers the fire. We crawl under the massive broad-leaf plants of our shelter and settle into the hammock. All that protects us from an attack are flimsy leaves and a sheer netting, and yet that feeling of safety returns.

Darkness blankets the both of us, shrouding good intentions and conversation topics better left ignored. I haven't been able to shake the loneliness I heard in Manuel's voice when he talked about his constant traveling. I knew he'd gone out for a mission; I learned all about it after the fact. Ana was always planning on sending someone to every corner of Inkasisa to secure allies. Not once did I think Manuel would volunteer for the mission.

"You kissed me," I say softly. "And then you left for three years, and I never once got a letter from you. I didn't even get a goodbye. *Why?*"

He sits up abruptly, and the hammock swings wide. "I'm going to sleep out there."

I let out a bitter laugh. "Am I so awful that you'd prefer to risk the jungle?"

"No," he says. "*No.* You're not awful. You're—" There's a long, drawn-out pause, and then he loudly exhales and all of his words come out in a rush. "Catalina"—I startle at the use of my name—"I messed up. I *never* should have kissed you, never should have spent time with you the way that I did. I'm a guard, you're my sovereign. So please drop the subject. Don't look for something that isn't there. Nothing can ever happen between us." He leans forward, his voice dropping to a harsh whisper. "I need you to respect my wishes. Can you do that?"

It's in that moment I realize how much hope I'd had for him and me. I'd clung to it for three years, that elusive wisp of hope, and with his words, it fades into the nothing it always was.

"You should have said goodbye."

He sighs. "You're right, I ought to have. But I didn't trust myself. I'm sorry, Catalina. For all of it. Can we proceed as . . ." He breaks off, clearly uncertain what label to use.

"Friends?" I ask dryly.

He hesitates and I nudge his knee. "That feels too familiar—"

"Manuel, *compromise* is a delightful word. I think you ought to get better acquainted with it."

And for the first time since I've laid eyes on him in this awful place, he laughs. "Yes, all right. Friends."

We settle into a silence that almost feels companionable, even as disappointment clings to every corner of my heart. Even the hidden parts. I want him to be more than just my friend, more than just my guard. But his feelings have clearly changed in the three years we've been apart. I need to respect his wishes and somehow convince my heart to move on. The only thought that remotely cheers me is his willingness to be friends.

And friends aren't afraid to apologize to each other.

CAPÍTULO

once

By the next afternoon, we're still hopelessly, frustratingly lost.
We snake deeper into the jungle, plucking mangoes and avocados, peeling and eating them as we walk beneath the tangled
green arches. Every time there's a clearing among the treetops,
Manuel looks for the hill with the dip in the middle, but we
never find that particular landmark again. Instead we pass by
a myriad of stone pillars nearly swallowed up by thick vines
and roots.

Manuel never loses the tightness in his shoulders. While
the hand gripping the handle of his machete is steady, the skin
around his knuckles is white.

"You're worried," I say, breaking his rule of silence. We
haven't seen any Illari in what feels like days, haven't encountered
anything enormous with teeth either. He's killed a few snakes,
pointed out tarantulas as big as my palm, but other than that,
the jungle has been quiet. Eerily so.

He must agree with me, because he replies, though it's barely
a whisper, "I'd prefer it if we knew where we were going."

At all times, I walk behind Manuel as he clears a way forward, that great weapon of his swinging. He doesn't turn to face me, but I can hear his frustration all the same. "That's not the only thing bothering you," I say.

Manuel is quiet for a long moment. Just when I think the conversation is over, he slows down enough for me to catch up. "You're right," he admits. "I've traveled deep into the jungle and always, *always*, I've encountered the Illari. I've run from them, fought them, and hidden under their noses. But we haven't seen any since the caimán."

It seems like a blessing to me. "And why is that a bad thing?"

"It must mean there's a greater threat. I've said it'd be wise to fear what the Illari fear . . . and the longer we're lost, the more chance we have of stumbling upon this evil."

His words are scary, or they ought to be. While I certainly don't want to run headfirst into what's confounding the Illari, a small part of me appreciates that Manuel is finally confiding in me. Talking to me as if I weren't his charge but a regular traveling companion. "What do we do then?"

Manuel rolls back his shoulders. "We keep walking. To stay still in this place means courting death." He shoots me a quick look. "I'm frightening you, aren't I?"

I lift my chin. "Yes. But I can take it."

He smiles and keeps pace with me.

We walk for hours and hours. Everything looks the same. At least to me, anyway. Manuel huffs irritated noises as the time passes. The strain takes its toll. Worry settles onto my shoulders and presses hard. How will we ever find Paititi? Every step might be taking us away from the Illari, away from any hope of convincing them to march on La Ciudad, and closer to what threatens the jungle.

We might be risking our lives for nothing.

Still, we press on.

My legs are sore, and the mosquitos are rampant, buzzing in my ears, flying in front of my face. The trees become taller and taller, until not even pockets of sunlight poke through, ensuring everything below my feet is dead or decaying. Clumps of dirt and mulch squish underneath my boots. The air *feels* wet and sticky, and murderously hot.

But somehow, none of my misery prevents me from seeing the marvelous. This verdant forest houses some of the strangest things I've ever seen. Manuel shows me a vivid green leaf that when mashed and mixed with water creates a purple dye. I wish he would have warned me—both of my hands look as if I've dunked them in beet juice.

Then there are the birds in every color imaginable. Rainbow-hued parrots and determined hummingbirds sweep above us. Monkeys and sloths are constant features—as are the capybaras and armadillos. I want to spend time with all of them, but Manuel keeps us at a quick pace. The bottoms of my feet are raw, and before long I'm hobbling along, limping over tree roots and puddles deep with mud. Wonderful. More blisters.

I try not to complain, but after an hour of this, the pain becomes excruciating. The blisters on my heels return with a vengeance. When I scramble over a log and land on the other side, a moan escapes me. Manuel immediately turns. "What is it?"

I shake my head, not wanting to be weak or a burden anymore. Both of which I feel keenly.

He narrows his gaze at me. "¿Qué te pasa?"

"Nada," I mutter, slowly walking past him. "Let's keep going."

Manuel snakes his arm around my waist, and together we move forward. He's half carrying me with one arm, while his free hand thwacks at the dense greenery clogging the way forward. "You're limping again."

"Barely."

"You can hardly stand."

"Stop exaggerating."

He stops and glares down at me. "I never exaggerate. We have to find a dry place so I can look at your feet."

"I'm fine—"

"Stop lying to me," he says calmly. "You're so stubborn."

"And you're bossy."

His brow creases, but we resume hobbling. I won't admit it out loud, but his support is the only thing that's keeping me upright. Mist curls around us like a tight fist, a dangerous blow to our sight. Manuel's Moonsight gleams through the jungle and at last we find a cave, nearly hidden by several tall oaks. He peers inside, the soft glow coming from his gaze illuminating the interior. The walls are jagged and damp. Wild mushrooms grow between the crevices.

I stumble inside and Manuel gently lowers me to the ground. He kneels in front of me and unties the leather laces, then pulls both boots off. I wince, tucking my chin toward my chest, fighting tears. Even that hurts.

"Condesa," he murmurs, examining my feet.

Angry blisters near bursting mar my heels and the tops of my toes.

"How long have you been hurting?" he asks quietly.

"Not long."

His face tilts up toward mine, grim and serious, anger deep within the dark pools of his eyes. "Try again."

"Several hours."

"You can't keep things like this from me. Blisters can lead to infection, and that would be catastrophic here."

"I didn't want to be weak," I mumble.

"It's not weak to address sores on your feet." He stands and glances over his shoulder to the cavern entrance. The trees gently sway from the current of wind sweeping through the jungle and whistling through the cracks in the cavern wall. "You need more poultice, but I've run out. I can go out and search for the ingredients, but it means leaving you here."

I swallow and glance down at my feet. "Do what you have to do."

"Take out your dagger and stab anyone or anything that comes in here. I won't be gone long. Ten minutes, that's it." He waits for my nod and then rushes out. I gingerly lean against the wall, the dagger in my lap. The wounds at my back still hurt, but not as bad as before. I shift slightly, angling away from a bit of stone poking against my back. The air inside the cave smells stale and I wrinkle my nose, trying to focus on my surroundings instead of the abject fear that pulses under my skin. Along the wall are shimmering veins of turquoise, and I trace them with my index finger.

At last Manuel returns carrying a bundle of aloe, bananas, mangoes, oranges, and wild duck. He really did collect everything in ten minutes. If I wasn't so hungry, I'd be annoyed by his efficiency. The only thing I would've brought back is another blister—if I came back at all. My mouth waters at the sight of the feast. He sets to work, gently spreading the cool liquid on my feet, and I let out a groan of pleasure. He hands me the fruit. I peel everything and drop it into his wooden bowl, mixing it all together to create a salad. We polish it off as Manuel cooks the pato over a fire. It's delicious: smoky and charred on the outside, tender meat on the inside.

The stone is hard underneath my crossed legs, and slightly damp, but with my belly full, I couldn't care less.

"Should we keep going?"

Manuel shoots a swift look in the direction of the entrance. While not exactly night, there still isn't enough light. He shakes his head and settles against the craggy wall, his eyes open and alert, flickering from one end of the cave to the other. His eyes glow like twin fires in the dim light, illuminating the shadowy corners of the cave. Silence descends, heavy and obliterating. I'm worried, and I know he is too, despite how hard he's trying not to let it show.

"You can tell me what you're thinking," I say. "I'm not going to fall apart."

He clasps his hands in his lap, brooding. "I'm wondering if the Illari have been following us and I just haven't been paying attention."

"You?" I tease. "Not paying attention?"

His lips soften into a grudging smile. "I was arrogant when I first walked into the jungle. After a few days, I learned never to let down my guard. Which is why I can't stop thinking about the Illari."

"It will be easier to press forward when they aren't breathing down our necks."

"Whoever or whatever killed all those birds was evil." He hesitates. "A dark kind of magic."

"Do you mean like the human who transformed into the caimán?"

"That's the Pacha magic of the Illari. I saw one of them transform into a large jaguar—which I killed when it was distracted by you."

I gasp. *That was a person?*

He nods. "I told you the Illari are people steeped in magic from Pachamama. More than anywhere else in Inkasisa, this is her domain, like Luna reigns over the night. The Illari worship the earth goddess just like the Llacsans do. And here she's gifted her children with ways to protect the land and the lost city."

"What happens if we can't find Paititi?" I ask.

He doesn't answer for a long moment. "Ask me again after we've exhausted all avenues."

"But I'm asking now."

"And I'm telling you, it's much too soon to ask that question."

I swallow my frustration, but even so, a glare still escapes me. "Do you enjoy provoking me?"

"No," he says frankly. "I hate worrying you. We ought to sleep. Tomorrow we'll wake up early and set off."

"I'm not tired. Can you tell me more about how you spent your days here in the jungle? Eight months is a long time."

He shifts and stretches out his long legs, crosses them at the ankles. "At first I tried to find Paititi. If the rumors are true about the city being made of gold, I thought for certain they'd have the resources to have an effective army of warriors. But every time I thought I was close to finding it, I'd encounter one of the Illari. I've only just realized they were protecting a bridge near the hill with the dip in the middle. I made several attempts to cross the bridge, but none of them worked. That's when I tried to discover a way out of the jungle."

"Why do you think they've remained hidden all these years?"

He shrugs again. "It might be about the gold. A good enough reason not to let the world know what you've found hidden in the mountains."

I scoop up the last orange segment in the bowl and pop it into my mouth. "The gold must be there. Otherwise, why remain hidden?"

Manuel reaches for the pack and yanks out the hammock. He spreads it out on the ground. "Here, you can rest first." I scoot over and lie down, my head near his outstretched legs. He shifts away.

"They're foolish if they think no one else will come looking for their city. It's only a matter of time."

"Yes," he says thoughtfully. "I think they're fully aware that time is running out for them."

My eyes drift closed at his words, and before I fall asleep, I can't help thinking how nothing lasts forever.

The next morning we're up and out of the cave at dawn. During the night, Manuel gave me more aloe to rub on my feet. He'd let himself sleep for an hour, and then we'd switch back again. I don't think either of us slept well, but at the very least, nothing with teeth snuck into our cave. We trek uphill, hoping to get high enough to find the spot Manuel's looking for. It's the landmark closest to that bridge we need to cross in order to find Paititi.

I drop my pack and stretch my arms up high above me. Manuel bends and scoops up my bag, holds it out for me to take. "Do not put your belongings on the ground."

Reluctantly, I slip the strap over my shoulders.

"Something nasty might crawl in there," he explains.

I bounce my pack higher and nod. The last thing I need is for a scorpion to make a new home within my things.

A shimmery glint catches my attention. There's a small patch of flowers nearly buried by vivid green brush. I stride forward, arrested by the glimmering petals. Manuel follows and falls down into a squat. Using his machete, he gently uncovers the silver flowers. They're incandescent and glowing, as if made from the finest crystal. My breath catches.

"Have you ever seen anything so beautiful?" I reach out to touch the soft petal, but Manuel snatches my wrist.

"What have I told you about touching things?"

"But it's so pretty," I protest. "Look, it's entirely delicate. *I* might hurt it."

"Not that delicate." He points at the ground with the tip of his blade. "Tell me what you see."

I bristle at being told what to do, but I drop my gaze to the jungle floor. Underneath the shrub, the ground is covered by an iridescent dusting. It looks dead, frozen, and void of any color. Manuel smells the petals, then drops even closer to the shimmering ground. "The flowers are killing the soil. Look—"

"I see that." My pleasure turns to outrage. How could something so beautiful destroy the land? "What should we do? Can you uproot it?"

"We shouldn't touch it." His expression turns thoughtful, considering. "I wonder if the Illari have seen this? I can't imagine they're happy with its presence."

"What do you mean? It's not from here?"

"I've never seen it before. I think it could've been brought to the forest by someone who didn't care about the consequences. They might've simply been careless—but I don't think so. My gut tells me this flower is hard to come by."

I nod approvingly. "So it stands to reason that whoever got ahold of it knew what it could do."

"Exactly."

What kind of stranger would bring something so destructive into the jungle? And for what purpose? A sudden thought makes me gasp. I reach out and grasp Manuel's arm. To my surprise, he doesn't flinch. Instead he encourages me with a small smile. "What is it?"

"I understand why the Illari haven't killed us yet."

He raises a brow.

"What if they think you brought the flower?"

Manuel tilts his head to the side. "Even more reason to do me in, wouldn't you think?"

I shake my head. "Not if they want to learn where you got the flower, and what you're planning on doing with it. It's what I'd do. I wouldn't want to kill the only person who might know how to destroy the flower and reverse the damage." I clear my throat and realize that I haven't had anything to drink in hours. "Is there any water?"

He jumps to his feet and searches the area for bamboo. When he returns, he hands me a cup. "You might be right. But that doesn't explain all those birds dying at the same time."

"We won't know for sure until we have an actual conversation with the Illari."

"Which they may not want to have," he points out grimly. "They may shoot us on sight."

But I get the sense that he's wrong. Otherwise, we'd already be dead. It's not like two people—who have been mostly lost—are hard to kill.

The Illari are up to something; I can *feel* it.

We drink from bamboo stalks, and as the water touches my lips, a butterfly lands on the wooden cup. Her wings are a vibrant red, with iridescent veins creating a shimmering pattern that literally takes my breath away. She's a tiny thing, no bigger than my palm.

I slowly lower the cup from my lips. With my free hand, I reach toward her with my index finger. She doesn't move, and as I'm about to coax her onto my hand, I stop.

Manuel's warning: *Don't touch anything.*

I shoot him a glance, surprised to see him watching. He suddenly grins, and his brown eyes become warm. He's pleased I've remembered his lesson, especially after my near miss with the flower. I lift a brow in question.

"Butterflies don't harm humans."

Again, I stretch out my finger for the butterfly to climb on, and a moment later she does, her wings fluttering. I gleefully show Manuel, whose smile hasn't faded but only stretched wider, as if we were the former Catalina and Manuel living behind the stone walls of the Illustrian keep, sometimes friends.

"What shall I call her?"

He seems bemused by this. "Consuelo?"

I make a face. "I had a Great-Aunt Consuelo who always made me brush my hair one hundred times every nigh—" A sharp pain flares at my finger, burning hot. The feeling travels up my arm, into my chest—smothering.

"What just happened?" Manuel demands. "Condesa?"

The butterfly sinks her teeth farther into my skin, sucking blood. I try to shake her off as the fire spreads to the rest of my body. I clench my jaw as her incisors dig into my skin again. Tears prick my eyes. Manuel grabs my arm and cuts her wings— but still she feasts on my flesh. Finally he yanks the butterfly off, throws her onto the ground, and steps on her.

My index finger has two deep puncture marks and is bleeding profusely, dripping onto the jungle floor. Manuel rips at the bottom of his tunic, producing a long strip. He binds the wound.

"Does it still hurt?"

A shape materializes near his shoulder, paper-thin wings fluttering in the sharp heat of the jungle. "Manuel!" But I'm too late. The butterfly lands on his shoulder, and he hisses sharply, yanking her off. He bats at another one near my ear, and another at the top of my hip. It's only then that realization dawns.

I look up to hundreds of bloodsucking butterflies riding the warm wind above us, circling like vultures.

CAPÍTULO

doce

I see the girl first.

Between the oak trees, shrouded in a greenish glow cast from the broad leaves. She's slight, with dark hair bound into a single braid. Her body is painted in vibrant colors, a thousand wings decorating her skin. Manuel and I barely notice as she transforms into a butterfly; we're too busy smacking at the insistent creatures fluttering above our heads. There are hundreds of them, swooping from behind broad palm leaves. Manuel shoots me a quick look. It only takes me a second to understand: We'll be eaten alive if we don't run.

We race away from the cloud of furious insects, our arms flapping over our heads, trying to protect our necks. The swarm of butterflies persists and a few catch up as I struggle with tangled roots and vines spooling at my feet. Damn being careful or quiet, damn whatever we accidentally touch. There's another prick on my upper arm, then one on my right leg and one on my left, close to my knees and ankles.

The burning sensation blazes up and down my body, making

my head swim. I yank the creatures off me, and blood drips down my arms and legs. Manuel glances over his shoulder, motioning for me to keep up.

Another butterfly lands on my exposed skin. And then another. I slow my pace, tears streaming down my scorched cheeks. I'm burning alive, set on fire from the inside. Manuel doubles back for me, his eyes yelling *don't slow down, don't give up*. He swats away the little monsters, hissing as one sinks its teeth into his palm. He plucks it out, throwing it to the ground, and then takes my hand, now slick with his blood. I don't stop to think how disgusting that is. Somehow I push through prickly leaves and jagged-edged palms.

We are too slow.

There are hundreds of them.

And then—just ahead, something made of stone looms between the trees. Manuel guides me toward a square building, both of us still swatting at the hungry butterflies. Vines devour the exterior of the building, covering patches of black stone. We clear the trees and race up the front steps. I'm half aware that I'm running straight into what looks like an abandoned temple. The entrance is tall with a curtain of thin leafy vines blocking the way through.

We bolt past the plants, and they swing back into place. The butterflies can't drift in after us, and the realization makes my knees buckle. I sink onto the stone floor, sweating from every pore, bleeding and fighting to keep the fire under my skin at bay. Manuel drops down next to me, in the same miserable state. He drags in air, but on his exhale, he sits up and frantically grabs a hidden butterfly near my ankle. The rip of flesh and fabric rents the air and I groan. He steps on the insect with his left boot and then swivels around to face me. His hands run along my arms and legs, urgent and methodical. Satisfied I'm butterfly free, he lifts his gaze as my vision blurs.

Exhaustion covers me like smoke intent on smothering life. Manuel shakes my shoulders. "Condesa!" A second later he smartly slaps my cheek. My eyes fly open. "Don't you *dare* fall asleep on me." His fingers dig into my skin. "Stay awake. Talk to me. Look for more of them; I might have missed one."

There's a shaft of light coming from somewhere above, landing in a triangular shape in the center of the room. There's enough light to see his expression as he examines my face. His dark eyes softly glow in the shadowy chamber. I return the favor, and when we're satisfied there aren't any more insects feasting on our blood, we bind the wounds as best we can, and then lean back against the cool walls, exhausted.

"I feel as if I've walked through fire." My mouth is dry. I lick my lips and swallow. "Have we been poisoned?"

His lips flatten, and there's a grim set to his shoulders. "Possibly."

My heart stutters. "What do we do?"

Manuel reaches into his sack, the movement slow and almost clumsy as he struggles with the flap. He rummages inside the bag, and finally pulls out a small bottle filled with honey. He pulls the cork stopper with his teeth and then holds out the jar to me. "Dip your finger and dab honey on every single one of your wounds."

"What will this do?"

"A healer in one of the villages I spent time in used this when treating similar bites." He dips his index finger and spreads the gooey liquid on the irritated patches of his skin. I do the same, addressing the ones I can easily touch. "Every time I've used the honey, it's helped the affected area." He replaces the cork and tosses the jar back into his bag.

"Have you tried it for poison?"

"No," he says shortly.

I don't have any experience with poison. The idea of dying slowly, growing weaker and sicker, makes my stomach twist painfully and the breath catch at the back of my throat. My fingers curl into a tight fist, as if readying a fight against an invisible enemy.

Manuel nudges me with his knee. "We're not dead yet, Condesa. Keep breathing—slowly. Let the honey do its work, and we'll take it from there."

I concentrate on keeping my panic at bay. My body is tense, strung so tightly that I fear I might snap. We sit for long minutes. I don't know how much time passes. But the waiting doesn't make me calm; it only fills me with dread. What if we're getting worse?

But then something inside me shifts. The burning sensation slowly fades, leaving a dull ache. Without meaning to, my head drops onto Manuel's shoulder, and he immediately stiffens. It's noticeable enough for me to move away from him, my cheeks flushing.

He stands, using the wall to support his frame. Then he peers into the room, squinting a little against the stream of light. There are three pillars each situated an equal distance from one another, framing a triangle on the floor. They are covered in ornate carvings, and standing on the tops are marble statues. Each of the statues is different: One is of a pregnant woman, the other a young man, and the third a woman with a gentle motherly expression. They all face away from one another.

I stand, my knees shaking and my head spinning. Manuel casts a quick glance in my direction. "Are you all right? You've lost a lot of blood."

"So did you," I say with a wan smile, my gaze roving the chamber. It feels old, the air stale and smelling of damp stone. "What is this place?"

"There are a few of these buildings in the jungle. I've come across at least four, but never stepped inside." His hands skim the wall. "We shouldn't stay long."

"What about the butterflies?"

"They might be gone by now," he says. "I don't like the idea of staying in here—we're too vulnerable. If the Illari come . . ."

I shudder. "You're in charge."

This makes him pause, a grudging smile bending his mouth. "Am I? Is that what you think?"

"You don't remember what you said to me in the cave?" I deepen my voice. "'Do exactly what I tell you; if I tell you to run, do it. If I tell you to act like a monkey, do it. If I tell you to walk backward and—'"

"I said *nothing* of the sort." He rolls his eyes. "And I don't sound the least bit like that," he says, exasperated. "But I'm pleased to hear you *are* paying attention."

More than he knows. It's impossible not to notice how he's filled out in the shoulders, developed muscles along his arms. I flush and avert my gaze. I feel his attention on me, a somewhat curious, perhaps even baffled air about him. He wants to know why I'm blushing. I squash the urge to look in his direction, and instead walk to the curtain of vines. But when I try to walk through, I'm met with a wall of stone. I step back, confused.

This is the entrance, isn't it?

Manuel comes to stand next to me and sweeps the vines aside with his machete. The blade scratches the stone. I slap my palms against the rock and push—but it's heavy and won't move, not even an inch. Manuel imitates my stance, placing his hands close to mine.

"All right," I say through a clenched jaw. "Now push."

"I *have* been." He shifts and leans against the wall, using his shoulder to help me shove, gritting his teeth and groaning with effort.

We might as well have tried moving a mountain with a shovel. The rock wall won't budge. I back away, blinking at it, expecting it to disappear or evaporate or both. I look around the room, but there's no other doorway. This is the only way out.

And it's blocked.

A whisper of panic clings to my voice. "Manuel."

He drags a long hand down his face. "That's our exit. I know it is."

"What could have happened?" I hate the panic in my words, hate it, but I can't help it. "Why didn't we hear it move? It's stone. Shouldn't it groan as it moves? Or does it screech?"

He stares back at me coolly. "Condesa."

"Right. Not important."

Manuel squats in front of the wall, peering at the edge of the stone. "Looks like the door came up from the ground. There's a gap here, and that's why we didn't hear it."

"Walls don't just rise without help."

"I'm aware," he says mildly. "There might be a lever or a pulley somewhere. Why don't you search the opposite wall, and I'll look over here?"

A reasonable suggestion. But it sits heavily at the back of my throat, difficult to swallow. "I don't think whoever trapped us in here will have done us the courtesy of also providing the way out."

He stands, his hands on his hips. "Would you prefer to do nothing?"

His tone is stubbornly calm—and I want to shake him. We're trapped in a temple! We aren't carrying a lot of food, and there's not a morsel to be found in this chamber. I walk right up to him. He keeps utterly still, like one of the statues up on the pillars. "I'm scared."

"There's no reason to be just yet. We haven't explored all of our options. I'll tell you when it's appropriate to panic." He gently turns me around. "Go over there and see if you can find anything interesting."

Sometimes he can be infuriatingly right. I look around the room, studying every corner and crevice. The carvings on the pillars depict suns and moons and flowers whose roots travel deep into the earth. As I walk the chamber, a round shadow ensnares my attention. Three of the walls have them—the only one that doesn't is our former entrance.

"Manuel," I call over my shoulder. "Ven aquí."

He walks to me and together we analyze the dial. It's a wheel made of smooth white marble, with three long dashes filled with gold and carved deep into the center of the stone. Manuel attempts to move the dial to the left and then to the right, but it won't budge, no matter how much he tugs. I step away from him and examine the dial on the next wall. This one is also made of the same marble, but it has two dashes. The third wall has one dash.

Manuel attempts to turn the two remaining wheels, but neither one budges. He walks around all three pillars, his finger tapping his lip lightly, his head tilted back to examine the statues. I walk up to one of the pillars. The carvings are truly beautiful, deep fissures as wide as my hand, all working together to create a scene from nature.

We walk around the room several times. I discard idea after idea, each as impossible as the last. Manuel attempts to turn the wheels on the wall in a different order, but that doesn't work. An hour might have gone by, maybe more. My stomach decides to loudly wake, growling impatiently, the sound reverberating in the small room and crashing in my ears. Exhaustion seeps into my bones. The shaft of sunlight turns silver. Night has fallen, and it's Luna's turn to reign. But her light barely illuminates the chamber; the corners are dark, shrouded in shadow. The only other light comes from Manuel's softly glowing eyes. I have to lean close to the walls in order to study the feathery cracks, searching for some clue.

Finally I slump against a wall and slide down. "Manuel, come sit."

He looks over at me from examining one of the dials. "What is it?"

"You need a break."

"I do?"

I nod. "We've been on our feet all day."

He walks around one of the pillars and gracefully sits next to me, making sure there's a respectable distance between us. Of course. "If you'd like to panic now, I think it might be the time for it."

"Are you panicking?"

"I might tomorrow."

I glance over at him. "How much food do we have?"

He hesitates. "I have an emergency stash of nuts. That's it." He turns his head to face me. "You can have it all."

It's as if someone has doused me with frigid water. I sputter at his words, part disbelieving, part mad with panic that we might die here, slowly starving once his *emergency* reserve is all gone. "What are we going to do? How are we going to get out of this?" With each question, my voice rises. And for the first time, I notice how small this chamber is, how dark and forbidding.

We are in a tomb.

I sip the air and it tastes stale and wet. "What if they just leave us in here? Is there enough air for the both of us?"

"There's a hole in the ceiling."

"I can't die in here! What about our people? The throne?" I struggle to my feet, but he reaches for me and places a firm hand on my shoulder, keeping me on the ground. He places one calloused palm on each of my cheeks, his dark gaze boring into mine.

"Look at me," he whispers.

My heart thunders against my ribs, rattling bone.

"Catalina."

A whoosh of air escapes my mouth. I gulp more in, my chest

rising and falling in quick successions. My body shakes, my teeth clacking against one another. "I'm so—so scared."

"Did you know I love horses?" Manuel says suddenly.

His words reach me from far away, a sharp tug that momentarily stops the hitch in my breath. "W-what?"

"We had a farm before the revolt," he continues. "Just outside of La Ciudad. When my parents were off for the season, we'd go out on horseback and get lost for a week or two in the mountains."

My heartbeat stutters and then slows. "You've never talked about your father."

Manuel lets go of me and settles against the cool stone. "He died when I was six years old—during a routine visit with a tribe from El Altiplano. I still don't know what happened exactly, and the mystery made us all sick. The not knowing used to keep Sofía up at night. Mother spent more and more time training soldiers; I think because, if she stopped for one moment, she'd notice his absence . . . and then the revolt happened." He pauses, his shoulders tense. "Sofía and I worried we'd lose Mother, too."

I reach out and place a soft hand on his arm. The war has taken so much from us. My parents and cousins and aunts and uncles. People who made up my large family, all murdered in an afternoon. I carry their faces with me, and the memory keeps my hatred of the Llacsans burning.

"What was your father like?" It's a question I wish people would ask *me* sometimes. But no one really does, and why would they? The pictures I have in my mind of my parents are blurry, smudges on a blank canvas. I wish I had known them better. But all I have left are vague recollections. The scent of flowers in Mama's garden and Papa's scruffy beard against my cheek.

"He was a big bear of a man. Told stories during mealtimes and always ate second helpings. He didn't like to dance, but he loved listening to my mother play the guitar. He was honorable."

My breath quiets, no longer violently shaking my chest. "What's your favorite memory of him?"

Manuel tips his head back and shuts his eyes. A long moment passes, and I think he may have fallen asleep. His chest rises and falls in a steady rhythm, his hands lightly clasped in his lap. His long legs are stretched out, crossed at the ankles. He's calm, composed, and in control. I can't help staring at him as I wait for him to speak.

"I was small for my age," he whispers. "My mother worried about my size a lot, wondered why I wasn't growing. But Papa never did. He'd pull me onto his shoulders, carry me around until I felt like I was a great giant. He promised me that I'd get to be that tall one day." His lips twist into a sad smile. "I didn't, obviously. But once Mother told me I'd reached his height, that was tall enough for me."

He slowly reopens his eyes and stares unseeingly out into the dark room. "I volunteered for many of the missions into La Ciudad simply to be able to ride the horses outside of the keep. I could never go fast enough on our side of the bridge."

"And did you volunteer on your mother's mission to secure allies to get away from me?"

Manuel shifts his gaze to mine, and he keeps it there. "Yes, I did."

There's no need to ask him why. I think I understand what he can't explain—he'd felt something for me back then, when we were younger and the outside world hadn't yet intruded into our bubble. That kiss shattered the illusion, and Manuel's profound sense of duty and honor prevented him from going further.

Just like it does now.

I tilt my head back until it rests against the cold stone. This place is terrifying, with its musty air and dark corners that hide secrets. Exhaustion clings to my bones, and I fall asleep, and as I do, I picture a yawning pit. Dark and black, with no escape, smothering me as I slowly starve.

CAPÍTULO

trece

My stomach wakes me. The growl reverberates through the room, and at my core I feel completely empty. As if I haven't eaten in days, weeks. I shake Manuel, and he sits up, yawning and rubbing his eyes. For some reason he appears more tired than I've ever seen him, even though I know we both slept through the night. Not that it was very comfortable; stone makes for an appalling bed. Manuel peers at me, assessing me in the same way I study him. There are bruises under his eyes, deep caverns stained purple.

"I'm hungry."

He nods. "Me too—ravenous." When he stands, I'm surprised to see him sway on his feet. He has to fling his arm out to keep himself upright. "Condesa, get up."

I struggle to get to my feet, my back sore and stiff. My limbs are heavy, and I'm weirdly lightheaded. I don't want to move from my spot on the floor. "I feel terrible." A thought strikes me. "Could it be the butterflies, after all? Perhaps the honey didn't work."

The blood drains from his face. "Maybe."

"We might seriously be poisoned."

"If we are, we have to get out of here," he says grimly. "There are plants that help with infection, but we won't find any in this temple." He slaps his face, once, twice. "I'm struggling to stay awake. Vision is a little blurry."

He doesn't seem to be talking to me. I use the wall to help me up to my feet. Once again, Manuel walks the chamber. His Moonsight makes his eyes softly glow like a fire blazing against the night. I watch him from the corner of my eye, wanting to make sure he's all right. I wish I could reach out to him, but I know he'd look at me in alarm. Touches like that aren't allowed between us. I walk to the base of one of the pillars, once again studying the carvings on the stone.

The answer lies here somewhere, I'm sure of it.

I lift my chin and study the statue at the top. This one is of Luna, looking off into the distance, as if watching over her faithful subjects. There are stars in her flowing hair, and her robes are decorated with the different phases of the moon. My gaze lowers and a potent whisper nudges me closer. A feeling, a rush of discovery that suddenly raises the hair on my arms.

There are cracks embedded in the stone that look as if they're part of the design. My feet can definitely fit into these cracks, as if they're not only meant to complement the design but to serve a purpose, too—a kind of beautiful, ornate ladder.

I reach for the stem of a flower that's curling out from the stone and place one booted foot between the cracks. I lift myself up, finding another flower stem to hold on to. This happens again and again until I'm all the way up to the top of the pillar.

The effort takes a toll.

I'm panting, nearly gasping for breath. I have to sit down again, my legs dangling off the side of the pillar like fallen banners.

"Condesa," Manuel asks from below. "Are you all right?"

"I only want to sleep," I mumble, rubbing my eyes. "I could drop to the ground and not get up for years, I think."

"Damn those butterflies. We have to find a way out—"

"How much time do we have left?"

"No sé," he says grimly. "I've never encountered Consuelo before."

My fingers cling to the edge of the pillar until my knuckles turn white. No food, perhaps not enough air, and we're both slowly dying from poisonous butterflies. The odds aren't in our favor.

And I'm too tired to panic.

I stand on wobbly knees, holding on to Luna's cool surface. There's enough room for me to walk around the statue, its height reaching my shoulders. I study the intricate detail, marveling at every fold of Luna's clothing.

And then I see it.

The statue sits on a raised circular platform. When I place the slightest pressure on the statue, the whole thing rotates—but only if I go against the clock. Manuel comes to stand at the foot of the pillar, his face upturned, the length of his neck exposed.

"The statues move," I call down.

He darts over to the pillar with the statue of the pregnant woman at the top. He climbs faster than I did, and in no time he stands at the top and spins the platform counterclockwise. He looks over at me. "What do you think?"

I bend closer to Luna, trying to find something—

"Look to see if she's wearing a pendant!" I point to the

necklace hanging around our goddess's neck. "Mine has a round disc with two dashes on it."

Manuel spins the statue and then exclaims, "This woman is wearing a crown and on one of the jewels, I can see a single dash. Condesa, I think this is meant to be a depiction of Pachamama. The earth goddess of the Llacsans."

"Why is she pregnant?"

"Because the tribes believe she's a symbol of motherhood and fertility. The earth gives life every season."

I point to the last statue. "Mine is certainly Luna, and if you're correct, then that pillar has to be their sun god, Inti."

Manuel quickly climbs down and then dashes over to the pillar. Once again he makes quick work of the climb, even though he's breathing heavily from the effort. When he reaches the top, he walks around the marble, studying every detail. "There's an amulet on his wrist with three dashes!"

"All right," I say, and I'm happy to feel a fluttering of excitement. "We're definitely onto something. The dashes match the dials on the walls. I bet you have to turn the dials in the correct order, starting with the first dash, and then the door will open again. Why don't you do one and two, and I'll take care of three?"

I climb down, careful not to slip, and then run toward the corresponding dial with three dashes. "I'm ready!"

"I'm not," Manuel says. "The wheel with one dash won't turn."

My shoulders slump. "I really thought that was it."

"It was a good idea," he concedes. "What are we missing? All of this has to relate somehow."

We try each wheel on the walls again, but none of them move. Even reversing the order doesn't work. Hunger drives me around the room, searching for an answer, willing one to appear. But there's nothing. Finally we slump onto the ground again, backs pressed against the wall. Both of us sweating, exhausted, and panting.

"Do you want to eat the nuts?" Manuel asks. "Enough to curb your appetite?"

"Are you going to eat?"

"No."

My stomach grumbles and I actually glance down at it and glare. "Then I won't either."

"Have my portion," Manuel says.

A fissure of alarm sweeps through me. "When I eat, you eat. Always together. Stop thinking that you're not important."

"You have to survive and I don't."

I can't stand his tone. Matter-of-fact, far removed, as if he's already decided that he won't make it out of the jungle alive. I hate that he's thinking that.

"I'm not going to survive without you. That's the unvarnished truth, so I suggest you eat when I do."

He pushes back the dark hair falling at a slant over his brow. "Well, *of course* I want to live. But we may not have the luxury of walking out of this building together." He deliberates for a moment and then reaches inside his bag, pulling out a cloth bundle tied up by a leather string. He hands it over to me, and I carefully unwrap the fabric. My stomach growls at the sight. There's a large pile of assorted nuts: walnut, macadamia, and the enormous castañas de Pando. "You need to eat, Condesa."

I grit my teeth, ignoring the loud rumbling of my stomach. "Only when you do."

Manuel glares at me but eats a handful. "Happy?"

"Now that you've stopped being morbid, yes."

"I'm not being morbid," he says. "I'm being *practical*. This is our reality."

I can't talk about this anymore, can't imagine Inkasisa without Manuel in it. I spent years wondering about his life beyond the walls of the Illustrian keep. Hated the miles and miles between us, not knowing if he was all right. I pluck a castaña and enjoy its smooth, buttery taste. I eat several, one after another, thankful to have something in my belly. "Tell me about the people you met during your travels around Inkasisa."

He blinks at the subject change. "¿Por qué?"

I nudge his shoulder. "Because you've been everywhere, and for most of my life, I've lived within a fortress. You've probably fallen in love, and the most I've done is kiss boys at the keep."

He faces me, outrage dawning. *"What?"*

I can't help the sudden thrill that makes my body shiver. "I was curious. Nothing else happened, not that it's any of your business."

"They ought to have left you alone." A scowl tugs at his mouth. "I knew they admired you, but I never once thought anything was happening."

I offer a dainty shrug. "I can be quite persuasive."

He shoots me a dark look.

"Will you tell me about them? About falling in love?"

"For someone who's expected to make a strategic match, you sure talk about love a lot."

"I'm not currently in a position to make a strategic match, am I? Who'd want to marry a deposed condesa?" I raise a brow. "You're avoiding the question."

"I had a job to do. I couldn't afford to develop feelings for anyone."

"So you've been alone these three years? No girl to keep you company?"

"I didn't say that."

My mouth snaps closed.

"There was someone, but I was never in love," he says finally. "That was the problem. I needed access to a tribe in the Tierra Baja, and I used her connection to their leader. She figured it out, but by then the damage was done. I'd broken her heart."

"I hope you apologized."

"Why would I do that?"

"You didn't tell her you were sorry you used her?"

"No." He seems confused by my question and my outrage. "Because I *wasn't* sorry. I could not fail my mission. I'd do it all over again if it meant there was a chance to gain an ally against Atoc." He hesitates. "She's a sweet girl, and I'm confident there'll be someone else who deserves her."

His tone doesn't sound like himself. There's a current of regret hidden under each vowel. Almost wistful.

"But it bothers you all the same," I say quietly. "To have used someone like that."

"No. I told you—" He breaks off at my raised eyebrow. Then his lips tighten as he dips his chin a fraction of an inch.

"It bothers me too," I say. "The people who have worked so hard to put me on the throne. We've lost so many over the years.

It never gets easier. I want to take care of them all, but I keep asking them to risk their lives."

He reaches for my hand, but then changes his mind and drops his palm so it rests flat against the stone. "You're worth it."

I think about Ximena, and how she changed sides. She would have rather supported my enemies than see me on the throne. "It's hard to believe sometimes."

"Most of the good things are," he says, and his voice is kind and warm, like the softest tunic against my skin. "Try to hold on to them when you hear them."

"Did you ever find any allies?"

His mouth twists. "No one wanted to openly move against the king. Too afraid, or too far removed from La Ciudad. They remembered the earthquake."

The earthquake. Atoc's Pacha magic, the ability to shake the ground beneath our feet. He destroyed whole sections of the city. Hundreds died. And as if that weren't enough, he found an enchanted gem that had the ability to call up ghosts.

Warriors who didn't bleed.

I'd held that weapon in my hands. Victory had been in my hands—literally. I'd even called up the ghosts.

Then I *dropped* it.

Manuel studies me carefully. "Did any of those boys hurt you?"

I make a face. "Of course not. I was only curious." And maybe it's because we're stuck in here without a clear way out, and the possibility of starving looms larger with every passing minute, I decide to venture close to the line he's drawn between us. The one that's meant to keep me acting appropriately. "All the other boys flocked over, but you kept your distance."

"I'm surprised you noticed," he says, and he sounds almost amused. "There always were a few of them surrounding you. Even when they ought to have been practicing."

"Were you jealous?" I tease.

"Perhaps," he says coolly. "Perhaps not."

My heart flips. I want to provoke him. Flap the unflappable Manuel. Find hidden treasures in his conversation. Sentences I could hold up to the light and marvel at every word. But I stay silent and fight to respect his wishes and not bring up something he'd rather not talk or think about. I force my attention back to the chamber and the three pillars topped by the three statues.

"We might die in here."

He's angry now. "You're not going to die. I won't let you."

"I might, Manuel, and there won't be anything you can do about it."

A long moment passes, the both of us glowering at each other. Then he lurches to his feet. "The hell you will. Come on. The answer is here somewhere."

I hold up both hands, and he reluctantly helps me to my feet. He walks to the closest pillar. Once again, I walk around all three columns, this time studying the statues and the carvings along the sides.

This is merely a puzzle, a kind of riddle.

I only have to take in the whole picture and remember the facts, clearing out everything else. Manuel's heartache over his family. My mission to find the Illari. My own broken heart. I sweep all of that to the side.

Think, Catalina. *Think.*

All of the statues are the same width and height. The three gods are all wearing robes, facing away from one another, and somewhere on them they are carrying an item of importance. A crown, a pendant, and an amulet.

Perhaps the answer has something to do with that?

I step away from the three pillars, wanting to stare at them all at once. When I do—I *finally* see it.

"Manuel," I say. "Why do you suppose the statues are on platforms that spin?"

He comes to stand next to me. "I don't know."

"There has to be a reason," I muse. "Otherwise, why not set them on the flat surface at the top of the pillar? Why have them move at all?"

"All good questions," he says, taking off his hat to smooth back his hair. "Any ideas?"

I contemplate the three pillars and their corresponding statues until something shifts in my mind and an idea strikes.

Manuel studies me. "What is it? What do you see?"

I point to the statues. "They're dressed identically, and their faces resemble one another. As if they're a family—which is monstrous. But look, the artist who carved them designed them as a matching set. They somehow . . . belong to one another."

He tilts his head. "Right. I see it. But I still don't understand what we're missing."

"I'm getting to that. Right now they're all facing away from one another, and it looks wrong. Weird, even. They spin for a reason, so logically there must be a correct direction. If we turn the platforms and have them face one another, the dials might finally work."

"But there are three of them. How do we get them to face one another? It's not possible."

I frown. "True. I wonder if they need to be looking toward the center of the room, instead of away from it. Almost as if they're pointing to something."

"But there's nothing in the center," he says, walking over the marked floor. "Only this symbol."

"It can't hurt to try." I point to the moon goddess. "I'll spin Luna. You take care of Inti and Pachamama."

"All right," he says, studying the dials on the walls. "I bet the correct way to turn the wheels is counterclockwise, just like the platforms."

I run to the moon goddess's pillar and climb up so I can spin the platform around with the statue gazing toward the center of the room. By the time Manuel does the same for the other two, I'm already standing in front of the wheel that has one long dash down the middle.

He looks over at me and nods.

I turn the wheel counterclockwise and it slowly gives under my fingers. "It's working!" I finish the turn and then run over to the third dial. Manuel spins his wheel with two dashes, and then I complete the turn for the last one. We meet in the middle of the chamber and glance at the vine-covered wall, and then slowly approach it, as if it were feral. I swing the vines to the side. The wall of stone is still there.

We're still trapped inside.

catorce

The sound of rock scraping against stone rents the air. We stare at the wall, but it still doesn't move. I spin away, searching for the source of the noise, and walk toward the pillars.

"Manuel!"

He rushes to my side and we gape at the floor—specifically at the triangle-shaped pattern in the center of the chamber. Whatever we did with the wheels, it's propelled the stone to move, revealing a deep, dark hole. I walk slowly toward it, but Manuel stops me and pushes me behind him. "Let me check it first."

I resist rolling my eyes. He carefully makes his way over to the pit and peers into the flat darkness.

"Well?"

"There's a ladder carved into the wall. I think we're meant to climb down." He leans farther, his gaze narrowed. My heart hammers against my ribs.

Loud screeching destroys the quiet.

Manuel drops to the ground as a blur of wings flies out from within the hole. I scream. My knees give way, and I stumble to the floor. The bats swarm above my head, thundering loud, as I crawl toward Manuel. I reach the edge of the hole and gasp. There's no light at the end. I can't possibly go down there. A bat swoops to my level and tangles in my hair. Manuel yanks it free, and I wince. Then he places his feet over the edge and onto the first step. Another creature lands on my shoulder, claws piercing my tunic, sinking into my skin. I rip the creature away, and my clothing tears.

Manuel disappears below and I follow him, my body shaking. I lower each foot, trusting there will be another rung, another groove. The stone is cold under my fingertips. We sink lower and lower, the bats shrieking and circling above. I glance over my shoulder and down toward Manuel.

He looks up, his eyes glowing. "¿Estás bien?"

I don't know how to answer that question. Fatigue is a constant thrum deep under my skin. I can't speak anyway—terror locks my jaw tight. He seems to understand and resumes moving. Our breaths collide in the narrow tunnel, tangling as they hit the jagged stone. Manuel makes a huffing noise of surprise.

"There're no more steps," he says. "I'm going to let go—"

"No!" I cry. "What if—"

"Condesa," he says firmly. "I'll call out if it's safe."

I catch the moment he loosens his fingers. Wordlessly, he disappears into the dark. There's a splash and then silence. "Manuel? Manuel!"

"I'm all right!"

My shoulders sag, and I press against the rock. I lower myself to the last available slot, and hesitate.

"It's all right," he says. "You can let go. I've got you."

My arms shake. Another opportunity for me to drown. I can't seem to escape the water in this damn jungle.

"Come on!" he yells. "You can do this."

I let go. The wind tears into my hair as I hit the water. It's freezing and it slashes my skin. I come up sputtering. Manuel swims to me, wraps his arms around my shoulders. Then he guides us forward; I can feel his legs kicking near mine. I help him by treading water, imitating his free hand. He glances around, his dark eyes glimmering, providing the only source of light. All around us are craggy walls, uneven and bumpy. The smell reminds me of mushrooms drenched by a thunderstorm.

"No entiendo," I say, my teeth chattering. "Where can we go?"

He leads me to a protruding ledge big enough to hold on to. I reach out with both hands and cling to it for dear life. Then Manuel drags in a big sip of air before sinking below. For a terrible moment I'm alone in this space. Only the sounds of my breathing interrupt the soft water lapping against the rock. It's pitch black without Manuel's Moonsight. And then he breaks the surface.

"Anything?"

Manuel shakes his head, inhales again, and disappears. He does this three more times before finally finding something. "There's a tunnel—but I don't know where it leads or if there's anything on the other side. I can go—" He stops, his lips twisting. "I can go, but I might run out of air looking."

I reach for his arm, wrap my hands around his wrist, and tug him nearer. He lets me close the distance between us. "You can't risk it."

He tilts his head back, and I follow his gaze. Our drop came from directly above us, about twenty feet. There's no way we can climb back up.

"No," I moan. "What if you drown?"

He doesn't say anything. We both know this is our only option, and I hate it. Because if he doesn't come back, the only available thing for me to do is tread water until I can't stand the dark anymore. My breath hitches in my throat.

"There's a way out of here," Manuel whispers. "I feel it in my bones."

I'm not ready for him to go.

I can only stare at his face. Grim and decided. He's as serious as I've ever seen him. He's only waiting to give me time to get used to the idea of him not coming back. Of him dying. I clench my eyes.

They fly open when I feel his rough palm against my cheek. "I won't let anything happen to you."

"Manuel." I lick my lips, and suddenly I can't speak anymore, even though there're so many things I want to say to him. But those words remain deep in my heart, afraid to make their journey out into the open where anyone can hear. "I'm thankful for you," I say finally, and while I mean every word, disappointment lances my body. I want to tell him how I really feel. But I also need to respect his choice, even as it kills me. Because the way he's looking at me now, with his hand against my cheek, is incredibly tender and almost beckoning me to reveal my secret.

"Shhh," he says. "This isn't goodbye."

He creeps closer, the water pulsing between us as if it were a heartbeat. His fingers glide up my shoulders. Surprise keeps me from moving, but then I press my body against his. Manuel's luminous eyes widen a fraction, and then he smiles small. Almost shy.

The words rip out of me. "You were the one whose kiss I wanted most," I whisper. I tilt my chin upward, and his glowing gaze drops to my mouth.

"If I don't make it back . . . you need to know." He bites his bottom lip, and his uncertainty is the most endearing thing I've ever seen. "If I were free to choose what I wanted, free to be *anyone* else, I'd pick you. Over and over again, I'd pick you."

He gently moves my hands until they grip the craggy wall once more. I'm not ready to let go of him. "Manuel. Espera."

But before I can say anything else, he disappears.

My fingers dig into the stone. The soft huffs of my breath sound like thunder in my ears. The water laps against the rock, a steady rhythm that echoes my heartbeat. Should I go after him? I don't want to be alone in this chamber for another second. What if he doesn't come back? The cloying, dank smell assaults my nose.

My fingers loosen on the ledge. Manuel might need my help. Even now he could be fighting for air, fighting to return to me.

There's a sudden swell of water and I gasp. He reappears, panting for air. Tears flood my eyes. I let go of the ledge and clumsily swim toward him, reach my arms around his shoulders.

"Estás vivo." I choke back a sob. "You're alive."

Manuel squeezes my waist and a slight tremor goes through him. Then he releases me, and I recognize the change in him. His guard is up again—but the words can never be unsaid. We both know that. "There's another room at the other end of the tunnel." His voice becomes matter-of-fact. "You'll have to swim fast."

"I'm not a strong swimmer," I say, fighting panic. "You know that."

He gently shakes me. "Do you want to live?"

"What kind of question is that? Of course I do."

"Do you want to become queen?"

I try to shove away from him, but he holds on tightly. "You know I do!"

"Then you'll have to swim to the other side. It's the only way. You can do this, Condesa—you have to."

"But—"

He glares at me and my protest dies.

"Are you ready?"

"Of course not," I wail.

A hint of a smile bends his unyielding mouth. He takes my hand and I inhale until my lungs expand and burn. Then we dip below and Manuel points in the direction of the tunnel. The water is a deep well of gloom. He tugs my hand, and I kick my legs wildly. With my free arm, I push against the water, fighting to go forward. We reach the tunnel together and swim through. But the walls narrow, and Manuel pushes me ahead. I never stop kicking, not even when my lungs start burning.

The mouth of the submerged cave is small, and I use the edge to push myself out. I feel rather than see Manuel behind me. Then he's beside me, holding my hand again, and we kick to the surface. I come up sputtering, wiping the water from my eyes. This chamber is filled with soft rays of sunlight. The ceiling has plants poking through cracks in the rock formation.

"You did it," he says with a broad smile. "I'm so proud of you."

My heart burns as my cheeks flush. I look away, overwhelmed.

"This way," Manuel says, gesturing toward the edge of the pool. My movements are still awkward, but I manage to stay afloat on my own. I haul myself up, crawl away from the water, and warily get to my feet.

The cave is smaller than I first realized, maybe half the size of the room with the pillars. Behind us are long stretches of hanging vines, varying in thickness. Manuel marches over to the thicket and sweeps them aside, revealing another tunnel.

He looks back at me, then stills, his mouth caught in surprise. His eyes flicker down to my feet and then back up to my face, and warmth spreads over his cheeks. He clears his throat and averts his gaze.

I scrunch my brow and glance down. My tunic and pants stick to my skin, and every line and curve is visible. But instead of feeling embarrassed, I grin. He catches my smirk and his face turns to stone—but his cheeks are still stained red.

Somehow I know if I tease him about it, he'll only further withdraw behind that wall he's erected between us. It's the first time I've ever caught him admiring my body. When his gaze isn't perfectly respectful, his eyes only focus on my face. If there was ever a boy I'd want to stare, it's Manuel.

"Let's go," he says, and vanishes behind the green curtain. I trudge after him, unable to rid the smile from my face. I've never seen him blush.

The walls of the tunnel are just as craggy and uneven as the cave we left behind. But there are roots and plants covering most of the rock, and warm, muggy air clings to my skin. We keep walking, Manuel ahead, lighting the way forward with his Luna-blessed sight. I push myself to match his long-legged stride. Which is a mistake—my body is inexplicably weak. As if I've been hungry and sick for days and days.

"I wonder how long we have before the poison kills us."

He looks at me in alarm. "Have you gotten worse?"

I consider his question. "I haven't, actually. I feel the same as when I woke up."

"I think if we were poisoned, we'd steadily get worse." He pulls back the sleeve of his tunic. "None of the bites are infected or swollen."

I wrinkle my nose. "So then what could it be?"

He doesn't answer right away. "The jungle has all kinds of magic in its veins, Condesa."

"But this building is man-made."

"Doesn't mean it can't be affected."

"Well, say it is the building. What magic is at work? What's making us sick?"

He runs his fingers along the wall. "There might be something in the air. But it's definitely magic. It doesn't make sense that we'd both be feeling this poorly after one night."

I shoot him a sidelong glance. "You know I wouldn't have survived the swim without you, right?"

"It's my job," he says, but the words are softened by a small smile that deepens the lines at the corner of his mouth. He reaches out and tucks a long strand of wet hair behind my ear. My heart stutters. "Condesa, about what I said—"

I abruptly stop walking and hold up my hand. "Wait. You shared how you felt, and I think I deserve the right to speak my piece. For you to hear it without retreating. That's fair, isn't it?"

He hesitates, but then nods.

"I don't know what the future holds or if we'll ever make it to Paititi. But until we do, I'd like us to be who we are. We might die in the jungle and this might be the only time we'll have together. It seems a shame to waste it when we both know what we clearly want."

He studies me, quietly considering.

I clear my throat. "Well? What do you think?"

After a second of deliberation, Manuel holds out his hand. I can't stop my grin from reaching ear to ear. We resume walking, and I swing his arm playfully. He glances at our clasped fingers, as if he can't quite believe what he's agreed to.

But he doesn't let go.

At last we reach the cave opening. I walk out of the tunnel, letting out an immense sigh of relief. I immediately drag in a lungful of warm air. The sun is out, peeking through the tangle of leaves overhead. We're a few feet from the cavern entrance when Manuel stiffens beside me and drops my hand.

I look around. "What is it?"

He doesn't register my question, just stares straight ahead. I follow the line of his gaze.

A lone woman stands at the base of an enormous tree trunk, dressed in forest-green pants and a black-and-white checked tunic.

The Illari tracker.

Manuel unsheathes his machete and steps in front of me. I peer over his shoulder, my body rooted to the spot, as if I've suddenly become one of the oak trees surrounding the tunnel entrance.

The girl dismisses my companion *and* his blade, and she has the temerity to move a single step closer. Her hair is bound in a single black braid, and it swings over her shoulder, curving around her skin like a snake. She has wide-set eyes, and a dusting of freckles peppers her high cheekbones. She's taller than the woman we saw earlier with the butterflies.

"Not one more step," Manuel snarls, raising his weapon.

"You don't make demands," the girl says. She speaks the old language of the Llacsans and Lowlanders. I have some knowledge of their tongue. Hopefully my accent won't offend anyone.

She stands alone and without a weapon in her hands. Rays of sunlight cast parts of her body in a bright glow. She's younger than I originally thought. Perhaps a touch older than Manuel. Her bare arms are smooth, deeply tanned, and toned. A bow is strapped to her bag, and even from where I'm standing, I catch sight of feathered arrows kept in a leather pouch.

I place a soft hand on Manuel's arm, tight and strained, ready for action. "Calm," I whisper into his ear.

The woman takes another step.

Manuel growls at her. I tighten my hold, my fingers digging into his skin. This is what I want—a chance to talk with them. Space to have a conversation, present my case. I'm about to open my mouth when a dark shape materializes behind her, crouched low. The shape draws closer and my heart kicks.

A spotted jaguar.

This is why she's not unnerved by Manuel's steel. Or his growls, for that matter. She has a beast at her side. Hunched under her fingertips, ready to pounce, to sink its knife-tipped teeth into our throats.

"I mean you no harm," I say in Quechua. "I wish to speak to your village leader regarding an urgent matter."

She tilts her head, once again drawing closer, the big cat climbing the steps. "Why have you come into our jungle?"

I move out from Manuel's shadow. He shoots me a quick look. "I need help against an adversary."

Her face shutters. "We are not interested in war." She turns away.

I rush after her. "Espera! Wait!"

The jaguar lunges for me, teeth first. Manuel yanks me back, and I'm saved by mere inches.

The woman snaps a command—I can't make sense of it over the roar of my heart. The jaguar snarls but backs down, settling onto his haunches, his lambent gaze on mine, tracking every breath, every move.

"Por favor, I've been looking for you. For the Illari."

"We do not want to be found."

"I know," I continue. "And I can understand. I've been kept a secret for most of my life."

"You're a secret?"

I nod. "*Por favor*. Don't leave, and hear what I have to say."

"I have been waiting a week for you to leave the temple. I'm impatient to go home."

"A *week*?" I turn around and look at the building, as if it will somehow lessen my confusion. "That can't be right; we were only in there for a day."

"A week," she repeats. "What do you wish to tell me?"

"Perdón," I say, switching to Castellano. "But I still don't understand."

She sighs. The woman continues in Quechua, but she clearly understands the language of Inkasisa. "Time is a funny thing in that building. I couldn't believe you chose to run into that one when there are others."

I gasp. Our exhaustion makes sense. Our bodies went a week without food or water. No wonder we had trouble focusing.

"We were in danger," Manuel says in perfect Quechua. I nearly jump from surprise. But of course he'd know the language—traveling around for three years from one corner of Inkasisa to the other. What had I thought? That he was on vacation?

I shake my head. My mind can't move past the notion that we lost an entire week inside the temple. What's happening with my people back in La Ciudad? Maybe they've forgotten me, or worse, believe I've given up on them?

"I need help. There's a powerful threat in my home city—the same threat that drove your people into the jungle all those years ago. I'm begging you to take me to Paititi."

She's as still and remote as the trees surrounding us. But something I've said has arrested her attention. The subtle narrowing of her gaze—eyes that glow amber gold in the sunlight. Her fingers clench on the tufts of hair atop the jaguar's head. "You have a choice before you," she says at last. "Head back the way you've come, and you may live. Continue, and risk death."

I glance at Manuel, panicked. If I don't keep going, if I don't keep trying, what does that say about me? My people will live under another Llacsan. Another enemy. My family will never be avenged.

Everyone thinks I'll eventually disappear. Slink off into a quiet existence, defined by my inability to lead. My weakness. I don't want to be that person. I don't want to give up.

I've come so far.

"I must stay," I say in Quechua again. "Will you escort my companion to the jungle border? His safety is important to me."

Manuel looks at me with impotent fury. "Your *companion* won't be leaving."

"There is one more test," the woman says. "If you live, I will take you to Paititi myself. Will you follow me?"

"*One more test?*" he asks, realization dawning. "The caimán? The butterflies? Were those tests?"

"Decide," she says, her gaze flickering to mine, confirming our suspicion.

I inhale. "We'll follow you."

She nods and then makes a loud clicking noise. The jaguar

instantly becomes alert and follows her away from the cave. I hoist my pack and trudge after her, one eye on our guide and the other on Manuel. His face is set, but in the depths of his eyes there's something else. Something I don't expect at all.

Fear.

The woman doesn't speak, or encourage conversation. She doesn't hack her way through the tangled brush, but somehow finds a path, bending and curving her body around thickets of trees and clumps of jagged-edged leaves. Several times she glances over in my direction, often after I've made a noise—not even *that* loud of a sound—and she frowns, as if I'm walking and breathing wrong. It seems there's only one way to walk properly in the jungle. Whatever it is, Manuel has mastered it. He moves quietly, his machete sheathed, mimicking her movements. A born predator, like the jaguar following on the heels of the Illari tracker.

She never looks at Manuel in disapproval.

We trek deeper into the unknown, the surroundings changing gradually. Plants become brighter and fuller. Trees loom larger, and the vines curling around branches become longer and thicker. I don't recognize any of the fruit hanging above our heads, or even the scent of the forest. The damp smell of decay turns sweeter, less rotting, and my nose doesn't wrinkle as much. The sounds are the same, however: croaks, hoots, grunts, and buzzing. There is a constant cacophony of leaves rustling and water rushing, glazing rocks and splashing the muddy banks.

And always, the inescapable heat. Sweat clings to my skin, coating every inch in a wet, sticky sheen. Mosquitos lap up my blood—tiny monsters, all of them.

But the jungle never fails to be wondrous as much as it is dangerous. Even in the gloom, howling monkeys traverse overhead, sloths with their young slowly reach for the next branch, and everywhere are the jewel-tone birds, fluttering and singing. I want to hate this place as much as it hates me.

But I don't.

There's magic in every inch; the forest creates a powerful enchantment—though I can't see it. I can only feel the subtle currents of Pachamama. This is her domain; she is the giver of life and beauty, nurturing every beast and insect.

The woman leads us to a clearing next to a pond with a small island in the center. Overhead, the stars have come out and Luna shines brightly from her throne in the sky. Her rays glide over my skin, and I shiver from the cool embrace.

"We'll rest here," the Illari tracker says.

"¿Cómo te llamas?" I ask.

She ignores my question. My cheeks flush as we head onto the sandy bank, imperfect, with numerous jagged rocks marring its surface. Manuel cuts down bamboo, and I look for firewood, bringing back whatever I can find that isn't sopping wet. She takes the bundle from my arms and lays it above a stretch of broad leaves. Using two rocks, she somehow coaxes a small fire to life. Manuel hands out bamboo cups filled with fresh water, and then ventures to the lake, once again with a long bamboo stalk, one end carved into sharp prongs. I settle onto the sand near the fire, even though it's blazing hot, and sip from my cup. The jaguar curls next to the tracker, its gaze on my every movement.

Manuel returns carrying a long catfish writhing in his arms. While he prepares the fish for cooking, I study our guide as she rests by the fire, her big jungle cat pressed against her legs. She stares at Manuel, a slight furrow between her black brows, as if she can't quite figure out what he's doing here. He's not a member of a tribe, his weapon is Illustrian, but he also carries a slingshot, which he's never had to use. The jungle seems to accept him, and in return he respects its majesty. He's a blend of the land and people who have shaped him these last three years.

"How far is the next test?" I ask.

No reply to this. Manuel seems to know to keep silent, but I'm not built that way. When I'm nervous, I chatter. But even her foreboding expression deters me from asking another question.

I catalog her features. Study every line of her compact frame. The tracker's tunic is beautiful, the hem finished with a black-and-white fringe that grazes her skin. On her feet are soft leather sandals, and her trousers look lightweight and of good quality. The circlet of gold on her brow intrigues me. Is she someone important in the lost city?

The silence stretches. I can't take it. "Is Paititi far from here?"

Her gaze flickers to mine. "You may not see it at all. No sense in talking of my home village."

"I'm only attempting polite conversation."

"You make too much noise," she says, and then tilts her head back to gaze up at Luna.

I try not to be hurt by her words and her tone, even as they scratch my skin. When she reaches for her small pack, I expect her to pull out a weapon; instead a small canvas sack appears in her fingers. She reaches inside and grabs a glittering dust from within.

Moondust.

I've never seen it unless made by Ximena, a byproduct of whenever she'd take to the loom and weave with strands of moonlight. A magical ability gifted to her by Luna—*our* goddess. How does this girl have access to moondust? Have they captured an Illustrian weaver?

Another thought blazes through my mind—scorching hot. Could Ximena be here in the jungle? But no. That's impossible. She stayed behind in La Ciudad. We parted ways as enemies.

Manuel brings the fish over to the fire, along with his pan. When he sees the sparkling powder cupped in her hand, he pauses, and then his glowing gaze shoots to mine.

"How did you come by moondust?"

The woman ignores my question *again*, and I hiss out an impatient breath. When she throws the dust into her eyes, I gasp. Her dark eyes turn silver, gleaming from across the fire pit. She lifts her hand, her index finger pointed, and traces the sky. My blood runs cold. I've done the same gesture before. Hundreds of times. Every night, probably. It's what I do when trying to read the stars.

She's a seer. She has to be. But even as she surveys the heavens, my body refuses to accept the truth. Despite the heat coming from the fire, from the steaming jungle a few yards away, I shiver. I thought Luna only blessed Illustrians; I thought we were her chosen people. Set apart and gifted by her awesome powers.

But here's an Illari reading Luna's celestial message.

I reach into my pack with shaking hands. Pull out my dented

telescope and peer up into the sky. My breaths are erratic pants. I don't notice when Manuel hands me a slab of cooked fish on a leaf. Don't notice when he hands me another bamboo cup. All I care about is what I can see though the narrow window of my scope. But Luna doesn't speak clearly to me. The lines between the stars shift and fade, messy letters that don't make sense or form any legible words. I lower the telescope, fighting tears.

The woman stares at me steadily, her eyes no longer silver.

"She hides from you," she says. Then she picks up her fish and settles away from the fire, a few paces from the pair of us, the jaguar jumping to its feet and settling in the space between, an effective and deadly barrier.

"Try eating," Manuel says softly from his place on the damp sand. "You might feel better."

The fish is crisp in my mouth but tastes like ash. Manuel sits next to me, his leg pressing against mine. I glance at him in surprise, and he merely smiles. The Illari tracker catches the movement, and then turns away from both of us, finishing her meal in silence, every now and again feeding the jaguar bits of her food.

"Do you think she's taking us to the bridge?" I whisper.

Manuel's lips flatten. "I'm sure of it, but hopefully our experience will be better than the last time I attempted to cross."

"What happened?"

His eyes flicker to mine. "My nose was broken."

I make a gesture with my hand, signaling for him to continue. Manuel sets his plate and cup down. "It was two, maybe three months after I arrived in the jungle. I'd tracked one of them to the bridge." His lips twist. "But it was a trap. I almost made it to the other side when arrows came flying from every direction. I turned around—got hit twice, and then fell forward and broke my nose on one of the wooden slats."

I grip his arm. "How are you alive?"

"I fell into the water," he whispers. "The current carried me away, and the Illari left me for dead. It's not a memory I like to dwell on. Now do you see why I wanted to spare you before?"

Fear shoots an icy blade through my veins. "What if this is another trap?"

Manuel gazes at the tracker, considering. "It might be. While she sleeps, we can make our escape."

The decision doesn't come easily. Whatever happens, we have to cross that bridge. She's offering to escort us, to take us right to the entrance. If we go alone, we might get shot, but if we accompany her, there's a small chance they'll let us cross.

"We go with her."

Manuel nods, resigned.

We resume our study of the tracker, who pays no attention to us. She's done eating, the jaguar regarding us with baleful eyes, and after a moment she resumes her study of the stars.

"Why does Luna speak to her and not to me?" I swat at a mosquito. "Why does she have moondust?"

"No sé, Catalina." He eats his fish, every now and again turning to stare at the girl worshiping the moon. "But maybe if we pass this next test, we can ask what Luna thinks of our mission. She might offer you more guidance."

I flinch and squeeze my eyes shut. I have loved Luna all of my life. For her ability to conquer the night, for the way she's blessed every one of my people with gifts, small and big. She is constant and loyal and true. I reopen my eyes. The woman starts to hum, a soft smile bending her lips, her chin pointed upward, and the moonlight kisses her cheeks.

When I look down at my dirty clothes and hands, every part of me is tucked in shadow.

dieciséis

We set off early in the morning as the sun rises over the verdant-green canopy, setting golden fire to each leaf. The woman spends a few minutes staring at the first rays of dawn, and I get the sense that she's greeting the sun god. Inti wakes up slow and steady and warms everything within his reach. He's a deity I thought only the Llacsans worshiped—but it seems the Illari are a trifle cavalier with their affections, loving the earth and the sun and the moon, too.

It feels wrong.

Greedy, almost, to want blessings from all three of them. My thoughts tumble in my mind, tangling like unruly vines, poking holes in my thoughts. Because even if I think it's wrong, it clearly *isn't*. Luna favors the Illari tracker. Has shone down upon her, communicated with her, and blessed her with an extraordinary gift.

But not me. My magic barely works. And it bothers me, profoundly and deeply.

What's wrong with me, that I can't be trusted with more?

Our guide turns away from the water and gathers her things. I do the same, shoving everything back into my pack. Manuel hands me another bamboo cup.

"You're not drinking enough water."

"I'm not doing enough of anything," I mutter.

His brows rise at my mulish tone. "Sleep well?"

"Terrible. You?"

He shoots the woman a quick look before returning his attention to me, and I'm astounded to find his smile is rather sheepish. "Last night was the first night I slept soundly since arriving. With her close, I knew I could depend on her to wake me if there was any trouble."

My face falls. He can't let down his guard while with me—not even to sleep well. I'm that much of a burden. A tremendous weight on his shoulders.

Manuel studies me. "Condesa."

"It's Catalina," I say flatly. "I thought we'd moved past the title."

He gives me a look that's mired in exasperation. "What's bothering you?"

I can't begin to answer that question. There's so much my heart is carrying—hopes and dreams for my people, fed by an unquestionable thirst to prove myself. My fear of failure grows heavier every day, weighing me down and wanting to fold me into the hard earth. "Everything feels heavy, Manuel. We don't need to talk about it; I know we have to keep moving."

I turn away—but in a flash, he reaches for my arm and tugs me toward him. Before I know what's happening, he wraps both arms around me and holds on tightly. "You didn't think you could swim, but you did. You've walked miles, climbed a cliff, and slept in a cave. It was your wits and resourcefulness that got us out of the temple. You may not think you're a survivor, Catalina, but I do." And then he presses a soft kiss high on my temple, near the hairline. It happens so fast, in the space of a blink.

He releases me and averts his gaze, suddenly shy, and it's a good thing too, because I have to pick my jaw up off the ground. A hopeful flutter sweeps through my body, from the top of my head down to the tips of my toes. The warmth of his embrace clings to my skin. I shiver, trying to hold on to the sensation.

I'm still standing in the same spot, my fingertips grazing the place where he'd *kissed me*, and as he brushes past, for a moment I swear, I *swear*, I catch sight of an amused glint in his dark eyes. I shake my head, trying to remember where I am, what my name is, and what my age is. If someone asked me any of those questions, I wouldn't be able to answer. Not even if my life depended on it. I hoist my pack higher up on my hip and hurry after Manuel and our guide, my heart thrashing against my ribs.

She's up ahead with her jaguar, leading us again, taking us farther away from the jungle border, even though the way out is long gone by now. I ought to be glad that we have a guide to Paititi, but last night changed things for me, and I can't help feeling that I'm walking into something I couldn't have anticipated or planned for.

Who am I kidding?

I hadn't planned for any of this. Not my exile or seeing Manuel again after three years or looking for the lost city. I hadn't planned on my best friend betraying me, or discovering how useless I am outside of the Illustrian fortress. It's a painful truth that sits heavily on my shoulders, so immense that I'm sure I'll fall over from the weight.

Lost in my thoughts, I don't notice clearing the tree line and almost walk right over a cliff. Manuel snatches my pack and yanks me away from the edge.

"That would have been tragic," I say, and laugh.

He's not amused. "Quite."

Down below is a wide river, roaring thunderously, and on the opposite side is another jagged cliff, at a lower height than ours. It's covered in trees and thick vines and a riot of flowers in every color of the rainbow.

Our guide glances in our direction. "Stay here." She vanishes back into the jungle and returns with a thin liana vine looped around and around her right shoulder. She pulls out one of her arrows and ties the end of the vine to it. Then she draws her bow and deftly lets her arrow fly, streaking across the gulf and smack into a tree on the other side.

Manuel lets out a low, appreciative whistle. Even I'm impressed, despite myself. The tracker then secures the other end of the vine around a thick tree trunk on our side, pulling it taut. From our side of the river, the vine slopes down at a steep angle.

Then the tracker drops to her knees in front of the jaguar, pressing her forehead against its neck. I cringe at the sight, knowing the beast won't hurt her, but I'm scared all the same. It purrs loudly and then scampers off into the jungle with a final look in our direction that I interpret to mean: *Hurt her, and I will hunt you, outsiders.*

"Do what I do." The Illari stands, picks up a branch from the jungle floor, and jumps off the cliff. Holding either end of the bark, she zips down to the other cliff. The tracker lands on her feet, then turns around and waves for us to follow.

I watch in horror the entire time. Manuel bends and finds two branches, and then uses his dagger to cut off any smaller pieces sticking out.

Wordlessly, he hands one over to me. "You're next."

My mouth goes dry. "I don't think I can do this."

"You can and you will."

I peer over the edge to stare at the churning water below. I'm not afraid of heights, but even so, my knees are shaking. What if the vine snaps? What if I lose my grip and fall? I've become a better swimmer, but I'm no match for the hungry river.

There's a lump at the back of my throat as I take the branch. "I can't believe I'm about to do this."

"I can't believe half of the things you've done."

I raise my brows. "What do you mean? Anyone would have done what I did. A dog has that kind of survival instinct."

He lowers his chin and levels a hard gaze at me. "Condesa, most people would have given up by now. But you've refused to. You are my queen."

I can't muster even a thank-you. I can only gape at him. Then he beckons me over to the vine and demonstrates how to hold the branch.

"You only need to hold tight," he says. "The vine and the branch will take care of the rest."

I nod and I let his words sink in. Back at the Illustrian keep, no one else knew I was the real condesa, so they couldn't encourage me. Ximena and Sofía were supportive, but not in the way I needed. They understood the circumstances were inevitable: I was going to reclaim the throne. Perhaps they thought I didn't need to hear affirmation.

But I do.

I grip the branch the way Manuel showed me, and draw close to the edge. The wind tears at my hair, and the river rushes past, snarling. I take deep sips of the warm air.

"It helps if you jump," Manuel says from behind me. "Suerte, Catalina."

I glance over my shoulder. He's utterly calm and adorably ruffled with his dirt-streaked clothes and tousled hair. I want to rush into his arms and feel his embrace again. But I force myself to turn around.

I take the leap.

My stomach swoops as I fall for half a second before I'm jerked upward as the vine keeps me from falling straight down. I zip across the wide river, feet kicked up and my fingers clutching the rough bark. I let out a cry—but it's not one of terror. It's something between a laugh and a yell, and even to my own ears, the sound is a happy one. The wind teases my hair, and my tunic flutters behind me like the tail of a beautiful bird. Much too soon, I reach the other side, and I veer toward the large tree where the other end of the vine is secured. At the last moment, I let go and drop to the soft jungle floor, rolling until I come to a stop.

The tracker looms above me, a speculative gleam in her eyes. "You enjoyed that."

It's not a question, but I nod anyway. I more than enjoyed it. I want to repeat the entire experience over and over again. My body thrums with barely contained energy, and every beat of my heart against my ribs is joyous. I scramble to my feet and watch Manuel's crossing. His face is set, matter-of-fact, and when he lets go, he lands on his feet at a run. When he doubles back, he glances over at me, as if to make sure I didn't break anything. And when his gaze lifts to mine—*he winks at me.*

I am breathless.

Our guide motions for us to follow, tucking herself into the jungle, embracing its song. I follow after her, and Manuel brings up the rear. We travel single file for most of the day, though it's impossible to tell the hour under the dense canopy. The heat coats our skin, and sweat dampens every inch. My clothing smells disgusting; there's no other word for it. I want to bathe, but I'm afraid to go in the water, afraid of the creatures waiting for prey. Every mile or so, we stop to drink. The Illari woman disappears and returns with large nuts, ripe bananas, and several avocados. We eat and drink our fill and continue the trek deeper into the jungle. Or perhaps we're already as deep as we can go. Perhaps we've arrived at the heart.

We hike up a small hill, and when we reach the summit, the view forces me to still, demanding to be enjoyed. The jungle is immense, stretching in every direction for miles and miles. The noise is deafening from up here, monkeys howling at the top of their voices, birds calling to one another, and insects buzzing. It is an amazing, humbling sight. I glance at Manuel, who stands at my elbow, arrested by the scene.

"Is it weird that this place is starting to feel like home?"

He answers without looking in my direction. "Yes."

I can't help but laugh. Somehow this dangerous place has

forced its way into my heart. The magic it hides, deep within its belly, the vibrant colors and glorious river, and the stern mountain in the center, lording over it all. My gaze snags on a stretch of white forest. The trees glint silver, as if sprinkled by moondust.

"Is that *snow*?" I ask the tracker.

She looks at me carefully. "No, no es nieve."

"Then what is it?" But as soon as the words are out of my mouth, a memory comes rushing back. We found a similar stretch of silvery leaves surrounding an equally silvery flower.

"You would know, outsider."

"¿Cómo puedo yo saber?" I ask, baffled.

Her hands curl into tight fists. "That part of the jungle is dying."

I return my attention to the affected area. For some unfathomable reason, she's implying that I'm responsible. "I don't understand."

Manuel steps closer to me. "Speak frankly, Illari."

The tracker straightens her shoulders, lifts her chin a fraction of an inch. "It's this way."

She marches from us, down the other side of the hill. I pull my brows into a swift frown. "What do you think that was about?"

"No idea."

"But she seemed angry."

His expression turns grim. "Furiosa."

CAPÍTULO

diecisiete

The Illari tracker takes us to a massive statue of a vulture, made entirely of stone and painted the purest white. It's double the height of the temple, hidden at the base of the hill and surrounded by a moat with the darkest water I've ever seen—the color of night without Luna's twinkling companions. A single wooden-slat bridge permits entry. I'm suddenly reminded of the Illustrian fortress. We, too, had a bridge, enchanted by Ana. What kind of protection will this bridge have? I turn to Manuel, but his attention is on the swirling water. He clenches his jaw.

"I never thought I'd see it again," he says.

Realization dawns. *Oh*. This is the bridge he'd hinted at earlier. The one he refused to talk about.

The tracker steps forward and points to the wooden platform. "You must cross here. No one will shoot."

"Why am I allowed to cross this time?" Manuel asks.

She jerks her chin in my direction. "We are interested in the stunted seer."

I glance at Manuel and mouth, *Stunted?*

"You're not coming too?" Manuel asks, his voice deceptively calm. He inches closer to her, as if readying to attack should he not like her answer.

"Both of you first."

There's no room for argument in her tone. I stare at the statue with its outstretched wings lowered to a spot on the ground, the fierce expression carved into the face of the stone. "This is the last test?"

The tracker nods. "If you pass, I will have no choice but to take you to Paititi."

I walk to the bridge—it gently sways over the river, perhaps ten or fifteen feet above it. The fall won't kill me, but the caimánes might. There are three of them, lounging in the water, patient and trusting that food will come their way.

I lift my foot to take the first step, but Manuel stops me. He glares at me and gently sets me aside so he can go ahead of me. But I don't let him.

I grab onto the sleeve of his tunic. "It has to be me."

I'm not made of porcelain. This is the farthest I've been from home, and I'm still alive. Much to everyone's surprise.

Even my own.

Manuel studies me carefully, and I meet his assessing gaze without flinching. His face shifts, and he beams back at me, full of pride. A warm glow spreads throughout my body. Then he moves away from the bridge, and I walk forward, head held high.

"Be careful," he says.

I hold my breath for the first step—it wobbles beneath my weight, and I fling out my arms to grip the ropes on either side to help my balance. They're rough under my palms. I walk forward as the bridge swings wildly. Through the cracks of the wooden boards, I catch sight of something long and black peeking through. When I'm halfway across, I look down at the water below. The caimánes have gathered underneath my feet. I freeze, noticing for the first time how old the wood looks. Nearly rotted through, some planks. The next one might give under my weight.

"Keep going," Manuel says at my heels. "Slowly."

Shuddering, I force myself to move forward, skipping the next board, and as I do, the monsters follow my movement.

"We're almost there," he says. "If you fall, I'm coming after you."

I take another step. "Is that supposed to make me feel better?"

"Well, at least you won't be lonely down there."

His tone is almost teasing. Manuel *never* teases. I look at him in shock. "You're in a good mood for someone mere feet away from a black caimán."

He stares uneasily at the creatures in the dark water. "Or maybe I'm trying to distract you from the danger."

One of the monsters leaps, jaws snapping loudly, and then falls under the surface with a loud splash. My fingers tighten on the rope. "Your plan isn't working."

"Just keep moving, Catalina." He points to something over my shoulder. I spin around, surprised to find that we're only a few steps away from the end. I walk forward, bending my knees to keep myself in rhythm with the swaying bridge. It's a mercurial dance partner.

Five more steps.

Below us, the caimánes snap their teeth. A soft whimper escapes my mouth and drifts down. The next wooden slat looks as if it might disintegrate with a gust of wind. I step over it and bring my other foot forward, breathing a sigh of relief, but then—

The slat beneath my feet shudders and cracks and disappears.

I fall through, barely snatching onto the next plank. My fingers dig into the wood, my feet swinging frantically beneath me. I let out a sharp scream as the rope snaps and the wood strains against my weight. The caimán leaps, clearing the water and aiming for my feet. Its jaws slam together, just missing the toe of my boot. The creature smacks the water with a roar. Another leaps and I jerk my legs up just in time.

Manuel darts forward, using the rope to keep balance as he leans forward, his palm extended toward me. "Calm, Catalina. Reach for my hand."

The wooden plank beneath my hands shudders, and there's a loud tearing noise.

"Ahora," he says firmly.

I reach with my right hand as the plank cracks and splits. Manuel grasps my hand as the slat drops and I sway forward, my legs careening against the underside of the other wooden slats with a loud thud.

"Other hand," Manuel says.

I do as he says and he yanks me up and over to the other side, closer to where we need to be. He hauls us both onto our feet and swivels me around. I'm shaking as I continue walking, but this time Manuel keeps ahold of my hand. Every move costs me an hour of my life. At one point I don't think I can move another inch; I'm so terrified of falling through again. He bumps me from behind. I take another step and then another. When I reach solid ground, I let out a ragged sigh of relief.

But there's a sudden shift in the air. A dangerous quality that sinks into my bones. The hair on my arms stands on end.

"Catalina," Manuel whispers in a hoarse tone. "Ven aquí."

From the corner of my eye, I catch sight of movement on the opposite side of the moat where we left the tracker. I turn around and as I do, Manuel slowly pitches toward me, as if wanting to shield me from what's coming.

We are surrounded by people wielding bows and arrows. There must be about fifty of them of various ages, all dressed in black-and-white tunics. Standing on the other end of the bridge is our traitorous guide. Her arrow is aimed at the level of Manuel's heart. I clutch his arm.

"Go to the foot of the statue," she calls coldly. "You'll know what to do."

"If we don't?" Manuel asks.

All of them shift and aim for him. In a second he'll have fifty arrows embedded in his body.

"We'll go," I say, tugging at his wrist. He backs away from the bridge, each step careful and measured. I lead us toward the immense vulture. The base is a triangle-shaped platform with Quechuan words carved into the stone. Beautiful etchings depict hearts—some appear dark, others are painted white. With a soft hand, I trace one of the patterns and study the massive outstretched wings made of the same stone. The wings curve and dip in the middle, a deliberate design, but I don't understand what we're supposed to do.

"What do you think?" Manuel asks.

"There are a few words here." I lean forward, squinting in the dying light. "'Be weighed, but once, so the jungle may know if you're true.'" I glance back up. "I think we're meant to sit on the wings."

"It's a scale," he says. "And if we're found lacking, they'll shoot us."

I glance back toward the bridge. Several of the Illari have crossed over, their weapons notched. I didn't hear them make a sound, never even felt them. I fight to keep my panic at bay, but it sweeps into my senses, and my breath comes out in shallow puffs. Manuel unsheathes his machete, much good it will do him from this distance.

"We have to be weighed," I say. "It's the only way."

"One day," he mutters, "I'd like to not fear for my life while in your company."

"Nonsense. You're not afraid of anything."

He hesitates before slowly returning his attention to me. Dark eyes troubled. There's a current of confusion and dismay hidden in the deep lines bracketing his mouth. As if he's just realized his worst fear and it involves me. "That's not true."

"What are you afraid of?"

His lips flatten. "Not the time."

A small smile threatens to tug my mouth, but it's overruled by the widening pit deep in my belly. I might die in the next few minutes. I try to figure out how we can climb up onto the wings. And then I see the way up, subtle and nearly hidden by the great feathers. The statue has steps carved along the side of the vulture's body.

"I'll go first—"

"Absolutely not," Manuel snaps, and before I can say another word, he races up the steps and settles onto the middle of the right wing. Terror seizes my body, the blood rioting in my veins. The Illari press closer, until they're only a few feet away from me, but I barely notice. I can't tear my gaze away from Manuel.

He sits cupped in the great wing, and waits. And then the head of the vulture *moves* toward Manuel, peering at him with coolly assessing eyes. My breath lodges at the back of my throat. Manuel stares up at the bird, unwavering, a stubborn set to his shoulders. He grips his blade, readying to start swinging at anyone who comes near him.

I thought I loved him when I knew him at the Illustrian keep. But this person has captured every corner of my heart. His bravery and loyalty, his exasperating sense of duty. And right now, in this moment, as he glares with unflinching confidence at an enchanted statue.

I clutch at my arms, terrified of losing him.

There's a loud grating noise as the vulture's left wing descends to the ground and Manuel is lifted higher. The vulture has weighed his heart and deemed it worthy for life.

I sink to the ground, my ears ringing from my heartbeat thrashing against my ribs. I was prepared to fight all of the Illari. Manuel climbs down the stairs, loud, furious stomps. I expect to see profound relief cut into his features—but his dark eyes are twin fires, blazing and angry. He scowls at the crowd of people surrounding us and then at the statue.

It's my turn to be weighed.

There is no hope of escape.

Manuel offers his calloused palm to help me stand. I take it, feeling the reassuring strength of his hand, and then I brush past him. With shaking knees, I climb up the steps. My mind crowds with thoughts of my failures. I'm responsible for Sofía's and Ana's deaths. I'm the reason why Illustrians have died, terrified of starving because I didn't know how to manage our food resources. If I'd been stronger, maybe Ximena would have seen a worthy queen. Instead she saw a weak royal incapable of leading. I want to plead my case to the statue, defend myself against the damning evidence. But I remain quiet and push my hysteria down into the depths of my soul, where it might never be found.

Not even by magic.

By the time I reach the right wing, it's returned to its original height, waiting for the next heart to be judged. I scoot onto the middle, tuck my legs close, and inhale deeply, willing myself to remain calm. The Illari raise their arrows and aim at my face, my stomach, my legs. If I fail this test, it'll be a massacre.

Manuel tilts his head back. "Catalina."

My name is a soft caress, and I shiver as the sudden warmth beats away my fear. I lean forward to catch his eye, and raise a brow.

"You are worthy," he whispers.

I'm thankful to be sitting, and for half a second I forget that I might die, might bleed all over this white stone. The vulture moves its head and faces me. I force myself to meet its hard gaze, but my hands are laced tightly in my lap, fingers turning bone white. The blood drains from my face as I keep my mouth shut, even as protests bubble up to the surface.

You are vengeful and proud, a voice inside my head whispers.

A soft gasp escapes from my lips.

You have been wronged, but you are doing wrong yourself. Change is within reach, a fine balance. If you ignore the signs, you will fail and lose everything and everyone you hold dear.

My stomach twists.

Even now your heart is closed.

But it is not evil.

The stone groans as the vulture's head turns away. My stomach lurches as the wing moves. I can't watch it happen, can't look to see Manuel's disappointment.

"Look," he says breathlessly.

I force my eyes open, sure to find arrows flying. But the wing is high up.

Relief swoops into my heart, and I want to curl up as tremors rock my body. There's a loud thud as someone races up the stone steps. Strong hands grip my arms and pull me forward. Manuel drags me off the wing. He hugs me tight, my cheek pressing against the rough fabric of his tunic. My knees buckle, but Manuel won't let me fall. Together we climb down to face them all.

The Illari lower their arrows, stash their bows. Our guide walks forward, a tentative smile on her lips. It's the friendliest expression I've seen on her, and while I ought to return the gesture, I'd rather dissolve into a puddle.

A magical statue believes my heart isn't evil—it's broken and wounded and scared—but it's not evil. After everything, this test felt the hardest.

The tracker meets us at the foot of the stairs. Manuel stares at her coldly, holding me tight against his side. Her smile stretches. "I am Chaska."

dieciocho

Walking through the jungle with the Illari is different from when it was just Manuel and me. For one, the sense of danger is dulled. I'm not worried about predators or getting lost. Now I fear the men and women watching us with wary eyes. They touch my ratty tunic and braid. One of them takes ahold of my hand and examines my fingernails and smooth palms. I look to Manuel in alarm, but he silently shakes his head.

Keep silent. Play along.

There's no harm in their examinations. At least they aren't pointing their arrows at us anymore. Manuel stays close. Ever watchful—in case their goodwill only lasts so long.

The sun dips lower in the sky and the mosquitos remain ever vigilante. The Illari warriors melt into the shadows of the jungle, disappearing suddenly and without warning. Here one minute. Gone the next. It happens so quickly, I could have missed it had I blinked.

I search in every direction for hints of their black-and-white tunics, for red fringes and feathered headdresses. "Where have they gone?" I ask Chaska.

"To their posts," she says. "They guard the outer territory of Paititi. But we haven't lost all of them." She gestures behind me, and I whirl around to find three warriors remaining. They are bare chested and covered in paint, red and deep purple. I nod at them, but none respond.

"How many warriors are in Paititi?" Manuel asks.

"As numerous as the stars," she says simply.

My brows reach my hairline. "So many as that?"

"We won't be driven out of our homes again."

She's talking about the Llacsans, of course. Hundreds of years ago they conquered the land near Qullqi Orqo, the great mountain that once held all of the silver in Inkasisa. The Illari ran for their lives into the jungle, never to be seen or heard from again. My people had come in some time after, taken that land from the Llacsans, and founded our capital, La Ciudad Blanca.

We held on to that for four hundred years, until the revolt led by Atoc ten years ago. My family will forever be known as the Illustrians who lost their people their home. The thought sits heavily in my stomach, an indigestible lump.

I'm so close to arriving in Paititi, so close to asking for their help. What if they don't listen? What if they hear my plea and dismiss it altogether? Now that the moment is quickly approaching, I can't think of anything else. What does the lost city look like? Who will I have to convince? The Llacsans conquered *them* hundreds of years ago. I can only pray to Luna their anger burns as bright as mine.

Now that we've passed the third test, Chaska's demeanor warms. Instead of walking ahead, she walks at my side, breathing the same air under the shady trees. The scent is sweet and thick, like the darkest of honey slathered onto a bit of toast.

"Every day in the jungle, you must ask Pachamama's permission to be here," she says. "If you don't, you might anger her, and she won't treat you kindly. One of her many spirit children might give you trouble."

"What spirits?" I ask.

"The most powerful is Duende, a mischievous being. Powerful enough to trap you in another realm."

"I've never heard of that word—or the spirit."

"It means 'goblin.'"

"And the earth goddess controls the goblin?"

"Pachamama does not." Chaska gently sweeps aside a thick vine blocking our way. "There is no control here, outsider. Only balance. Everything is carefully weighed. We all have a place. I did not think you belonged—you cannot bear the heat, I suspect you are a bad runner, and you're unable to take a deer or even a rabbit. But the vulture king says you're worthy. We shall see."

"I would appreciate it if you called me by my given name." I have nothing else to say. Every word is true. I want to remain angry—for her putting us through those tests, for pointing out my shortcomings—but I can't blame the Illari for defending themselves. Not when my family couldn't maintain our people's safety from the Llacsans.

I chance a look behind me. Manuel follows along in our wake, his weapon in his hands. He meets my gaze and jerks his chin to the right. I look to where he's indicating, but all I can see are more mammoth trees tucked side by side like books on a shelf.

¿Qué? I mouth.

Manuel rolls his eyes. "Watch where you're going."

I turn around in time to catch myself before stumbling over a massive root.

We continue on the pathless green, and my mind circles back to the spirits Chaska mentioned. I think about the bloody butterflies and the sorcerer by the river who transformed into a caimán. Every incident felt like a defense against our presence. We are not wanted here—and yet the vulture gave his permission for us to stay.

Why?

Chaska guides us through a valley of branches and bark and rainbow-colored flowers. Hummingbirds shoot past, and spiderwebs glimmer high over our heads, draped across the branches like mosquito netting. Butterflies tangle in the sticky web, and I shudder as I pass. Chaska points to a large rubber tree covered in sap. At the base is a colony of inch-long black ants. Their sharp, squeaky noises make my skin crawl.

"The izula ant," Chaska says. "Careful of that one. The worst pain I have ever known. Lasted a full day before I got my mind back."

I quickly step away from the tree, and she laughs.

"They are guardians of the jungle. We use their poison against our enemies."

I raise my brows. "Do they obey your command?"

Chaska shoots me a pitying look. "We do not *command* the creatures of the jungle. But we know what they can do and hope they will act in the way Pachamama made them to act. That is the best we can hope for."

"I'm still confused."

"You do not listen," she chides.

I'm about to respond when a sudden blast of cold wind slaps my cheeks. It's frigid, and a chill skitters down my spine. "Did you feel that?"

Chaska nods. "It comes from the dying part of the forest."

Manuel narrows his gaze. "The area we saw from the hill— we're close?"

She raises her brow and beckons for us to follow. We do, if a little grudgingly. I don't think I'm going to like what she has to show us.

As we walk, we're bathed in a golden light with a greenish hue, our clothes cast in the same color, as if the jungle has enchanted us. The wind turns colder, and at first I welcome winter's touch— let it kiss my mouth, dust my eyelids, and tousle my hair.

But then its kiss turns into a feral bite.

I fold my arms across my chest, trying to shield my body from the blast. Under my feet, the jungle floor turns brittle white. I blink a few times, not understanding or believing what I'm seeing.

It's utter and complete desolation.

A massive oak tree has fallen over and taken down several others with it. They lie broken and frozen across one another, locked in a frigid embrace. My teeth chatter as we follow Chaska past the cemetery of giants. Beyond, the decay stretches out, killing anything in its path. The jungle may not be a friend of mine, but I'm devastated regardless. It's only after a few more steps that I finally notice what's missing—other than the heat and the color green.

"Why is it so quiet?"

"Nothing lives here," Chaska says.

She's right. I haven't heard a single hoot or croak or roar since we crossed into this eerie plain. I study the terrain and pick up a handful of the white-smudged dirt. I expect it to be freezing, but it's not. Only the howling wind is. The ground feels gritty like coarse sand, almost silver in color, and gives off a subtle shimmer. It reminds me of something, but it's so cold, I'm having a hard time thinking straight.

Even the Illari guards tremble. They gather around us, alert and watchful. I can sense they're uneasy with our distance from cover. The wind lifts the dust beneath our feet and thickens the air, blurring our vision. We can hardly see ten feet in front of us. I tip my head back, frowning. It's a clear night, but because of the swirling dust, it's impossible to catch sight of the stars or Luna herself.

"Diosa." Manuel walks over to the fallen trees. "They're dead, and covered in the same dust as the ground."

I startle and glance down at the palmful of dirt cupped in my hand. That's what the sand reminds me of—Ximena's moondust.

"You see the similarities too?" Chaska asks, catching the look of sudden understanding on my face.

I nod. "It doesn't feel like moondust, though. The dust is normally softer."

Chaska doesn't comment, merely studies me thoughtfully—her head tilted to the side, the lines across her brow deepening.

"What happened?" I ask. "What killed these trees?"

I think about that odd silver flower, the one that had taken root. Is it possible that the Illari haven't seen it? In this part of the forest, it'd be impossible to pinpoint the source. But the section Manuel and I saw was small—surrounding that one plant. It's on the tip of my tongue to tell Chaska, but something holds me back. There might be a better use for the information.

"A very good question, traveler. I don't know the answer, but whatever caused this, it's not of the jungle. It came here like you did. An invader."

"I'm not an *invader*," I say. "I'm a visitor. I'm here because I need help."

"Your people are conquerors. Destroyers of culture and traditions. Murderers and thieves."

I flush. "The Llacsans are your enemy. Not us."

She lifts her chin, dark gaze flashing like sudden streaks of lightning against a black night. "We are never happy with war."

It's not as if I am either. "I understand," I say.

"When did this part of the jungle change?" Manuel asks. His tone is coaxing and soft.

But Chaska is unfazed and impossible to charm. She points a finger at me. "It started right before *her* arrival." She turns away and walks off in a huff as my mouth drops to the jungle floor

Manuel's lips tighten. "I don't like this."

"She's abrupt, but I don't think she'll hurt us."

"I'm not so sure," he says in a hushed voice. "They're hiding something. I can feel it."

I shiver—from fear or the chilly night, I don't know. I walk up to Manuel and slide my arms around his waist. He slowly wraps both arms around me, and I smile against his chest. I'll never get used to this—Manuel without his armor, thinning the wall he's built.

His deep voice makes his chest rumble against my cheek. "You asked me what I fear."

I pull away far enough so that I can look up into his face.

"I'm afraid of the day when you'll need me, and I won't be there."

"Why won't you be there?"

"Because I don't know what's waiting for us in that city."

A shiver tears through my body. He lets me hold on to him as tightly as I need. The thought of neither of us walking back out of Paititi makes my heart thump painfully against my ribs. Manuel watches me silently, and after a long moment his gaze drops to my mouth. He pulls me closer. I reach up and curl my hand around the back of his neck. I forget about where we are and who we're with.

"Why do all of my terrible decisions involve you?" he whispers.

I grin as he dips his head.

"Travelers," Chaska calls from several feet away. "We must go."

Manuel freezes, a hairsbreadth away from my lips. "Damn it."

I open my mouth to tell her to wait just *one minute*, but Manuel covers my lips with his hand. "Not a good idea."

"How did you know what I was going to say?" I ask after I step away.

"Because I felt the same," he says. "Come on."

I take one last look at the desolated jungle then hurry after Manuel, the cold seeping into my bones. And my heart. We're almost out of the dead forest when someone cries out—in pain. Manuel immediately comes to my side and raises his machete. Ahead a few paces, Chaska whirls around and gracefully drops to one knee, an arrow already notched in her bow.

Her lips part. "One of the guards is missing."

My stomach lurches. She's right—the two remaining guards spin, their spears raised as they cry out for their missing companion. In every direction there's only dense, dusty fog shrouding the dead wood.

"I don't understand. He was just *here*," I say.

"Shhh," Manuel says. "Let me listen."

Chaska remains on the ground, arrow moving steadily, her gaze narrowed. She hisses something in rapid Quechua, but I miss it. We are still and quiet, and I'm painfully aware of my weaponless state. If only I had *something*—

Pale hands reach from within the fog and yank another guard into the thick mist. The Illari warrior goes screaming. The noise rattles my pulse, makes it leap and race. Manuel takes my hand and drags me away as Chaska shoots her arrow. There's a loud thwack as it hits a tree. The remaining guard runs after his friend, hollering a war cry.

Everything happens so fast. I don't have time to think, concentrating only on staying upright as I'm pulled back into the vivid green of the jungle, hot and steaming and completely alive. Long minutes go by, Manuel panting at my side, his weapon raised. We stare into the cold, waiting for our companions. Chaska finally bursts into view, searching frantically for the missing guards.

"Have they come?" she demands.

I shake my head. They have not.

Diecinueve

Chaska reluctantly motions for us to continue our journey. As we trek farther into the lush green land, my skin warms up. I welcome the heat. My teeth stop chattering, and I can feel my toes again. Even the jungle song warms my heart, the trill and chirps from birds filling the air.

But we do not slow, or linger. Chaska constantly looks over her shoulder.

"Manuel," I mutter. "I don't understand. What took them?"

He has no answer, and neither must our guide, because she, too, remains silent. We move at a brisk pace, and slowly, the sense of danger drops to a persistent thrum in my veins. It's hard to remember the frigid cold when you're sweating profusely. From somewhere above, a monkey follows our trek and occasionally drops fruit in front of my feet. Apples and oranges, a mango. I pick up each and smile up at the generous creature, with its walnut-colored fur and white ears.

I am enchanted.

The first bite of orange makes me groan. The tart flavor bursts in my mouth, and even as the mosquitos flutter in my face, they don't lessen the enjoyment. I hand Manuel and Chaska a slice, and we eat orange after orange as we walk, the juice making our fingers sticky. The terrain slopes downward and my ears pick up the sound of running water. My stomach lurches. I've had enough adventures with water to last a lifetime.

We reach the sandbank, and I immediately search for caimánes. Chaska veers toward a thorny grove of plants with long leaves and stems, and then drags a canoe from within the tangled brush. It's about as tall as Manuel, perhaps around six feet. There are three wooden benches inside. I help push the boat off the muddy bank, careful not to step a toe in the water. Chaska and I climb in from opposite sides. Manuel pushes us off then jumps inside. There are two oars tucked along the edge of the canoe, and when Chaska attempts to pass me one, Manuel holds out his hand instead.

"I'll do it," he says.

She shakes her head. "She'll never learn if she doesn't try."

I take the oar. "I've paddled before."

Chaska smiles. "Then you'll only get better." And then she dips the oar into the water, barely skimming the surface. After a few clumsy attempts, I manage to imitate her movements and we glide toward the middle of the river. A large shape leaps up from the depths and lands with a loud splash.

"Look!" I exclaim. Manuel leans outward, his hand curling over the slim railing, to see where I'm pointing as another one jumps out of the water.

"Pink river dolphins," Chaska says. "Legend says they are the guardians of the underwater city of Encante."

My jaw drops. "Does such a place exist?"

"Seeing as I cannot breathe underwater, it's hard to know for sure," she says wryly. "Those who are invited never return to the land."

"Then how do you know that's where they've been?"

"Because we have seen the pink river dolphin transform into a man." She sinks her oar into the water. "The jungle has many mysteries. Now, help me steer."

I resume paddling, and it strikes me that I'll never discover the many secrets hidden in this place—I won't be here long enough. The idea makes me unaccountably sad. I shake off the feeling and concentrate on doing my part. Luna's light slips off the boat's wooden frame, washing it in a cool glow. The water churns, and I have to fight to keep our canoe straight and true along the current.

"A caimán follows us," Manuel says calmly from behind.

I whirl around in my seat. "How big?" I don't know why I ask. If it were only one foot in length, I'd still be afraid.

He keeps his attention focused behind us. "Nine feet maybe."

"Respect him, and he will respect you," Chaska says. "Continue paddling, traveler."

"Catalina," I mutter, but do what she says. Manuel half turns his head toward me, the corners of his mouth kicking up, and my heart does an odd flip in my chest. The careful boundaries he's placed between us have melted away. As if he's realized that things may look very different in the future, and there's no sense in putting up walls where there need not be any.

We continue on our journey, the caimán following our boat like the long stretch of tail dragging behind a lizard. We make turn after turn on the flat, wide river, curving around bends and floating past smaller inlets that bleed from the main one.

Manuel misses nothing, studying every turn of the canoe with great interest, while keeping one eye trained on the caimán. I'd bet my life he could lead us back to where we first embarked.

Chaska directs me to take a left turn, and the moment we do, a large waterfall comes into view. She maneuvers us closer. The roar fills my ears, thundering loud and constant as it pours into a plunge pool. Rocky outcroppings jut forward on either side of the falls, and moss clings to the thick tree trunks. The waterfall is several feet wide, a frothy, angry wall daring adventurers to come closer. Branches peppered with thick leaves hang above the pool, forming a dense canopy. We draw closer, and the mist slides against my skin, dampening my hair. I try to override Chaska's movements, but she's quicker and stronger.

"Straight," she says. "We go through."

"Through?" It seems I can never escape the water. What if the boat fills up too quickly? We might sink, and as far as I know, there might be other monsters waiting below.

"I won't repeat myself."

Manuel drops a light hand onto my shoulder, and I immediately relax. I might be caught in a whirlwind, but he manages to calm the storm. He'll keep me safe. I hand my oar over to him as Chaska gives me a reproachful look, then I clutch either side of the canoe.

"I'm not a strong swimmer," I tell her.

She isn't surprised, nor does she seem to care. She swivels around on the bench, once again facing forward. We pass under the waterfall curtain and the beating hammers the top of my head, my shoulders, my lap. Water seeps into my shoes, fills the boat *and* my ears, slicks my hair to my scalp. When we come out on the other side, I'm spluttering and shaking.

I blink to clear my vision and gasp. We're in a cave. Ahead, several other canoes bob against the edge of a rocky pier. Two people wait with spears, dressed in shades of dark blue, with long sleeves and gold fringe at the bottom of their tunics. On their feet are leather sandals with straps that climb all the way up to their knees. Thick belts around their hips store slingshots and knives, and strapped to their backs are bundles of feathered arrows.

Neither of them are smiling.

Chaska and Manuel guide us closer to the pier, and the two Illari help attach the boat to a wooden pole with a short length of hemp rope. I climb out, fumbling and wobbly, and without the assistance of either of them. Manuel leaps out—gracefully, of course—and stands close to my side, staring down the men.

Once Chaska is out of the canoe, they turn and head into a tunnel, lit by blazing torches every twenty feet or so. I'm sopping wet and my shoes make a squishy noise with every step. Manuel is drenched too, but his movements are still dead silent. The walls of the cave are bumpy. In every crack, fingerlings of tree roots fight through. Water drips from fissures in the ceiling. The smells of wet stone and spongey greenery coat everything.

The opening of the cave widens, and excitement pulses in my blood. I'm about to present my case to the Illari. I'll have to convince them to help me reclaim my throne. What will I say? I've only thought about surviving, about getting here. I discard one thought after another, praying to Luna that the words will come.

They don't. My mind is blank—a crumpled-up piece of paper, every line a rotten idea.

Manuel glances over his shoulder and stops when I do. He raises his brow. "All right?"

"I'm going to have to speak to their leader," I whisper.

"You're just *now* thinking of this?"

"Of course not. Only, until this moment, I hadn't thought it'd be a reality."

Chaska doubles back for us. "We must press on."

Manuel turns to her and says something low and fast in Quechua. She blinks up at him, nods once, then backs away, giving us space to talk.

"What did you say?" I ask.

"I told her that you needed help with the language," he says. "You want to sound respectful to their leader."

"Oh."

"Explain what's happening." He tilts his chin downward. "You look pale."

"I'm nervous."

"Anyone would be," he says gently.

"What happens if I can't convince them to help me? I've been standing here, trying to figure out what to say, and I can't think of anything that doesn't make me look inexperienced or desperate."

"You are inexperienced and desperate."

I glare at him. "Not helpful."

"Then what do you want to hear from me, Catalina?"

"All I want is for our people to have their homes again, with a queen they recognize. An Illustrian who will look after them." I avert my gaze from his. This next part is hard to say. "I don't want anyone's deaths to have been in vain. What will happen if they turn me away?"

"You will figure out what to do next."

"How do you know?"

A faint smile softens his mouth. "You thought of *this* scheme, didn't you?"

"I would never have gotten this far without you."

His smile stretches into a grin. "That's very true."

"Can I ask you a question?"

Instantly his expression sobers. "What?"

"Do you really think I'm inexperienced and desperate?"

He nods, and my shoulders slump. I turn away, but pause when his next words come, in nearly a whisper. "But that's not *all* I think."

I wait, holding my breath. "How else would you describe me?"

Manuel ponders my question, the silence stretching between us. I keep my attention on a particularly gnarled root grazing the wall.

"Brave," he says at last. "Determined. Intelligent. Unsure. Lost and angry. Sad, too, I think. But you hide it well."

I raise my brows. He's right, of course. I knew I was angry about the exile and the betrayal, but I didn't realize the weight of my sadness until he pointed it out. I miss Ximena. Not the decoy, or the warrior. I miss my friend.

I swallow hard and slowly face him. "You see all of that, huh?"

Manuel nods.

I draw closer, and his warm brown eyes darken with an emotion I recognize because I'm feeling it too—longing. A sharp wisp of desire pierces my heart. He slowly dips his head, his attention solely on my mouth. *Finally.* Three long years of hoping and wishing for this moment. His lips are whisper soft against mine. The slightest brush of his mouth.

He pulls away, and we stare at each other in amazement. I stand on my tiptoes, wanting more, but he stiffens at the sound of approaching footsteps, his gaze flickering over my shoulder. Chaska comes back into view. I hastily drop my heels back onto the ground, my cheeks flushing.

The corners of her mouth turn downward.

Manuel draws away from me, a little line forming between his brows. The Illari tracker stares us down, holding herself rigidly, not even attempting to hide her disapproval. A flare of annoyance spreads within me. I shoot Manuel a quick, puzzled look. I can't understand the Illari seer's reaction to us.

He gives me a reassuring smile, and then addresses the Illari. "Lead the way."

Chaska nods once, and gestures for us to continue following the long, curving path of the cavern. As we brush past her, she says, "I'd like a word with you, ranger."

Manuel stops, his brows rising. "With me?"

Another swift nod.

I pause, unsure. But Manuel urges me forward gently. "I'll be right behind you, Catalina."

Reluctantly, I press on, but I glance over my shoulder right before I turn a corner. Chaska has her feet spread apart, hands on her hips. Her lips move in a furious whisper. With every word, Manuel's countenance loses all warmth. His shoulders tighten, his jaw clenches. Then he slowly folds his arms across his chest as his face turns stony and resigned.

What is the Illari telling him?

One of the guards beckons me to continue. My footsteps are heavy as I follow him, questions swirling in my mind. Perhaps I'm not wanted here after all. Maybe they'll turn us out without hearing my case. My mouth feels dry as worry seeps into my bones.

The tunnel is long, and the damp smell of mushrooms and wet rock assaults my nose. Somewhere behind me, Manuel and Chaska's approach grows louder and louder. I want to demand answers, but we've reached the end of the path. At the cave entrance, I stop, unable to move another step. The view is incredible. Hundreds of torchlights line curved paths, dotting hills and neighborhoods. Moonlight glows down into the sprawling city below, and I can see some of the buildings spilling outward in a decadent display. They are all white, and the roofs glint golden against the guttering fires. Dividing the city in two is a curving river. I can hear the water even from where we are way up on the ledge. There are people milling around, heading to their homes, sitting around various campfires that look like giant flaming stars set against the dark curve of the hill.

Paititi.

veinte

Chaska jerks her chin toward a dirt path leading down toward the city. We follow the Illari, and the path turns to cobbled stone under our feet. Manuel stays behind me, and though I can't hear him, I can feel his presence. His steps are in tune with mine. Torches guide us. We descend stairs made of solid rock, continuing on, following switchback after switchback, until we reach the bottom of the hill. The city bobs into view.

It looks nothing like I imagined. I pictured people eating off golden plates, living in solid-gold dwellings. The roads were supposed to be cobbled with gold too. How silly of me! This place is breathtaking in its organized simplicity. Functional, protected, and hidden. It has to be, if there truly is gold to be found within.

There are more people waiting for us by a cluster of white circular buildings with golden roofs and handsome doors. They're made of wood paneling and arched at the top. One of the Illari steps forward, a girl close to my age.

"I am Nina," she says in Quechua.

"Mi nombre es Catalina Quiroga," I say, choosing to speak in Castellano. "This is my friend Manuel."

"Bienvenidos a Paititi," she says. "Our king regrets being unable to welcome you himself, but he sends his regards."

Since she doesn't offer the king's name, I don't ask for it. He might be vain and expect me to know it already.

"Will you please follow me?"

Manuel and I both step forward, but Nina shakes her head. "Only Catalina."

"We stay together," Manuel says firmly.

"Even for bathing?"

Manuel blushes to the roots of his hair. When he nods, I almost fall over. Nina merely smiles and beckons for us to follow.

"I'm sorry—I won't leave you alone until I know it's safe to do so," Manuel says under his breath.

"I don't mind." I reach for his hand, but he steps away, gaze averted from mine as if he can't stand to look at me. I let my palm drop, and I fight to keep the hurt out of my voice. But I don't succeed. "What is it?"

Manuel motions for me to walk ahead, his expression remote and grave, and then he lags behind with our newest guides. I resist looking over my shoulder as he strikes up a conversation. In the space of a walk, something has shifted between us. Once again I wonder what the Illari tracker told him.

We keep to the outskirts, though the paths are also well lit. Chaska has disappeared, along with the other two guards. Only the three women remain with their guards. Our attendants are dressed in long tunics and open-toed sandals. Their dark hair is worn long and loose, reaching their waists.

Part of the river has broken away to form a round pool. Stone steps lead down into the clear water. The pool looks like the moon, and the steps form a crescent shape alongside it. Guttering torches provide enough light to showcase the deep azure of the water.

Next to the pool is a small building, also round and white. Nina disappears inside and comes out with baskets for both Manuel and me. Each is filled with fresh clothing, a bar of soap, bundles of mint leaves, and rough cotton towels.

She gestures toward a large flat rock next to the pool. "Leave your clothes there. We'll clean them for you." She wrinkles her nose as she assesses my shirt and trousers. "Or burn them."

"Burn," I say with a small smile. "Definitely burn it all."

Manuel stands a few feet away, as if he dare not draw any closer. He's frustrated; I know it from his tense shoulders and annoyed huffs of breath.

"I'll let you have your privacy with each other," Nina says.

Something in her tone makes me blush again. But then Manuel's flat voice cuts the night. "I'm only her guard," he says. "I'm sworn to protect her."

She shrugs. "But you still need privacy, yes?" And before I can say anything else, she and the other women disappear. I face Manuel, clutching my basket. We study each other—there's hope on my face; I can *feel* it. But he's as stiff and formal as ever, wearing his sense of duty like a heavy cloak.

I hate it and don't understand it.

"You can—" he begins just as I start to say something. We both stop awkwardly.

I strive for a light tone. "Do you think there are piranhas in there?"

A reluctant smile tugs at his mouth. He shakes his head. "Go in first." He turns around, hands gripping either side of his basket.

He doesn't need to tell me twice. I haven't had a bath in what feels like *forever*. The soap smells heavenly, a blend of citrus scents. Perhaps mandarina and naranja. I undress and throw the soiled garments onto the flat rock. Then I sink into the pool, the cool water coming up to the bottom of my chin. I bend my knees and let it close over my head.

When I reappear, I call out to Manuel. "The water is perfect. You don't have to wait until I'm done. I won't look." I tuck myself under the surface so only my head and neck are visible, then face away from the steps.

"Don't turn around," he orders.

"You're safe from me, Manuel."

He mutters something, but I don't catch the words. The sound of him undressing rides on the subtle breeze. I shiver and sink deeper into the water.

"I'm in," he says softly.

I face him and nearly laugh. He's as far away from me as he can go, clutching the bar of soap like a weapon. He regards me fiercely, his expression clear: *Don't come any closer.*

I hate being told what to do, and the urge to cause ripples across his still demeanor nearly overwhelms me. I want to yank open the doors to his shuttered expression, let enough light in to reveal all of his secrets.

"I can't keep up with your moods," I say.

"No one is saying you have to."

"But they affect me," I say. "One minute, I'm your friend. The next, I'm not. Sometimes you smile at me and seem to enjoy it. But then there are the smiles that come against your will. I *hate* those. Manuel, what did Chaska say to you?"

He remains stubbornly silent—trapped in a pool with me, nothing but water between us.

I look away and search for another topic of conversation. "Have you ever been swimming with a girl?"

His shoulders tighten. "This isn't suitable conversation."

"I bet all the girls were madly in love with you, no matter where you went."

"Why?" he asks, exasperated. "Why on earth would you think that?"

"Well, look at you," I say.

He glances down at himself, at the puckered scar on his shoulder, his calloused hands, and the dirt under his fingernails. Then he returns his attention to me, his face perfectly straight, but his voice has a subtle note of amusement. "What am I supposed to be looking at?"

I try not to roll my eyes, but it's seriously difficult. "You're taller than any boy I've met, you look great in a pair of pants, and your jawline . . ." I let out a little laugh at the startled look on his face. "But more than all that, you're constant and loyal. Always calm—except when you lose your temper, which isn't often, but for some reason, it's usually with me. I always feel perfectly safe when you're near, like everything will turn out all right in the end. There's so much about you to love."

"But there's no point in falling in love with me, is there?" he asks.

"It might be fun," I say, striving for a light tone, even as my heart flips.

He flicks water at me. "Think harder."

"Will you tell me what's wrong?" My voice drops to a whisper. "What's changed?"

"Maybe I've come to my senses, Condesa."

I make my way toward him, the water rippling against my moonlight-touched skin.

He eyes me warily, as if I were a predator. "Chaska told me about the king."

That stops me. "What about him?"

I'm only a foot away from him. We stare at each other for a long moment. He's breathing hard. From annoyance, nerves, I can't tell.

"His name is Sonco," he says flatly. "He's looking for a wife."

Is that all? I shrug. "So he's looking for a wife. Why does that upset you?"

"Chaska told me how much they value seers here. She implied that you might have a lucrative future in the city." He swallows hard. "You could be his wife—"

"Now, that's ridiculous."

"Is it?" he counters. "Take a moment and consider it."

Everything in me resists, but the idea takes root unwillingly. The tribe thrives within the jungle, guarding untold riches. They clearly have an army—one I need desperately. I am a condesa without a throne, and here's one available. I've been hoping for their help to march against the Llacsan queen. I just never imagined I could do it newly crowned myself.

It's enough to push me to the other side of the pool. Manuel watches my retreat, half approving, half sad. "I knew you'd see the benefits."

But even as I stand as far away from him as I can, I still want him. "I need to think."

"What is there to think about?"

I throw up my hands, splashing water. "I don't know. My feelings for you, maybe?"

"You'll move past them."

"Kindly refrain from telling me about my own sentiments," I say stiffly. "Manuel, there might still be a way for me to acquire an army without my having to marry him."

He inclines his head. "Maybe. This one is the easiest."

But he doesn't sound convinced, and even I have to agree that marrying Sonco would be a neat and tidy solution to all of my problems—all of my problems, save one. Manuel folds his arms across his chest. I hate how far he's drawn away from me. I think about everything we've gone through, how he's pushed me to my limits, encouraged and supported me.

I don't want to give him up just yet. I glide forward, my toes skipping against the soft sand. Manuel stares at me in alarm. "What are you doing?"

"You know what."

He shakes his head. "I'm *wrong* for you. You know I am, and that's why you're pushing this to happen when it can't. Not ever."

I step forward and he sucks in a deep breath. His gaze drops to where the water laps against my neck. Drops lower to the swell of my breasts.

There might not be another time. I've been dreaming of a future that may never come to pass: ruling a kingdom, reconciling with my people, honoring my parents' memory. And here's Manuel, dependable, strong Manuel, who feels the same way I do. Here's a future that still might happen.

"I know what I'm doing," I whisper.

He leans closer, his expression tortured, and runs a light finger down my cheek. "You'd be making a mistake with me. You're—" He breaks off and half turns toward the steps.

I don't hear anything. "What is it?"

"Shhh." He pushes away from me. "They're returning."

"No one is coming. You just want the conversation to end."

Manuel glares at me as Nina and the others return. When they see that we're still in the water, they quickly turn around. "It's growing late," Nina calls out. "Unless you two would prefer to remain—"

"No," Manuel says. "I'm coming out." He shoots me a pointed look and I turn around.

The words said between us drift into the night, incomplete.

I'm given an ankle-length tunic to wear. The cotton fabric is light and soft against my skin, the shade a fierce yellow. Gold geometric patterns are stitched across the upper half, the sleeves lined with matching fringe. Manuel is given a tunic of his own, but his ends at the knee. Our sandals have a wide leather strip near the toes. The shoes don't fit, but it's better than stuffing my sandy feet into my boots.

I quickly braid my wet hair and then twist it into a bun at the top of my head, tucking the end between the thick coils. When I'm done, Nina guides us back to the smattering of buildings I saw by the bottom of the hill. She points to the larger of the four.

"Condesa, you'll be staying here."

"Gracias," I say.

She turns to Manuel. "If you'd like, you can sleep with the other guards."

He glances at the building. "As her guard, I'd prefer to remain close to my sovereign. I can station myself outside her door."

I roll my eyes. "You'll have to sleep sometime."

"We have men who patrol throughout the night," she explains. "I assure you, she'll be perfectly safe."

Manuel appears torn but tucks his chin. "I'll remain on watch tonight."

"Certainly," she murmurs. "I'll have someone prepare you a bedroll."

Before I can say anything, Manuel thanks her. I shoot him an exasperated look.

"I'll be fine if you want to keep quarters with the other guards."

He scowls at me. "I'll be with you."

I throw my hands in the air, but that only makes him more unyielding. The strong lines of his face tighten between his brows and at the corners of his eyes. Exhaustion hits me squarely in the face. "I'm too tired to argue with you."

"Yo también."

Nina watches us both with an amused expression. "I'll return for you in the morning. We hope you sleep well."

"Gracias." I push open the door and step inside, but Manuel remains outside. Half a dozen flickering eucalyptus-scented candles line four window ledges. A basket filled with mango and achachairú sits on a wooden table. I peel the skin off the latter and suck on the tangy fruit, enjoying the sweet lemon flavor. There's a plate of boiled turtle eggs and dried beef, and a bowl of sliced marraquetas to snack on as well. Off to the side sits a narrow pallet made of bamboo with a large animal fur draped across it. No sheets or pillow, but it's so hot, I don't think I'll need either one.

The cot looks more comfortable than a cramped hammock.

Potted plants give the room a cozy, homey feel. A small fireplace completes the setting. I notice a large clay pot with matching cups sitting next to the food basket. I lift the lid to find cool fresh water and a ladle. I pour myself a cup and drink it down. Then I have another, but slower, savoring the feel of the cold liquid sliding down my throat.

The door opens, and Manuel steps inside. "They're asking if you'd like anything hot to eat."

"No, I'm too tired," I say. "¿Quieres agua?"

He nods, and I hand him my cup, still nearly full. He sips from it, studying me over the rim.

"Is it possible for us to be just friends?"

Manuel hesitates. "I don't know."

"I still don't want to fight." I sigh. "You're being stubborn."

"*I'm* being stubborn?" he asks, incredulous. "We've been acting inappropriately. I'm your guard, and I ought to have never shared my feelings with you. Never should have kissed you—"

My jaw drops. "That kiss—which wasn't really a kiss, by the way—"

"I know what a kiss is," he growls.

"You thought it was inappropriate?"

"I have a job to do." He slashes the space between us with his free hand. "You *know* that."

I wince. I keep forgetting that part. My safety is his responsibility. "We don't know anything right now. So, fine. Their leader is looking for a wife, but what if he already has his eye on someone? It's pointless to argue over something that hasn't happened yet."

He shoots me an aggrieved look. "And in the meantime, we risk our hearts?"

I sigh. "I'm exhausted."

"So am I."

I drag a long hand down my braid. "You don't have to stand watch. Sleep in here—"

"I'll sleep on the ground outside."

The *ground* is made of packed dirt. He'd rather sleep on dirt than next to me. "All right."

He finishes the water. "Their king is a great warrior. The people love and respect him because they loved and respected his father."

"Why are you telling me this?"

Manuel stares into the empty cup. "He sounds like a good man."

"How old is he?"

"Younger, I think." Manuel pauses. I get the sense he wants to say more, but he must change his mind, because the silence stretches. "Good night, Condesa."

I try not to flinch. He lowers his chin, a swift acknowledgment, before closing the door behind him. He leaves me standing with my heart splintering. I thought I'd gotten past his wall, but it's solidly back in place, with a moat around it. I drag in air, willing my body to stop trembling. I shake away my hurt, my confusion, and think about the Illari, who I have to convince to help my cause.

An Illari I might have to marry in order to get what I want.

CAPÍTULO

Veintiuno

The next morning, I'm up and ready before they come to get us. It's time to meet with their leader. I'm chewing on mint leaves when a loud rap sounds on the door. Manuel waits on the other side.

"Sleep well?" he inquires politely.

His expression is carefully arranged and nonchalant, nothing for me to question or poke. I can't stand it. "We're not doing that," I say firmly.

He takes a step back. "Doing *what?*"

"It's all right to show me what you're really thinking . . . how you're really feeling. I can handle your frustration."

Manuel drags his hand down his face. Peers at me through spread fingers. I can't discern his expression.

"What?" I ask.

He sighs. "You keep surprising me."

"Are you unhappy?" I lower my voice into an urgent whisper. "Tell me the truth."

Manuel lowers his hand slowly. "Yes."

"Then be miserable with me." I inhale sharply. "Because there is an *us*, whether you like it or not. I don't want to have another conversation until we know what we're dealing with. Fair?"

"Fair." He pulls open the door. "¿Estás lista?"

I glance down at my ensemble. I'm still wearing the long tunic from the night before, but my hair is at least dry, my face scrubbed of dirt, my hair rid of tangles. What I wouldn't give for a hairbrush to smooth it into a polished shine. I leave it long and loose, and it curls in every direction.

Manuel is dressed in a royal blue tunic with gold detailing and embroidery. He looks neat and clean, as if he hadn't slept on the ground. The Illari have given him leather sandals and a blade to remove his scruff. He looks young and more like the Manuel who left me behind three years ago.

Together we follow Nina and a couple of guards on a path that leads deeper into Paititi. The buildings become numerous, all with white-patched walls, and roofs of russet clay tiles, mixed in with a few solid-gold ones. The stone path splits into several directions, but we remain on the one heading straight to the center of the city. We cross a stone bridge, guarded by a golden statue of a jaguar on one end and a king vulture on the other. Both animals are rendered in motion, ready for attack, fierce expressions on their gleaming faces.

"What are your buildings made of?" Manuel asks.

"We mix white clay with a bit of straw and soil," Nina says. "When it dries, the material becomes strong. Our roofs are the clay found in the riverbank and the gold from our mountain."

Their mountain is smaller than ours, but equally majestic. It's dark and rocky, and while the peak isn't capped in snow, the rest is covered in handsome trees. A square temple made of black stone juts forward, as if part of the mountain itself. Gold pillars frame the entrance. I hope they'll let me peek inside one day. I slow down to walk alongside Manuel. His dark eyes flicker from one building to another, to the guards patrolling the market and back down the way we came, memorizing the route, not missing a single detail.

"Have you figured out a way to leave this place already?" I'm sort of joking, but when he nods, my laughter evaporates. "What, seriously?"

"This path will lead us back to the base of the hill." He points to a smaller path next to the market. "And that one leads to the farmlands. I imagine we can make a run for it from there."

"How can you possibly know that?"

"Because it ends at the market. How else will they transport their produce?"

"Is this how you think? All the time?"

"It's how my mother trained me to think."

At the mention of Ana, I reach over and place a soft hand on his sleeve. "I miss her too." Nina glances at us and urges us to hurry. My stomach twists at the thought of meeting Sonco—I still haven't thought of what to say. All I have is my truth, and I pray to Luna that it will be enough, or else my stay in Paititi will be very short.

Now that I'm here, I don't want to return to the jungle.

Once we're on the other side of the river, the path takes us to a large square protected by woven cloths hanging above and filled with wooden stalls. The cloths come in every color and I'm immediately drawn to the bright ambiance of the market. Everywhere people are dressed in a variety of tunic styles and leather sandals, and they mill around, selling produce and pottery, blankets and llama poop. A few call out to us as we pass, and while I long to explore, I keep up with our guide.

"We have many artisans here," Nina explains. "Tanners and weavers, butchers and dyers. But we also have farmers, each specializing in a different produce."

"How many people live in the city?" I ask.

"Enough," Nina says. She leads us off the main path toward a building, larger than the rest but just as white, the golden tiles gleaming in the sunlight. I step inside after her and squint against the sudden dimness.

There are dozens of people crowded in the room, clamoring to be heard. They're shouting, asking questions in Quechua, but it's not anger I hear threaded in their voices. It's something else, and it taints the room.

Fear.

Manuel and I press closer, trying to move forward through the crowd. Someone taps me on the arm, and I turn to find Chaska at my elbow.

"Stand over there." She gestures to the curved wall. "And *listen*." Then she disappears into the crowd.

I pull on Manuel's sleeve and guide him to the spot she indicated. There's room for both of us, provided we stand very close to each other, our hands almost brushing. He clears his throat and tucks his hands into his pockets. I survey the room, trying to peer over shoulders to see the Illari leader. A young man stands in front of the crowd, his hands in the air pressing downward as if trying to instill calm energy into the room. He's dressed in a red tunic that reaches his knees and a necklace made of hammered gold. On his fingers are bands of rings in the same style.

This must be Sonco.

Directly behind him, another man is propped up against the wall—one leg extended straight, the other bent at the knee, his bare foot slapped against the surface. His arms are folded across his broad chest. He's dressed in a plain white tunic—I say white, but there are more dirt stains than what's appropriate at a gathering such as this. He might be Sonco's personal guard. He certainly has the face for it.

It's been through war.

Three jagged scars slash downward from his left temple, the outermost line nearly running against his full bottom lip. His nose has been broken at least twice, and his hair is shorn close to the scalp—which also displays more ragged scars.

I avert my attention away from the Illari guard and pay attention to the young man dressed in red, who has somehow managed to quiet everyone. His tone is soft and almost soothing. There's a quiet power to his voice, despite how he appears to be only a few years older than I am.

"I know you're all frightened," he says. "As your leader, I promise I'll find a way forward. But we must work together. This latest news is alarming—"

"What's your plan?" someone asks.

"How do we keep our people safe?" another cries.

"Where is my husband?" a woman says. "It's been days."

"I mourn their loss," Sonco says. "And I'm hopeful they'll be found. For now, I ask that everyone remain calm. Turn to our gods for comfort. They will provide it, I assure you."

I hear the regret and sadness entrenched in every syllable. Manuel and I exchange glances. They must be referring to the parts of the jungle that are dying.

"However, we cannot be caught unaware. If the corrupted area grows, we must send more scouts."

"Another mission?" someone balks. "Didn't you lose good people bringing the strangers into our city?"

Several people turn to glare at us. I shift my feet and drop my gaze.

"This will be a different objective," Sonco says smoothly. "The group will only venture there to observe and report back their findings." He hesitates. "That's not to say it won't be dangerous."

"What about the dark magic?"

The hairs on my arm stand on end. I go up onto my tiptoes, trying to find who's asked the question. Manuel nudges me and points.

It was Chaska.

I look at Manuel and mouth, *Wow.* He nods, then his gaze flickers back to her.

"Did you hear the way some have died?" Chaska asks. "Their bodies torn apart. Arms and legs pulled from their sockets. That isn't the work of a wild animal. This is a monster the likes of which we've never seen. This threat is too close to the city entrance."

Sonco's jaw locks.

"If you send out another group, I'll be going as well," she demands.

But the Illari leader is already shaking his head. "It's much too dangerous. We cannot lose someone with your immeasurable talent. You're our only seer."

She stills. And then, incredibly, her head tilts and half turns toward where I'm standing. Manuel positions himself closer to me, frowning.

"She can't mean . . ." I breathe.

He scowls. "She absolutely does."

Sonco continues his reassurances. "This time we will send our finest trackers to learn more about the area affected. The more information we have, the better we can plan."

I nod along with him. It's a sensible strategy.

"Who will go?" he asks quietly. "I need five. Perhaps six people."

Chaska immediately raises her hand. Sonco shoots her a disbelieving look. "I said no."

She drops her arm.

No one else indicates they're willing to risk their lives for the mission. Dark magic? A monster capable of ripping limbs? I don't blame anyone for remaining quiet.

Then comes a gravelly voice from the front of the room. "I'll go."

For a moment no one says a word. Sonco's shoulders tense, then he halfway turns to the man behind him, leaning against the wall, his eyes closed. I honestly thought he'd been asleep.

"You've only just returned."

The man shrugs. His eyes are *still* shut. "You need men. I've gone before and at least know what to expect."

"Brother," Sonco says. "No."

The man's eyes fly open. This is the only part of his face that has any real beauty: His eyes are large and luminous, the color of golden amber, framed by thick black eyelashes that could be raven's wings.

Sonco must see something there because he angrily turns back around. "Will no one go with him?"

Manuel twitches next to me and I shoot him a sidelong glance. His sense of honor and fairness are on full display. His hand is up to his waist.

"Don't even think about it," I whisper.

He scowls. "They need volunteers."

"That doesn't mean it has to be *you*." I nudge him with my shoulder. "Who's going to keep me safe among these *strangers* if you're not here?"

Manuel immediately drops his arm.

A few more people's hands shoot upward, including the man standing next to me. He's older, and the frowning woman at his side is none too pleased. But his face tells me everything—he stares proudly at Sonco's brother, admiring and a little in awe.

Sonco acknowledges the three volunteers then once again turns to the man behind him. "Is that enough, Kusi?"

"It will have to be." He pushes away from the wall. "To the people coming with me, we'll leave tomorrow at dawn."

He resumes his position on the wall. Sonco gazes at him fondly, but there's something else in his expression too. It's the same way I looked at Ana every time she left for a mission into La Ciudad, searching for food or information—a perfect blend of pride and fear.

"Thank you for your time," Sonco says. "I ask that you return to your homes and for only the council to remain. We have guests I need to meet."

Kusi's gaze unerringly finds mine through the crowd. His attention catches me by surprise, and the only thing I can think to do is smile at him. I hope I look confident.

His face remains remote.

Everyone else shuffles out, glancing at us curiously. Many others frown, and I remember they've never had strangers among them. We're the first—perhaps in centuries—who've made it to Paititi. The remaining ten people sit on the floor in a circle. They leave two empty spaces for Manuel and me.

Together we sink to the floor and face the Illari.

Kusi drops next to his brother in a single fluid motion, his legs tucked close and coiled tight, as if ready to strike. On his right hand is a single thick gold band, engraved with a shape at the center, but I can't make out what it is from where I'm sitting.

He feels my stare and his gaze lifts to mine. Everyone in the room quiets, and I struggle not to drop my eyes. I don't want him to think me weak or incapable.

Even though I feel like I'm both—a sheltered girl trying to do a woman's job. How will I make my petition? What if the words don't come? Or worse, what if they come out wrong? Everything can change in the space of a breath. In the pause between two words.

I pray to Luna I'll get it right.

Chaska sits on the other side of Sonco.

"Primo," Chaska says, and I startle, recognizing the word for cousin.

They are all related. The similarities are there—same eyes and dark hair, same pronounced cheekbones and rich bronze skin.

"This is Catalina," Chaska says. "A traveler from La Ciudad Blanca. Her companion is her guard. He is called Manuel. She understands our language and speaks it passingly well. How do you wish to continue?"

"Castellano," Sonco says, and his voice is deep, the hottest cup of coffee and just as rich.

"Catalina is a seer," Chaska says.

At this, the Illari leader straightens. His dark eyes are speculative and assessing. I will my body not to fidget, to look regal and comfortable in my own skin. To not look like I've lost everything.

"But her talent needs to be developed," Chaska continues. "It's not where it should be, given her age. However, the vulture deemed her worthy of Paititi." She tilts her head. "The vulture deemed them *both* worthy."

Sonco raises an inky brow. "So, you are a seer."

"Yes," I say.

"But inept."

"I've been instructed on how to enhance my gift." I force myself not to glance toward my hands. It's true that I was educated, but I barely remember it.

Sonco listens quietly, shoulders straight and proud. He does not make any unnecessary movements or waver in his attention. There's nothing coy about this king, and intuition tells me to play the game honestly, or he might sweep me off the board entirely. "We do not welcome strangers here, outsider. Have you come to learn the ways of Luna?"

I blink, sure I've misunderstood. Did he just offer to train me? "I'm not sure what you mean."

"Your gift is a valuable one and it should not be wasted.

217

Among our people, the ability to predict the future is a rare one, and it is usually passed down through families."

"My great-aunt was a seer."

"Then you ought to complete your schooling *here*. There's much we can teach you."

It takes everything in me to not cry out in frustration. They expect me to learn about the stars from them? We are Luna's true children. "I have not come for lessons," I say stiffly.

"Then why have you come?" Kusi asks flatly.

"I know you don't invite strangers into your beautiful city," I say. "I'm thankful to be here. Truly. I don't come with weapons, but a plea."

"That much is obvious," Kusi says. On closer inspection, I realize that he's a lot younger than I first thought. It's his battle scars that give him the air of seasoned maturity. But the rest of his face is smooth and unlined, radiating health, except for where steel met skin.

"Brother," Sonco chides. "Let her speak."

But Kusi ignores the admonishment. He half turns toward Manuel, one warrior assessing another. "Then again, perhaps you are not as defenseless as you seem."

"She is my sovereign," Manuel says. "And I will protect her with my life."

"You were about to tell us why you've come," Sonco says.

"I've come because I need your help—and because it might benefit you as well."

He drops his chin, and I'm surprised to find the slightest smirk teasing the corner of his mouth. "You've come to the jungle *willingly*?"

My fingers tangle together in my lap. Everyone's gaze drags across my skin. A thousand accusing pricks. What if he knows of my fate—of what happened back home? That's impossible this far removed from Illustrian society. Again, my instincts are loud, clanging as sharply as bells. *Don't evade what he's implying. Meet his words with the truth.* I swallow and shake my head. "No, not willingly. I was banished to die here. On my own"—I shift my attention to Manuel—"but I found a friend, someone loyal to my family. I'm the rightful heir to the Inkasisa throne."

"So you are a princesa of the realm?" he asks. "An important, beloved member of your people?"

"I am no princess," I say. "I am a condesa, and the only surviving member of my family. They died a little over ten years ago, during the Llacsan revolt that ended with the queen's death."

"When one of the Llacsans summoned ghosts."

"How do you know this?" Manuel demands.

"We have our ways."

He means spies. My gaze immediately shoots to Kusi. He regards us with a slightly bored expression while Manuel studies him in return.

"Continue with your tale," Chaska says.

I take a deep breath. "The Llacsans not only called forth ghosts, their leader created a powerful earthquake."

"Yes, I remember." Sonco frowns. "We felt the tremors here."

"That man's sister now reigns over Inkasisa, a descendant of the people who drove your people from their homes. I'm asking you to lead an army against the city so we can reclaim what belongs to us."

"And split the kingdom in half?" he asks casually. "Or rule it together?"

My mouth is dry. "I'm sure we can think of an arrangement that works for both of us. It doesn't have to be marriage."

Sonco's eyes warm. "I never said a word about marriage, but now that you've given me the idea . . ." He trails off, considering. "The idea of having another seer in the family is certainly appealing. The gift is hereditary."

He means *heirs*. A child of his and mine.

The silence presses into me, as if I were standing between two stones. I'm painfully aware of Manuel, who hasn't taken a breath for half a minute.

I'm in the same state. Not daring to breathe while Sonco considers my request. The king tilts his head, silently communicating with Kusi, before he straightens. "I don't think helping you is in our best interest. At least, not in the terms you have outlined. We are a peaceful city, prosperous, and hidden from any dangers from external forces. Marching out will only allude to our location. I do not want to rule over a larger country. I do not need more land or wealth. My people are happy and that is enough for me."

I recoil in shock. He's denied me—but he can't. If I don't have their help, there's no chance of my ever going home. "Please, I ask you to reconsider."

"My brother said no," Kusi says coolly.

"He's not thinking this through." I turn to Sonco. "You don't understand. The Llacsans have murdered my family, my people. Driven us from our homes, our city. Everything we hold dear, our way of life, our culture is gone. They will become stronger."

"The jungle will protect us," Sonco says.

"I won't accept that." There's the slightest hint of desperation in my voice. I can't stand it. "The jungle will protect you? It's turning against you. Dying before your eyes. How long do you think Paititi will remain hidden? La Ciudad will only become more crowded, its borders expanding. It's only a matter of time before the Llacsans come looking for the gold."

"You have my answer. I will not invite war. Should it come, we'll be ready."

My heart crumbles, shattering into a million irredeemable pieces. What can I do now? There must be a way to convince him. There has to be—I need his army. In the deepest corner of my heart, I picture myself arriving in La Ciudad, a legion of soldiers flanking either side of my stallion. My people rushing out into the streets, calling for their true queen.

I've come all this way. I can't fail. My heart slams against my ribs as an idea takes root. The words are thick in my throat. Somehow I manage to speak them in a clear voice. "I'm open to the idea of marriage if you'll grant me access to your army."

Sonco's smile is kind. "But your skills as a seer may never fully develop. And I'm not interested in leaving this jungle, not even for a throne you claim you have a right to."

My lips flatten. I've failed. *Again.* "I'm very motivated to learn."

He senses my profound disappointment. "You're welcome to stay here for as long as you like. Stay until the day you die; it's fine with me. You may learn from Chaska, and perhaps one day you'll find yourself working as another seer we trust. Perhaps even among our own family."

Stay here forever? I look around at the solemn faces studying me. I never considered this might be an option. My hope was always to go back home, rescue my people, and fulfill my promise to them. I'm not the only one wanting vengeance. Manuel catches my eye—and his expression robs me of breath.

It's one of utter resignation, as if he thinks the marriage is a foregone conclusion. His belief that I'll become a capable seer is so palpable, I could cradle it my palms.

"You're making a mistake," I say. "Please reconsider."

"My offer of hospitality will have to be enough."

"For now. But I won't stop asking."

Kusi frowns. "You need to respect my brother."

"I mean no disrespect. I only ask that you consider this warning—from someone who has lived through war."

"Your warning will be considered." Sonco inclines his head. "But enough of this heaviness. We've never entertained nobility. We'll hold a feast in your honor." He raises a brow at his cousin, and she nods before he continues. "There's a full moon in three days. We'll have it then."

"Gracias," I say, surprised.

"Chaska will be your guide. Should you need or want anything, please let her know."

He gestures to one of his attendants dressed in a handsome tunic with a fringed hem, and they immediately stand and leave the room. Low chatter begins, and Sonco engages the woman on his right in conversation. I can't manage to look anywhere other than down at my hands, clasped so tightly, they're nearly white.

"I know this is hard for you," Manuel murmurs.

I nod. It's just like him to not mention how hard it must have been hearing my marriage proposal to Sonco. Manuel will put me first, in all things. That thought should comfort me, but it only makes me sad. I'm finally understanding how marriage to the Illari leader will help me carry out my plan to save Illustrians. So far, it's the best option.

"What do you need from me?" he asks.

Tell me I'm not a failure. That I'll find some other way to convince the Illari leader.

But I say none of those things. I'm afraid if I open my mouth, I'll only cry in front of all these people. So I shrug. Manuel doesn't say another word, only allows his knee to brush against my leg. I stare at that point of contact. Here sits one of my own, witnessing my failure, desperation, and inexperience. What kind of queen will I make if I can't secure allies? If I can't provide for my people or help them in a meaningful way? This was my chance to prove that my voice is strong enough to be heard.

But I wasn't loud enough.

The door opens and people carrying trays of food deliver everything into the middle of the circle. My mouth waters. Clay bowls are filled with pan-fried yuca, boiled potatoes, blended greens, roasted pig with crispy skin, and plátanos maduros drizzled with honey.

All of it looks delicious. None of it seems appetizing.

I can't think of eating with them, not when I must wear my disappointment on my face. When someone tries to hand me a glass of jugo made of sweetened lime, I refuse to take it. Manuel grasps the drink and gives it to me, saying my thanks for me.

"You need to have something," he murmurs. "I know you're upset, but you haven't eaten anything substantial in weeks."

I manage a nod. We're given a plate with generous portions

and enough juice to wash everything down. Once we're done eating, Sonco stands, and everyone else follows suit. He inclines his head toward me again, then leaves with his attendants at his heels. Only Manuel and Chaska remain.

"Regarding tomorrow, you have two options," she says to him. "You can train with our warriors, or join us for a tour of Paititi."

Manuel doesn't hesitate. "I'll train."

Though I'm surprised, I don't let my face show it. What happened to wanting to remain close? Does this mean he no longer considers the Illari a danger to me? He leaves without a glance in my direction, as if compensating for his attempts to comfort me.

Chaska places her hands on her hips. "Now that we're alone, I can see if I can fix it."

"Fix what?"

"Your magic. There's something wrong with it."

CAPÍTULO

veintitrés

All I can think about is my recent failure, but I have no time to think about how to convince Sonco, because Chaska leads me to another building, also white and round, and brings me inside. She shuts the wooden door behind her, and for a second I wonder if I ought to be nervous. My eyes adjust to the dim room.

A clear line of demarcation divides the chamber in half. On one side, the walls are painted the deepest hue of blue. Hammered gold plates cut into stars of varying sizes decorate nearly every square inch, save for the space designated for Luna, whose face wears a cryptic smile. On the other side, the room is painted a softer blue. In the center hangs a golden sun with rays that stretch from the ceiling to the floor. It's also made of gold.

From one end of the floor to the other are beautifully rendered flowers, ranging in shades of orange to lavender, with vibrant green stems and leaves. This entire place is a work of art. I slowly turn to face Chaska, really seeing her for the first time. Her full lips are stretched into a soft knowing smirk, black hair loose and swirling around her toned shoulders. Her tunic is the color of a red apple, with golden geometric shapes stitched across her chest.

"Did you paint this?" I ask.

She nods.

"It's beautiful," I say.

"Gracias . . . Catalina."

I smile as I step toward Luna's side, marveling at the beautiful constellations. The shapes make words in my mind, jumbled and confusing. I shake my head to clear my confusion, and I bite my lip. Even in a mural, Luna hides her voice from me.

"Can you read what it says?" Chaska asks.

I flush to the roots of my hair.

Her next words come out as a hush, the level of rustling leaves against stone. "You can't, can you?"

I stiffen. "Is this another trial? Another test?"

She stands next to me, her gaze on Luna. "Don't you want to know her? She *wants* to know you. She's been waiting for you."

"What do you mean? I've been reaching for her my *whole* life."

"Because you don't listen. You talk and talk, asking your questions, demanding answers. That's not how to use Luna's gifts. Her magic has no beginning or middle or end. You only want one part of the tale, when you need to listen for the whole story."

I whirl around, my hands on my hips. I'm unable to keep the frustration out of my voice. "You don't know anything about me! Who are you to say there's something wrong with my magic?"

"But there is," she says, confused. "It's as clear to me as it is to you. Why not try to figure out what's wrong? If you can prove to Sonco that your ability is proficient, then he might consider marriage."

Confusion flares within me. She's the one who first told Manuel about Sonco wanting a wife, and I don't understand why she'd want her cousin to marry an outsider. "Why do you want me to marry your cousin?"

She tilts her head to the side, considering. "I have never left this jungle because I am the only seer in Paititi. Long trips are impossible, and yet I long for them."

I look away. I can understand her yearning. Growing up the way I did, behind fortress walls, the outside world tantalized me, too.

"It will be better for Sonco to have another seer," she says, a hint of defensiveness in her tone. "The more information he has, the better he can guard our city against the rest of the country."

Her points make sense to me. Pressure builds in my chest. Everything hinges on my ability to develop my gift from Luna.

I fold my arms across my chest. Tears threaten to fall, but I don't want to cry in front of her. Ever since I can remember, the stars have kept their meaning from me. Occasionally a word or two becomes clear, but it feels like Luna's yelling at me, trying to get my attention, frustrated, somehow, that I keep missing something monumental in our communication. I barely remember the training I had as a little girl. My Great-Aunt Pastora only talked of the special relationship between the goddess and her children. It sounded like heaven to me—it still does. To a little girl who'd lost her own mother, the idea of a celestial parent looking out for me was the balm I needed.

Here's what I do remember: Always say a prayer before gazing upward; never come to Luna with a full head; quiet your breathing; be still; patience and dedication will do the rest.

My early education may have had gaps, but that doesn't mean what I learned at my great-aunt's knee was incorrect.

"Why do you think there's something wrong? I might be having a rough week." A rough *season*, more like.

"Because she told me," Chaska says.

I freeze, unable to breathe. My mind still can't fathom Luna blessing the Illari. Back in La Ciudad, the Llacsans worship only Inti and Pachamama. They have no love for my goddess, and I have no love for theirs. Both of them. Because the Illari were the original inhabitants of Inkasisa, I assumed the Llacsans had followed in their footsteps.

My lips are wooden, but somehow the words escape. "That can't be true."

"That's very rude," Chaska says sternly. "We have taken you in, clothed and fed you. My cousin has offered you a home when you have none. And you call me a liar?"

I flush and meet her gaze. "This is very hard for me to accept."

She tilts her head again. "What's hard about it?"

"Because—because I thought Luna only belonged to us! She's our goddess, our life. We have been blessed by her, and I didn't know—didn't think—she could love . . ." I trail off.

"Who? Other humans?" Her voice rises and it feels like a battering ram against my chest. "How *arrogant* of you. Why on earth would you think that you and your people have all of the goddess's attention and love?"

I splay my hands. "It's what I was taught. I don't know why only we heard from Luna, but that's been the way of it for decades. And the Llacsans didn't love the moon, worshiping only the sun and the earth. That was my normal."

"Who trained you?" she demands.

My voice wobbles. "An Illustrian seer. My Great-Aunt Pastora. She only taught me to communicate with Luna. But then the revolt happened, and she died in the earthquake. They all did. There was no one left, and so I had to somehow figure it out on my own. This blessing from Luna."

A blessing that feels like a curse. I can't say those words out loud, not while standing in front of her likeness. It feels disloyal, somehow.

Chaska's demeanor softens. "You carry a great weight, do you not?"

I nod, this time allowing the tears to fall. "I've let everyone down. I still am, I think."

"Then shouldn't you have an open mind? You owe it to your people to fulfill the gift Luna has given you. With respect to your great-aunt, she did you a disservice. Have all Illustrian seers been this irresponsible? A rare ability like yours ought not to be wasted. Especially out of ignorance."

I step forward and let my index finger graze the starry wall. For years all I've wanted was to be known by Luna—to understand her so I could share her celestial knowledge with my people. When I turn to face Chaska, my shoulders are straight, my chin high.

"What must I do?"

She smiles and points to the sun on the opposite side of the room. "Learn to love her familia."

I gape at her. "Family?"

"Inti is her brother." Chaska taps her sandaled foot on the ground. "And the great Pachamama is her mother."

The words seem to ripple in the air, hitting my body as if they were weapons of war. I want to duck and defend myself against such lies. But the serious expression on her face, so earnest and genuine, makes me pause. Can she be telling me the truth?

"I've never heard this version before."

"It's not a version," she says. "It's the truth. Can you accept what's in front of you?"

I tug on the sleeves of my tunic. "It feels like a betrayal of everything I've been taught. Of who I am—an Illustrian who loves the moon."

"You are still an Illustrian who loves the moon," she says. "But you can also love the sun, who shines down on you and brings all things to life. You can still love the earth, who nurtures your body and gives you a home. The three of them wait for you, Catalina. If you never learn, you'll never feel comfortable in your own skin. Misery and doubt will follow your every step. You need only open the door. Let go of your old teachings, and brave what you fear."

What does she mean, brave my fears? I'm here, aren't I? I've traveled all this way. "I have to think."

"When you do," she murmurs, "try to remember your people, and what would be good for them."

This room feels too small. I want more space to breathe, to mull over this strange information that somehow feels right and wrong. The idea of dismantling some of my core beliefs frightens me. I've stood on them for so long. Because there are some things I've always known to be true: Luna is the goddess of the Illustrians, I am the daughter of the murdered royal family of Inkasisa, and the Llacsans are my enemy. These are the pillars that make up my foundation and if I take one away, what will I have left?

What else do I have wrong?

"Say I do believe you . . . what must I do to learn about Inti and Pachamama?"

Chaska crosses the room and opens the door. "They are outside right now. Will you come?"

I step outside, feel the warmth of the sun, the solid ground beneath my feet. All my life, I've been looking for someone, wanting to understand who I am, this gift that's tormented and delighted me since I first glimpsed the stars shift. Maybe my resistance to Chaska's words have more to do with fear—there's safety in the familiar, even in my long years of disappointment.

But here's my chance. I only need to face my ignorance.

She takes me high up to a hill overlooking Paititi. The view is different now from what it was at night, but equally awe inspiring. Red and gold tiles glint in the sunlight, the buildings nestled close to one another in bursts, and surrounded by lush trees and the curving stone pathway. The river cuts through the city, a pale slash of blue water. It doesn't look like it houses any monsters.

To think this city was hidden for centuries, deep in the most dangerous place in Inkasisa. If everyone knew this place was real, they'd brave the jungle to see it for themselves. No, not just see it. Many would try to steal their secrets. Hunt their gold. Take their homes. It's the way of the world, to conquer or be conquered. The Llacsans ran the Illari from their lands, and my people swept in with our army and drove the Llacsans up to the mountains. Four hundred years later, thousands of Illustrians were killed, and those who survived lived in a fortress for ten years.

No one is blameless. The history of Inkasisa makes me sad when I think of all those displaced people, the lives lost while my ancestors forced them to mine Qullqi Orqo for silver. The years when we'd forced them to acclimate to our way of life. And for the ones who refused, they were pushed out of the city. We took and took and took from them.

Why have I never thought about them before? All I've ever seen was my own hurt, my own losses. The world is so much bigger than my pain.

We sit down on the ground, under the shade of a great rubber tree, the soft grass tickling my ankles and in between my toes. The sun's rays warm patches of my body, and the heat makes my shoulders tingle.

"Empty your mind," Chaska says in a lilting voice. "And close your eyes."

I do as she says, feeling ridiculous. Whenever I talk to Luna, my gaze is open and trained on the heavens. But this is her lesson, and I promised I'd clear my mind of ancient history.

"What do you feel?"

"My sweat dripping down my neck."

She flicks my shoulder. "Try again."

I picture the moment before I look into my dented telescope—how my breath goes soft, my mind clearing of worries. The same process is harder with Inti potentially listening. Time seems to slow as I let my breathing do its steady work, easing the tension from my shoulders, loosening my spine until it's as if I'm nearly boneless.

"That's good," she murmurs. "Picture the many things you are thankful for, what would not be possible without the sun or earth."

There wouldn't be much without the pair of them. Morning light as the sun dawns. Flowers to admire, cool water to drink. The scent of honey and the taste of sweet mango, when it's gone from green to red. Slowly, I feel a soft tickle near my edges, a shy and warm greeting. If I hadn't been sitting perfectly still, waiting for the moment, I would have missed it.

My eyes snap open, and I turn my head in Chaska's direction. "I *felt* something."

But her attention is on the patch of ground in front of me. "The earth goddess listened."

Where there were once only weeds and shards of grass now blooms a single yellow flower by my tucked legs.

I blink several times, but the flower remains. "Did I do that?"

Chaska lets out an exasperated huff of breath. "*No.* You turned to her, and she answered."

"But why?" I ask. "I've ignored her my whole life."

She plucks a blade of grass and lifts it up to her nose. "I sense a profound shift in the relationship between mother and daughter, brother and sister. It feels softer, as if there's been a . . . reconciliation in their divine familia. We might be part of that story, in some small way."

"I can't see how."

"Of course not," she says. "We're *human*. How can we fully know the ways of the gods? For now we must be open and listen, and be thankful for their gifts."

It's a start, a step in the right direction, though I sense the journey will be a long one. But I had felt Inti, I was sure of it—warmth curling around me like steam over a cup of hot tea. And then Pachamama's friendly flower. They want a relationship with me.

"What do I do now?"

She seems amused by this. "Continue the conversation. Every day may not be like this, but you know they are present, listening. Tonight, when you read the words from Luna, perhaps they will make sense. But if they do not, try again and again."

"I will." Happiness bubbles to the surface. Without thinking, I throw my arms around her shoulders. "Gracias, gracias, gracias. This never would have happened if not for you."

Chaska doesn't push me away, roll her eyes, or tease me as I would suspect. Instead she hugs me back. "That is very true."

I pull away, yearning to try again, to learn about these other gods who I've ignored for all of my life. I'm on the cusp of something immense, of finally understanding how I might be able to use Luna's gift as it was intended.

More than anything, I want to be useful. If I'm a capable seer, then I have something to offer Sonco. Once married, I can take the first steps toward becoming the kind of condesa my people can respect. Leading an army against the Llacsan queen is the perfect demonstration of how far I've come.

"You have much to learn still," Chaska says. "But if you give yourself the chance, I think you will make a fine seer."

My happiness dims. "What do you mean? Of course I'll give myself the chance."

"Will you be both a seer and a ruler?"

"I can do both," I insist.

"Of course you can," she says with a shake of her head. "But it doesn't mean you should."

I lean away from her. "Where is this coming from?"

She assesses me and says, "Luna."

"She spoke to you of this?"

"Some of your story has been revealed to me, yes."

"What parts?"

"Ask her yourself," she says, and her voice is kind, even as her attention draws toward the view of the city.

"I will."

We settle into silence, and while not uncomfortable, I wouldn't say it's companionable. At least not on my end. I once again admire the city set into the mountain's soft rolling hills. "You all have flourished," I say. "It's remarkable and inspiring."

"And we have known no wars," she says sadly. "But that might change in the near future."

It would change if they helped me. I'd be introducing them to something dangerous and terrifying. Death and destruction. Children left as orphans. Families ravaged. But what choice do I have? My people need their chance to get their homes back. I say in a small voice, "I don't regret asking for your cousin's help."

She turns to me, her black brows gathering together. "We face war here in the jungle, Catalina. It's coming for us whether we want it to or not. I have been trying to discover the source of the evil."

"What do you mean?"

"Something or someone is killing our jungle," she says fiercely. "It's awful dark magic, and it must be stopped before it's too late."

"Do you know how? What does Luna say?"

And for the first time, she sounds bitter. "Not one word."

The rest of the day is spent exploring. Chaska leads me to the market, where children learn how to weave tapestries and dye cloth from plants, their sweet little faces smiling and eager to please. We pass vendors carting husks of corn and bundles of coca leaves, and women cooking meals over outdoor fire pits. The city bustles with life, particularly the market, where beads are sold as necklaces and anklets.

By evening I've been fed by so many people—Illari who've opened their doors and invited me into their homes—that any more food and someone will have to roll me home. Chaska laughs when I tell her this, and bids me good night.

I don't want to go to bed, not even the slightest bit, so instead I rush back to my sleeping quarters and grab my telescope before climbing up the hill, yearning to talk to Luna.

That moment is now.

I settle onto the soft earth, away from the rubber tree so that I might see the stars more clearly. Down below, dozens of fires flicker in the night, people laughing and enjoying one another in the moonlight. I shut my eyes and wait for my heartbeat to slow. Gradually the noise fades away, until all I can focus on is my breath grazing against the back of my throat.

Slow inhale. Soft exhale.

My mind settles and reaches for the heavens. There is an answering calm that clings to my skin, seeps into my bones. I hold on to the feeling as if it were a lifeline. When I open my eyes again, I bring the scope higher and peer through it.

The stars shift, creeping across the inky night, finding one another in the near dark. Luna shines bright, guiding her children into formation. My heart kicks against my ribs as the constellations form—and stay.

Bienvenida, hija.

I drop the scope and laugh. I laugh until tears pour down my cheeks. Happy, relieved laughter that I feel all the way to my toes. When I'm calm, I once again bring my dented telescope to eye level.

The stars have moved again. Another warm greeting. It's as if I've stumbled across a cottage in a forest, my mother waiting at the threshold with a plate of toasted marraqueta and a cup of tea. She pulls me inside her home, asking about my journey, how I've been, and if I'm happy. The connection is strong, feelings of love and respect from both sides. She is a long-lost friend, one I've missed and yearned for, despite not really knowing her.

I tell her I'm sorry for my absence, but she brushes that aside. *I know*, she says. *I've always been here, ready and waiting.* Just when I think I might burst from happiness, a warning whispers against my cheek. My elation dims as Luna guides my eyes to a corner of the sky, shadowed and so far from where I sit.

The stars rearrange, lines shift to show the face of a young boy, desperately unhappy and alone. His hair is long, his lips thin, his nose pronounced.

"I don't understand," I murmur. "Have I seen this boy before?" He doesn't look familiar.

The stars rearrange themselves. *Yes*, Luna says. *Be careful when your paths cross again.*

Fear spikes my blood. I rack my brain, trying to remember this dangerous boy. When the constellations change again, Luna's tone is softer, a mother soothing the fears of her little one. I'm so engrossed in our conversation that I don't hear someone approaching until they're sitting beside me. I lower the telescope.

"I've been looking for you," Manuel says gruffly. "It's near midnight."

"Were you worried?" I ask, unable to keep the smile off my face. I've had my first real conversation with Luna. I could roll down this hill and laugh the whole way.

"You know I was." He stretches his long legs in front of him. "Tell me about your day."

So I do. By the time I tell him about Luna, I'm sure my eyes are shining with more tears. There's so much I want to ask her.

Manuel grins. "I knew you'd be able to figure it out." It's not until I see his smile that I realize just how tired he is. There are dark circles under his eyes. Deep lines carved into the corners of his mouth.

I bump his shoulder with mine. "You look terrible."

"And smell it too."

I lean over and sniff. "A little bit. But mostly you smell like sunshine."

He shoots me an amused look. "No one can smell like sunshine."

"Obviously, yes, because you do."

Manuel shakes his head, exasperated. He's never looked more adorable. Dark hair tousled, the blue of his tunic a handsome contrast to his olive skin. Brown eyes gazing at me warmly.

Maybe it's my success with Luna, and for once not feeling like a failure. Maybe it's because we're alone, with a spectacular view of the moon and stars and this incredible city. But I'm tired of not being able to talk about our feelings.

I scoot around until I face him, my legs crisscrossed. He stiffens, immediately wary. I don't care. "I've been in love with you for a long time."

He blinks.

"You'll say it's inappropriate, a passing emotion that will fade when I meet someone suitable. Manuel, I *have* met someone suitable. But if I don't tell you the truth now, then I'm afraid I never will."

A muscle jumps in his jaw. I reach for his hand and tangle my fingers with his.

"What are you thinking?" I whisper, half yearning to know, half terrified of his thoughts.

He hesitates, looking like a jaguar cornered. Any moment I expect him to lunge, teeth first. "He *is* going to accept your proposal. Why wouldn't he? You will become every bit the seer Luna has fated you to be. You're brave and determined, and loyal. It's only a matter of time before Sonco realizes who he has in his hands."

"He might never agree."

Manuel's fingers tighten against mine. "Of course he will."

I can't speak for a moment. Grief thickens my throat. "So this is it, then. We'll never have anything more besides our time in the jungle. We'll never become more than a condesa and her loyal guard."

He meets my gaze unflinchingly. "That's right."

I drop his hand. This is for the best, I know it is. This is how a condesa would comport herself; this is the kind of leadership my people will expect from me. Over and over again, I will have to set what I want to the side.

But I will have one more thing.

"I want you to do something for me."

He stares at me guardedly. "What?"

I lift my chin. "Kiss me."

He stills.

"Kiss me and be honest," I whisper. "Do this, and promise not to hold back."

"You might regret it."

"Never." I shake my head. "*Nunca.*"

"Then *I* might."

"It's your choice. Now or never, Manuel."

He glares at me, exasperated. I grin and he slaps both of his palms against his face, groaning. "That smile."

"What about my smile?"

"I can't handle it."

"Now I can't smile?" I ask, bemused.

He makes a disgusted sound, but it's not aimed toward me. I don't think.

We are both quiet and still, mere inches away from each other. I've kissed many boys, but looking at him now, at his proud chin and strong shoulders, at the scruff on his face and thunderous brow, butterflies dance deep in my belly. My body doesn't want to move.

He raises a dark brow. "Have it your way, then. But don't say I didn't warn you."

I smile, oddly comforted by his grumpiness. His scowl falters as I lean forward and brush my lips to his cheekbone. His warm scent envelops me. Sunshine. Palm leaves. My mouth slides across his broken nose, a soft feathery touch until I reach his other cheek and press another soft kiss.

He inhales sharply. "For the record, I think this is a bad idea."

"The record understands your hesitations. And thinks they're dumb."

He snorts. I smile against his skin, my mouth gliding against his cheek, and he groans. I travel up to both eyelids. More soft kisses there. He grips my upper arms and positions us so our lips meet. The kiss isn't gentle. It's a war between two stubborn souls. I get lost in the fight, thread my fingers in his hair, taste his frustration. He nips my mouth, pulls me closer, until I'm sitting in his lap. I'm winning the battle. His hands slide up to the back of my neck and he ends the kiss. Calls a truce. His eyes are open, and instead of anger, he regards me ruefully. "I surrender, Catalina."

"Does that mean you'll kiss me again?" I tease.

"Before this night is over, I will. I'm not quite ready to say goodbye." Manuel gently lifts me off his lap, sets me close to his side. We tilt our heads back, stare up at Luna, and her moonlight dances around us.

We sit, shoulder to shoulder for a long moment. There are only the soft croaks from the jungle frogs and the buzzing of mosquitos, the snap of a hot breeze that teases my unruly hair.

"I'm leaving for a short while," he says. "Perhaps a day or two."

I look at him sharply. "¿Cuándo?"

"In the morning with the dawn. I didn't want to leave without telling you." He pushes his hair off his face. "I'm going with Kusi to investigate the part of the jungle that has become affected."

"No."

"You'll be safe here. In fact, this is the safest place you can be, Catalina."

"But what about you? This mission is dangerous."

He shrugs. "Perhaps it is. Sonco doesn't like the idea of waging war because he doesn't know who the enemy is."

"You will come back, won't you?"

"I swear it."

"In time for the festival in two days? I've never seen you dance."

"Because I can't."

We spent very few days dancing in the Illustrian keep. Sometimes we danced on Ana's birthday because we pestered her to celebrate. "I'm sure I'm not a good dancer either."

"We'll return when we're done with the mission."

A terrible sense of foreboding washes over me, dampening the stars' brightness, dulling the scent of the flowers surrounding us. My eyes grow weary, and I yawn. Exhaustion sets in. And if I'm tired, Manuel must be doubly so. He hasn't stopped moving since the day he rescued me from that jaguar. "It's not your job to find answers."

"I have my reasons. Besides, it's the least I can do."

I poke his arm. "Why do I get the feeling you're not telling me something?"

"Oh, I have to share all of my secrets with you?"

"It'd be nice."

"That's not how this works."

"The old way isn't working for me."

He snorts. "But it was working for me."

"Come on," I say coaxingly. "What were you thinking, just now when your eyes got sad?"

"I smell like sunshine, but my eyes look sad?"

"You contain multitudes."

He laughs, and it dawns on me how rarely I've heard that sound coming from him. It's rich and full, and it fills up the night. I'll never have another night like this with him again. Just the two of us, sitting this close, having just kissed.

Manuel's chuckle dies as he catches sight of the expression on my face. He reads me easily, and his glowing eyes seem to dim. Or maybe I think they do because I want him to hold on to this moment and remember it forever, like I will.

"Come here," he says softly.

I lean forward, and his lips meet mine again. This kiss is nothing like the one from before: It's soft and sad, and I can almost taste the word waiting on his tongue. The one he won't say but means with all his heart.

Goodbye.

CAPÍTULO
veinticinco

The sound of the door creaking open jerks me awake. I blink into the dim room, turning around in the bamboo bed to face the door. Manuel pokes his head in.

I sit, wiping the sleep from my eyes. "Are you leaving?"

He nods. I climb out of the bed and shuffle over to him, throwing my arms around his waist. "Be safe," I mumble.

He grunts, and I lean away far enough that I'm able to peer up into his face. "That's it. That's all I wanted to say. Was that so terrible?"

His lips twitch.

My arms fall to my sides. "I'll see you when you return."

But things between us will be different then, and both of us know it.

Manuel seems to realize this too, because he doesn't move, one foot inside the building and another on the stone path that will lead him out of Paititi. Slowly, he tucks a wayward strand of dark hair behind my ear. I shiver at his touch, and his eyes heat. Then he backs away, as if I've burned him. I let him go without a word of protest. We've said everything that needed to be said. It's over.

I stand in the doorway, watching him go. He doesn't look back. I swallow hard, fight to keep my breath steady, and spend a few minutes admiring the way the morning light—fiery and golden—streaks through the sky. The sight calms me. The beauty of the jungle settles my frustration, soothes my warring heart.

Choosing Sonco is the best decision. As a condesa, I've done right by my people.

If only my heart felt the same way.

I shut the door and sag against it. I say a quick prayer to Luna that Manuel will return in one piece. And then another thought occurs to me. Feeling incredibly awkward, I mumble a prayer to Inti and Pachamama, too. The words are foreign on my tongue, but I push through. Then I go to my little cot and promptly fall back to sleep.

I don't feel the least bit bad about it.

There's a loud knocking on the door—*again*. I raise an arm as if to brush the noise aside. When it continues, I mumble a curse, stumble toward the door, and yank it open. Sonco stands outside, dressed resplendently in a purple tunic with blue and gold thread stitched at the collar and shirtsleeves. His polite smile stretches wide as he takes in the sight of my hair—which I'm sure looks fetching, given that I haven't brushed it in *weeks*.

"Buenos días. Did you sleep well?"

I nod. "I'm so sorry, but am I late to something?"

He shakes his head. "No. I just figured you'd be up. We all rise with the sun."

Right. Because they adore the sun god here. Or maybe they don't like wasting away the morning like I apparently do. As he stands there, it strikes me that he's probably expecting me to invite him inside. I'm sure my floundering looks foolish to the Illari king. "I appreciate your stopping by, King Sonco."

His dark brows pull into a frown. "Just my name is fine."

I laugh nervously. "Do you have a title?"

"Oh. No. We have no titles here." He tugs on the collar of his tunic. "Do you have a title you prefer? I haven't somehow offended you, have I?"

"If I did have a preference, it doesn't much matter anymore. My people aren't here. I've lost our home. The only loyal subject I have left is Manuel, and he's not really—" I break off with a rueful chuckle. "He's loyal."

If Sonco thinks my explanation is odd, he doesn't show it. "Would you like to join me for the morning meal?"

"Yes, give me a moment." I shut the door, walk over to the clay tureen, and splash water on my face. Then I grab a handful of mint leaves from a small bowl and quickly braid my hair. I smooth down my tunic and make sure the fringes are untangled. This is my moment to make a good impression. It never occurred to me that he'd seek out my company without attendants.

The Illari king makes space for me on the path, and together we walk side by side as the sky deepens to a rich blue with a smattering of thunderclouds brewing. The heat is ever present, and after a few moments sweat beads at my hairline.

"Are you sure you don't want to be addressed by your title?" Sonco asks.

I let out a humorless laugh. Considering that my people are miles and miles away, living under the reign of a new queen, do I still have the right to be called by my birthright?

Arriving here might change that.

"In this moment, I have no other name besides the one given to me by my parents."

"Then Catalina is acceptable?"

I nod as we slowly cross the bridge and pass the market. It's bustling with people selling maracuyá, papaya, potatoes, and other produce. Someone plays a melody by slapping a hollowed-out log, the soft drumming adding the perfect backdrop to people gathering under the shaded areas in the main square. The city has several different levels, with big stone steps leading to each one.

"And where are your parents now?" Sonco continues.

"Long gone." I wonder, at what age did that become easier to say? When did I stop crying through the night for them? I can't even remember their faces anymore. That memory was taken from me too. I only remember Ana and her lessons and plans—the never-ending scheming. It's what kept us alive all those years, stuck in that fortress, wanting our homes back. "What about your family?"

"A jaguar killed my father," he says. "Mother died giving birth to Kusi. He and Chaska are my only family left."

And I have no one. I watch as families cart their little ones on their backs, as mothers scold children and fathers smile with paternal pride—what my life could have been like, had I not lost my parents and the baby my mother carried.

Sonco studies me with a thoughtful air. "You carry sad memories."

"Doesn't everyone, if they live long enough?"

"True."

I shoot him a quick glance. I'm struck by the stern lines of his profile: an unforgiving jaw, thin lips, proud brow. His unyielding expression softens around the children and the mothers carrying sacks of dried food, bundles of cloth. He's handsome in an austere way. Sonco senses my assessment and meets my gaze.

"There isn't anything you wouldn't do for them, is there?" I ask.

"I've done my fair share to keep my people safe." He hesitates. "Which is why I won't change my mind about sending the army from Paititi."

I stop. "This city will disappear once it's found. The mountain will be mined, your people will lose their homes. I've seen what the Llacsans can do."

"I can't think of anything else until I figure out what's happening to the jungle. That's my immediate problem, not what might happen years from now."

What rotten timing. If only this threat weren't looming against their home. If there were something I could do to help them, maybe he'd reconsider. I don't know where to start in terms of planning, but the memory of what happened to the Illari guards flares to life inside me—their sudden disappearances, their screaming.

What exactly is out there?

We reach the building where I met him before and step inside. I'm surprised to find plates and bowls of food stacked on a red-purple-and-navy mat. Fried yuca, roasted pork cut into thin juicy slabs, smashed jungle yams, and a salad of diced tomato and onion mixed with some kind of white cheese. Sonco motions for me to have a seat.

I suddenly remember that I'm supposed to convince this king that marrying me would benefit us both. But we've only just met, and I know nothing about him. The only tangible thing I can offer is my commitment to being a better seer. Is that enough for Sonco? I try not to think about how I'm a disgraced condesa without an army of her own and whose people are battered and recovering.

I also try not to think about how badly I want Sonco to refuse me again. The thought takes root in my heart, refusing to let go. If I'm denied, then I'm free to be with Manuel.

But it'd be another failure.

I can't have that.

Sonco hands me a plate, and I immediately pile on a little of everything. "You have a hearty appetite in the morning."

I shake my head. "It's all the walking and climbing. Ximena is the one who—" I break off with a sudden flush.

He pauses in bringing the food up to his mouth. "She's the one who what?"

I take a bite of the roasted pork, and that first crispy taste nearly makes me swoon. Casually, I ask, "So, have you given any more thought to my offer of marriage?"

Sonco blinks. "You're trying to change the subject."

"It's a painful memory."

He resumes eating, but in between bites, I feel him assessing me. When he's finished, he leans back on his hands. My plate remains perpetually full. I can't seem to eat enough pork or plantains. And while it pains me to think of this, Ximena would love all of the food here.

"Are you going to answer my question?" I prod. "Or you can tell me what you're looking for in a wife."

"I *personally* am not looking for one." His voice holds a note of exasperation. "But everyone is encouraging me to marry their daughter or niece or cousin or great-aunt." He stops, considering. "Though I suppose it might be time to consider my options."

"The downside of being popular. Do you like any of them?"

Again, he blinks at me and I smother a laugh. It's part of my charm, I guess, getting away with mildly inappropriate questions. It's only Manuel who doesn't let me gain any ground. I'm immediately annoyed that I've thought about him again, and in the middle of this conversation. I need to focus on finding out what Sonco wants in a partner. I help myself to more food.

"That's a personal question," he says. "Are you involved with the man you're traveling with?"

I choke on the yuca. "You've made your point."

He smiles lazily, and I return it.

"I have to commend you for your ability to keep this city well insulated from the outside world," I say. "Just how large is your army?"

Sonco narrows his gaze. "You won't give up, will you?"

"I'm told I'm stubborn."

"The army is large enough that my people are safe from outside danger."

I lean forward. "And all the gold."

"Yes, I've been told people in Inkasisa will do anything for it—kill for it, enslave others to mine it."

I flush. It seems the history of my people is common knowledge.

The past has always felt like a distant memory, something that has nothing to do with me. I've only cared about what happened to my people, my family, our homes ten years ago. That felt real. But standing in this city—with their own valuable mountain—I can't help but think that if my ancestors had known about Paititi, they would have moved heaven and earth to find it.

The thought turns my stomach, twists my heart.

But I am not my ancestors. I'd rule differently. More fairly. Wouldn't I?

"That was a long time ago," I say. "My people are different now. You might trust us."

"Among the Illari, trust must be earned."

"How might I earn your trust? I don't have much time. My people need their leader. They want hope for the future, one that doesn't have a Llacsan queen lording over them."

"We have our own battle to fight here."

Once again, the idea of discovering the culprit looms larger in my mind. "Manuel mentioned that a new area of the jungle has been corrupted. Do you have any idea what's causing it?"

He shakes his head. "I was hoping you'd be able to tell me. At first I thought you might be responsible."

My back stiffens, and my hand flies to my chest. "Why would you think that?"

"You're a stranger with a bloody history."

"You shouldn't make assumptions about me."

"It was a logical observation, not an assumption. And besides, you're one to talk about making assumptions."

I sputter. "What's that supposed to mean?"

"I'm told the new Llacsan queen is honorable."

"How would you know such a thing?"

Sonco raises a brow. "The jungle is our home—we know every inch, the way in and out. What makes you think we don't have news of the outside world?"

My body stills, as if frozen by an enchantment. "Well, you've been misinformed. The new queen isn't honorable. Her brother killed my people. My parents. Destroyed half of my city in an earthquake with his Pacha magic."

"Exactly. *Her brother*. Not her. You've assumed she's a copy of her sibling."

I hate what he's suggesting. "Why do you think she deserves your respect?"

"She's welcomed everyone back into the city, opened up the castillo, and housed those without homes. Fed them and clothed them. The new queen is accessible and, by all accounts, kind."

The words scrape at my edges. "Have you forgotten what they did to the Illari? Why you're here in the first place?"

He seems amused by this. "Do you mean a thousand years ago? Give or take a few years? Incredibly, I've let that slight go."

"My people were virtually trapped in a fortress, supplies scarce, for ten years. It was the only way to stay safe against the Llacsans, who were always on the verge of declaring war."

"But her brother *died*." His next words are said gently. "Perhaps it's time to move on."

"I promised my people I'd give them back their homes and their way of life before the revolt." I wait for my usual anger to sweep through my body. But it doesn't come. Instead my words are laced with a tired, sad note. "What about what I've lost? My parents were murdered. Am I just supposed to let that go? Forget that I'm the only one in my family who survived the Llacsan attack? All I've ever wanted is to go back to the way things were."

Back to when my life made sense. When I'd had parents and aunts and uncles and cousins. When my home wasn't destroyed and I couldn't wait to be a big sister. My mother was a month away from giving birth.

"That's a silly thing to promise. Time only moves forward. No one can go back." He tilts his head. "Are you afraid of what will happen if you let go of your anger?"

I want to lie to him, but this entire conversation is unsettling and surprising. "I don't know if I understand your question," I hedge.

"Yes, you do. Without your anger, you'll have to grieve the loss of your family."

My throat feels thick. "I think I liked you better when we were discussing your impending marriage."

He picks up a clay cup, takes a small sip. "I'd consider marriage to you if you proved to me and my people that you'd make a fine leader. Becoming a capable seer is a step in the right direction."

For a moment I can't speak. He doesn't know how badly I want to be the answer to my people's troubles. Ximena didn't believe I could rule. Sometimes I don't think I can either. But his words spark something deep within me—the overwhelming urge to prove that I am capable, that I'm more than a sheltered girl, betrayed and banished.

The Illari king continues. "If we're to marry, you'd get your army outright."

I swallow hard. "Are you being serious? I can't tell."

Sonco puts the cup down. "I value the role of seers in our city, but unfortunately we only have Chaska. Perhaps her descendants will have the same gift, but I'm worried nevertheless. Everything I do is for my people—to keep them safe, to keep them *hidden*. Our scouts travel beyond the jungle border, but having reliable seers will help gather information from within the city. I'd do anything not to risk Paititi. Even marry a condesa without her throne."

There's a roaring in my ears. All I can think about is having an army to reclaim La Ciudad Blanca, my birthright. "And you'd really propose?"

Sonco shrugs, his voice light. "I might."

CAPÍTULO

veintiséis

The people of Paititi know how to live. The hours seem slow, and daily chores are finished by midmorning, followed by a long midday meal with their families. Children attend lessons in a group with experts in their fields, learning to weave and dye wool, and then in the late afternoon they train. All children are taught how to defend themselves with knives and arrows, axes and spears. Some of the children run around practicing shooting with their blow darts, nailing cockroaches scrambling across the dirt.

It's only later that I learn the darts are coated in poison.

The day is sunny and warm, the air scented by the sweep of immense trees surrounding the base of the mountain. People are friendly, if a little wary, so I smile at every person who looks over at Sonco and me strolling on the paths, as if there weren't a greater danger surrounding us. As if Manuel weren't risking his life trying to help the Illari.

Sonco and I walk through the market at a leisurely pace, and I admire the pretty beaded jewelry and woven mantillas. Several people are weaving long banners, and Sonco tells me they will be used as decorations for the fiesta. There's a stall filled with sandals, and a pair catches my eye. I haven't had new shoes in a long time, only the borrowed sandals and my worn leather boots. Ana said they were practical. But I adore pretty things, and the shoes people wear in Paititi are delicate and strappy, not meant for combat.

"You like these?" Sonco holds up the ones I'm staring at. The leather is a warm amber hue, with pom-pom detailing near the ankle. When I nod, he says, "You ought to have them."

I grimace. "I haven't any money—haven't had any in a long time, actually."

He looks at the vendor and asks in Quechua, "What will you have in exchange for these?"

The man is older, with heavily creased skin and graying hair. "You may have them free of charge."

Sonco smiles. "That's kind but unnecessary." He starts to remove the leather belt from around his waist, but the seller stops him.

"I insist."

The Illari leader inclines his head then presents me with the shoes, the vendor grinning. An uncomfortable flutter sweeps through my body, like the scattering of leaves rustling against a stone floor. My time with Sonco has been surprisingly pleasant. If I somehow end up married to him, perhaps it wouldn't be the worst thing.

"Would you like to try them on?" Sonco asks, effectively jarring me from my thoughts.

"Oh yes, of course." I walk over to a stone bench, kick off the borrowed sandals, and try on my new ones.

"Better?" Sonco asks.

"So much," I say.

"Well, I *do* have things to take care of today." His brow furrows. "But it would've been rude to leave without seeing you settled."

I shade my eyes from the sun's fierce glare. "Leave?"

"I'm going with a few others to collect the remains of those who didn't make it back from the last mission." His voice drops to a hush. "If there are any, at least."

"But isn't it much too dangerous to leave the safety of Paititi?" I'm surprised to hear myself asking about his welfare. "What if something were to happen to you?"

"To lead is to serve my people. I won't ask them to do something I wouldn't do myself. My position doesn't change the fact that Paititi is my home too. I will defend her with my breath and body and not hide behind walls."

Which is exactly what I've done all of my life. I've asked people to do things I wouldn't or *couldn't* do myself. I even had someone pretending to be me in order to keep me safe. Shame burns the whole way down to my belly. I try not to think of Manuel, try not to imagine his body broken and bleeding somewhere in the jungle. "How many have died so far?"

He considers my question. "Your guard left with the group, did he not?"

I nod.

Sonco rearranges his face into a neutral expression, betraying nothing, but I don't believe the sudden light tone he's striving for. "Why don't you enjoy the city? Someone will come around and invite you to dinner, I'm sure." He turns to leave, but pauses. His voice drops to a shy whisper, and there's a warm glint in his serious eyes. "I enjoyed our time together."

Then he walks off and I'm left wondering about that bashful quality in his voice. I would have preferred not to have heard it at all, preferred to keep things uncomplicated. I'd wanted to know exactly how much danger we were in.

But the answer to how many people have died at the hands of the Illari's nemesis remains a mystery.

I spend most of the day in the market, talking to the various vendors. Several invite me over to chat. I'm given tiny figurines—wooden blocks carved into llamas and miniature buildings, even some shaped like corn. I'm told carrying them around will bring me good fortune—a baby, for the hope I'll have a family one day; a building, so that I'll always have a home to return to; and an ear of corn, so I'll never go hungry. I'm not sure what the llama is for, but it's darling, so I keep it. Who wouldn't want a pet llama anyway?

My walk takes me around different residences, and close to gardens filled with avocados and bananas, oranges and lemons. Many Illari women sit around their front stoops, holding clay bowls filled with boiled plantains and slices of meat from a peccary. Another group munches on river turtles, their shells cracked and stuffed with peppers and roasted potatoes, while another crowd enjoys crispy paiche, a freshwater fish that has been marinated and cooked over an open fire. I try a little of everything, even after I'm too full to eat anything else, though several people insist.

I wander idly, stopping every now and again to chat with people passing by, and the sun continues its steady march across the sky. And while the sights are interesting, I can't stop thinking about what it will take to become a capable seer. Ximena once told me that all things get easier with practice, and now that I've learned the missing element when it comes to reading the constellations, all I want to do is read the stars.

But the sun persists in its relentless glare, so I vow to spend some much-needed time with Luna tonight. I continue exploring, getting lost amid the squat buildings peppering the path. Paititi is a city I could get lost in. Everything is simple and functional, and the food! I'm stuffed from the various offerings throughout the day. I alternate between rosewater tea and a sweet blended banana drink. I'm given plenty of cups of warm nutty coffee and it makes me think about Ximena. She'd *love* it here. She, too, entered a whole new world—living with the Llacsans, learning their ways, and by the end she chose them over me. I'm starting to think that maybe her choice was warranted.

By early evening I've learned half a dozen names and even tried helping a woman find her teenage son, who apparently disappears every and now again into the mountains. She laughingly waves me off, assuring me that he'll turn up when he's good and ready to return to reality. As I leave the market, I can't help but feel like I could make friends here. In the end, I have twelve invitations for the evening meal.

But all I want is for Manuel to return—to talk with him

about what he saw in the jungle, to untangle the mystery of why people are disappearing and dying. I turn the dinner invitations down and head back to my little home at the end of the path. An image of me living in this building with Manuel takes hold, makes my heart beat faster. It's strange how someone can weave themselves so thoroughly into the tapestry of your life, and it's only with their absence that you realize you're missing a crucial thread. My steps slow down during my walk home. Because I'm suddenly thinking of the other thread missing in my life.

Ximena.

It still hurts.

But not as much as it did when I first left La Ciudad in disgrace. Part of me has softened, and I can't explain why. It started when I was in the jungle. Like Ximena, I arrived in a whole new world, with a mission. Though hers must've been doubly hard because she lived among enemies. The Illari have treated me like an honored guest, despite being a total stranger—with failures known throughout Inkasisa. What had Ximena's life been like living with people who despised her?

I'm about to walk through the door of my little casa when the sudden blast of a horn comes from the top of the hill. I run for the path. Others join me, and soon there are many of us racing toward the bellowing horn.

They've come back.

Manuel, Manuel, *Manuel. Por favor*, I pray to Luna, *let him be all right.*

My heart pounds against my ribs as I race up the steps, making hairpin turns at every switchback. Voices drift down the hill, and I urge myself to move faster, my legs pumping. The other Illari villagers are at my heels, but I barely notice because Kusi comes into sight at the last turn. He's carrying one of the volunteers on a platform made of palm fronds and bamboo. Sweat drenches his face and dried blood stains his pale tunic. I fight my panic even as my arms and legs shake. Dread engulfs me. Slowly, I let my gaze drop to the figure on the pallet.

It's not Manuel.

It's another man, missing both of his legs—the man who was standing next to me that first night, with the young wife who didn't want him to go. My breath stutters deep in my chest. The pain he must be in. . . . He lies there, his mouth open and his eyes squeezed shut, in agony even in his sleep.

I'm ashamed of the relief I feel that it's not Manuel, but when I don't see him in the group, my heart seems to stop altogether. Kusi and another man brush past me and continue their descent. Soon a crowd of Illari encircles them, chattering all at once. I glance back as Sonco appears and embraces his brother, then helps him carry the injured man down the hill.

There are three of them—but where are the other two?

I'm breathing much too fast. My hands tremble, fingers numb.

Behind me comes the sound of a soft, helpless groan. I whip around in time to see Manuel and another figure turn the corner. Both are wobbling, as if the ground quakes beneath their feet. Manuel has his arm wrapped tightly around the young man's waist, propping him up. I race to the other side of the injured man and lift his arm so it rests across my shoulders.

Manuel shoots me a quick look, then glances away, concentrating on the barely lit path. The three of us move slowly down the hill. One dragging, stumbling foot after another.

"What's your name?" I ask the young man, hoping to distract him.

"Guari," he says through clenched teeth. "You are the princesa."

"Condesa," I correct automatically. "Did you eat any good food while you were away?"

He blinks at me, confused, as Manuel snorts. "You want to know what I *ate*?"

I wink at him. "Only if you want to tell me."

Guari stares at me, dazed. "Lots of bananas."

"You must have had to relieve yourself a lot."

"*Condesa,*" Manuel says, exasperated. "Behave yourself."

I lean forward and grin at him. A very soft, reluctant smile tugs at his mouth. We reach the bottom of the hill, and soon several people come and take Guari, guiding him straight to their healer.

I whirl to face Manuel. "And you? Do you need a healer?"

The torchlight along the path casts flickering shadows across his face, which is more tired and haggard than when he left. The bruises under his eyes are darker, and the lines across his forehead are even more pronounced. Smudges of dirt stain his cheeks and the bridge of his nose. "Estoy bien."

"Are you hungry?"

He nods. "I'd eat whatever you put in front of me. Twice."

We walk toward my home. He doesn't have a limp nor is he clutching his side. He really seems fine—exhausted, but hale and whole. "Was it awful?"

"Yes." He pushes open the door and stumbles inside. I light all the candles and soon my room is washed in a warm glow. I make him sit, and I'm about to go out again to find something for him to eat when I spot a platter on the table. The clay plate is filled with thinly sliced steak, pan-fried potatoes, choclo, and roasted plantains generously drizzled with honey. As soon as I hand him a fork, he starts eating and doesn't stop until everything is gone.

"¿Hay agua?" he asks in a quiet voice.

I jump to my feet and pour him a cup of water. He guzzles it down and when he's done, I pour him another. Then I sit across from him on the floor. "What happened to Guari?"

Manuel flinches.

My heart clenches. I reach over and place a soft hand on his arm. "We don't have to talk about it."

He hesitates, and I wait. And wait. And wait. Then: "It might scare you."

"Share your burden with me, Manuel. I'm your friend. Probably your best friend in the whole world."

I expect him to laugh, but he doesn't. Instead he's quiet and serious, clearly thinking something but unwilling to bring it out into the open.

"What is it?" I press.

His face flushes. "I know you meant it as a joke, but I think it might be true."

For once he doesn't turn away. He lets himself smile, and warmth spreads down to my toes. "Tell me what happened out there," I say quickly. "I can handle it."

"We set out early this morning. I expected the affected area to be close to the one you and I saw, but we trekked to a part of the jungle I'd never been to. We didn't stop walking the entire time."

His voice drops to a hush. My ears strain to hear every word. "This part of the jungle was totally gone—as destroyed and bleak as the patch of land we saw with Chaska."

"How had no one seen it before?"

"It's a part of the jungle they don't often visit," he says. "They have enough food and water in this area. They don't disturb or take from what they don't need."

"Then what happened?"

"I noticed a flower planted in the ground. Do you remember the flower we came across earlier in our journey?" When I nod, he continues. "Well, it was the only thing growing in the entire area. We were all standing around it when we noticed Quinti wasn't standing next to us anymore. He'd disappeared."

"Quinti is the injured man? The one who lost his legs?"

"Yes, that's him. We immediately started looking for him, then came this noise—gut-wrenching and awful, not the kind of noise an animal makes. It was kind of like a groan, but louder and angrier. Right after, Quinti screamed. We all went running in that direction, but whatever had attacked him had vanished. I've never been so scared. Any moment I expected the beast to return, even as we carried Quinti away. I couldn't stop looking over my shoulder."

"Did he get a good look at the monster?"

"He's been barely coherent," he says. "Muttering and crying from the pain. Kusi made him take something that sent him to sleep."

"What do you think the monster was?"

He shoves his plate away. "My best guess is it has something to do with that flower. It was glowing silver like—like Ximena's moon thread."

I gasp. "Could it be someone's magic—the ability to grow that flower?"

"I hardly think Luna would bless someone with a gift that destroys life."

"You're right," I say. "It's ridiculous." But as soon as the words are out, I can't help but latch onto the idea. Perhaps it's a gift that's been corrupted? My own gift was half complete because I didn't understand it. How many of us have blessings that we don't know how to use properly?

"I need to sleep," Manuel says, yawning. He stands and walks over to the end table that has several clean tunics neatly folded on top. He drags the soiled one over his head, and not for the first time, I admire the way his shoulder muscles ripple with movement. He pulls on a fresh shirt, and I look away, blushing.

It seems unfair for him to sleep outside on the ground when he's just come back from a harrowing experience. If it were me, I'd want to seek shelter within a safe space, tucked away behind strong walls. "Manuel, take the bed."

"It wouldn't be appropriate." But there's clear longing in his voice. His gaze sweeps the room, missing none of the little details that make the place cozy and warm. The sweet-smelling breeze, tart and floral, drifts in from the open window.

"We've slept near each other for days now," I say archly. "When's the last time you *truly* slept well? Comfortable, without fear of an attack?"

He hesitates, glancing toward the door. "I have to keep watch."

"You're allowed a night off," I say quietly. "No one would fault you."

The pallet is covered in the thick fur blanket, soft and inviting.

He seems to think so too, because he sinks down on top of it. The bamboo cot creaks as he stretches out his long legs. I freeze, unsure of what to do or say. I didn't actually think he'd accept. He must be *extremely* tired. I blow out all the candles, intending to pick up my telescope and seek Luna, but his voice stops me.

"Catalina," he whispers.

I startle at the sound of my name. "¿Qué?"

He doesn't say anything for a long, long time. Just as I'm about to reach for the telescope again, his voice cuts through the dark again. "Up here with me."

Thank Luna the room is pitch black so he can't see my huge grin. I stumble toward him, reaching out with my hands until my fingers bump against the cot. My hand glides along the soft animal fur, until he clasps onto my arm and slowly pulls me on top, straddling him. He reaches up to my face, softly tracing the curve of my cheek, then brushes the hair from out of my eyes.

"Manuel," I whisper. "I thought we ended this."

"We did," he murmurs back. "But I can't escape you no matter how far away I am. Why is that?"

I don't have an answer for him.

My eyes have adjusted to the shadows, and I can make out the warm glint in his eyes. I pinch his side, and he chuckles. Then he becomes serious, because it's Manuel, and he can't help but be responsible and dutiful. "I'm completely wrong for you."

"You've said," I mutter. Sonco's words rush into my mind. I ought to tell Manuel what we talked about. That I might have a chance of acquiring the army—through the possibility of marriage, if I were to only prove myself as a seer. Manuel would help me in a heartbeat. Because he wants me to fulfill my destiny as much as I do. That's who he is: Even if it broke his heart, he'd want me to be who our people need me to be.

But I keep silent.

The moment I say any of it, Manuel will back away for good. Here in the dark, with his hands on me, his raw vulnerability, I don't have the strength to end what's happening.

"I'm tired of trying to block out what I feel," Manuel whispers.

"Me too," I confess.

"I haven't been able to stop thinking all day."

"What about?"

"This," he growls, and pulls my head down, pressing his lips against mine, hard. He curves a strong arm around my waist, holding me flush as he deepens the kiss. Every thought I have escapes, until the only thing I can think about is the way he's holding on to me for dear life—how his mouth works like a drug. I slip my hands into his hair, curl a strand tightly around my finger.

Each of his kisses detonates my senses. As he slides his hand up my back, heat flares between us, potent and obliterating, and for a moment I forget where we are entirely. We kiss and kiss and kiss. He brushes the side of my breast, and we both freeze, lips whisking against each other, breaths ragged. Slow awareness creeps in. The sound of frogs croaking outside. The gentle breeze that sweeps inside, cooling my back, teasing my hair. His hard chest underneath my ribs.

"What am I doing?" he mutters to himself.

"Don't," I say. "Stop *thinking*."

"Clearly I already have, Catalina." He presses his hot mouth against the side of my neck and I shiver. Then he positions me against his side, my head tucked under his chin, and I drape my leg over him. I tell myself it's only for a few minutes. Just until he falls asleep. We lie quietly, the animal fur tickling the back of my neck and Manuel's steady breathing slowly lulling me to sleep.

During the night, I dream of monsters.

I wake sometime in the middle of the night with a jerk, pressed tight against Manuel's side. His body is hot underneath mine, and I shift out of his arms. He mumbles softly, his hand curling into his hair. He looks so young while he sleeps. I blink into the dark, trying to rid the nightmare from my mind, and focus on untangling myself from the fur covering. I can't *believe* I fell asleep.

How much time do I have left before Luna disappears?

Slowly, I stand, careful not to make any noise, but then my gaze snags on Manuel, dread blooming deep in the corner of my heart. For a second I can't move. The memory of his mouth against mine makes my blood feverish. Tonight was a mistake. I know what my duty is, but my heart refuses to cooperate. I need to give Manuel up, to let him go so that we can both move on. What kind of condesa will I be if I can't make sacrifices?

I have to end this for good.

Moonlight sweeps into the room, and I blink at the sudden light. I turn toward the window, frantic. Please, por favor, let it not be close to morning. My steps are soft as I peer outside, tipping my head back. The stars glint and shimmer against the inky night, freckles on a beautiful goddess. They move, slow and deliberate, nearly fading from view.

There's barely enough time.

There's a soft groan behind me and I spin around. Manuel sits up, wiping his eyes. "What's wrong?"

"Nothing. Go back to sleep." I fight to keep my voice cool and composed. "I'm sorry I woke you."

When I turn to look for my telescope, he reaches out and grabs my wrist. "Where are you going?"

"There's something I must do."

He swings his feet toward the ground. "Let me get my boots."

"Manuel," I say firmly. "I won't go far. Just outside the door, I promise. You need to rest."

He half groans, half yawns. "If you're not back in ten minutes, I'm coming to get you."

"Ten minutes. All right." But by the time I lace up my sandals, he's not only fallen back to sleep, his snores fill up the quiet room. I grab my dented telescope and pull open the door. The night is warm and scented by the surrounding oak trees. I walk along the path, searching for the best place to sit so I can work. I find an area close to my temporary home where nothing blocks the stars.

Normally I would clear my mind and only think of Luna, but this time I kneel onto the soft ground and say a prayer to Pachamama, too. I honor her commitment to providing food and shelter. I praise her creation, beautiful as it is dangerous and wild. My fingers dig into the ground, touching the velvety soil, tickling the grass. Peace settles deep into my soul, into my bones. I lift my dented bronze telescope and tilt my head back.

The stars shift and align to create perfect shapes. The image of the young boy returns. He's older now, his expression meaner, his lips curling in a snarl. He's been ostracized from his tribe, hunting alone and angry. He has no care for where he steps, angrily overturning rocks, butting his walking stick against tree trunks, scaring small rodents. For all his rage, I sense the despairing sadness clutching at his edges. And then the conversation shifts, the letters rearranging to paint a different picture. Paititi comes into focus, but it's tainted. A dark smudge on an otherwise bright landscape. And then the image of the boy returns, but now he's much older.

And he's still angry.

Luna wants me to see him this clearly for a reason. I narrow my gaze and think as the constellation shifts again. It takes me a moment to understand her message.

The telescope slips from my fingers. I know why the jungle is dying.

Quickly, I pick up the scope, hoping to confirm what I've seen, because I can't afford to be wrong. Every time one of my predications hasn't come true, the burning shame I felt nearly overwhelmed me. Oh, no one ever got mad, they understood, but I sensed their disappointment anyway. Ana and her children, but more important, Ximena.

I press the scope to my eye, but the sky has turned lighter, the stars growing fainter and fainter. I slap the ground and yell out a curse. I'm too late. I didn't see—but what does it matter? I know enough to warn everyone.

I jump to my feet as the early-morning light streaks through the sky, the sun following close behind. The cobblestones on the path glint golden as I race back to my building. From a distance, Manuel opens the door then shuts it behind him.

"Manuel!" I cry.

His face snaps to mine. When he sees me running, he reaches into his boots, pulls out a dagger, and races toward me.

"The flower is in Paititi," I say, coming to such an abrupt stop, I almost topple over. He holds out a firm hand to steady me. "It's inside the city; someone brought it in. But I don't know if it was a mistake. I just know it's *here* somewhere. But morning came before I could discover *where* it is—"

Manuel tucks his knife into its sheath. "Slow down." He guides me back onto the path, tucking my arm in his, and we quickly walk toward the heart of the village. "Start from the beginning."

I take a deep breath. "Luna showed me the flower was brought into the city. I think it might've been a merchant, but I dropped the telescope before getting the whole picture. I've got to tell Sonco what I saw. The fiesta is today."

Manuel looks around, and I do the same, finally noticing that Paititi is awake and bustling. Farmers gather food, cooks prepare meals, and everyone else helps set up the temple in preparation for dancing and playing music. Manuel and I take a flight of stairs that leads to another level of buildings. This looks like the residential district, with many doors open to allow the breeze to drift inside. Beyond the rows and rows of houses are more stairs.

"Do you know where Sonco might be?" I ask between panting breaths. These steps are accursedly tall.

"I assume the temple." He doesn't sound winded at all.

We climb up and up, my breath raspy and legs trembling, until at last the temple looms ahead. It's an austere square building with gold pillars flanking the entrance. I step inside the well-lit corridor, and despite the urgency of the message, I slow down.

The walls are made of immense stones cobbled together, and on either side the walls seem to press in. Nerves deep in my belly make themselves known. When I reach the end of the hall, it opens up to an immense cavern, a room carved into the mountain itself. Enormous pillars line the room, and at the foreground is a raised platform with a throne made of stone. Two seats flanked by immense slabs of granite are carved with lines of Quechua.

Everywhere people are prepping the great room for the festival. Flowers and tapestries decorate the walls, musicians set up a stage, and tables are brought in for the food.

From the corner of my eye, I spot Chaska carrying strips of dyed blue fabric. "There," I say to Manuel, but he's already walking toward her. She startles at the sight of both of us.

"I must speak with you," I say.

"Regarding? I have much to do." She frowns at me. "We all do."

"I know and I wouldn't be here if it weren't important. Our conversation must be private." I jerk my chin in the direction of a small alcove. "Can we talk there?"

For the first time, she really looks at me, then lowers her pile of fabrics and takes in my expression. Manuel nods to confirm what I have to share is worth it. She dumps the cotton onto a nearby table and follows us into the alcove. "What is this about?"

"Luna."

She immediately stills. "You read the stars."

I nod. "Last night. She—"

"Chaska."

We all turn to find Kusi coming toward us. He's drenched in sweat, as if he'd been training hard. "What did you need? I'm not hanging ribbons." He stops when he sees my expression. "I'm interrupting."

I shoot a quick look toward Chaska. "I'm afraid—"

But Chaska finishes: "Luna sent a message."

Kusi slowly turns to face me. "You read the stars? Was her message about the corrupted land?"

"Yes." Normally I'd hesitate to share something I've seen so quickly. Sometimes I'm wrong. At this, Kusi raises his hand and waves, wanting more of an explanation, but I hesitate.

Manuel nudges my shoulder. "Just tell them what you saw, Catalina."

I take a deep breath and hold it until my lungs might burst. I exhale, and make sure to sound calm. "Do you remember seeing the flower? The one that shone silver?"

He nods.

"That's what's killing the jungle. It's being planted in the wrong place." I tug on my bottom lip. "Well, I actually don't know if it ought to be planted at all—that part was confusing. What I know for sure is that the flower is involved, and someone is planting it around the jungle, searching for something. I keep seeing the image of a small boy, but each time I see him, he grows older. He's been hurt in his life, and now he's turned . . . cold. He wants power, and he's planning something with the flower."

"Why?" Kusi asks. "Did Luna say?"

I hesitate. "No, but there's more. Someone's brought the flower into Paititi. I don't know if it was an accident or if it was intentional. I ran out of time."

Chaska pales. "The flower is inside our city?"

"We have to cancel the fiesta," I say urgently. "Every corner of Paititi must be searched before the flower harms someone. A small child might get ahold of it and—" I break off.

Kusi's jaw tightens. "Did Luna mention anything else?"

I shut my eyes and let my mind wander to last night—the stars shifting miles above my head, the lines connecting and rearranging, the words written in starlight that I'd put together into a cohesive thought. "Flower. Danger. Corruption. Greed."

"And what's that?" Kusi asks.

"Those are the main points," Chaska says breathlessly. "Seers intuit the rest, based on how we feel and how Luna moves in our hearts. Think of it like a marker on a trail. Once you see it, you know you're in the right place."

"But those *markers* can mean anything!" he explodes.

"You're lucky that she caught what she did," Manuel cuts in coolly.

"Such is the nature of being a seer," Chaska tells Kusi. "Part of the blessing is also a curse. We do more interpreting than anything else. And it's a burden, that pressure of wanting to get it exactly right."

"I think the greed refers to the person doing this," I say softly. "I think it's their motive. But I don't understand how harming the jungle gets them what they want."

Chaska faces her cousin. "What do you think?"

"Haven't you seen this?" Kusi's tone is incredulous.

"Not one word," she admits.

My heart sinks. Perhaps I read the stars wrong, or maybe Luna wasn't really speaking to me. For years I've been mistaken; the stars have hidden their true meaning. Kusi continues assessing me, and I can imagine what he's thinking. Here's this stranger coming into his home with a history of failure and a punishment so severe, it meant her death. And now this same stranger brings a dire, threatening message.

"Well?" Chaska demands.

"We go to Sonco," Kusi says flatly. Then he latches onto my wrist, and I let out a surprised cry. "And you're going to tell him everything, seer."

It happens fast—one minute, Kusi grips my arm, and then he's flat on his stomach. Manuel presses his knee into the middle of his back. "Don't touch her."

I place a soft hand on Manuel's shoulder. "Let him up. I'll go to Sonco."

Kusi jumps to his feet, snarling. Chaska steps between them and glares at her cousin. "There's a threat to our city. Now's not the time to defend your ego." She hooks her arm around his and drags him away. Manuel and I follow, and it's only when we cross the temple entrance that I see the dagger in his hand.

veintiocho

We don't have to venture far to find Sonco. He's on the level below us, visiting with a few of the elder Illari. They're sitting around an unlit fire pit, telling stories, and I get the impression that Sonco does this regularly. When he sees us approaching, he excuses himself and comes over to greet us.

"I don't know what's happening, but the looks on your faces tell me I'm not going to like it."

Kusi prods me forward. "Tell him, seer."

The warning from the heavens comes out in bits and starts, and I end up rambling. Sonco listens without interruption, unlike Kusi, who prowls and paces like an agitated jaguar. When it's made clear that I'm the one who saw the message and not Chaska, Sonco frowns.

"Why wouldn't you have both seen the same thing?" he mutters.

"Luna has her reasons," Chaska says. "But if I were to guess, I suppose it's because Catalina has a lesson to learn."

I startle at this. "What do you mean?"

Chaska shakes her head. "We all have a path. I've found

mine, but you don't know yours. Luna might want you to handle this situation, for the simple reason that she hopes you'll discover yourself."

"That's an awful risk to take with people's lives," Kusi snarls.

"Luna clearly trusts her," Manuel says in a warning tone.

Part of me wishes she wouldn't trust me *that* much. If what Chaska said is true, then what am I supposed to learn? A small inner voice presses close, telling me that it might be about my choice—follow my heart or pursue my birthright. If I don't marry Sonco for his army, then any opportunity for the throne vanishes. What's left after that? Defeat and setting aside all of my training, the long years of studying for a role I'll never fulfill. Walking away from my title, the throne, feels like I'm giving up. But a small part of me yearns for that freedom—as terrifying as it is.

"Brother, we must act," Kusi says. "Cancel the festivities and have everyone search for the flower."

Sonco looks around as people sweep past, carrying woven baskets filled with food up toward the temple. Everyone moves at a fast clip and with a sense of purpose, lugging around decorations and musical instruments. Several have stacks of clay plates, others have jugs. Preparations are well underway, and to suddenly cancel might bring the morale down.

"If we cancel, we'll only make everyone nervous," he says. "I don't want to cause undue panic. The four of you can conduct a private search while everyone else prepares for the evening."

Neither Kusi nor Chaska refutes his declaration, even though they look like they want to. When I was living in the Illustrian fortress, we went through the worst food shortage. It was easier for me to hand out food without rationing it, for fear of people panicking about the lack of supplies. I wouldn't have the nerve to cancel the fiesta hours before it's supposed to start.

While the rest of the villagers prepare for the fiesta, the four of us conduct quick sweeps of the empty residences. Chaska and I pair off and search one level, while Manuel and Kusi search another. It was a bold choice pairing them together, but Chaska insisted it'd be good for them. Though most of the dwellings have only one to two rooms, it takes us most of the afternoon to search two levels of Paititi. There's still another district full of domiciles to work through.

After another hour, Kusi calls down from a level above ours. "Anything?"

Chaska shakes her head then looks toward the sun. "We can't miss the fiesta; our presence will be noti—"

"I agree," Kusi says, and his gaze flickers to mine. "Go get dressed. Your guard and I will keep searching."

"My guard has a name," I say coolly. Said guard sends me a quick smile from over the ledge. "And I can keep looking."

"You're the guest of honor," Chaska says. "It'll appear suspicious if you're late."

Reluctantly, I leave them, trudging down the many steps until I reach the lowest level. As I sweep through the market, I spot the lady whose son I helped search for closing up her stall. She stops slamming barrel lids and folding mantillas long enough to wave at me.

"Did he turn up?" I call out.

The woman rolls her eyes. "He'll turn up at the festival. If there's singani available, he's sure to find it."

I laugh and pick up my pace as the sun disappears behind the mountain.

After a quick bath in the pool, I return to my home and find that someone has left a long tunic for me to wear to the fiesta. It's patterned in the beautiful geometric designs I've come to associate with the Illari, all shades of red and pink and violet. The fringed hem skims the top of my ankles, and I love the way it looks when I spin. On my feet, I wear the lovely sandals Sonco gave me. I leave my hair down, curly and wild with a single orange flower as an ornament.

Manuel doesn't show up, so I walk alone back up the many flights of stairs, following a small crowd as the stars glimmer miles above our heads. I must've taken longer than I thought— the village seems mostly empty and quiet. My stomach gives off an embarrassingly loud rumble, and I cast a nervous glance around me. Everyone is wearing beautiful tunics in a variety of different styles and lengths. Most have fringe lining the hems and sleeves. Some Illari have feathers woven into their braids, or thick leather bands serving as hair decorations.

When we reach the temple, I'm surprised to see it already near capacity. There must be hundreds of Illari here, milling around, talking and eating. I search for my companions, but they haven't arrived yet. They must still be looking for the flower.

Several people dance in front of the musicians, who beat their drums and play the charangos. In the dance, women hop and skip in tune to the melody, holding a strip of fabric behind their backs, one end in each hand. They raise the cotton high over their heads and let it flutter above them like a wispy cloud. While they form a tight ring, men encircle them, crouched with their arms thrown out. Every leap from one foot to the other is followed by a resounding stomp and a mock punch. The rhythm is warlike and dangerous.

I've never seen this kind of dance before.

"Tinku," Nina, the bathhouse attendant, says to me. "It's a traditional dance. See how the men seem to be fighting? It's in praise of Pachamama."

"It's fierce," I say. "Beautiful."

The men keep dancing in the tight circle, and as they stomp by, I catch sight of a familiar face.

Manuel.

Manuel, *dancing*.

He moves perfectly, in tune with the constant beating of the drum and the other men parading in the circle, his leaps and jumps high. In all the long years I've known him, I've never seen him even tap his front foot. He lied to me!

"Want to learn it?" Nina asks.

I turn to her, my eyes wide. "Yes, *por favor*."

She tugs me toward a few other women waiting for their turn to dance, and soon they're all teaching me the moves. I stumble through most of it, laughing at the mistakes I make. For once, I don't think about the Llacsan queen or the dying jungle. I let myself feel the music, throwing my head back and giving in to the steps. I lose track of time as I master parts of the dance and botch the rest. It's the most fun I've had in a very, very long time.

Aside from kissing Manuel.

I notice him across the room, leaning against the wall, sipping idly from a clay cup and watching me. Our eyes clash. I know I should leave him alone, but I can't stop myself from staring. I crook my finger at him, and he smiles slightly before pressing off the wall and threading through the crowd. He reaches my side and I take his cup from him, drinking deeply.

"Sure," he says dryly. "Help yourself."

I return his drink. "The flower?"

He shakes his head grimly. "Nothing."

Fear pools in my belly. Did I somehow read the stars wrong? Perhaps Kusi was right and I'd been too hasty to share what I'd seen.

"Stop it," he says.

I raise a brow. "What?"

He gives me a shrewd look. "Doubting yourself. You read the stars right."

Timid laughter bubbles to the surface. I never know how to handle his trust, his encouragement. It's hard for me to see myself the way he sees me.

"You look handsome," I say, hastily changing the subject. His tunic is ebony with mint green and gold stitching. His long wavy hair has a few braids in it, the ends tucked into a bar of hammered gold.

"Where did you get gold accessories?"

He laughs. "Some of the men I've been training with lent them to me."

"Remind me to thank them."

Manuel flushes and looks away, but not before I catch the small smile bending his perfect mouth. "The flower is a nice touch."

"Gracias," I say. We shouldn't say such things to each other, but the words slip out easily. I fidget, lowering my eyes, trying to think of something safe to talk about. The weather or the food or maybe we can chat about how sloths are incredibly cute. We could have an entire conversation about his hair—no, *not* his perfect hair. Damn it.

"You look lovely."

This is the first time he's ever complimented my looks. I can't bear to hear another nice word from him. "Have you eaten?"

He shakes his head. "Was waiting for you."

"That's sweet."

Manuel grimaces. "I've never been called 'sweet' a day in my life."

"Come on," I say, hooking my arm through his. "You can berate my word choices while we eat everything in sight."

There are clay platters filled with every kind of fruit available in the jungle—guava and sliced oranges, mangoes already peeled and quartered, grapefruit and papaya. The main dishes are crispy stingray fins, grilled catfish, oven-baked tail of caimán, and roasted armadillo. Manuel says the taste of it is different for everyone.

"It's fishy to me, but to you, armadillo might taste like steak. It's a running joke around here."

I take a small nibble from his plate and confirm it tastes like steak. We stand off to the side, enjoying bites of food. I enjoy spoonfuls of rice paired with runny eggs and sun-dried beef—and it's all so good, it practically melts in my mouth. He grabs the fried yuca from my dish.

"So, Manuel . . ." I say in between bites. "How would you—"

He lowers his spoon. "I'm not dancing with you."

"You're not? Why?"

"Don't you think we've done enough things together?" he demands. "We've slept in the same bed, eaten off of each other's plates, and *bathed* at the same time. We've kissed—three times— and now we're going to dance? This is already too hard."

I want to dance precisely because I might not have another opportunity. But he's right. We keep walking right up to the edge, as if daring fate. But she's spoken and the way forward is clear—and it doesn't include Manuel.

And then something shifts in his face. The control over his features loosens, giving way to a stark, vulnerable look that robs me of my breath. As if he'd been thinking the same thing, realizing that we're at the end of the road, he and I. All that's left is to go our own ways.

"Let's dance," he whispers. "Just once."

We stack our used plates at the end of the table and turn toward the dancing area. He becomes quiet as we approach, but the music is a powerful master, issuing commands and demanding us to follow its loud beat. Manuel moves with the rest of the men in the outer circle, and I follow the women in the inner circle. Every time he passes me, our gazes collide. It's enough to almost make me forget the steps. I twirl and spin as Manuel leaps and jumps.

When the music slows, we're facing each other again, half laughing and half panting.

"You lied to me," I accuse. "You said you couldn't dance."

Manuel shrugs, a sheepish smile on his face.

I laugh, wanting to capture the moment in a bottle and relive it every chance I get. I'm still chuckling when Sonco walks up to us. "Good evening, Catalina," he says. "You look beautiful. The sandals look good too."

Manuel's face rearranges into a polite veneer.

"Oh, gracias, Sonco," I quickly say. "Have you met Manuel? Officially, I mean. We grew up together."

Sonco studies my companion. Both stand straighter, their shoulders rolling back, their chins lifting. Normally I'd find this kind of posturing funny, but Manuel's completely locked up. Retreated behind an impenetrable door.

"It's nice to meet you, Manuel. Thank you for keeping the condesa safe." There's a pitch to Sonco's voice that's meant to cause disruption. The Illari leader faces me, effectively cutting Manuel out of the conversation. "I have something else for you." His words come out hesitant and a little shy.

"One gift is enough," I say firmly. "You'll spoil me."

"Two gifts will hardly rot your character."

He digs into his trousers and pulls out a gold necklace with a large crescent moon charm dangling at the end. It's made of hammered gold and roughly half the size of my palm. The jewelry is the loveliest I've ever seen. This is quite a present.

"I can't accept it." I take a step backward.

"Nonsense." Sonco carefully places the necklace over my head. He studies my appearance. "It matches your tunic perfectly."

I glance down at my clothes. "Did you leave this for me?"

Sonco nods. "I wanted you to have something new. You're the guest of honor, after all." He holds out his hand. "Will you join me for a dance?"

Even though it's the height of rudeness not to reply at once, I sneak a glance at Manuel. He's turned away, his face is too hard to read.

"Sorry, was I interrupting?" Sonco asks.

It's on the tip of my tongue to say yes, but Manuel stops me cold.

"Not at all." His tone is the perfect blend of courtesy and respect. "The condesa was just mentioning how she loves to dance."

The Illari leader immediately holds out his arm.

Manuel slowly distances himself, creating boundaries once more. Blood rushes to my face, fills my cheeks.

Manuel inclines his head to Sonco, and then to me, as if we were a matching set of nobility, bound together by our titles. Then he walks away as Sonco tugs my arm toward the crowd of people dancing, unaware that my heart splinters into a million pieces.

As soon as my dance with Sonco is over, he leads me to one of the small alcoves, his hand engulfing mine. I chance a quick look at the temple entrance, but there's no sign of Manuel. Sonco clears his throat, and I return my attention to the Illari king.

"You care for your guard," he says.

My cheeks warm, but I don't deny it.

He studies me carefully and quietly. As each second passes, dread pools in my belly. I know where this conversation is going, and I'm not prepared for it. I'd hoped finding the flower in the city would be enough to prove myself. I don't want to marry him, but I do need his army.

"I've been considering the matter and have come to a conclusion that *feels* right to me," he slowly begins. "I think you can thrive here, Catalina. I am looking for a capable seer with a true heart, who would make a fine partner." He smiles briefly. "I regret the feelings you have for another, but I hope, in time, we might have a successful and effective union. I'd have another seer in the family, and you'd have your army."

My breath hitches at the back of my throat. This is what I've wanted, what's pushed me through the hardest days in the jungle. The reason why I kept going. He's offering me a position most would die for—a chance to rule Inkasisa, and a say in the governance of the people of Paititi. It's more than I dreamed of. What's more, he's under no illusions about the match. This is a business arrangement, nothing more.

"Will you consider my proposal?" he asks quietly. "I believe it's a practical solution to your predicament, and your blessing from Luna will help keep Paititi safe."

For some unfathomable reason, Ximena pops into my mind—her determined face, the scowl she wears when wielding a dagger. She didn't think I could be queen. But as I stare at Sonco, I wonder if I twisted her words so that they sounded like disapproval instead of the advice of a friend. I close my eyes and her voice rings loudly in my ear: *I love you, you're my best friend, and I* know *you. If you forget the throne, you'll be free to be the person you're supposed to be. Can't you understand what I'm saying?*

At the time I didn't. The only thing I heard was that she didn't think I had enough iron in my blood to be queen. She thought me weak, someone who cared too much about what others thought. And perhaps some of that is true, but with miles between us, with the passing of time, her words don't sound like a weapon against me.

Suddenly the idea of another war doesn't sit well with me at all.

"Catalina?" Sonco asks in a gentle tone. "What do you think?"

I slip my hand from his.

I rush out of the cavern and race down the hall, my sandals angrily slapping against the stone. I burst out into the warm night air, Luna shining down on me, embracing me as if I were a long-lost child. I stalk toward the steps, barely noticing the call of the moon.

"Catalina."

I jump a foot and spin wildly at the sound. Manuel steps out from the shadows and walks into the light, his expression calm and controlled. I want to shake him, drop him in a river and wash off that impervious mask.

"I'm astonished you'd wait for me. I thought you'd run."

Like you did last time, and I didn't see you again for three years.

"I didn't want you searching for me at all hours of the night, potentially getting lost or hurt."

What a reasonable and logical statement. It sits at the back of my throat, nearly choking me. "Well, you have something to say, I'm sure of it."

"I do," he says, and jerks his chin away from the corridor entrance. "Take a walk with me."

"I'm not sure I want to."

He overturns a rock with the toe of his boot. I frown. Unnecessary gestures don't fit him. He's usually controlled, his movements economical. "There are things I have to say."

"I won't stop you from saying them."

We take the flight of stairs down to the bottom level and walk idly on the path, meandering through the different districts. No one is around. It's just us and the moon and whatever words the stars have carved against the black night. Manuel keeps several feet between us, and it takes everything in me not to yell or cry.

"I did a lot of thinking out here while you were dancing—"

"Of course," I mutter.

For a moment his eyes flash. Triumph blazes deep in my veins.

"—and I've come to a decision."

I brace myself, and his face softens, only just. Enough to slay me.

"Sonco is interested in you. From what I can tell, and from what others say about him"—he breaks off, swallowing hard—"he's a good man who will take care of you. You need to give a relationship with him a chance. He's the ruler of Paititi; you could do worse. I think there is a very real chance he will marry you, but not if I'm around."

By "worse" he means himself. And the thought makes my blood riot. I stop on the path, my eyes wide in shock. We're standing right in front of the entrance to the market. All the stalls are closed up, the lids of baskets tied down, the woven mats rolled up, the food stored away. "You are worthy."

"Not of you."

"*Yes*, you are."

"Catalina." He folds his arm across his chest. *"No."*

"¿Por qué?"

"It's the wisest move for you to make. I'm honor-bound to do right by you, to respect the title you carry and the position you've been groomed for. It can't be wasted on me."

"Wasted?"

"You'll be safe here," he continues, as if I haven't spoken. "I thought you were open to the idea of marrying him?"

"I've changed my mind."

"Catalina, consider all of your options. What do you want more than anything?"

I don't hesitate, even as the word surprises me. "You."

He flinches. "That's not true. You want the throne. And this is how you'll get it, by marrying into a powerful family with an army. *Think* about it. Even if your mission in La Ciudad doesn't succeed, you'll still be in a position of power here, and safe."

This is the moment to tell him that I've already turned down Sonco, that I've already chosen a future that doesn't result in war. It's time I trust the friend who's spent a decade of her life pretending to be me, risking her own life. Ximena chose to support Tamaya for a reason, not because she found me lacking, but because she knew Luna had a better path for my life.

I am a seer. Not a queen.

I bite my tongue. If Manuel doesn't trust what I want and doesn't stop making decisions for me, then we'll never work. I want him to be with me because he wants to, not because I've given up the throne. I want him to have faith in who we are together.

He takes both of my hands, his voice pleading. "I'm a ranger. You have a chance here for real security, something I'll never be able to give you. My name doesn't come with power or a title or money. My whole life has been shaped and forged to protect you, and this is the best way of achieving that." He swallows hard and looks away. "Give him a chance. He's fair and decent."

Yes, his words are sensible and perhaps even honorable—I'm *really* starting to hate that word—but there's a raw quality to his voice that I find particularly interesting. I take a step forward and he stiffens.

"Would you ever lie to me, I wonder?"

"I might to protect you."

"I'm not an infant," I snap. "And I'd like to ask you a question, but only if you give me the courtesy of treating me as an adult."

He glowers at me. "What is it?"

"Do you love me?"

"Hell," he says, and then lets out a low curse. "I'm not answering that."

I wait. Only the frogs croaking and owls hooting break the sudden quiet.

"You know I do, damn it," he snarls. "Do you think this is easy for me? It's not. Do you think I don't have emotions? I do. Don't make this harder than it has be. Let me move on in peace."

A cavernous pit opens in my heart. He's not going to fight for me—for us. I can hardly believe it. "This is really your decision, Manuel? The only option you see is for me to marry Sonco?"

It's as if I've employed the worst kind of enchantment and turned him to stone. The blood leaves his face, leaving him pale, and his eyes darken into thunderous pools. He is deadly quiet, and then his lips twist. "He can provide for you in a way that I can't." He sweeps his arm wide. "Look what he has, Condesa—a kingdom, loyal subjects. A powerful army. You're his match. It's clear to everyone but you."

"At least he has the courage to reach for what he wants. At least he isn't a *coward*." My voice turns sour, as if I've dredged it through lemon juice. "Manuel, you don't need to say another word. I understand you quite well."

He flinches, steps away from me as if my words are a blade. Tears run down my face. I've hurt him. I've hurt us both.

"I'm not a coward for acting in the way I've been trained to act," he says stiffly. "I'm not a coward for being the best guard I know how to be. I can't believe you'd say that to me, knowing how I *feel*. I should never have entertained—should never have acted on my emotions."

"There's nothing more to say." My voice cracks. "I'm sorry it had to end this way."

"Me too," he whispers.

Neither of us moves or speaks or even blinks for several long, torturous seconds. It's over, really over, this time, but I can't make myself walk away.

When the screaming starts, I blink stupidly, as if our argument, Sonco's proposal, and this whole night were nothing but a terrible nightmare. Manuel reacts faster than I do, racing toward the temple. I follow at his heels.

"Go back!" he yells.

"Don't you tell me what to do," I snap as I dash into the cavern. People are rushing past me, shoving to get away from whatever is happening inside. My mouth goes dry as I draw closer to the fiesta. What is happening? Is there an attack?

"Damn it, Catalina. I'm still your guard!" Manuel roars, weaving in and out of the crowd.

Another horrifying bellow echoes in the tunnel. We burst into the main room in time to see a young man approach an Illari woman who's cowering under one of the tables. His too-pale skin glimmers in the torchlight as he bends and drags the poor woman out by her hair. Someone else attempts to deter the attack, but the pale man slams a fist into their stomach, catapulting the Illari into the wall with a sickening crunch.

Then the pale man rips the arm of the Illari woman clean from her body.

Blood and bone splatter.

Manuel shoves me behind his back, reaches into his boots, and pulls out two thin blades. He lunges forward, swiping at the pale man. He's only a few years younger than me. There's something odd about the way he moves, and his hands—they look charred. As if he's dipped his palms in coal.

A woman to my right screams and faints. I drop to my knees as recognition sets in. I *know* this woman—she was the one who'd lost track of her son. The one I helped search for. In horror, I look to the pale boy, who's being restrained by Manuel and Kusi and now several guards. Sonco rushes forward and gives the order to kill him.

It's done in seconds. Manuel digs his blade deep into the boy's neck and twists sharply.

I avert my gaze, gagging, my eyes prickling with tears.

When it's over, the poor woman is carried off. I don't envy the nightmare she'll wake up to. Sounds come at me from a great distance, dim and hard to decipher. I feel as if I'm trying to push through a heavy stream, the water roaring in my ears. And it's slow going. In the chaos afterward, in the mess of people leaving, faces pale and withdrawn, Chaska finds me, eyes red-rimmed. "His name was Urpi—fifteen years old."

"This is my fault," I whisper. "I should have consulted the stars more, searched harder this afternoon."

But Chaska shakes her head. "It's no one's fault. Come—Sonco wishes to speak to us in private."

We follow the crowd down several levels until we reach the room where Sonco conducts the affairs of the city. Several elders are already sitting on mats, while Sonco is in quiet conversation with his brother. Manuel sits with a few guards. At my entrance, his eyes lift to meet mine.

Then he quickly looks away.

My heart batters against my ribs, a relentless assault. Chaska motions for me to sit next to her along the wall. I lean my back against the cool stone. I cross my legs, and press close to the seer. She doesn't seem to mind. Everyone converses in hushed tones until Sonco clears his throat and we all look to him. For guidance, for answers, for comfort.

He speaks in a halting, disbelieving voice. "Earlier I learned that a flower had appeared in Paititi—a flower that's responsible for killing parts of the jungle. It infected Urpi and turned him into . . . into a monster. The man we've known since birth was lost to us. I grieve for his family."

His attention remains solely on the elders, who are wearing tunics the color of night, golden stitching at the collars and cuffs. On their feet are leather sandals with straps that crisscross up their calves. Feathers dangle from the ears and long braids of the women.

"A tragic day," one of them says. "What's your plan, son of Saywa?"

"With your blessing, I suggest that a small group go into the jungle and investigate the flower. We have a seer"—Sonco gestures toward me—"a visitor who's been communicating with Luna. The goddess has given her information about a mysterious individual planting this flower throughout the jungle. When we have more information, I'll send out the army to vanquish this evil and rid it from our home."

The elders confer among themselves. The rest of us wait, breaths filling our bellies.

"You have spoken, and we agree."

Sonco inclines his head. "Gracias."

I stand, but before I can leave, the Illari king motions to Chaska, Kusi, and me. "A word, por favor."

We wait as the elders file outside. Manuel follows them without a look in my direction. But his shoulders are tight, his jaw set, hands stuffed into his pockets. He's closed off, tucked away behind that indomitable fortress of his. It takes me only a second to realize what his posture means. Normally he'd insist on staying with me, keeping a close eye on me. But he's handed me off, believing I'm in capable hands.

It wouldn't surprise me if tonight's his last night in Paititi.

The thought makes me want to crumple in a heap on the floor. But Sonco clears his throat, jerking me back to the present moment.

"I think we need to keep this party investigating the flower small. Kusi, pick two guards to join us—no, don't give me that look, brother. I'm going. Chaska is too, and"—Sonco glances at me—"and I'm hoping you will."

I raise my brows. "Me?"

He nods. "I'd like all the help I can get."

Kusi frowns but keeps silent. I can feel his disapproval. It's Chaska who gives me a reassuring nod and I want to say yes. But what if I make things worse, what if I lead them astray? As quickly as the thought formulates in my mind, I shove it aside.

I can do this.

"I'll do it," I say, my voice shaky. "But you'll owe me a favor." I smile to let Sonco know I'm teasing.

But his response is somber. "It would only be fair."

"Oh, I was only—" I begin, but the Illari king waves me off.

"Go and prepare. We'll depart at dawn."

As I leave, Kusi, Chaska, and Sonco fold into a tight embrace. Every line of their bodies touches, and together they represent the youth of the Illari, the hopes of their people. Leader. Warrior. Seer.

Manuel finds me the minute I exit the building.

"You're still here," I say, surprised.

"I wouldn't leave without saying goodbye."

The effect is instant. My hands start shaking. I pull them behind me, keep my chin lifted and my eyes clear. "That was fast."

He scrubs his face with a long drag of his hand. "It's for the best. I did what I said I'd do—brought you to Paititi. You're in good hands, this city is well protected, and you'll be marrying the king." He pauses. "It's time for me to go. I've probably stayed too long as it is." He drags in air. "I've kept my vow to you."

So it is. There's nothing more to say. I step forward and he tenses. I swiftly kiss his cheek. "Take care of yourself, Manuel."

His lips twist, a sharp grimace. "I'll escort you back."

I nod, exhaustion forcing my eyelids to droop. We walk in strained silence, only the quiet song of the jungle disturbing the tense air between us. I want to ask him what he'll do, where he'll go. But those details will only hurt me. I don't need to know what kind of life he intends to build without me.

"Can you do something for me?" Manuel asks suddenly.

I glance at him curiously. "What?"

He stops in the middle of the path. We're close to home, and the path is empty. The odd monkey howls somewhere in the distance, an owl offering an accompanying hoot.

"Don't go on this mission," he says, the words coming out rushed. "It's too dangerous. Chaska is going; she's a seer. Let her read the stars."

His protectiveness is showing. Old habits are hard to vanquish. "I can't stay behind. Luna wants me to go. I can feel it."

"Will you just think about it?"

The long hours of the day weigh heavily on my shoulders. I lower my chin, and let out a low sigh. I don't have it in me to argue, so I tell him what he wants to hear.

I lie.

The next morning, I'm ready by the time Chaska knocks on my door. I step out of my room and look for Manuel. He'd slept outside, but now he's nowhere to be found. He might be in the pool, getting one last bath before venturing into the jungle. It's such a great idea, I wish I'd thought of it, but I'd collapsed on my bed the moment I stepped inside my snug home.

And cried.

It's still dark outside, birds chirping and twittering. Chaska is carrying a bundle of clothing for me: dark trousers, long-sleeved tunic, leather belt, and my boots, cleaned and polished to a sheen. In her free hand is a large cup of coffee. I nearly fall into it with relief, enjoying the strong bitter taste that somehow rids the last remnants of sleep. She gives me privacy while I change, and when I step back outside, carrying only my dented telescope, I'm also given a small pack, tightly woven and slightly heavy.

"Dried food, cup for water, hammock and blanket, and netting," she says. "You said you know how to use a dagger?"

"I'm not that helpless," I snap.

She raises her brows.

"Sorry," I mutter. "I didn't sleep well."

Chaska peers at me. "I can see that. I'll carry the dagger for you—don't want you hurting yourself."

I blink at her.

"You do need something, though—a light weapon within easy reach." Chaska thinks on it then hands me a leather strap attached to a quiver full of blowgun darts.

"I have no idea how to use these." I reach for one of the darts neatly stacked against one another, feathers on one side, the other sharpened to a point.

"Careful. They're dipped in poison from the rainbow frogs."

My hand drops away. "I'm going to poke myself with this, I just know it."

"We should go," she says, turning.

I follow her, hoisting my pack. We meet the rest of the group at the foot of the stairs, and start climbing as the sun slowly kisses the horizon. Kusi leads the way, Sonco at his heels. I'm incredibly surprised that he's come, given how dangerous this mission is.

Chaska notices me staring at the brothers. "It was the worst argument I've ever heard between them. In the end, Sonco chose to act as an older brother—not as the leader of the Illari."

I study the members of our party. Along with Chaska, there are two other young men, both lean and carrying spears and slingshots. Manuel is nowhere in sight and I try not to dwell on what his absence might mean.

But I know he's long gone.

By the time we reach the top of the hill, the sky has brightened to a dewy lavender. It stormed sometime during the night, and raindrops cling to every curling vine and blade of grass, glimmering in the sunlight like gems. Chaska walks ahead of me, and when she stops abruptly, I swerve to avoid crashing into her. I peer around her shoulder to see why we've stopped.

My heart snags, as if caught on a nail.

Manuel kneels on the ground, rummaging through his pack. At the sight of us, he slowly stands, slinging his belongings over his shoulder. He looks perfectly unrumpled, dark tunic clean and free of wrinkles, broad hat wiped of any dust and dirt, hair damp. "Buenos días."

He hasn't seen me. I shift farther behind Chaska. Maybe he won't notice until it's too late. It's a desperate, foolish thought, but it doesn't stop me from hiding in her shadow.

"I wanted to wish you luck," Manuel says. "Buena suerte."

"Shame you couldn't join us," Kusi says. "Are you sure you won't reconsider?"

Manuel shakes his head. "It's time for me to go."

"Safe travels," Sonco says. "Need anything?"

Again he shakes his head. I expect him to leave, but he lingers. "Will you return to the same place as last time?" Manuel asks.

"Yes, but this time we have our seers to help guide us forward."

Manuel tilts his head, and a faint line appears between his brows. "Seers?"

"The condesa will be joining us," Sonco says.

Manuel's voice comes out flat. *"Why?"*

"Ask her yourself," Kusi says.

Chaska moves out of the way, as do the others, parting down the middle until Manuel has a clear view of me. The blood drains from his face, leaving him unnaturally pale. His hands curl into fists around the straps of his pack. He takes in my clothing, the quiver of darts around my chest, and he visibly winces. "She's *not* going. It's too dangerous."

"It's her decision," Sonco says. "Luna has been communicating with her, and we need her on the journey to guide us." He slaps Manuel on the back as he brushes past. "We must go; we're losing light."

The group moves as one, passing Manuel, but when I'm within reach, his hand snatches my wrist. "Catalina. What are you doing? You said you'd stay behind." I try not to show how his touch affects me, but for a moment I'm reminded of when that same hand cupped my check. Was that only yesterday?

"I have a way to help them, so I will," I say.

"Why must you both go?"

"Because Luna is communicating with *me*, but if something should happen, they'll still have Chaska to rely on."

"This isn't worth your life," he whisper-shouts. "When you marry Sonco, he'll give you an army. Don't put yourself in this kind of danger."

"I'm not marrying Sonco," I say calmly. "And I'm not doing this for an army. Paititi will be my home, and I'll do whatever I can to protect her."

His jaw drops. "What are you talking about?"

"I've had a change of heart," I whisper. "My whole life, I was told I'd be queen. I never questioned that path. Until I *finally* realized that I can choose to stop pretending to be someone I'm not."

Manuel tightens his grip. "I don't understand."

"It's simple, really," I say. "The answer has been in front of me this whole time, and I didn't see it because I'm stubborn. I'm a seer, not a queen."

"Fine," he says. "Fine. But *stay* here where it's safe. Por favor."

"I'm not your job anymore, Manuel." My voice softens. "I release you from your position as my guard."

His expression shifts, his jaw going slack, as if I struck him.

I march away, quickening my speed to catch up to the others. Their quiet voices echo in the tunnel. It feels like I was just here—the spot where I'd kissed Manuel looks exactly the same—but as I hurry along, my throat constricts. I meet up with the others at the dock, marveling at the roar of the waterfall, feeling every note of its song in my bones. The two guards peer into the boats and when they tip one onto its side, a family of black snakes falls into the water. We climb into the boats—Chaska, Kusi, and I in one, Sonco and the other men in the second—and just as we're about to push off, Manuel comes running, footsteps thundering, and leaps into my canoe.

He lands next to me, and the boat rocks from side to side. I clutch the rail and glare at him. "You couldn't have taken an empty one?"

"No!" he shouts furiously over the bellowing cry of the water. "I couldn't."

We push away from the dock and glide through the falls. The water slaps against my skin. We come out the other side, and the jungle's sinister face welcomes us back.

"For a second I didn't think you were coming," Kusi says to Manuel.

He scowls at me. "I go where she goes."

"Excellent," Kusi says at last. "Can you keep an eye on the caimán following our boat?"

We follow the river as it hugs and curves around the muddy banks of the steaming jungle. I stare into the dense green foliage, my heart heavy as I remember what it's like to trek through the trees, a thousand predators lurking under every rock and leaf. The river is black enough that I can't see through its inky surface, but I know there are creatures looking back at me.

Manuel hasn't said a word since we left the waterfall.

We leave the canoes on the bank, cover them in wide palm fronds, and mark the location by crossing a few branches nearby. I pull my feet out of the mud that's sucking me down to the tops of my boots. So much for polished leather. Kusi leads the way up to the tree line and we follow in single file, Manuel directly behind me. Under the canopy, the suddenly dim light makes my hair stand on end.

I'd forgotten about the jungle's eerie green glow.

Manuel's lessons rush back to me—*don't lean on anything, don't touch anything.* Snakes hide among fallen logs and branches, fire ants crawl on stems and tall grass, tarantulas nest in shadowy holes in the ground, and bats duck behind thick leaves. The jungle wages war against all of us, Manuel's warnings my only shield.

We march on, quiet and alert. In every direction things crawl, fly, hiss, and grunt. At no point do we stop for a rest. It's too dangerous, even when traveling with the Illari. They might make their home here, but the jungle is still the ultimate predator. The only true king. Every now and again, Manuel plucks a fruit and wordlessly hands it to me. I ignore his offerings and take a fruit for myself, careful not to touch or step on anything lethal.

There's no sense of time, another thing I forgot. Because the canopy is so dense, I don't notice the late hour until it's suddenly incredibly dark, the fog curling around the trees obscuring my sight. Kusi holds up a hand and we stop.

"We make camp here," he says.

Someone tends to a fire while another ventures off to hunt. I hope he brings back a platter of fried yuca and eggs over an enormous serving of rice. Manuel and I set up our hammocks. He makes sure to pick a pair of trees that is close to mine. I'm painfully aware of his presence, even though I refuse to look in his direction. He's made his feelings perfectly clear.

We gather around the fire, passing dried beef, hardened cheese, cups of bamboo water, and hunks of slow-roasted rabbit meat. Sonco and Chaska fill in the details about the mission and my involvement. When they're done, we're all quiet. The two guards eat their fill and stand to take up the first watch.

"How far are we from the corruption?" I ask Kusi.

He points in the opposite direction of the river. "We have another full day of walking ahead of us if we move briskly."

"Are we safe here?" I hate how my voice trembles, but there's no denying the fear clinging to my skin, making goose bumps flare up and down my arms.

"Only Luna knows," Sonco says.

I shudder, wishing for reassurance, but not finding any in his troubled expression.

"Then we're just observing?" Manuel asks. "We're not actually venturing into the corrupted land?"

"That's up to Catalina," Sonco says. He briefly eyes the distance between us, his brows pulling together into a stern line. Manuel and I share a log, but he's on one end and I'm on the other. "And whatever Luna tells her."

I clench my wooden cup, the last drops of water clinging to the bottom. What if Luna doesn't have another message for me? What if I'm not as helpful as I hope to be? I shakily stand and walk over to my pack. The telescope is on top, and it feels heavy in my hands.

Footsteps clamor through the brush. Branches snap. Leaves rustle. Everyone jumps to their feet, weapons raised. Manuel is at my side in an instant. "Pull out your weapon."

I stuff my telescope into my belt. As for weapons, all I have are the darts dipped in poison. When I show him, his brow furrows. "That's it?"

"Chaska has my dagger."

Manuel is about to reclaim it when there's another loud crash. "Over there!" Kusi exclaims, his spear raised. A figure bursts into our camp, huffing. I let a blow dart fly, and it lands nowhere near him. A second later I'm glad for it. He's one of the guards.

"Where is Sayri? Has he come back?"

Chaska steps forward, her arms raised. "Calm down. He's taking the first watch."

"No," the man replies, frantic. "We were together, but there was a noise—I turned around and *my brother was gone.*"

"He can't have disappeared," Kusi says. "He might've walked away to relieve himself."

"I looked," he says, panic threading his words. "I looked *everywhere*. Called his name. Made a racket. But he's nowhere! Help me find him, please."

Chaska looks toward her cousin. "What do you think?"

"I'll go with him to search," Kusi says. "The rest of you stay here. Protect the camp. Keep the fire blazing, your weapons close." He and the guard disappear into the tree line, and for a horrible moment I have a feeling I won't see either of them again.

"He didn't say what kind of noise it was," I mutter. Was it a scream? A growl?

What's hunting us?

Manuel clenches the handle of his machete. I reach for my telescope again, but he catches my movement. A snarl escapes him. "Don't even think about it."

"But Luna might offer guidance."

"The nearest clearing is a ten-minute walk away. We stay together, with the fire."

I stuff the scope back into my bag.

We wait for what feels like hours, until at last, *at last*, the pair reappears. Kusi looks to Sonco first, a slight shake of his head. My stomach drops. Sayri hasn't been found.

"We're going to attempt another search in the morning," Kusi says. "For now no one—not even the watch—steps out of sight."

He motions toward Manuel and me. "You two sleep first."

Sleep? How is anyone supposed to sleep with a monster on the loose?

We each settle into our hammocks. Mine swings wildly until I slam a foot down to keep it steady. Manuel checks to make sure I'm safe before climbing into his. I stare up into the dense canopy of trees, tangles twisting like long limbs, ready to choke the life out of anyone who draws near. I remember the loneliness and terror I'd felt that first night in the jungle. It was a miracle I'd survived at all.

Manuel says softly, "Catalina."

"What?" I whisper back.

"I won't let anything happen to you." There's iron in his vow. "Try to sleep."

I avert my gaze and turn away from his hammock. Somehow sleep claims me after all.

The next morning we look for the missing guard. Kusi keeps us all together, searching beyond our campsite. I get down on my knees, peering into the thick greenery surrounding a massive tree trunk. A tarantula creeps on a long palm frond and I shudder, drawing away. Manuel stays close, lifting tangled vines, trying to forge a path through the dense jungle.

We look for an hour, but there's no sign of Sayri. And then someone calls, a few feet away.

"Over here," Chaska says.

She points to the ground. To something half hidden underneath a tight cluster of ferns. I step closer, Manuel at my elbow. Kusi and Sonco join us.

Someone lets out a smothered cry. I think it might be me.

Sayri's bloody leg rests against a massive rubber tree.

Ripped clean.

We spend hours searching for the rest of him. But there's nothing else. By the early afternoon, with most of the day behind us, Kusi pulls aside Sayri's brother. Their exchange isn't easy to watch. Kusi remains firm while the guard breaks down, crying out in his desperation. He pounds his chest, wipes his steaming eyes.

Chaska comes to stand by me. "We can turn back."

I glance at her, my eyebrows rising. "Do you want to go back?"

"This is terrifying—and I've lived in the jungle all my life." She bites her lip. "But we haven't learned anything important. I don't want to face our people empty-handed."

I know the feeling. Which is why I won't go back. Besides, at this point it feels safer to stick together. Kusi and the guard finish their conversation, and we resume our trek toward the dying part of the jungle, drawing closer to danger.

To the unknown.

We make camp later that evening, and once again I pull out my dented telescope. Manuel is standing on the other side of the roaring fire, but he looks over as if I've called his name. His gaze drops to the scope in my hands, and he frowns.

"I'm going," I say, my heart hammering against my ribs. I'm scared to wander away, but I have to consult Luna. She might provide advice—or direction.

Manuel shakes his head.

I prepare for another argument, but I'm saved by Kusi. "We passed by a small clearing. Not too far of a walk."

Manuel shoots him a look of profound disgust. "It's dangerous. Why don't we all pack up and spend the night there?"

"Too vulnerable to attack," Kusi says. "But we could use Luna's guidance."

"I'll go with her," Chaska says. "I'll have my weapon."

"I go where she goes," Manuel says. His expression could scare off a jaguar.

The three of us leave, walking away from our companions, away from warmth, and plunge deeper into the sinister forest. Manuel hacks at the dense foliage. I'm two steps behind him, carefully moving around thick sludge streaking through the green carpet. The ground emits a damp, mildewy scent. Liana vines loop down, and a few times I mistake one for a snake. The clearing comes into view, and Manuel stiffens as the trees become sparse, the protection growing thinner. Moonlight shines through the smattering of leaves, casting a delicate pattern onto the mushy green earth.

He sweeps the area and huffs out an annoyed breath. "How long will this take?"

"Long enough," Chaska says.

"Helpful," he mutters, then warily walks around the perimeter.

I pull out my scope then spend the next few minutes quieting my heart, calming my spirit. My breaths are intentional, slow and deep, brushing at the back of my throat and filling my lungs. My shoes sink into the earth, taking root. I say a soft prayer to

Inti, for the warm days; to Pachamama, for nurturing life; and to Luna, for lighting the darkness.

Then I lift my scope and peer through it, trembling. Dimly, I'm aware of Chaska doing the exact same thing.

Please guide us.

The stars move, connecting and reconnecting, shifting and turning to fit against one another, forming shapes that only Chaska and I can see and decipher. Each word is a blow to my chest.

Enemy. Power. Near. Consume. Unnatural.

The message doesn't change, and I feel the quiet assurance of Luna's presence. Tucked in every glimmer of moonlight that kisses my skin and grazes my cheek. *Hurry*, she seems to whisper. *Hurry.*

"I don't understand—hurry where?"

Chaska looks over at me. "That's one of the words I see too."

Manuel draws near, his brow puckered. "What's the word?"

"Words, multiple." I finger the end of my braid, letting the strand tickle my lips and chin. "*Enemy, power, near, consume, unnatural,* and *hurry.* But . . . they don't fit together. Almost like—like they're meant for two different people."

Manuel is quiet while holding up his machete and surveying the area. I pace around, carding through ideas and impressions, gut feelings and intuition.

"By *enemy,*" Manuel asks, "does she mean the person who's planting the flower?"

"It has to be. I don't know who else Luna could be talking about. But why doesn't she just name the culprit?"

"With Luna, everything is carefully measured," Chaska says.

"Intentional. She doesn't pick random shapes; it's all supposed to mean something. She gives me the words, and a seer is meant to form the rest of the story. Perhaps the name doesn't matter. After all, it could be someone we don't know. And in that case, what difference does a name make?"

He lets out a low whistle. "A lot of room for error. Not to mention pressure."

"Shhh," Chaska murmurs. "Let us think for a moment."

"I'm close to understanding," I say as I continue pacing. "I can feel it."

"Would you mind standing still?" Manuel asks. "So I can keep an eye on you while looking out for . . . jaguars."

He doesn't say *monster*, and I'm glad for it. I stop walking, my arms flapping. "I'm missing something, or maybe I'm feeling *too* much. I have so many options, so many ways I can interpret her—" My eyes widen when I'm hit with a flash of realization. "It's the flower."

"Yes, we know that already," he says.

"No, I mean the flower isn't meant to be *consumed*." I reach out and grasp his arm. "The monsters are people who've consumed the flower. The plant not only corrupts the earth but human flesh, too."

"Of course," Chaska says breathlessly. "Poor Urpi must have eaten it."

"How is that possible?" Manuel demands. "Where did the flower come from?"

"I don't know but—"

A harsh, long scream rents the air. Manuel spins in the direction of camp, shoulders tightening. "Stay here—"

"No," I whisper, suddenly understanding the urgency. "They're coming—"

Chaska bolts out of the clearing, shouting for her cousins. She disappears into the brush. Another bellowing shriek follows, full of agony. My stomach lurches, and I sag against Manuel, feeling Luna's frantic breath against my edges.

"I can't leave them," he says.

"Neither can I."

He grasps my hand and together we run toward whatever horror our friends face.

CAPÍTULO

treinta y dos

I pump my legs, racing after Manuel, ignoring all of his lessons. I touch branches and vines, stumble over a log. My feet kick up leaves, no doubt disturbing the homes of tarantulas and poisonous frogs. When the glow of the fire looms ahead, Manuel spins and hauls me behind a tree.

"What are you—"

Manuel slaps a firm hand over my mouth, his fingers dry, unlike my sweat-slicked ones. His face is as calm as ever, and for the first time I wonder if it's because he knows that if he shows fear, I'd be too frightened to go on. He peers around the vast tree trunk. Moss clings to the branches overhead, and I brush aside a clump, staring at Manuel, at the part of the jungle within my sight, and at my own weaponless hands. The only thing I have on me is my telescope and those useless darts.

He removes his hand and speaks, his voice a mere strip of sound. I have to lean in to hear him at all. "Don't move from this spot. I'll be close by."

I nod as he walks away, vanishing into a thicket of tree ferns.

I blink back tears, struggling to keep calm. An army of ants climbs up the long line of the trunk, disappearing into a gaping black hole. I take a half step away, shuddering. Leaves drip tears onto the top of my head. It takes everything in me not to run for my life, screaming at the top of my voice. I clutch my stomach, spinning in a slow circle, half waiting, half dreading for the monster to come.

I wait for minutes. Every second feels like an hour.

Fear keeps me upright, rigid and tense. I can't believe I didn't take my weapon from Chaska. Foolish, foolish planning. I pray to Luna for Manuel to come back. I'm so desperate, I'm about to get on my knees to beseech the canopy when I hear it.

Someone moans close by.

Human.

I slowly turn, my ears straining at the hushed noise. I creep away from the tree, my heart thundering against my ribs as I will myself not to panic. Manuel hasn't returned, watching for the monster, trying to find our friends. Another groan punctures the night. I drop to a squat, gently unfolding leaves until I see streaks of blood glistening on the jungle floor. There's so much of it. Spread over ferns and vines, mixing with the muddy ground. I crab-walk forward until I find someone's warm hand under a brush of greenery.

Without thinking I reach forward, grasping the open palm. "It's all right now. I'm here to help." The words are a whisper, barely teasing my mouth. I brush the rest of the leaves aside—notice the bone and blood on the other end—and let out a scream. I drop the hand and kick away, my boots slapping mud everywhere.

Tears carve tracks against my cheeks.

It's one of the guards.

"Catalina," Manuel says from above me, frantic. "Get up. We have to move." He notices the palm and blanches. "Can you stand?"

No way. The bloody limb is a mere foot away from me.

Manuel tucks his hands under my arms and hauls me to my feet. His face startles me. Sweat greases his hairline, drips down the sharp planes of his face. His tunic is soaked through, forearms glistening in what little moonlight pokes through the canopy of trees.

"The others?"

"I can't find them," he says grimly. "We're going back—"

Someone crashes through the jungle near us. The heavy panting roars in my ears. Branches snap. Manuel shoves me behind him, machete raised, reflecting the light from his luminous eyes, glowing bright against the flat black.

Kusi stumbles through a gap in the trees, his clothes stained with mud—no, not mud—blood. His spear is clutched in his hand, and quivers holding blowgun darts cross his broad chest. He's ready for war.

"Where's Chaska?"

"She's not with you?" I ask.

"¡Mierda!" Kusi cries. "She went with you, didn't she?"

"Yes, but she ran ahead the moment the screaming started," Manuel says.

"What do they look like? The monsters?" I'm amazed I have enough saliva in my mouth to speak at all. "Did they look like poor Urpi?"

"Barely human," he says, his face pale. "Bodies turned white. Cold skin."

His flat voice heightens my fear.

"Where is Sonco?" Manuel asks. "We found one—part of—" He breaks off, his expression pained. "One of the guards is there. Sayri's brother."

The Illari follows Manuel's line of sight and lands on the bloody limb. His face twists, the warrior brother barely containing his rage.

"Is the monster gone?" I ask. "What should we do?"

"*Monsters.* There're several of them," Kusi spits. "They came after you left. We all fought so Sonco could run back to Paititi, round up the army—"

A bloodcurdling scream cuts him off.

Chaska.

We race toward the sound, leaping over twisted roots buttressing up against massive tree trunks. We run through towering saw grass and hanging vines, through utter darkness, Manuel leading the way with his Moonsight. The green of the jungle is an ocean hiding slithering creatures, monsters with the strength of ten men, and animals with sharp teeth. I try not to think of what I'm stepping on or what's flying around me.

"Chaska!" Kusi roars, bolting around Manuel.

He kneels beside a shaking form—it's Chaska. He lifts her halfway. The expression on her face is stark terror, her skin ashen and pulled tight over her cheekbones. She stares at me blankly from red-rimmed eyes. Above us, several king vultures peer down with their beady eyes, patiently waiting for dinner.

Luna's breath glides across my skin, raising the hair at the back of my neck. *They're coming.*

"Manuel," I whisper, fear searing my throat, stabbing my belly.

Four of them melt into view, surrounding us. They're all bare chested, bodies turned pale white. Only the tips of their fingers are dark, their nails sharpened into lethal points. They carry bows and arrows, swords in sheaths. What's left of their clothing is tattered and dirty. Their sinewy muscle is tense, holding back, but ready for violence—for death. Every one of them has Moonsight, lambent gazes staring with unguarded hunger. They've been blessed by our goddess.

Blessed—*or cursed.*

Black tattoos are etched across their bodies. It's a language I know—constellations. I read the words carved into their flesh: *Child. Gift. Blessing.*

I press close to Manuel, my hand a death grip on his arm. Kusi slowly pulls Chaska to her feet, and she slumps against him. *Luna. What is this?*

From the dense foliage comes another figure—a man covered from head to toe in an eggplant-purple robe. Long black hair sweeps past his shoulders, and in his bronze hands he holds a sword. He regards us coldly, his lips twisting into a sneer. "Drop your weapons."

The pale creatures lift theirs, ready to unleash their hunger. We drop our spears and daggers, but I clench my telescope, refusing to let it go. He said weapons, and this isn't one. My heart slams against my ribs, my arms trembling at my sides, completely useless. The man in the purple robe studies my companions, then his attention lands on Manuel and me.

"Illustrians." A catlike grin stretches across his thin mouth. "Interesting."

He snaps his fingers. One of the monsters removes an arrow

from his pack and notches it in his bow. I'm frozen all over as the monster levels the weapon at my heart.

Manuel stiffens next to me, breathing softly. "What do you want with her?" His voice is unimaginably calm.

"Answers," the man rasps out. "Step forward, girl."

I glance at Manuel, who doesn't take his eyes off the creature training his arrow on me. He gives me an imperceptible nod. But my feet remain rooted to the ground. The monster growls at me, his strong arm pulling back the bow.

"Catalina," Manuel says.

The robed man's gaze sharpens and latches onto mine. When his laughter cuts the air, I actually wince. It's an awful, grating noise that makes every inch of my skin crawl. "Catalina? Catalina Quiroga?"

My jaw drops. "How do you know my name?"

"I know all about you." He steps closer, and his eyes travel up and down my body, lingering on my dark hair, my face. "You two could have been twins," he adds, almost as an afterthought.

I freeze. He can only mean one person—the girl who acted as my decoy for nearly my entire life. The idea of her being anywhere near this man sends a shiver down my spine. I don't like the mean curve to his mouth, the anger hidden in his eyes. "You know Ximena?"

"We've met," he says with a grim smile. "Imagine running into you here, of all places. What brings you?"

"I was banished to the jungle by the Llacsan queen."

"And the Estrella?"

Shame eats at me. "I lost it to Ximena. It was destroyed."

"A pity," he says. "But there's a small chance you might have some value. The daughter of nobility, a member of the royal family who ruled Inkasisa for centuries. I imagine you either have enemies or admirers. Come over here—I won't hurt you."

I blanch. Manuel steps in front of me, his calm veneer fracturing. The instant he does, there's a whistle of wind and a sharp thud. Manuel hisses loudly, bending forward. I kneel beside him and gasp. An arrow pierces his right thigh, blood blooming from the wound.

Manuel shoots a quick look at me, his face contorted in pain: *Hold it together. Don't fall apart.*

I straighten helplessly, my hand at the center of his back. Manuel reaches behind his leg and breaks the shaft close to the wound without so much as a whimper, and then throws it on the ground at the man's feet, who appears pleased by Manuel's defiance. His thin lips frame a cold smile, and fear squeezes my heart. I don't like the way the robed man assesses Manuel, as if he were a prized warhorse.

"You'll make a fine warrior."

Manuel frowns as Kusi asks, "Who are you?"

The man considers the question. "I am a priest."

Recognition slams into me. This is *Atoc's* priest, his loud shadow, master of vicious magic. Memories flood my mind. His many attempts to cross the magical bridge dividing the Illustrian keep from Atoc's army. His use of torture and control to force our people to let him pass.

"This man is dangerous," I say. "He's capable of terrible magic."

The priest shoots a quick look in my direction, and he seems almost amused. "So you *have* heard of me."

"What do you want?" Kusi asks.

"Many, many things," the man says. "But for now, the way to Paititi will serve. Which of you will give it to me?"

Kusi's face turns mutinous.

The priest casts his eye around. "Pachamama has blessed me this night. I have an Illustrian royal and a handful of Illari warriors to join my army." For the first time I notice a small leather pouch at his hip. "You've all been a nuisance, standing in my way, distracting me from my plans, but once you swallow the flower, you'll become immortal." He points toward Manuel. "You first, Illustrian."

"It's not meant to be consumed," I say. "Can't you see that you're bringing death—"

"Your companions will eat the flower," he says.

I gape at the priest. Horror pools deep in my belly, buzzes through my jaw and teeth, locks my knees. "No. Por favor."

He scowls at me. "No? Do you know the way to Paititi, then?"

I shake my head. "I can't even tell you where north is."

"Pathetic." He turns toward Kusi. "And you?"

"I will not," Kusi says.

He snaps his fingers.

Kusi leaps forward but abruptly stops, clutching his throat. He's immobile, his eyes growing wider and wider. He claws at his throat, opening and closing his mouth, unable to drag in air. One of the monsters carries a writhing Chaska toward the priest, unfazed by her kicking and clawing. Manuel holds up his machete, standing in front of me when another figure races forward, a blur of movement, his legs pumping furiously to save his brother in time.

Sonco.

I let out a smothered cry. Manuel sweeps his machete in a wide arc and lops off the head of one of the monsters. The decapitated body falls forward, but no blood spills from the gaping hole between its shoulder blades.

And then something grips me. I can't move my hands or feet. Fingers won't curl, knees won't bend. My blood seems to freeze under my skin. I can't even move my neck.

The priest stands in the middle of all of us, bodies frozen mid-movement. The only ones in motion are the monsters. Sonco's dagger is inches from piercing the priest's heart. He was so close: Another step forward and the weapon would have done its job. The priest stares at the Illari leader coldly and then rips the weapon out of his hands.

He drags the blade across Sonco's neck.

We are all frozen, unable to cry out or rage. Sonco attempts to look in his brother's direction, but he's trapped in his statue-like state. The angry line at his throat waits to be free of magic, to widen and release the king's lifeblood.

It's too horrifying for words.

The priest lifts a finger. Whatever magic holds Sonco in place releases him, and he slumps forward, his eyes wide open, blood gushing from the gash.

I can't see Kusi's face—his body positioned away from mine, still clutching his throat, utterly trapped in the priest's magic. Tears streak down my face.

The people of Paititi have just lost a good man.

The priest lifts another finger. The magic vanishes. I drop to the ground, shuddering. Everyone else follows. *Thud, thud, thud.*

The monsters encircle us. Kusi stares in horror at his brother—his mouth formed into a silent scream.

"I hope you understand that fighting is futile." The priest snaps at one of the creatures. "Pick up the girls."

A monster yanks me by the hair, bringing me to my feet. I accidentally brush against its arm and I shiver. The body is bone white, cold to the touch. Dark eyes gaze at me, and its jaw closes with an audible snap. Curling brown-black hair falls to its shoulders. I keep staring, sure there's something familiar about this face, and it takes me a while to finally understand that I recognize the monster.

Rumi. The vigilante.

Treinta y tres

The priest surveys the jungle and wrinkles his nose. He slaps a mosquito against his neck. "We leave for camp. Immediately." He crooks his finger, and Kusi and Manuel lift to their feet. "My men will carry the girls. Should you attempt anything, it will be their lives."

He marches forward. Manuel and Kusi follow, half dragged, half struggling against the priest's magic. They have enough freedom to move only their legs. Rumi swings me over his shoulder, keeping a firm hold on the backs of my thighs. The other monster attempts to do the same with Chaska, but she fights him, scratching and kicking, until his hand grips her throat and squeezes until she faints.

This is how we travel up the hill.

My only line of sight is the ground and Rumi's tattered pants sinking into the mud, the muck splattering up his legs. I cry the entire journey to the dead part of the jungle. What possessed me to think I could help in any way? This is all my fault. I'm a worthless seer—how could I not have seen this? Luna might have been trying to tell me more, but because of my inexperience, I missed crucial information. Sonco would still be alive if I'd known to demand he stay behind.

How many more people will I put in danger?

The ground transforms under Rumi's feet. From green to gray to white. From alive to dying to dead within a few steps. I try to lift my head by pushing against his back, but his hold across my legs tightens and I wince. We walk on, the cold settling into my bones. By the time we stop, my whole body shivers, teeth clacking against one another from the bitter air. Each howl of the wind tears into my flesh.

Rumi drops me and I land painfully on my side. The dust lifts and then settles around me. I try not to breathe any in. It smells of nothing—devoid of any hint of life. Terror raps against my chest, rattling bone, making my fingers tremble.

The priest wipes his eyes, yawning. Our walk took a toll—or maybe it's his prolonged use of his magic. The land is barren and bone dry. There are several cages made of tall bamboo stalks, fortified by liana vines. Manuel and Kusi are thrown into separate prisons. Both immediately attempt to rattle the stalks but there's no give, and more monsters appear to guard them. Every time Manuel or Kusi reach for the bamboo, a creature jabs its spear between the bars, pushing the men back.

Kusi's face twists in horror. The monsters are dressed in Illari-style tunics. These people must be the missing scouts.

"Catalina, you're with me," the priest says. "Take the other girl and lock her up."

"¡Espera!" Manuel cries. "Take me instead."

Rumi wrenches me toward a large tent made of fabric and

leaves draped over bamboo. Inside there's a simple woven mat on the ground and a narrow cot covered in mosquito netting.

The priest follows me in, breathing down my neck. I jump away, trembling.

He gestures toward the ground. "Siéntate."

I carefully lower myself, my gaze flicking past his shoulder to the tent opening. How far could I go before he uses his magic on me?

He observes me shrewdly. "You won't get far."

There's a small basket by the cot and from within it he pulls out a bottle of wine and a clay cup. He pours himself a full glass then settles across from me. "Rather interesting," he says, "facing you here. Clever strategy to send a decoy to the palace in your place. Was that your idea?"

I shake my head, shuddering at the sight of the deep burgundy wine staining his lips. "It was Ana's."

He tilts the cup back, takes a long sip. His fingers clutch the cup possessively. When his cold gaze settles on mine again, I notice the smirk. "I remember Ana. Your general. She's a screamer. Did you hear how she died?"

I wince, looking away.

"Atoc pushed her into a deep crack in the earth. She screamed the whole way down. A bit dramatic, if you ask me." He studies me—my skin ravished by mosquito bites, my hair in thick tangles, my clothes damp with sweat. "You've lost everything, haven't you? The throne. Your friends. And eventually your freedom, when I sell you to the highest bidder."

"Who will want me? I have no land, no title."

He shrugs. "When you've lived as long as I have, survived

against all odds, you learn to take whatever is available. No opportunity is wasted."

"Why are you doing this?" I ask quietly.

He rubs his eyes and then finishes the rest of his wine. Again I can tell he's drowsy from the use of his magic. And again my gaze skitters to the entrance, the fabric fluttering gently against the bamboo.

The priest's low chuckle makes the hair at the back of my neck stand on end. He lifts a single finger. My throat constricts, and I reach up, wanting to pull away whatever is blocking air from my lungs. But I feel only skin.

"Have you guessed my magic? Nothing to say?" The priest smiles coldly. "Not too bright, are you? At least your decoy knew how to stand up for herself."

I flush hotly, even as my body yearns for sweet air. It wants to live. I know what kind of awful magic runs through his veins. But the words stick at the back of my throat. I'd been afraid of him for years after hearing about all of his exploits against my people. What horrors did Ximena face at his hands?

The priest leans forward. "I can control blood. Stop a heart from beating. Swell a throat, thicken it with blood. Force a person to jump off a cliff, drown in a puddle of water."

I stare at him in horror as I clutch my throat. He drops his finger and I drag in a mouthful of cold air. I cough and gasp, fight to control the rapid beating of my heart. I have to keep him talking, learn as much as I can. Expose a weakness. My mouth is dry, but I somehow manage to choke out, "I've never heard of this kind of magic."

"A rare ability in the little village I came from," he says

absently. "Have you ever visited the Lowlands?"

I shake my head.

"Skip it," he says. "A smattering of huts, no road or wealth of any kind. I wanted more for my people, my family, but they were content in their small corner of Inkasisa, content with being forgotten."

My eyes narrow. That weary bitterness feels familiar. I've seen it on someone else too, a hazy picture in my mind. "I know your face."

"Of course you do," he says coolly. "I was there the day you lost it all."

He's right, but it's more than that. This is the boy Luna tried to show me, the one who grew up lonely and isolated. Without companions or family. "You lost your parents when you were young."

The scowl vanishes from his face.

"We have that in common," I say softly. "But that's where our similarities end. Maybe you thought the people would like you better if you brought money into the village. But it didn't go that way—they feared your magic. Even though you didn't ask for it."

The priest folds his arms across his chest.

My throat thickens, unnaturally. A voice inside tells me to speak up, to share that I understand some of what he went through as a boy, wanting a friend, a home of his own, for his tiny village to make it onto a map. "That must have been terribly lonely for you."

His hold on my blood thins. I inhale deeply, filling my belly with air.

"You don't have to do this."

"You think you know me because Luna shared my past?" His fingers dig into his arms, and the veins in his throat become more pronounced. "I don't need saving, Condesa."

I chance another look toward the tent entrance, trying to see if one of the priest's men waits outside. But I don't see anyone.

"I wouldn't attempt it," he says in a voice colder than the bitter breeze howling against the tent. "Or have you forgotten I have your friends locked in cages?"

He's toying with me, provoking me, as if I could possibly fight back against his magic. Any attempt would be futile and we both know it. He wants to watch me fail. "You obviously want to say something to me, so say it."

"I want you to answer a few questions about Paititi."

"Why should I?"

He points a crooked index finger toward the cages outside the tent. "Consider the lives I hold in my hands."

"You're going to murder them anyway," I say bleakly.

"But think about how I could do it. Tell me what I want to know, and they die peacefully; resist, and I will turn them into monsters for my army. It's your choice."

Two terrible choices. I stare at him—the thin lips, the pulled-back hair, the razor-sharp cheekbones, the hungry eyes. He'll ruin their lives and in the most horrid and wretched way imaginable.

"What do you want to know?"

"Where do they keep the gold?"

I blink at him. "*Gold?* This is what you're after?"

He is silent and not amused by my caustic tone.

I decide to be honest with him. "The roads aren't made of the metal you seek. People wear an odd bracelet or necklace, but that's it. Some buildings use gold on their roofs, but the legend of Paititi was grossly exaggerated."

He lifts his hand, and I'm blown back, rolling out of the tent and landing in a messy heap. The wind is knocked out of me. I pound my chest, coughing, and scramble to my hands and knees. My fingers dig into the cold earth, desperate for purchase.

"Catalina!" Manuel roars, his hands clutching the bamboo. One of the creatures jabs a spear toward him, and Manuel jerks back, cursing loudly.

I jump to my feet without thinking, only wanting to be near Manuel, even if I have to be in that cage with him. But the moment I take a step, I'm lurched backward again and dragged through the mud and inside the tent, kicking and screaming as I go. The priest's magic forces me onto my knees in front of him.

"Try again."

"I never saw gold—not in the way you're imagining. There aren't piles of it lying around!" I cry, trying to fight his magic. But it's as hard as iron. "This is a fool's errand."

"There has to be," he snaps. "I cannot face him empty-handed."

"Who? Who can't you face?"

He releases me and I slump to the ground. "What pact have you made?" I ask. "With who?"

"The king of Palma," he says stiffly.

I think back to Ana's lessons about the neighboring countries. Inkasisa is landlocked, surrounded. After the revolt on La Ciudad—the capital city—Manuel reported seeing soldiers pressing into our borders, testing our weaknesses. But Atoc pushed them back. It was now his younger sister's problem to deal with overeager kings.

One of them being from Palma.

Notorious for their ambition and greed, with a power-hungry monarch bent on conquering his imagined enemies. My family kept him appeased by sending chests filled with silver from our mountain. What was his name? I hadn't thought about him in a long time, so concerned about my own revolution against Atoc's iron grip on my throne.

"Fuentes," I say under my breath.

"What was that?"

"The name of your . . . employer. What will he give you in return for the gold?"

The priest leans forward, a slick grin on his face. "The Inkasisa throne."

I'm removed from the tent, the priest wanting sleep. I expect to be taken to one of the empty cages near the others, but instead Rumi yanks me away from them, and Manuel stares furiously at my captor. I drag my heels, but his grip is tight and painful on my wrist. I'll wake up with bruises tomorrow.

We reach a dark pit and he yanks me forward so hard, I'm surprised my arm doesn't pop out of its socket. I stumble into the hole and land with a sharp thud on my side. Pain shoots up and down my leg. A grid of bamboo stalks slams on top of the pit opening. I scramble to my feet, my fingers digging into the moist earth. The space is claustrophobic, dirty, and damp, smelling of rotting mushrooms.

"Let me out!"

But no one comes.

Damn it. I don't dare sit on the ground. Who knows what might take a sampling of my flesh? I let out a miserable sigh. It's pitch dark, save for the moon and stars. A gasp rushes from my lips. My hand flies to my pants pocket—the priest never asked me to empty them. Perhaps he thought me too helpless.

I dip my shaking hand inside and pull out my trusty dented telescope.

My knees buckle in relief. Prayers fall from my lips—to Luna, Inti, and Pachamama. I beg for their help. No amount of breathing can slow the drumming of my heart. But I shut my eyes, focusing on quieting my cluttered mind, ridding it of the deafening chatter, terror, and doubt. I fill up my lungs with frigid air, and it's ice against the back of my throat. I wait for the pulsing thrum, the delicious sense of peace, wait for my goddess.

I lift up the telescope. The stars have moved since I last looked. I squint, making sure I'm reading every word right.

Consume. Consume. Consume.

I lower the scope and pull at my bottom lip with my teeth. What does it mean? No answers come. Even as I stand stock-still, barely breathing, listening for Luna's soft whisper against my cheek.

There's nothing.

Something bites my leg. A sharp sting that I feel everywhere. I look down and screech—ants crawl under my boots, hundreds of them. I stomp on them, my breath coming out in freezing puffs of air. I scream when more come, remembering what Chaska told me about the ant that burns flesh, the feeling as if you're being stabbed.

Someone peers down—Rumi the monster, by the shape of his outline.

"There are ants in here! Please let me out!"

I shudder, rubbing at my tunic, scratching my legs. The image of ants crawling all over my skin pierces my mind, and I let out a whimper. The only thing I can do is keep marching all over them throughout the night.

But they bite me anyway, and by the time morning comes, dozens of welts cover my legs.

That's nothing compared to the dread that snakes up my spine at the sight of the priest, looking down at me, refreshed, magic full and ready to be unleashed.

Rumi pulls me out of the pit, hauling me up and dragging me across the frozen ground. He yanks me upright by my hair. I cry out from the pain blazing against my skull, and he twists me around to face the bamboo cages. They're empty, but my friends stand beside them, held utterly still by the priest's magic. Manuel's eyes flicker toward mine, and I read the anguish in them. Rumi and a couple of other creatures encircle us as the priest looks on with an impatient scowl.

I'm bone weary. Barely able to stand. Above, the day is gray. Thunderclouds hang heavily, ready to slam a wet fist onto earth's waiting face. The conquered sun is nowhere to be seen; not even one ray of light reaches the ground. The cold is a villain all on its own. Biting and sharp against my skin.

"I'm running out of patience," the priest says. "Here are your options. One of you will tell me the way to Paititi. If not, you'll be killed or forced to join my army. It will be easy to find the city once I destroy the jungle. How will the city remain hidden without the trees and animals blocking my way? Now, which one of you will break first?"

Kusi and Chaska remain silent. Manuel shoots me a quick look—one the priest doesn't miss. When he snaps his fingers, Rumi grabs Manuel and forces him to his knees. I rush forward, enraged, but Rumi holds me at bay. All traces of him are gone. I keep blinking to unsee the feral hatred in the depths of his dark eyes. But it's still there, inches from mine, breathing cold air into my stunned face. Rumi—Ximena's friend. The boy she's enamored with.

This will break her heart.

Kusi is dragged to his knees then pressed shoulder to shoulder with Manuel. Chaska scrambles toward me, and no one stops her. We press close, her fingers digging into my arms. But we look to each other and make a split decision.

We won't let the priest have Manuel and Kusi without a fight.

I jump onto Rumi's back and tightly grip his cold throat, but he throws me off as if I were a doll. Chaska fares better. She lands a resounding kick to a monster's face. But another slams a fist into her side—high, near her ribs. Chaska howls and drops to her knees, clutching herself. Then she's yanked up, her arms dragged behind her. She kicks backward, but she's held down by two monsters. Rumi locks me in a tight hold. I squirm, trying to break free.

The boys are unnaturally still—the priest's magic again. Only their heads are allowed to move.

"Stop!" I scream, struggling. "Stop! Por favor—*no!*"

Rumi wraps a strong arm around my waist, his claws tearing into my tunic. The long line of his body is pressed to mine, and it feels as if I'm standing against a block of ice. The priest draws something from his leather pack. It's a bruised flower, the petals crushed but glimmering. "Do you know what this remarkable plant is called?"

When neither boy responds, the man smiles. "In seconds that stubbornness will be a thing of the past." He cradles the flower as if it were a baby. "This is killasisa."

A jolt of surprise skids across my skin. It means "moon flower" in the old language.

Moon flower.

Recognition flares in Kusi's eyes. "It's not meant—"

"Cease talking," the priest says coldly.

Manuel's expression is stricken. I've never seen him this way before. A deep well of cavernous shadows mars the skin under his eyes. His lips press together in refusal, but the bleak cast to his face displays his sudden understanding: He won't be able to keep the flower out of his mouth. Wary resignation settles onto his countenance. I want to run to him, save him from his fate. Manuel turns his head, his lips moving, and through my tears I struggle to understand what he's saying.

Then at last I hear it.

"Te amo, Catalina."

He is utterly calm. His words thrum down the length of my spine, and a heartbreaking smile stretches his lips.

"Let me go! Please!" I say between sobs, and try to break free.

But it's too late.

The priest plucks a single petal. I squeeze my eyes shut, and when I open them again, he's forcing it between Manuel's closed lips. He plugs Manuel's nostrils and waits for him to gasp, then he sticks his crooked fingers into Manuel's mouth to shove the petals down. I scream and scream until my voice is gone. Despair hits every inch of my body, and I bend, clutching my sides. Until I am numb and feel nothing, until the best part of me falls away.

I cannot live through this.

The transformation happens quickly. Manuel slumps to the ground, his skin changing, starting with his mouth and spreading like wildfire to the rest of his body. He groans as his fingers lengthen, his nails deadening into lethal claws. I understand the transformation now. That flower is of the moon—a gift Luna sent down but never used, and was probably left forgotten until this madman found it. It's as foreign and alien as the moon itself—cold, gleaming white against the heavy black of night's armor.

Manuel slowly stands, rolls back his broad shoulders, and tilts his head toward the priest. Kusi looks on in horror. Manuel has become a monster of the moon. A victim of this ill-used gift turned into a curse.

With no cure.

When his dark eyes meet mine, it's only a cursory glance. An assessment of the danger I pose, and nothing more. There is no recognition. No heat in his gaze, no soft smile to his mouth.

He's gone.

Lost forever.

I stop struggling, and Rumi releases me with a grunt. I drop heavily to my knees. A chasm opens within me, devouring every one of my feelings, hungry to swallow me whole. I can't breathe. It hurts too much.

The priest shoots me an irritated look. "Are you ready to show me the way to Paititi?"

Somehow my lips remain closed. My heart may be broken,

but I will not give up the way to the city. I've lost the person I love the most, but I will not give up.

"You think the worst has been done to you?" the priest asks. "I'm in control here, Condesa. And I will continue to take from you until you break." With a swift smile in my direction, the priest motions for Manuel and points a long crooked finger at Chaska. "Another friend of yours?"

He means to turn her also. Another friend. Gone forever.

Manuel steps toward Chaska. She pales and backs away, but the priest lifts a finger and she freezes. "You have a chance to save her," he says coldly. "Tell me how to get to Paititi."

Chaska swallows hard. The muscles in her neck strain—she's trying to break free of the priest's magic. "Don't say anything, Catalina. *Do not.*"

Tears stream down my cheeks as Manuel takes a step closer, and another. Pale hands lifting. The priest releases his hold on Chaska and she stumbles.

"I'll have him torture her first," the priest says. "Rip out each limb—"

My fingers clutch the pale ground until they grow numb. "Stop, please stop."

Kusi struggles against the priest's magic, his veins pronounced along his neck. "I will murder you for this!"

"No, I don't think you will. This is your last chance to tell me where the city of gold lies."

"Don't say anything," Chaska says quickly, shaking as she tries to back away from Manuel.

I can't stand to look at his cold hatred. If he knew what he was about to do, it'd break his heart. Manuel charges, and somehow

Chaska ducks from his reach. He lets out a guttural roar, then turns and swings a great arm. It clocks her in the chest and she flies backward.

"Manuel!" I scream. "Don't do this!"

I leap to my feet and rush between them, holding up my hands in a pleading gesture. "Listen to me. Listen to my voice. It's me, Catalina."

The priest laughs. "You could be his mother; it makes no difference."

I lock eyes with the monster, but the warmth has vanished from his, replaced by a cold emptiness that widens that chasm inside me. He snaps his teeth at me.

"You don't want to do this," I beg. "Manuel. Por favor."

The monster reaches for my throat—I jump back, but he takes ahold of my wrist and sends me flying. I land on my side with a sharp thud. Pain shoots down my body. Somehow I get to my knees and crawl toward Chaska. Try one more time. "Manuel, *please*!"

He doesn't look in my direction, doesn't respond at all to his name. I crumble—he's well and truly gone. And he's about to murder someone in cold, cold blood. He stomps over to Chaska, who attempts to scramble away.

"Don't!" I yell, even though I know it's useless. I shakily get to my feet and take a few steps before Rumi snatches me again. "Manuel, *por favor*!"

Kusi's face is nearly purple, but the priest's hold never wavers.

Manuel bends over, shoves Chaska's hand away. His claws pierce her flesh—

She screams—

I push to my feet. "Priest! I will take you to Paititi!"

The priest stops Manuel, who straightens. Chaska lies moaning on the ground, clutching her chest. Blood seeps through her fingers. I rush to her side, dropping to my knees. Several puncture wounds mar her chest where Manuel dug in his sharp fingernails. Her face is ashen, her eyes screwed shut in pain.

"Chaska," I plead, lifting the hem of her shirt to stanch the flow of blood. "Don't die, don't die."

My gut twists, acid coating my tongue. When the priest looks over at me, my stomach clenches painfully. He crooks his finger, and Rumi drags me before the priest.

"Your turn, Condesa." He bares his teeth. "Don't you dare lie to me. I *feel* your blood, the pulse in your neck. I will know if you speak false."

Shame builds, nearly smothering. There's no course left, no one to turn to. I don't have the slightest idea on how to get to Paititi, but if I don't say something, the priest will have Manuel finish off Chaska and Kusi. If I lie, he'll do the same.

"Paititi is hidden behind a waterfall," I say at last.

The priest locks his jaw. "Do you think I'm a fool? There are *thousands* of waterfalls in this jungle."

Manuel approaches from behind, then stands beside me, his gaze intent on his master. He looks almost the same—if not for his bone-white skin dotted with inky constellations, and fingers that looked like they've been dipped in soot.

I blink. Something presses close, hovering as if riding on the air I breathe—the smallest, most desperate whisper, the level of leaves rustling on a shy gust of wind. I shut my eyes and inhale deeply.

There.

Luna's silver touch kisses my cheek. Tickles my ear and tousles the wisps of hair at my temples. She swirls around me, a feathery touch, wanting my attention. Begging me to notice her.

I do.

She murmurs secrets into my ear. Her voice grows louder as she tells me what I need to know: of things that happened long ago. Names and places. I am drowning in information. Picturing a priest in a castle hiding behind a false name. He lived among the Llacsans, pretended to befriend them. When I reopen my eyes, I know what to do. Adrenaline pulses in my blood. Spikes my heart rate like a fever. The priest stares at me, his head tilted to the side. "What's your magic, Condesa?"

For the first time in hours I have a reason to smile. "I am a seer, Umaq."

He blinks at the sound of his name. "Where did you hear that?"

"From Luna," I say. "And she isn't happy with you."

"You lie," he says stiffly, but fear claims his face. Deep grooves march across his forehead, and the corners of his mouth tighten. A long silence follows. I don't dare drop my gaze to the crushed killasisa petals in his palm. Luna once again whispers in my ear. Her words settle into my belly, fortifying me for what's to come.

Consume. Consume. Consume.

He raises his hand as if to throttle me, but I can't let him use his magic. I glance toward Kusi, who's ready to pounce should I distract the priest enough to loosen his hold. Then I glance at Manuel—I wish I'd put the truth together sooner.

"What else did she say?"

I ball my hands into fists. "You will die a painful death at the hands of your enemy." He pales, and I wait a long beat. "You will not survive me, Umaq."

He steps back, his jaw slack and his gaze as wide as twin moons on his face.

Kusi leaps to his feet—

Umaq raises his free hand, but I'm already moving toward him. He stops Kusi in his tracks, but I slip close enough to wrench a single petal from his grasp. He lets out a cry of surprise, too dumbfounded to do anything but stare as I swallow it whole. The magic tastes sweet on my tongue, like a crisp morning scented by gardenia and water rushing over polished rocks. And then it transforms into something else entirely—shimmering and silver.

I taste the stars.

Bubbly and sharp, the feeling spreads to every inch of my skin. I am filled with rays of moonlight, a majestic power, the light that always conquers shadows. Everyone steps away from me—the priest, Kusi, and the monsters.

I am Luna, and she is me.

Treinta y Cinco

I feel Luna's presence in every corner of my body, and her quiet power makes me tremble. Magic zips down my spine, shoots sparks from my fingertips. My skin becomes pale, my vision sharper. Her wisdom and generosity infiltrate my soul; her love for humanity coats every inhale and exhale. She becomes stronger, and I struggle to hold on to myself. There's a whisper of fear present in the back of my mind: I'm scared to disappear—what if I never come back?

Let go, Catalina. It's the only way.

I do as she says, surrendering myself fully to her magic. To *her*. It's as if I've relinquished the reins of a too-fast carriage, sliding to make room for another person.

Luna takes charge.

The priest snarls and raises both hands. Killasisa petals flutter to the ground, and I wince at the sight. I *never* meant for the flower to cause harm. It was a gift for a loyal mortal whom I loved. I see people give flowers to one another all the time, and I wanted to extend the same courtesy. Inti had been right, as he usually is. My brother and I fought brutally. He says I'm too impulsive, that I interfere too much. It's taken me centuries to see the damage I've done by narrowing my regard to only one group of people. I wanted them to forget about my brother and mother; I wanted to be the only one they worshiped.

The time has come for me to make things right.

The boy named Kusi rushes forward, ready to knock Umaq off his feet.

"Wait," I say, my voice holding all the music in the night.

Kusi slows to a stop, his expression transformed by his rage. He listens because he senses the power beating near my pulse points.

Umaq lifts his hand higher, outrage dawning. "You shouldn't be able to speak."

His voice is an annoying buzz in my ears. The force of the heavens fills my veins. Triumph blazes, fiery and red-hot. The priest snarls and snaps his fingers, urging his monsters to rip me in half. Irritation flickers through me. This small human has no love in his cold, misshapen heart. He'd started on this path by wanting better for his tribe, but sank into just wanting *more*. Why can't mortals ever be satisfied? My gaze lands on all the turned men, and my heart bleeds for them.

I am their goddess. They are my children, and not meant for this world.

The priest blinks stupidly. "Kill her! Kill her!"

They don't obey, and Umaq's jaw drops. He spins, rage contorting his features, and lifts his hands. His magic skims against my edges, picking and teasing, trying to find a weakness. It won't find any. I step forward as a flash of satisfaction flares at the sight of his gaping mouth.

"What are you?"

"You cannot run from your fate," I say coldly, and for half a moment I let my eyes fill with moonlight. The priest's jaw slackens.

"Mercy! Please, I beg you. I can be useful to you," he pleads. "I can help you, moon goddess. Talk of your greatness, spread your legend throughout Inkasisa. Everyone will fear you, respect you. Isn't that what you want? To never be forgotten? You will be the most revered diosa because of me. Consider!"

"If you're not going to use your heart," I cut in softly, "then you won't mind my taking it."

I lift my palm and a sharp beam of moonlight cuts through the skin protecting his ribs. The razor-edged light slices upward, and the priest drops to the ground, clutching his chest, trying to stop the blood from leaking out. None of his efforts will work. The light cuts right above his heart. Flesh gives like butter. My finger moves again, this time downward. His screams rent the air, destroying the calm night. Blood gushes between his fingers, stains his robe, the white ground. One more cut ought to do it. I slash my hand. The priest falls backward, his arms swinging wide as he smacks the earth.

The priest is no more.

There's a soft moan, and I turn, recognizing the voice. The girl Chaska lies a few feet away, clutching her wounds. I walk to her, my palms shining. Magic pours from my fingertips and light envelops her. Her breathing becomes steadier.

"Is that better?" I smooth a lock of hair from her face.

The girl's eyes widen, her lips moving, but not a sound comes out.

"Rest now," I say, and Chaska's eyes drift closed. A wave of tenderness washes over me. The girl within me wishes to have the reins back, but I'm not finished yet. My children wait for me. Something must be done, for they cannot stay here.

No. Please. Don't take Manuel, please.

I hear the request and worry my lip. The girl and I blend together, our hearts beating as one, our breaths coming from the same lungs. My hands are hers, but they shine silver with the power of the moon. "They belong with me now."

Please.

My eyes fly open at the sudden wave of emotion that crashes into me. Feelings I'd long since forgotten: love, longing, desperate hope. The paralyzing grief of loss.

Please, heal him and Rumi.

"Catalina?" Kusi asks in a gruff voice.

I stare at the human. A friend. A leader of men. Then I glance at the one called Manuel, and my heart wrenches, nearly splitting. Slowly, I walk toward him, place my hands on his, and speak the language of the stars. His skin warms under my fingers, turning scorching hot. The cold bleeds from his body, slowly disappearing. When he blinks, it's the face of someone who's woken from the deepest sleep.

"You are needed here." I smile broadly at him, and for a moment I'm not sure who is the one truly grinning.

A faint line appears between his brows. "Why are you talking strange?" He spins around, takes in the dead priest. "What's happened?"

Kusi stands in front of Manuel, anger radiating off him. His heart is noble—I don't worry what he will do. But in case he needs the reminder, I whisper into his mind: *He didn't know what he was doing to your cousin.*

Kusi blinks at the invasion, and when he looks at me, I smile. "She will live. She only needs rest as her body heals."

The tension in Kusi's shoulders loosens, and then he nods.

Manuel glances between us, that line deepening. "Will someone tell me what's going on?"

"He will," I say, nodding in Kusi's direction. Then I turn away and work my magic on the other corrupted humans, transforming them back to themselves. I sink my hands into the earth and enjoy the satisfaction of seeing it come to life. Green spreads and expands in every direction. Trees are righted, flowers bloom, and while I can't bring back to life the many animals who've died, I'm confident others will once again make their homes in this part of the jungle.

"It's Catalina," Kusi insists. "But also *not* Catalina."

"You're not making any sense," Manuel whispers furiously. "What's happened to her?"

"I think it's Luna."

Manuel sucks in a deep breath.

I laugh lightly then face the last mortal still locked in his corrupted state. Recognition flickers through me, and the girl nudges me forward, urging me to take his hands. In moments he returns, and confusion sweeps into his face.

"It's a very long story," I say. "It's Rumi, isn't it?"

His lips part, and like the others he sputters and stills when he sees the bodies littering the ground. "Yes, that's me. Don't you remember?"

I smile. "Kind of."

The poor mortal appears more confused. Best let him piece together what happened—the girl is impatient to speak with her love. Though he isn't reverently watching me like he ought to be, there's respect in his gaze. A calm assurance that I am loved and honored by him. But there's a question, too.

"What is it?" I ask.

"Thank you for what you've done. . . ." he says.

I bow my head. "You're welcome."

"But will you leave her?" He swallows. "Please."

I raise my brows.

"I'm grateful," he says quickly. "But I need her here with me."

The girl in me flushes, and the sensation makes me smile. "I am already leaving."

The night in another part of the sky calls me forth. The shine on Catalina's hands dims until there's nothing but her own flesh and blood. Manuel tentatively steps forward. I take one last look around, then turn my gaze to the edge of the jungle, to the stars glimmering high above another village.

I blink at the sudden vastness in my mind, in my heart.

"Catalina?" Manuel whispers. He slowly reaches for me, but I move his hand away and leap into his arms. He startles and then squeezes me tightly.

"I thought I'd lost you," I say.

He pulls away enough to stare into my eyes. "I'm here now."

I hold on to him, needing the strength of his arms, the steady beat of his heart. It's over, it's finally over. Manuel looks around, the lines around his eyes tightening. He has questions, but I can't form the answers right now. Sadness clouds my vision as I stare down at Chaska, her clothes stained a deep red. She sleeps profoundly, her chest rising and falling in even breaths. The goddess didn't say how long her rest would last, but I trust that when Chaska is ready, she'll wake.

"What happened to her?" Manuel asks.

"Another day," I say with a quick glance at Kusi.

He looks over and nods.

We make our way back to Paititi, and while the mood isn't exactly somber, it isn't happy, either. We've lost too many people to celebrate. It's an odd group: strangers bonded over a horrifying experience. Introductions are made quickly, and the night we spend in the jungle is filled with food and cups of bamboo around a roaring fire. No one talks. Kusi and Manuel venture off to try to find Sonco's body, but the jungle has swallowed him up. Only Manuel's machete is found. When they return, I hug them both—much to Kusi's shock.

We set off early the next day, the sun barely greeting us through the dense canopy.

Exhaustion is a relentless taskmaster, and by the time we reach the waterfall, I can barely walk. We find the boats where we left them, hidden under palm fronds, the new home to snakes. Manuel tucks me inside the canoe closest to us. I sit on his lap, no longer caring if there's a black caimán following us, or a school of piranhas swimming beneath the wood.

We glide under the curtain and water pounds the top of my head, pours into my ears. Manuel clutches me tight, and then we're on the other side. For a stupid moment the word *home* infiltrates my mind.

Home.

I shake my head and stumble out of the boat.

"Do you need me to carry you?"

"No," I mumble, straightening my shoulders. "I can walk

down all those steps, no problem."

Manuel laughs and scoops me into his arms. "You don't have to."

Rumi glances at us, a slight smile on his face. Kusi and I tell him parts of the story, the ones that aren't too painful to speak out loud. And we hear his harrowing tale. "We were attacked on the way out," he says. "One minute, I was walking toward the jungle border; the next, I couldn't move. Not even an inch." His voice drops to an angry rasp. "And then Umaq appears in my line of sight and shoves something into my mouth. I don't remember the rest."

"I'd like to know how he survived in the jungle for so long," I say.

"Umaq can control the blood running in every human and animal," Rumi says promptly. "What enemy of his stands a chance?"

I tuck myself closer to Manuel's side, the itchy fabric tickling my cheek. "I want a bath."

"You'll get one," Manuel promises.

I lean closer, and pull his head lower so I can whisper in his ear. "With you."

He pulls away, blushing the deepest shade of red. He gives me a rueful smile right before kissing me hard, his hold tightening as if he never wants to let me go.

Fine by me.

Later, after we've all bathed and slept, we meet in one of the buildings to eat. It's just us, the survivors, except for Chaska, who slept through the night, the deep slumber of healing. Being in this room without her is so strange. My conversation with Sonco feels like forever ago. Every and now again my attention snags on Kusi, whose face turns bleak when he thinks no one is looking. There's a haunted line to his mouth, despair etched into the curve of his cheeks. I understand his grief, and so when he meets my eye, I give him a sad, bracing smile.

Even though I know it's not enough—nothing will ever be.

We eat rice mixed with dried beef, seasoned with a blend of dried herbs and several fried eggs cracked over the top. I have two helpings of everything, and then load another plate full of fruit: maracuya, duraznos, and frutillas. Manuel sits next to me, a haunted gleam in the deep well of his dark eyes.

His fingers tighten around a clay cup filled with jugo de durazno.

"What is it?" I ask softly.

"What if Chaska never wakes?" he whispers, his lips twisting.

I grab his drink, set it on the mat, and take his clammy hand in mine. "Luna said she will. We need only time and patience."

His jaw clenches, but he squeezes my hand and then lets go so he can eat. Chatter hums throughout the meal, subdued, as talk circles around the next few days. There are funerals to arrange, people to mourn, a city that needs to meet and accept their new leader. Kusi bears all the discussion with a stony expression, as if, were he to allow one crack to form, all the emotion he feels would pour out.

He will need help in the coming days, weeks, months.

When we're done eating, Rumi sets his clay bowl onto his woven gold-patterned mat then clears his throat. "I've been gone from home a very long time. I must get back to La Ciudad."

Kusi bobs his head and says, "You will have whatever you need for the journey, as well as an escort out of the jungle. But you're sure you don't need to rest for a few days more?"

The healer shakes his head, briefly meets my eyes. "There's someone who's probably worried sick about me."

I smile, feeling almost shy. How can I possibly hate him? If I hadn't been wading through sludge searching for the wrong thing, I could've had something better. A life of my own, being what I was called to be. Something truer to who I am. When Luna and I shared the same breath, I realized that I was meant for something great—just not a throne or a kingdom that already has a worthy ruler.

My decision rings true: I am a seer.

"Kusi," I say, and he raises a brow. "You're the leader of the Illari now."

His expression made of stone and hard earth never falters. He nods.

"Umaq mentioned he'd been working with the king of Palma, promising him gold from the lost city of Paititi. Luna shared a vision with me—one day Palma will invade Inkasisa, searching for your home. They'll destroy everything in their path."

"This will happen?" Rumi asks, his voice hoarse.

I nod. "One day."

"What must we do?" Kusi asks, a muscle in his jaw ticking.

"When the time comes, we must all work together to save Inkasisa."

Kusi studies me silently. "I will fight alongside you, sister."

"There's one more thing," I say shyly. "Sonco said that I was welcome to stay here. I don't want to assume—"

The new king of the Illari places a firm hand on mine. "Sister, stay as long as you like."

My gaze flickers to Manuel. He winks at me and then asks the Illari leader, "Does that include me as well?"

"If it must," Kusi says dryly.

Rumi stands, wiping his pants of any crumbs. He's grown paler and thinner since that day when he'd left me to fend for myself. I'd been angry and scared, filled with resentment and bitterness. But now, looking at him, I feel only concern. "You should have another egg. Or three."

"I need to get going." He hesitates and then blurts out, "Would you like me to take a message to her?"

I set aside my clay cup and plate and slowly stand. "I'd like to come with you. If you'll let me."

"You're leaving?" Kusi asks. "I thought you were staying."

"I will come back, but there's something I have to do first." I gaze out the window, in the direction of where I think La Ciudad lies. Manuel eyes me shrewdly and chuckles quietly to himself. He turns me around, ticking my arm to another window.

"It's this way to Ximena."

three weeks later

The castillo looms ahead, at once familiar and terrifying. Blindingly white and austere. Memories flood my mind—of playing with my father in the main courtyard, running around and getting the hem of my skirt filthy. I'd been royalty then, someone respected because of the family I'd been born into. And now I arrive without a title, without family. But with friends, and an ability to read the stars.

More than enough for me.

The tall iron gates stand before our small party, forbidding entry. No visitors unless approved or invited. This is a terrible idea. She won't want to see me—I didn't even say goodbye. If I remember walking away from her, she certainly will.

I could have said goodbye.

Manuel leans forward, tightening his hold around my waist. "It'll be fine. I promise." He digs his heels into the horse's side, and we gallop forward until we're a few feet away from the great walls.

Several guards dressed in bold red tunics peer down at our upturned faces. "State your name," one of them calls down.

Rumi lets out a sharp whistle, high and then low. The minute they see the healer, they give a great cheer, and the iron bars groan as they lift, one slow inch at a time. The sound of the chain rattling disturbs the quiet, and I concentrate on that instead of on my racing heart, battering my ribs.

Manuel clicks his teeth and our party lurches forward into the main courtyard. A brightly-hued llama peers at us, lips smacking indolently. This isn't any kind of llama I've ever seen. Vibrant red strands of wool are woven throughout his hair coat, along with shimmering glimpses of moon thread. I'd know Ximena's work anywhere. Manuel takes a step back, eyes widening.

Rumi throws us a wink. "Careful, he spits."

As if to prove his point, the llama takes a step toward us and lobs a hairball at Rumi, who's only response is to send the animal off with a fond smile.

Manuel dismounts, then helps me down. When my toes skim the ground, he leans forward and presses a light kiss on my temple. "Remember when you flew between two cliffs?" he asks. "This is going to be much easier than that."

"So you say," I mutter. "I'd rather face a caimán."

"Don't exaggerate."

"I *never* exaggerate."

Manuel snorts, then clasps my hand in his. The rest of our party dismounts, and a stable hand comes running, the fringe of his poncho swinging around his skinny legs. I'm unsure of where to go or what to ask for. My throat is dry, and I'd like a pitcher of jugo all to myself. Rumi marches past other wooly creatures—a slow moving sloth, a fierce looking jaguar, and an anaconda curled around an ecstatic bunny—toward a pair of great wooden doors. They suddenly fling open, and a girl bursts through.

It's her.

Dark hair flying behind her, her eyes fixed on the healer. She wears loose-fitting trousers and a billowing tunic stitched with big florals in vibrant shades of purple and red. She doesn't carry a weapon, and her feet are bound in leather sandals. No more boots with hidden daggers. Rumi spreads his arms wide, and I expect her to hug him tight, but instead she smacks his stomach.

He lets out a grunt, and then laughs, bending over to scoop the furry sloth into his arms. He makes soothing noises, and the wooly animal slowly raises his arm to Rumi's cheek.

"Where have you been?" she demands. "I've been worried sick! A *week*, you said. If it wasn't for Tamaya—"

"Reina Tamaya," Rumi corrects, his lips twitching. "Por Dios, show some respect."

"Don't you dare be cute," Ximena says, aghast, but her eyes dance in merriment. "Why are you so thin?"

The healer winces. "The situation in the jungle got a little out of hand."

"Rumi, what happened? You've been gone for weeks!" she says, wrapping her arms around his waist, careful not to squish the sloth. "And tell me about Catalina. Is she—"

I step forward, half wanting to save Rumi from further scolding, and half because I'm impatient to see her up close. I've never seen her this happy, this free. She carries herself differently, less stiffly, as if she's comfortable in her own skin now.

"Hola, Ximena."

She abruptly stops talking. Her eyes widen, and she slowly turns around. Manuel squeezes my hand then lets go. I swallow hard, taking in the sight of her. The wind teases her hair, and her tunic billows around her like a flag. Some of the old tension returns, her back straightening, her shoulders tensing.

Behind her, the door opens again and Reina Tamaya steps out into the sunlight, squinting in my direction. She's just as beautiful as the last time I saw her, despite the long scar following the curve of her cheek. I swallow hard, my lips going dry. Should I bow or kneel? I'm frozen to the cobbled stone, unsure. For some reason, she doesn't seem surprised to see me. She drops her hand, and a knowing smile stretches her lips. I dip my chin, the slightest inclination of my head.

Then the reina winks at me, as if she already knew I'd survive the jungle, that I'd somehow make it back to this same castillo that houses so many of my old memories.

Ximena looks between us. "Catalina?" she whispers, cataloging the brightly woven Illari tunic I'm wearing, the gold jewelry around my neck, the gift from Sonco. Across my body I carry a leather satchel, and her attention snags on my dented bronze telescope. "You look different."

I'm suddenly aware of my travel-stained clothes and limp hair. "I must be a sight."

She waves her hand impatiently, in a gesture so familiar that tears gather in my eyes. "No, I mean—" She clears her throat and laughs awkwardly. "I meant, you *seem* different."

"I am." I clutch my hands tightly together. "I'd like to explain how much."

Her smile grows—hesitant, a bit watery. She takes another small step toward me.

And I meet her halfway.

acknowledgments

Sometimes I still feel like this is all a dream. That I didn't just have another one of my stories published, and I'll wake up to work on that query letter once again. But thankfully I have so many wonderful people in my life, reminding me that this is real.

A ginormous hug to my agent, Sarah Landis; I'm so glad we found each other. Here's to many more stories together. I can't wait! <3

So many heartfelt thanks to everyone at Page Street Publishing. To my editor, Ashley Hearn, who knows exactly what this story needed and for her deep love of Consuelo. It figures your favorite character would be a murderous butterfly. Many hugs and thanks to my publicists, Lauren Cepero and Lizzy Mason; editorial assistants Franny Donington and Tamara Grasty; copy editor Kaitlin Severini; managers Marissa Giambelluca, Hayley Gundlach, and Meg Palmer; publisher Will Kiester; and the wonderful sales team at Macmillan. Huge thanks to Meg Baskis for helping me bring the cover to life.

To my drafting partner, Rebecca Ross, thank you for swapping chapters with me as we furiously wrote every day to meet our word count goals. You are an angel for reading—and liking—my messy drafts. To Shea Ernshaw, my adorable sugar monster, I'm so thankful for our friendship.

To my sweet friends and professional Voxers: Adrienne Young, Kristin Dwyer, Adalyn Grace, Shelby Mahurin, and Rachel Griffin. For all the laughs, support, and encouragement, I will forever carry every word. My world wouldn't be the same without any of you in it. Love from the bottom of my heart. I'll see all of you in Asheville—no arguments.

A huge thanks to my friends who love me, cheering me on while I'm traveling, on deadline, or missing supper club. You know who you are! Love forever! <3

This book could not have been possible without the many conversations I had with my dad, asking him about his life in the jungle. He grew up in the Bolivian Amazon, born and raised in a small village that was inaccessible by road. To go anywhere, he had to go by river. Dad, I am in awe of who you are, and this book is for you. Thank you for the wild stories; I'll cherish them forever. Momma, mil gracias por tu apoyo. Te quiero mucho! Rodrigo, thanks for hand selling my books to everyone in your life (Hi, Apple employees!). It means so much to me. Love you!

Andrew James, every book is possible because of you. Thank you for loving and supporting my dream, for not blinking an eye when I'm in my pajamas for a straight week and for making sure I get out of the house to see the sunshine. Thank you for knowing exactly when takeout is needed and for reading whatever I put in front of you. Eres el amor de mi vida. I love you. <3

To my readers—you'll never know how thankful I am for you: for every review, like, retweet, and story reply. I am SO grateful for all of you.

about the author

Isabel Ibañez is the author of *Woven in Moonlight* (Page Street), which received two starred reviews and earned praise from NPR. She was born in Boca Raton, Florida, and is the proud daughter of two Bolivian immigrants. Isabel is an avid moviegoer and loves hosting family and friends around the dinner table. She currently lives in Winter Park, Florida, with her husband, their adorable dog, and a serious collection of books. Say hi on social media at @IsabelWriter09.